seizure

Also available by Kathy Reichs

Kathy Reichs
Seizure

arrow books

For Hannah, Madelynn, Brendan, Brittney,
and Brianna, my Texas critics.

Published by Arrow Books, 2012

1 3 5 7 9 10 8 6 4 2

Copyright © Kathy Reichs, 2011

Kathy Reichs has asserted her right under the Copyright, Designs and Patents Act,
1988, to be identified as the author of this work.

Published by arrangement with the original publisher, Razorbill,
an imprint of Penguin Inc First published in hardback in 2011 by

William Heinemann
The Random House Group Limited
20 Vauxhall Bridge Road, London, SW1V 2SA

www.randomhouse.co.uk

Addresses for companies within The Random House Group Limited can be found at:
www.randomhouse.co.uk/offices.htm

The Random House Group Limited Reg. No. 954009

A CIP catalogue record for this book
is available from the British Library

ISBN 9781784754730

Printed and bound by Clays Ltd, St Ives Plc

MIX
Paper from
responsible sources
FSC® C018179
www.fsc.org

Penguin Random House is committed to a sustainable future for
our business, our readers and our planet. This book is made
from Forest Stewardship Council® certified paper.

PROLOGUE

Cannons thumped in the distance.

Boom! Boom!

Final, frustrated salvos that faded with the dying light.

Wind screamed and lightning slashed a bruise-purple sky. Thunder clapped. Rain drummed the heaving forecastle deck.

Nervous shouts ricocheted as the crew struggled to trim the mainsail. Instructions. Curses. Prayers.

Revenge crested an enormous wave, then listed hard to port as a massive gust shoved her sideways. Timbers groaned. Voices bellowed in panic.

The pirate ship vibrated with an unnatural hum, moments from capsizing.

Seconds passed. Eons.

Then, mercifully, *Revenge* dropped into a deep trough. Shielded from the fierce gale, she slowly righted herself.

The deck leveled.

The shouts morphed into dark laughter, the giddy excitement of those pulled back from the brink. Backs were slapped. Grins spread like plague.

To all but one.

A tiny figure huddled alone on the quarterdeck, clutching the stern rail. Her body was drenched. Wind danced her hair, ripped at her shirt, bandana, and velvet waistcoat.

The woman had no complaints. The deadly storm was speeding *Revenge* to safety.

Her gaze scanned the trailing horizon. Anxious. Searching for enemy sails. Hoping not to spot them.

Then *Revenge* mounted another gargantuan wave.

There they were. A trio of black cutouts against the heavy, dark clouds.

Two were sloops similar to *Revenge*. Nothing they couldn't handle. But the third vessel was trouble.

English.

Frigate.

Bristling with thirty cannons.

Bullocks.

Calico Jack's men were good fighters, true pirates all. But they were no match for such a warship.

Revenge ran for her life.

Moments later the woman saw sailors scurrying the decks of the pursuing ships, frantically reefing sails.

Slowly the trio dropped back, swung about, and reversed course.

As it turned, the massive frigate fired one last broadside. A futile gesture. The range was far too great.

The woman finally smiled.

The approaching storm had soured the chase for the Crown's small fleet.

Her relief was short-lived, replaced by other worries.

Escape had a price.

Revenge's bowsprit was pointed into the heart of the rising tempest.

Anne Bonny watched a colossal breaker crash over the bow. Jack's crew had dodged the hangman's noose, but the sea would have the final say.

They'd had little choice but to chance the storm. Not after blundering into the British patrol. Frankly, Bonny was amazed *Revenge* had eluded the colonial authorities yet again.

Third time this year. The net is tightening.

Weeks earlier, the Charles Town militia had cornered *Revenge* while she was anchored off the Bahamian coast. Jack's men had awakened hungover and surly. They'd fought as best they could, but *Revenge* had nearly been forced against the rocks. Escape had been a very close thing.

And now they tempted fate in violent waters.

Bonny slumped to the deck, arm looping the rail for safety.

So tired. Tired of running.

For a moment, Bonny's eyes drifted shut. Unbidden came the image of Laughing Pete, his body crushed by a British cannonball.

Her lids snapped open.

A storm had saved *Revenge* this time. Climactic luck. How long could such good fortune hold?

Of late, the gallows loomed large in Bonny's mind.

So few of us left.

She saw faces, recalled names.

Stede Bonnet had been captured on the Cape Fear River, hanged at White Point in Charles Town. Rich Whorley had mistaken militia boats for merchant ships and paid with his life. Charles Vane had been hanged at Gallows Point, not ten leagues from where she now slumped.

Even Blackbeard was dead, killed in battle off the Carolina coast.

Yet Jack refuses to see.

Bonny raised her eyes to the topmast, where Calico Jack's banner flapped wildly. A black field, a white skull, two crossed cutlasses.

According to Jack, the flag announced he was always ready to fight.

He thinks we can go on pillaging forever. Even as they pick us off, ship by ship.

Bonny shook her head.

The other captains understood. Black Bart Roberts and Long Ben were already on the run. The rest would follow. Colonial power was increasing in the Caribbean. More warships. More troops. More control.

The golden age of piracy was drawing to a close. Any fool could see that.

Our way of life is ending. I won't end with it!

Bonny thought hard. Decided.

Pushing from the rail, she scurried amidships. Years at sea had made her adept at traversing the pitching, rolling deck. Rain pummeled her head and shoulders as she dropped through a hatch into the vessel's underbelly.

Dark. Dank.

Two pirates guarded the forward compartments. At her approach the men stepped aside, careful to avoid giving offense. Anne Bonny was not to be crossed. She needed no one's permission to visit the treasure hold.

Thunder boomed, shaking *Revenge* to her keel. Ignoring the storm, Bonny pried open a rough-hewn wooden door, passed through, then closed it behind her. She was alone, a rare luxury on a ship at sea.

Bonny took in the cramped chamber. Sacks of wool and tobacco lined one wall, piled next to oil casks and giant barrels of rum. A strongbox was bolted to the portside boards, filled to the brim with gold and silver coins.

Random objects filled what little space remained. Two leather chairs. A Spanish suit of armor. Jewelry boxes inlaid with rubies. Crates of English muskets. A set of ornamental brass sconces.

Anything of value, pirates will take.

Bonny smiled sadly. She was going to miss this line of work.

But she intended to survive.

Determined, she shifted aside a crate of perfume and two trunks of women's clothing, revealing a wooden chest secured by a stout iron lock.

She didn't open it. No need. She knew what lay inside.

This one is mine, Jack. The rest is yours.

But where to hide it?

Bonny's brow furrowed in thought.

Then the smile returned. Wider this time.

Perfect.

It would take patience, she knew, and luck. But she had plenty of both. And wouldn't *that* just goose the others?

Bonny chuckled softly. God, she loved being a pirate.

Jack is a fool. I must speak with Mary. Tomorrow.

Amused by the daring of her plan, Bonny retraced her path along the narrow passage and up the ladder to the main deck. The raging storm nearly forced her back down the rungs.

Night had fallen. *Revenge* was running in total darkness.

Bonny staggered to a rail and grabbed hold. Around her, crewmen struggled with lines and sails. She gazed out at the roiling ocean, oddly calm. She'd made her decision. Nothing would go wrong.

Two phrases winged through her brain.

That chest is mine. God weep for anyone who tries to steal it from me.

Revenge sped over an endless parade of enormous, frothing whitecaps.

Speeding Anne Bonny on her way.

North.

PART ONE:

BROKE

CHAPTER 1

SNAP.

The rush was electric, like grabbing the third rail in a subway tunnel.

My blood raced, molten lead careening through scorched veins.

Pain.

Disorientation.

Then power. Limitless power. *Visceral* power.

Sweat exploded from every pore.

My irises sparked, flashed golden. Glowing yellow disks encircled bottomless, inky-black pupils. The world sharpened to a laser-fine crispness. My eyes pierced like daggers.

My ears buzzed, then honed to supersonic clarity. White noise filled my head. A beat. The dissonance coalesced into a symphony of distinguishable ocean sounds.

My nose awoke, whisked patterns from the summer breeze,

deftly read the coastal scents. Salt. Sand. Sea. My nostrils sifted the delicate nuances.

My arms and legs quivered, smoldering with caged energy yearning for release. Unconsciously, I bared my teeth in animal delight.

The feeling was so incredible, so potent, that I panted with the pleasure of it. I wanted to live in that moment forever. Never stop. Never return.

I *flared*.

Beside me, Ben grimaced, dark eyes clamped shut. Muscles tense, his powerful frame trembling, he tried to flare by sheer force of will. Failed.

It doesn't work that way.

I kept quiet. Who was I to give advice? In the end, I didn't understand our powers any more than Ben. My control wasn't much better than his.

Not once I freed the wolf.

○   ○   ○

I suppose you're wondering what I'm talking about. Or you've already decided I'm nuts and are slowly backing away from this book. Can't say I blame you. A few months ago, I'd have done the same thing.

But that was before I changed. Before a microscopic invader altered my biological software. Before I evolved, became something more. Something brand new. Something primal.

Here's the short of it.

A few months back, a nasty supervirus infected my friends and me. The organism wasn't natural. It came straight from a secret laboratory, created during an illegal experiment. And this bug had a taste for human carriers.

How did I get so lucky?

An unscrupulous scientist, Dr. Marcus Karsten, cooked up the germ. He was my father's boss at Loggerhead Island Research Institute. In a mad dash for cash, Karsten crossed two types of parvovirus, accidentally creating a new strain that was contagious to people. Unfortunately, we caught it from a wolfdog named Cooper, Karsten's test subject.

Don't get me started.

Anyway, I was sick for days. We all were. Then things got weird.

My brain would snap like a rubber band. My senses would go berserk.

At times I'd lose control, unable to suppress sudden animal instincts. Scarfing raw hamburger meat. Stalking a caged gerbil. It was the same for the others.

When the dust settled, my friends and I were forever altered, down to the core. The vicious pathogen scrambled our cellular blueprint. Rewrote our genetic code. Canine DNA barged into my human chromosomes and made itself at home.

It's not easy, living with wolf instincts buried inside your double helix.

But our condition is not without certain . . . *benefits*.

I'll be blunt. My friends and I have special powers. Superhuman abilities. Hidden, but very real. You heard me right.

We're kind of a big deal. Or would be, if we could tell anyone about it, which we can't. Not unless we want to learn about human dissection. Up close.

We call the power "flaring." That's the best I can describe the sensation. I burn up inside, my mind warps and snaps, and then *boom*! My powers unleash.

I'm learning to control my abilities. At least, I think I am.

Okay, *hope* I am.

Heck, I'd settle for just knowing what they are.

I understand the basics. When I flare, my senses go into hyperdrive. Sight. Smell. Hearing. Taste. Even touch.

I become faster. Stronger.

More alive.

Viral.

That's what we call ourselves. Virals. It seemed appropriate to have a group name after becoming a gang of genetic mutants. It's good for morale.

There are five Virals total. Me. Ben. Hi. Shelton. And my wolfdog, Cooper, of course. After all, he was patient zero.

The upshot is we Virals can tap the physical powers of wolves. But not always when we want them. And sometimes the changes come unbidden.

To be honest, we have no idea exactly what happened to us, or what we can do to fix it. Or what will happen next.

But one thing is certain: we're different. Freaks. Disambiguations.

And we're on our own.

○   ○   ○

Ben's frustration grew with each passing moment. Angry, he ripped off his black T-shirt and threw it to the sand, as if the garment alone was foiling his efforts. Perspiration covered his deeply tanned skin.

I turned away so he wouldn't see my already glowing eyes. Didn't want to increase his aggravation. Ben Blue in a mood is no fun for anyone.

Hi crouched just beyond Ben. A chubby kid with wavy brown hair, he wore a red Hawaiian shirt and green board shorts. Not exactly stylish—or even matching—but classic Hiram Stolowitski.

He stared down the shoreline, having long since lit his own flare. Of all the Virals, accessing the power came easiest to Hi.

"I see you, Mr. Rabbit," he whispered to himself. "You can't hide from Wolfman Hi."

"Good work," I deadpanned. With my powers unleashed, his every word was crystal clear. "Taunting a helpless bunny. That's a worthwhile use of our flare time."

"He taunted me first." Hi's gaze remained glued to his target. "By being so darn cute! *Aren't cha?* Aren't cha cute, you *fuzzy wittle guy!*"

My golden eyes rolled. "We're *supposed* to be practicing."

"Then practice your vision, Lady Buzzkill." He pointed. "Fifty yards. Third dune from the tree line, the one with all the cattails. *Typha latifolia*. Brown fur, speckled. Black whiskers. It's an eastern cottontail. *Sylvilagus floridanus*."

Hi loved showing off his knowledge of natural history almost as much as he liked conducting scientific experiments. Both traits were inherited from his father, LIRI's head mechanical engineer.

Then Hi mock-squealed, his cheeks reddening. "*Oh*! And he's got a bunny friend now, too!"

We stood near the northern edge of Turtle Beach, on the west coast of Loggerhead Island. The interior forest loomed to my right. To my left stretched the Atlantic Ocean, unbroken all the way to Africa.

I focused on the spot Hi had indicated, a rough patch of cattails and salt myrtle at the wood's edge. My gaze zeroed. Locked.

The scene leaped forward with awesome clarity, beyond anything a human eye should be able to see. I could make out every leaf, every twig. Sure enough, two snuffling rabbits were tucked inside the foliage.

Half a football field away.

"Your flare vision is fantastic," I said. "Better than mine. I can't make out their whiskers from this distance."

Hi shrugged. "Then I've got you beat with one sense, at least. I don't hear as well as Shelton, or have your schnozzaroo."

Beside me, Ben grunted. Growled. Shook. He still couldn't light the lamp. His eyes remained closed, but his mutters had shifted to four-letter words. Unpleasant ones.

Observing Ben's struggle, Hi scratched his chin. Glanced at me. Shrugged. Then he quietly slipped around behind Ben.

And, without ceremony, kicked him in the ass. Hard.

Ben toppled forward into the sand.

"What the hell!?!" Ben surged to his feet and advanced on Hi with clenched fists. His eyes now blazed with yellow fire.

"Take it easy, slugger!" Hi backpedaled, both hands in the air. "I was only getting you mad enough! Had to be done."

So far, Ben could only tap his power when enraged. Like now. He looked ready to remove Hi's head.

"Stop!" I yelled, anxious to prevent a homicide. "Ben, you're flaring now. It worked."

Ben paused and flexed his hands, noticing the change. Scowling, he nodded at Hi. Hi gave a big thumbs-up, grinning from ear to ear.

"We've *got* to figure out a better way," Ben muttered, "or I'm going to end up thrashing one of you guys. I may pound Thick Burger here anyway," he said, gesturing toward Hi.

Hi chucked Ben's shoulder. "Hey, you're welcome pal. Anytime."

Faster than thought, Ben grabbed Hi and wrapped him in a vicious bear hug. "Smart-ass."

Hi sputtered, gasped for air. "Back off! I don't like you that way!"

Ben laughed. Then he lifted Hi over his shoulders. Effortlessly. My jaw dropped.

Ben spun Hi overhead like a chopper blade. Once. Twice. Hi turned a pale shade of green. Lime? Teal? Shamrock?

"I'm gonna puke!" Hi warned. "DEFCON One!"

Ben bounded to the waterline. Heaved.

Hi flew like a ragdoll, landed face-first in two feet of surf, sputtering and cursing.

Ben grinned wickedly. "I think I've got it now. Thanks."

"Ungrateful." Hi blew water from his nose while surveying his sopping clothes. "But I'll admit, that was kind of awesome. You get *strong*."

Hi tried splashing his attacker, but Ben danced away, hooting. Then Ben sprinted down Turtle Beach, leaped the sand dunes, and disappeared from sight.

"Wow," I said. "He's fast, too. Much faster than me, even flaring."

Hi slogged back onto the beach. "I let him win. He needs the self-confidence."

"Right."

"Hey, I'm a giver."

"A saint."

It was good to see Ben laugh again. Smiles had been rare since the Heaton case. The media firestorm had burned out quickly, but our parents were not so easily distracted. We'd each been grounded for most of the summer.

And I mean *grounded*. The adults had been savvy enough to

hit where it hurt. No visitors, TV, or phone. Not even Internet access. It was brutal, like living in a cave.

With no chances to meet or even discuss our abilities, I'd begun to quietly freak the flip out.

The virus was a wildcard rampaging through our bodies. *Anything* was possible.

Was the sickness gone for good? Had our powers stabilized? Did anyone else know about Karsten's secret experiment? About Coop? About us?

I'd been trapped with these questions for weeks. Alone.

The isolation hadn't been good for my nerves.

Ben escaped first. The senior Blues never paid much attention to discipline. My parole came August first, after nearly two months served.

Good behavior? More like constant moping. I just wore Kit down.

Hi had finally talked his way out last week. That surprised me. Knowing his mother, Ruth Stolowitski, I thought he'd be last for sure. Not so. As far as I knew, Shelton was still on lockdown. Apparently the Devers had zero tolerance for criminal behavior, regardless of justification.

Make no mistake, I was still on probation. Strict. Kit was watching me like a hawk. At least, he thought he was.

Once Hi shook free, the three of us began trekking out to Loggerhead every week. We needed to practice, safe from prying eyes. The isolation was ideal. And, right under my father's nose, I could visit the island without suspicion.

Loggerhead is held in trust by Charleston University. Very few have permission to visit. Luckily, dear old dad works here. So do the other Virals' parents.

Kit Howard is a marine biologist working at LIRI, the university's on-site scientific station. One of the most advanced veterinary facilities on the planet, LIRI consists of a three-acre walled compound nestled on the islet's southern half.

That's not all. Loggerhead Island is a full-fledged primate research center, with troops of rhesus monkeys roaming free in the woods. No permanent buildings exist outside the main complex.

The habitat is as close to undisturbed as possible for a prime hunk of real estate lying just off Charleston Harbor.

A perfect place to fly your freak flag.

This was our third practice session, and we'd begun to notice slight differences in our abilities. Strengths. Weaknesses. Variations in style and finesse.

But the powers were complex, our grasp of them far from complete. What I didn't understand would fill the ocean. Deep down, I suspected we'd barely scraped our full potential.

An explosion of sand reclaimed my attention.

My gaze fastened on a bouncing shape, moving wicked fast. Zoomed. Tracked. Unconsciously, my muscles tensed, ready to spring.

Then, recognition.

Ben, flying across the sandbank, a wild look on his face.

A second later, I knew why.

He was being chased.

CHAPTER 2

Cooper exploded from the dunes, fur sticking out in soggy spikes.

The wolfdog puppy chased Ben down the beach, yapping like mad.

"Not so quick, are you Coop?" Ben shouted over his shoulder as he cut left, racing for the surf.

Coop skidded to a halt when Ben dove into the ocean. Thwarted, he barked and raced back and forth.

"Here boy!" I called.

Coop tossed one last yip at Ben before trotting to my side. Then he shook furiously, spraying seawater everywhere.

"Blech!" I wiped salty droplets from my face. "Thanks for nothing, mongrel."

Coop looked pleased. I think. Hard to tell with dogs.

Hi, already doused, was nonchalant. "Did the bad Indian

throw you in the water, boy?" Taking a knee, he ruffled Coop's ears. "Been there."

Hi was referring to Ben's claim of ties to the Sewee, a North American clan folded into the Catawba tribe centuries ago. He'd even named his boat *Sewee*.

"I feel your pain," Hi continued. "Thanksgiving was a huge mistake."

Coop licked Hi's face.

"Not nice," I joked. "You'll sour Jewish-Sewee relations."

"It's true, I take it back," Hi said. "Our peoples have a rich history of mutual respect. Long live the alliance!"

I noticed movement in the corner of my eye. A wisp of gray passing through the forest. Sniffing once with my supercharged nose, I teased a scent from the air.

Warm fur. Hot breath. Musk.

Wolf.

"Look alive, Coop. Your mom's here."

"What?" Hi craned his neck. "Where?"

Three animals stepped from the trees. Whisper, the matriarch, was a gray wolf. A gorgeous, regal animal. All silver, with a hint of white on her nose.

Her mate, a rogue golden shepherd, stood by her side. I'd taken to calling him Polo. Behind them paced Coop's older brother, another wolfdog hybrid. I'd dubbed him Buster.

For a moment, the pack watched the scene on the beach. Then Whisper barked once. Cooper sprang to join his kin. Reunited, the family loped into the forest.

"Have fun!" I called.

I was happy to let him visit his folks, but Coop lived with me now. Whitney and Kit just had to deal. So far, so good.

Well, sort of. Coop and Whitney weren't exactly best friends.

Shrug. The opinion of my father's annoying girlfriend was extremely low on my list of concerns.

"Did you smell her?" Hi asked.

I nodded. Downwind, I'd picked up Whisper's scent at thirty yards.

"Amazing." Hi stripped off his shirt, wrung it out. "Score one for your honker."

"Thanks, I think." I cocked my chin at Hi's substantial midsection. "Nice abs."

"Yeah, I work out twice a month. No exceptions. But stop hitting on me, it's embarrassing."

Hot day. Not surprising for mid-August in South Carolina. I wiped my forehead. My sweating talent was in full effect.

"Shoot." Hi blinked, his eyes back to normal chestnut-brown. "I lost my flare. Stupid Ben."

"Can you get it back?"

"I'll try." Hi's face went blank in concentration. His pupils focused on nothing. Seconds ticked by. A minute.

Hi shook his head. "Still can't burn back-to-back. Not since . . ."

He trailed off. I didn't press. I knew what he was thinking.

The only time we'd flared twice in a row was at Claybourne Manor. The night when, somehow, I'd *forced* it on the other

Virals. When I'd stepped inside their minds.

I don't know how I did it. Had never been able to repeat the trick. Not for lack of trying. But no matter how hard I strained, I couldn't reconnect. Couldn't recapture that odd feeling of *oneness*. The cosmic link that broadcast my thoughts and let me hear theirs.

The close bond of a wolf pack.

"Do you want to try again?" Hi asked. Hesitant. I knew that this particular power gave him the willies. Same went for Ben and Shelton.

"Try what?" Ben joined us, water dripping from his shoulder-length black hair. "Are you talking about telepathy again?"

"It worked once," I said. Defensive.

"Maybe." Ben frowned. "Maybe not. It might've been part of the sickness."

When our powers first presented, we'd been slammed for days. A terrible, soul-crushing illness that left us weak as kittens. The major symptoms eventually subsided, but random oddities continued to afflict us.

Would the symptoms ever disappear for good? I had no answer.

But the current topic of conversation was an old argument.

"It wasn't the sickness," I said. "I felt a real connection, even with Coop. We're linked now."

"Then why can't you do it again?" Ben had no patience for things he couldn't understand.

"I don't know. Let me try now."

Never one to wait for permission, I closed my eyes, slowed my breath. Tried to crawl backward into my psyche.

I pictured the Virals in my mind. Hi. Ben. Shelton. Even Coop. Then I forced the images together, into one shape. A single unit. A pack.

Something twitched inside my brain. A tiny surge, like a breaker flipping. For a brief moment I felt my mind *push*, find resistance.

An invisible wall separated my thoughts from others outside my being. Encouraged, I shoved again in a way I can't describe. The barrier buckled, yielded slightly.

A low hum filled my head. Then it fragmented into murmurs, like hushed voices in a distant room. Coop's form appeared in the center of my consciousness, but vague, indistinct.

As suddenly as it formed, the bond frayed. I heard a thud, like a book slamming shut. The image slipped its tether and dissolved into cerebral darkness.

SNUP.

Blink.

Blink blink blink.

My eyes opened.

I was slumped in the sand, flare long gone.

Hi's voice broke through. "Cut it out, Tory! You're going to faint again."

Ben and Hi took my arms. Eased me back to my feet. Held on until satisfied I wouldn't collapse again.

"Let it go." The nimbus faded from Ben's eyes. "The mind

talk was a delusion. It's making you crazy."

Before I could disagree, a voice carried down the beach. Our heads whipped as one.

We were no longer alone.

CHAPTER 3

"You jokers could leave a note next time!"

Shelton strolled up the sand, hands in his pockets. Short and skinny with thick horn-rimmed glasses, he wore a blue Comic-Con T-shirt and oversized white gym shorts.

He also wore a lopsided grin. Shelton knew he'd startled us.

"Well, well, the caged bird sings," Hi said. "When did you bust out?"

"Pardoned this morning." Shelton wiped sweat from his dark chocolate brow, a gift from his African American father. The high cheekbones and hidden eyelids came straight from his Japanese mother. "I figured you'd be out here. And I can guess what you're doing."

"Tory's trying to play mind-bender again," Hi said. "She ended up face-planting on the beach."

Shelton's grin faded. "Can't we just pretend that never

happened? I can't sleep as it is." One finger nervously spun a key ring containing his prized lock-pick collection. A hobby of Shelton's that often came in handy.

"Pretend it never happened?" I scanned their faces. "We need to *understand* the changes. We can't just ignore them. What if we have more reactions?"

"I know, I know." Shelton's palms came up. "I'm just freaked out. I tried flaring a little, when my parents were gone. I still have no control. Then I caught a cold, and for two days I was sure the virus was killing me."

Ben nodded. "Even when I *can* flare, the powers are never the same. Or stable."

"We'll get there." I sounded more confident than I felt. "We just need practice."

"Or lobotomies," Hi muttered.

"But we experiment *nowhere* but here." Ben's gaze traveled from Viral to Viral. "Loggerhead is safe, but we have to be careful. It's too dangerous to use our powers where someone might see. Agreed?"

Everyone nodded. Our fear of discovery was ever-present. The ramifications of being caught were too horrible to contemplate.

"We can only trust each other," Ben finished. "Never forget that."

"Enough doom and gloom." Hi slapped Shelton's back. "How'd you find us, anyway? Expert tracking skills?"

"I ran into Kit at LIRI." Shelton turned to me. "Your dad's

looking for you. He told me to find ya'll and bring everyone back ASAP. I think something's up."

"Great," Ben said sarcastically. "What'd we do this time?"

"They probably heard about your assaults on me and the dog," Hi said. "You're looking at hard time, pal. Hope it was worth it."

"It was."

I whistled. A few beats, then Coop burst from the scrub, circled us twice, and shot down the beach.

"Well, no point guessing," I said. "Let's go find out."

Ten minutes later we reached LIRI's back gate.

Entering, we secured the barrier behind us. We'd forgotten once, and curious monkeys had spent a night testing doorknobs. Not good.

Around us, a dozen modern glass-and-steel buildings gleamed in the midday sun. Arranged in two rows, they faced each other across a central common. A concrete path bisected the grounds on its way to the main gate and, eventually, the dock. An eight-foot fence encircled the whole complex.

We paused outside Building One, at four floors the largest structure on the island. In addition to LIRI's administrative offices, Building One also housed the marine biology laboratory, my father's little fiefdom.

A tiny alarm piped in my brain. Something felt off. The facility seemed hushed, and strangely empty for a weekday.

Coop barked once, shattering the stillness. I placed a hand on his head.

"Easy, boy." Ear scratch.

Kit emerged from the building. Fast. Too fast. He must've been standing in the lobby, watching for me. He eyed his watch, impatient.

"That's my cue. Later guys."

Nods and grunts in response.

Spotting me, Kit strode forward. We met at center court.

"Hey kiddo! Ready to head home?"

Uh oh. False bravado, laid on thick. My BS sensors triggered. Why was Kit trying so hard to be cheerful?

"Sure," I said. "Is something wrong?"

"Wrong?" Kit pulled a face. "No! *Pssh*. Relax."

Nonsense answer. My anxiety skyrocketed.

Kit was avoiding something, but I held my tongue.

The crossing was weird. Cooper sat beside me on Mr. Blue's shuttle boat, his large head resting in my lap. Kit kept the conversation light, focused on trivial subjects.

So why the parental summons? By the time we reached Morris Island, I was on high alert.

A note about Christopher "Kit" Howard. He's my biological father, but I call him by his nickname. Not Daddy, or Pappy, or Father, or Sir. We've known each other less than a year. For now, it feels like a good fit.

I came to reside with Kit nine months ago, after a drunk driver killed my mother. The shock of losing Mom had been doubled by meeting "Dad." I'd barely had time to grieve before being shipped hundreds of miles to my new home.

Hello Carolina, good-bye Massachusetts. Whatever. I'd only lived there my whole life.

Kit and I are still figuring each other out. We've made progress, but there's a *long* way to go.

"Home sweet home!" Kit stepped onto the dock and made a beeline for our front door. I followed, baffled. Home sweet home? Seriously?

Most of LIRI's senior staff lives on Morris Island, in a row of townhomes owned by Charleston University. Constructed on the remains of Fort Wagner, an old Civil War fortification, our tiny community is the only modern structure for miles. The rest of the island is a nature preserve held in trust by CU for the state of South Carolina.

Morris Island is pretty far off the beaten track, even for Charleston. An outpost on the ass-edge of nowhere. I live in almost total isolation. Tough at first, but I've grown to love it.

"Come on, Coop." I slapped my side. "Let's get the news. Whatever it is."

When I arrived, Kit was seated in the kitchen, toying with a napkin. His eyes met mine, darted away. Shooing Coop to his doggie bed, I took a chair at the table.

"You're clearly uncomfortable," I said. "Spill it."

Kit opened his mouth. Closed it. Crumpled the napkin. Tossed it. Put his face in his hands. Rubbed his eyes. Looked up. Smiled.

"First of all, we're going to be fine. There's nothing to worry about." One hand made a chopping gesture. "At all."

"Okay." Now I *was* worried.

"There's a *chance*, that maybe, *possibly*, I might . . ." Kit searched for words, ". . . lose my job."

"What!?! Why?"

"Budget cuts." Kit sounded miserable. "Charleston University may have to shut down the whole LIRI facility. Obviously, that would eliminate my position."

Bad. Very bad.

"Close LIRI? Why would they do that?"

Kit sighed. "Where do I start? The institute is in turmoil. We've had no director since Dr. Karsten . . ." awkward pause, ". . . left. The press has been brutal. Rumors are flying about Karsten running unauthorized experiments, maybe taking corporate bribes."

I sat bolt upright. That hit *way* too close to home.

"Unauthorized experiments?"

"They found a new lab in Building Six," Kit continued, oblivious. "Secure. Unregistered. It had a ton of expensive equipment, but no records. Very strange. We have no idea what Karsten was doing."

My heart went hummingbird. Parvovirus. Cooper. Our illness. *If anyone ever found out . . .*

I clasped my hands below the table to hide the trembling.

Coop sensed my unease. He popped from his bed and padded to my side. I stroked his head absentmindedly.

Wrapped in his own private gloom, Kit didn't notice my agitation.

"The recent publicity caught the eye of some environmental groups. Now they're protesting the 'monkey abuse' on Loggerhead Island."

"But that's stupid!" For a moment, I forgot my own distress. "The monkeys aren't *abused*; they aren't even disturbed. It's observational research."

"Try telling them," Kit said. "We offered a tour of LIRI to ease their concerns. No dice. They don't seem worried about facts, or that these animals have no place else to go. They just want to scream, 'monkeys in captivity!' and shut us down."

Kit leaned back and crossed his arms. "But that's all secondary. Bottom line: CU lacks the funding to keep LIRI operating. The bad economy has gutted the budget."

"How big is the shortfall?"

"Huge. The trustees have been told to make deep cuts, and LIRI is extremely expensive to run and to staff."

"Tell them to close something else!" Sharp. I didn't care. Dominoes were falling in my head. The inevitable conclusions terrified me.

Again, Kit avoided my eyes. "That's not all."

I waited.

"With LIRI closed, the university won't keep these townhouses." He waved an arm wearily. "We won't be able to stay here."

Ice traveled my spine. I didn't want to hear what was coming next.

"We'll have to move." His shoulders tensed. "I'm sorry,

but there's no other way. There aren't any jobs for me in the Charleston area. I've looked."

"Move?" Barely whispered. It didn't seem real.

Kit rose, crossed to the living room, and gazed out the bay window. Beyond the palm-tree-speckled common, waves lapped softly at the docks below. The tide was slowly rolling out.

"I can't afford Bolton on my own, Tory. Not without the LIRI subsidy."

The other Virals and I attended Bolton Preparatory Academy, Charleston's oldest and most prestigious private school. Hoity-toity. Very expensive.

As an incentive to live and work so far from the city, CU picked up most of the tuition for parents working out on Loggerhead.

"Don't worry." Kit turned and locked eyes with me. "I saw some listings online that might work. I've already contacted a lab in Nova Scotia that needs a marine biologist."

"Nova Scotia?" I stared, dumbfounded by the turn of events. "Canada? We're moving to freaking *Canada*?"

"Nothing's decided, I just thought—"

"Stop!" My hands flew to my ears. "Just stop."

Too much.

Too fast.

I stormed past Kit, up the stairs, and into my bedroom.

Slammed the door.

My face hit my pillows seconds before the tears began to flow.

CHAPTER 4

The pity party was short.

I flew to my Mac, powered up, and had iFollow running in seconds.

I needed the other Virals. Now.

iFollow connects groups online. When users log in from a smartphone, the app will track the movements of all group members on a city map. The program also has file sharing and social networking functions. It rocks.

We still use it, despite everything. We need a way to locate everyone in a pinch. To watch each other's backs.

I checked the map, posted a message, then switched to videoconference mode.

And waited.

Shelton popped onto my screen first, head bobbing, making me slightly queasy. A motor hummed in the background.

A check of the GPS confirmed my guess. A red orb indicated that Shelton was just off the coast of Morris Island, inching north. He'd activated face-to-face from his iPhone.

"Did you hear?" Shelton asked, voice panicky.

"Yes. Where are you?"

"On the shuttle." His pitch climbed the scale. "Everyone at LIRI's getting fired! My dad just told me."

"I know. Kit said the same thing."

My spirits sank through my shoes. I'd held a vague hope that Kit had somehow gotten it wrong. Overreacted. But Shelton confirmed the awful truth.

"What will we do?" Shelton tugged his earlobe, a nervous habit. "We'll all have to move away."

Before I could answer, my screen divided into thirds. Hi appeared on the left, framed by his bedroom walls. Huffing and sweaty, he'd clearly run to his computer.

"Oh crap. You guys know, too." Wheeze. "Can you believe it?"

I shook my head, at a loss. I hadn't felt this powerless in a long time. Not since Mom died.

"Did you get all the details?" Hi asked.

"What details?" I felt a new surge of worry.

"According to my dad, the problems run deeper than just CU's operating budget. Apparently the whole state is broke. The legislature is trying to liquidate assets they've deemed nonessential."

"What does *that* mean?" Shelton asked.

"The state may seize and sell Loggerhead Island. Developers have been salivating over those beaches for decades."

"No!" I snapped. "They can't!"

"They can," Hi said. "My dad called a friend in Columbia who said a deal is in the works right now."

"Don't they have to vote on something like that?" Shelton asked. "Loggerhead is technically public property, right?"

Hi shook his head. "CU has title, and the legislature already has authorization to sell university assets. They can move forward with a sale any time they want."

"Given all the bad publicity, the state kills two birds with one stone." My fingers curled into fists. "PR bullshit."

"It gets worse," Hi said. "Morris Island may also be on the block."

"No way." I couldn't believe it.

"Think about it," Hi said. "Morris is even hotter real estate than Loggerhead. It's closer, has a road, and is three times bigger."

"And since CU also holds title to Morris Island," Shelton concluded, "it's fair game too. That's some slick dealing. Bastards."

"They'll build freaking *condos* over our bunker," Hi grumbled. "So fat seniors from Hoboken can tan by the pool."

"Goddamn it."

Blasphemy, but right then, I didn't care. My world—the new one I'd struggled so hard to create, to make work—was crumbling.

My computer screen restructured into four quadrants. Ben scowled from the sofa in his father's rec room.

"You heard?" Shelton asked.

Ben nodded tightly.

"What about Whisper and her pack?" I said. "Or the sea turtles? Around five hundred rhesus monkeys live on Logger-head. What about them?"

No one said a word.

The real-world answers were terrible.

Hi broke the silence. "Laws protect the turtles somewhat, but Whisper's family isn't really supposed to be there. The monkeys are worth big bucks. They could be sold to anyone, even medical research companies."

Tears burned the back of my lids. I choked them off. Going to pieces would accomplish nothing.

"My parents say we'll have to move," Shelton said quietly. "They're looking for new gigs right now."

"Mine too," Hi mumbled. "I hate change."

I rolled my eyes. "Kit is looking at a job in Nova Scotia."

"Canada?" Despite everything, Hi chuckled. "Have a good time, *eh*? Don't fight with any moose. Meese. Whatever."

"Shut up." Against all expectation, I giggled. At least I had my friends.

For a while.

"We can't let them split us up." Ben's first words.

His finger pointed at me from the screen. "You say we're a family. A pack." His arms folded across his chest. "A pack never gives up its own. Ever."

I was surprised. Quite a speech for Ben.

"He's right," Hi said. "I can't handle making new friends. Not my forte. Plus, where would I find new superpower-wielding mutants to argue with?"

"And let's not forget the dangerous part," Shelton added. "We don't know what's wrong with us, or what's gonna happen. I don't know about you guys, but I can't deal with this flaring thing solo."

Bobbleheaded nod from Hi. "I'm not getting dissected like some lab rat. You guys are supposed to watch my back."

Then, almost as one, the boys looked at their screens. Directly at me.

Huh? I was the youngest. The only girl. Why was I in charge?

No matter. I was in total agreement.

If I had to lead, then I would lead.

This seizure will not happen.

"We're going to need a plan," I said. "Fast."

CHAPTER 5

I'd forgotten my French project.

The end-of-year presentation, worth a third of my grade. Due today, I'd done nothing. So I stood before the class, panicked, faking a speech I hadn't prepared.

But I couldn't think of a single word. It was as though I'd never heard the language. I fidgeted, miserable, searching for something, *anything* to say.

Je m'appelle Tory. Parlez-vous français?

How could I have been so careless? I'd never pass now. My entire transcript would be ruined. College. Grad school. Everything down the drain.

Giggles rippled through the audience. Smirks. Points. Muffled laughter. Confused, I glanced down.

I wore Mom's old bathing suit, a ratty one-piece with a flimsy skirt stitched to the waist. It couldn't have been more out of style. Or place.

Mortified, I tried to cover myself. With my hands, my book. My cheeks flamed.

Where are my clothes!?!

Classmates howled, pounded desks. Hiram. Shelton. Jason. Even Ben. In the back, Chance Claybourne stood beside Dr. Karsten, glaring with angry eyes.

Too much, I couldn't take it. The door. The hall. Escape. I ran.

I rounded a corner into a dark, narrow corridor. A strange odor stopped me. It was musky, like wood chips and freshly turned earth. Confused, I scanned for the source.

Lockers lining the hall began to rattle. Doors bulged, gave way. Hundreds of chickens burst forth. Squawking and flapping, they milled at my feet. The noise was thunderous.

Where to run? What to do?

The mass of poultry pressed tightly. Beady eyes zeroed in on my throat.

Adrenaline arrived in buckets. And with it, something else.

A crimson streak split my vision. My brain expanded, then contracted to a point. I trembled uncontrollably.

Fur sprouted on my arms, my legs. My hands melted into paws.

Oh no! No no no no no!

Claws sprang from my fingers. A low growl spilled from deep in my throat.

The wolf was emerging.

This time, *all the way*.

A hand closed on my shoulder. Terrified, I spun, shoved blindly. The figure crashed to the floor.

Kit looked up at me with startled eyes. He wore a tuxedo, now a ruin of grease and feathers.

"Tory, I made breakfast!" he shouted.

I shook my head, uncomprehending, starting to hyperventilate.

He can see me! Kit sees what I really am!

I howled in dismay.

"Tory! Breakfast!"

I sat upright in bed. Kit's voice echoed on my eardrums. I heard bacon frying, smelled burned toast.

Ah.

A dream. A terrible, f'ed up dream. I don't even *take* French. *Hablo español.*

I rubbed the heels of my hands into my eyes, trying to wipe away the nightmare. Covered in sweat, lower back aching from tension, I felt more tired than when I'd gone to sleep.

"Tory! Get down here now!"

"Blargh."

Slinging aside covers, I trudged to the bathroom. Brush. Swish. Spit. Comb. Morning ablutions completed, I plodded downstairs.

Shocker.

Kit had set the table. Placemats. Silverware. Napkins. Glasses of ice water and OJ. Plates heaped with eggs, bacon, sausage patties, and grits. He'd even filled a pitcher with milk and set it on ice.

Someone was clearly overcompensating.

"Well, well," I said. "Is there a birthday I don't know about?"

"Nope. Just time I started feeding my daughter properly. Toast will be ready in a minute. The first batch didn't cooperate."

Cooper was following Kit's every move. Hopeful. He glanced over when I entered the kitchen and yapped once, but stayed rooted in place. The prospect of human food trumped my appearance.

"Sellout," I muttered.

Coop kept his eyes on the prize.

"The mutt can spot a master chef when he sees one." Kit dropped a piece of bacon to the floor. Tail wagging, Cooper devoured the offering.

I shook my head. No chance this would become routine. But hey, you know what they say about gift horses. I tucked in with gusto.

Thirty minutes later my stomach was full, and I barely remembered the nightmare.

"I'll be at work all day," Kit said, "but call me if you want to talk. Everything's going to be fine."

"Sure."

"I'm serious." Kit forced eye contact. "I got an email this morning about another position, and this one's in the U.S."

"Progress."

"It's a bit farther away, but a *much* better job. Science adviser to a major fishery. Great pay."

My eyebrows rose. "Farther? Where?"

"Dutch Harbor, Alaska. The online pictures are beautiful. Scenic. Rustic."

My forehead hit the table. Struck a beat.

Bang. Bang. Bang.

"They've got wolves there," he added lamely.

"Alaska?" I sat back. "Now it's *Alaska*?"

"Think of the adventure!" Kit smiled, but his eyes betrayed anxiety. "The Last Frontier!"

"Are you messing with me? Say yes."

"Nothing's settled yet, obviously. All I know is they liked my résumé."

"How much would it take to keep LIRI operating?"

I'd given the problem some thought. Fundraisers? Donors? Surely something could be done.

Kit frowned. "Ten million, annually. Minimum."

Ugh.

"There's nothing we can do? No trustees to beg? Letters to write?"

Kit shook his head. "It's just too much money. CU can solve its fiscal crisis and fix a PR disaster with one pen stroke. To them, it's a no-brainer."

Silence. Not much to say.

Kit grabbed his keys and headed for the door. Hand on the knob, he turned.

"Chin up, kiddo. We'll land on our feet. You'll see."

With that, he was gone.

"Chin up, my ass."

Coop padded over and nudged my palm. I scratched his ears, but even the wolfdog failed to brighten my mood.

Loggerhead Island was home to so many animals. Whisper, Polo, and Buster. The rhesus monkey troops. A centuries-old sea turtle colony. Hundreds of other species. Lives would be uprooted, possibly destroyed. All so the university could save a few bucks.

I thought of the LIRI scientists and staff. Everyone would get the ax. My friends and I would be scattered across the country. Our pack destroyed.

Enough.

We had to preserve LIRI. Had to save Loggerhead Island.

There was simply no other option.

Kit said it would take millions?

So what.

Time to find them.

Somewhere.

CHAPTER 6

"How would you like to make thousands of dollars, from the comfort of your very own living room?"

Hi read from note cards. He wore a white button-down shirt, navy clip-on tie, and tan slacks. Business casual. A quick glance at his audience, then he resumed his presentation.

"What about cash? Fabulous homes? *Luxurious* vacations?"

Hi searched the group for receptive faces. Found none.

"You can't be serious," Shelton groaned, eyes returning to his laptop. "I'd nearly hacked the Ben and Jerry's website when you called. We could've been eating free Chunky Monkey right now. I've got to start all over."

After cleaning the kitchen, Coop and I had walked to the bunker. Hi wanted a Virals meeting. With a sinking feeling, I began to understand why.

Shelton and Ben slouched on the window bench, sporting identical frowns. I sat on the rickety wooden chair beside the only table. Coop was curled at my feet.

The furnishings weren't exactly *GQ*. But what our clubhouse lacked in amenities, it more than made up for with privacy.

Built during the Civil War as part of Charleston's naval defenses, our bunker once guarded Morris Island's northern tip. Buried in a sand hill overlooking the harbor mouth, the sturdy, two-room wooden dugout is practically invisible.

No one else remembers it exists. The place is our fiercely guarded secret.

Sensing resistance from the bench sitters, Hi turned his charm on me.

"And you, Miss? How would you like to be your own boss? To earn more in a month than most people do in a year?"

My snort was sufficient response.

Hi soldiered on. "Join our team at Confederated Goods International, and you too could realize the dream of being—" dramatic pause, arms swept wide, "—a *millionaire!*"

With a flourish, Hi dropped a folder onto the table. Inside was a stack of papers printed off the Internet.

I did a quick perusal.

"There's nothing in here but clip art," I said. "Images of yachts and sports cars. This page is just a giant dollar sign."

"Ridiculous." Snapping his computer shut, Shelton grabbed a sheet at random. "Silver-haired men standing in front of mansions they don't own, arms around models they don't date."

Shelton tossed the folder to Ben, who didn't bother to catch it. The pages scattered across the floor.

"Now, now!" Hi continued quickly, reading from a new card. "I can tell you're excited to get started on the home business of your dreams. Just sign our 'personal empowerment agreement,' and we can open your path to financial success!"

"This is a rip-off, dude." Shelton scooped up a sheet. "Twenty pages, and I still don't know what these people do. But here's a JPEG OF A DIAMOND RING. VERY HELPFUL."

"You sell their products or something," Hi said. "'Just as good as available in stores.' I pay a small start-up fee and find three people to work for me. Then those people—you guys—each find three more people—"

"That's a pyramid scheme, you dope!" Ben smirked. "It's a scam."

Shelton shook his head. "Oldest trick in the book."

Hi flipped through his index cards, selected one from the back.

"I'm sensing you might be hesitant to embark on this new phase of your life," he began. "But don't let fear of the unknown—"

Hi ducked as his folder sailed inches above his head and exploded against the far wall. "Hey!"

Coop shot to his feet, startled, growling everywhere at once. I arm-wrapped his neck to calm him.

"Great." Hi began gathering the strewn papers. "You just ruined our marketing department. That's more overhead."

"Oops," Ben said.

"It's a classic rip-off, Hi." I corralled the last few pages. "We won't make any money. Get-rich-at-home programs never pan out."

"Fine." Red-faced, Hi pulled off his tie, untucked his shirt. "But we need to raise cash somehow."

"We need to *make* money," Ben said, "not lose our own in the process."

"And we need a lot of it," I muttered, stroking Coop's back. "Millions."

I told the others what Kit said over breakfast. "What about bank robbery?" Hi scratched his chin. "I mean, how hard could it be? We're pretty good at breaking into places, sneaking around. Plus we have superpowers. Sort of."

"Try again." Ben.

"Bank heists are a *little* out of our league," Shelton agreed. "I don't want to move away, but a prison cell? No thanks."

"Well we need *some* kind of plan," Hi said. "We can't allow ourselves to be split up. I don't want to be a freak alone. Been there, done that. I like having friends."

His voice dropped. "And this virus terrifies me."

For a moment, I felt as hopeless as Hi sounded. What could four teenagers possibly do?

"Stop whining, hippie." Ben crossed to Hi and mussed his hair. "We'll figure something out. But no spazzing inside the bunker. I won't allow it."

Hi swatted Ben's hand away. "Why, because that's *your* specialty?" But he was grinning. Sometimes, Ben knew exactly what to do.

"I got an email from a Nigerian prince." Shelton kept his face straight. "Apparently I just send him my bank account info, and he deposits a bunch of money. Can't see how it could go wrong."

"The lottery," Ben said. "Let's just play Powerball."

"Vegas?" Hi suggested. "I've got forty bucks and a fake moustache."

"Great ideas all around," I deadpanned. "But we *do* need to come up with something. We have to fight this."

The others nodded, but offered no serious suggestions. They were just as stumped as I was.

"And now I have to go." I sighed. "Keep me in the loop."

"Now?" Shelton asked. "You just got here."

My eyes rolled on their own accord. "I have a cotillion event. Some yacht-club charity fundraiser thingy. Whitney is insisting, and Kit took her side."

Three wide smiles.

"Oh shut up."

CHAPTER 7

Half an hour later, a surprise waited at the dock.

Ben. With *Sewee* primed and chugging.

"I'll give you a ride."

Unexpected. When I'd left the bunker, Ben hadn't indicated any interest in my afternoon. But he'd readied the boat while I changed.

Down the pier, Ben's father sat in a lawn chair beside his vessel. With Kit at work, Tom had agreed to ferry me into town.

But now Ben was here. For some reason.

"Fine by me." A wry smile crossed Tom Blue's lips. "But you don't have to ride with my boy if he's bothering you, Tory."

Ben scowled, reddened, but kept quiet.

"No, that'd be great," I said quickly. "Thanks, Ben. Thanks anyway, Tom!"

Ben cast off with more haste than usual. I could hear his father chuckling as we began to pull away.

"Where to?" Ben asked.

"Palmetto Yacht Club. On East Bay."

"I know where it is," he said curtly.

Okay then.

We rounded Morris Island and motored into Charleston Harbor. As we passed the point, I tried to spot our bunker among the sand hills. And failed, as always. Good.

Ben picked our way through a tangle of sandbars. Since he practically lived in his boat, I let him choose the route. He seemed to know his way around every islet in the Lowcountry, and there were dozens. Hundreds.

It was midday, and blazing hot, so I was thankful for the ocean breeze. The sharp tang of saltwater filled my nose. Seagulls circled over us, squawking. A pair of dolphins cavorted in *Sewee*'s wake. God, I love the sea.

"You look nice," Ben said stiffly, keeping his eyes on the horizon.

"Thanks." Awkward.

I was wearing the Katey dress by Elie Tahari. White, with golden metallic floral embroidery. Trendy, expensive, and not mine. Another designer number I could never afford.

What can I say about the grand southern tradition of cotillion? Defined as a social-education program for young people, it's really a suffocating nightmare engaged in by elitist brats. At least, that's been my experience.

We were *supposed* to be learning the fundamentals of courtesy, respect, communication, and etiquette, along with the art of social dance. Instead, silver-spoon prigs lounged around comparing price tags and munching pâté.

Cotillion also presented endless wardrobe problems, and I lacked the necessary firepower. Kit's insufferable girlfriend, Whitney Dubois, had so far solved the dilemma by borrowing dresses from her friend's boutique. The accompanying jewelry— this time a sterling silver charm bracelet and matching Tiffany necklace—belonged to the salon-tanned wonder herself.

I hated playing dress up, but at these fêtes it was best to blend in. Even if it meant accepting Whitney's pricey, stylish attire.

Blargh.

Ben throttled down to pick up speed. "How many of these events do you have, anyway?"

"Not sure. I think maybe two or three a month."

As part of the nightmare, I was scheduled to make my debut next fall. Thanks to Whitney, my fate was sealed. I was doomed to rub elbows with the city's junior elite not just at school, but also on my own time.

Double blargh.

As we shot across the harbor, passing Fort Sumter on the right, Ben kept a careful watch for larger vessels. *Sewee* is a sturdy boat—a sixteen-foot Boston Whaler runabout—but against a cargo ship she'd be kindling.

We reached the peninsula in just under half an hour.

"There's your snob warehouse." Ben pointed to the yacht club. "I'll drop you as close as I can get without a trust fund."

Wonderful. If this ticked him off so much, why offer me a ride in the first place? I didn't want to be here, either.

Ben was being even more moody than usual. Sullen. Almost angry. I couldn't understand why. If I hadn't known better I'd have said he was jealous, but Ben Blue had zero interest in attending a lame cotillion party. So why the attitude?

My iPhone beeped, sparing me the need to reply to Ben's comment.

Text. Jason. He'd meet me on the dock.

"That the blond meathead?" Ben asked.

"Jason's not a meathead. What's your problem with him anyway? He's helped us before."

Ben shrugged. "I'm allergic to jackasses."

We glided into the marina in frosty silence.

As surreptitiously as possible, I glanced over at Ben. He sat in the captain's chair, his long black hair dancing in the breeze. He wore his standard black T-shirt, cutoff khaki shorts, and a scowl that seemed permanently locked in place. With his dark eyes, copper skin, and muscular frame, he had the sleek, toned look of a jungle cat.

It occurred to me that Ben was an attractive guy, even when brooding.

Hell, *especially* when brooding.

"There's the dork now." Ben's voice snapped me back to reality.

Standing on the pier was Jason Taylor. Tall and athletic, he had white-blond hair and sky-blue eyes. The Viking-god type. Pure Scandinavia.

Jason was Bolton's star lacrosse player, and superwealthy—his family owned a ritzy estate in Mount Pleasant. He could've been an elitist jag, but his open, honest personality made him one of the most popular kids in school.

Basically, my polar opposite.

One of my lab partners from last semester, Jason inexplicably had taken a special interest in me. While flattered—and, frankly, stunned—I wasn't sure if his attention pleased me or not.

Don't get me wrong, Jason's great. He'd step in when the cool kids mocked me or the other Virals. Still, he didn't haunt my dreams or anything.

I should probably throw myself at Jason. Dating him would keep the Tripod at bay. Of course, that would mean being around them all the time. No thanks.

"Nice tie on Thor," Ben said. "Guy looks like a cell phone salesman."

One thing I *did* know for sure: Jason and Ben did *not* get along. I'd never understood why, but these two were oil and water. Every time I'd brought it up, Ben just changed the subject. Boys.

Was Ben jealous of Jason for some reason?

The contrast between the two could not have been starker. Night and day. Literally.

So which do you prefer?

The thought was startling. Prefer? Where did *that* come from?

"Tory!" Jason strode to the boat. "Ah, and Ben." Tight smile. "Always good to see you."

"Ditto." Ben flipped a line at Jason's head. "Make yourself useful."

"Sure." Jason ducked, but deftly caught the rope. "But why tie up? I assume you're not staying."

Ben's scowl darkened. Jason didn't usually go there.

Holding the line in one hand, Jason offered me the other. When I'd stepped onto the dock, he flung the rope back onto *Sewee*'s deck.

"Adios." Jason had already turned his back. "Safe ride."

Wordlessly, Ben reversed engine and chugged *Sewee* away from the pier.

"Thanks, Ben!" I called. "See you later!"

Without turning, he threw me a wave.

Jason took my arm. "Shall we?"

I didn't move. "Can you two *try* to play nicer? This is getting ridiculous."

"Sorry about that." Jason grimaced, embarrassed by the lack of manners he'd just displayed. "But you saw him throw the rope at me. Plus, it's baking out here. Let's get inside; the buffet just opened."

"You and food." I allowed myself to be led. "Is that the only reason you attend these parties? Free apps?"

"One of them." Half smile. "Now march."

◇   ◇   ◇

The Palmetto Yacht Club was tucked away on the eastern edge of

Charleston's downtown peninsula, where East Bay Street became Battery. Four sturdy piers jutted into the water, hosting a swarm of seven- and eight-figure pleasure vessels. The club's main building was a majestic three-story horseshoe of old brick and new stucco. Its wings surrounded a long, manicured lawn with a spectacular harbor view.

The day's fundraiser was an outdoor event. Though the mid-August heat was stifling, ancient magnolias and ocean breezes kept the spacious common reasonably cool.

For most, anyway. I was already sweating. Naturally. Tory Brennan, Olympic-level sweater.

As I walked beside Jason, I peeked inside several of the white canvas tents that formed two rows on the lawn. Art auction. Raffle. Each venue had its own theme. Based on the level of activity, the American Heart Association could expect a healthy deposit.

Expertly coiffed debutantes mingled with their upper-class beaus as well-monied parents looked on approvingly. The atmosphere reeked of privilege, extravagance, and self-satisfaction.

I couldn't have felt more out of place.

Jason beelined to one of the trestle tables, presumably worried that shrimp cocktail was a scarce commodity. And I was alone again. Of course.

I pulled sunglasses from my purse and slipped them on, hoping polarized lenses would mask my misery. Determined to make the best of a crappy situation, I walked a slow circuit, searching for friendly faces.

Found zip. In fact, things were worse than usual. I recognized classmates, but none said hello.

I could feel eyes on my back. Sensed whispered exchanges. I moved faster, as if a quicker pace had some tangible benefit. But there was nowhere better to go.

Distracted, I nearly took out a waitress. She stumbled, one arm flailing, crab cakes shifting wildly on her tray. I hopped backward, shades falling to the grass.

"Sorry!" I snatched my glasses, trying for invisible.

Massive fail.

Behind me, I heard snickers. Snuck a quick look.

Three junior boys, all lacrosse players.

Blood rushed to my head. My face burned with embarrassment.

Flash.

Bang.

SNAP.

Damn.

CHAPTER 8

The flare struck hard.

My senses vaulted into hyperdrive, exploding all at once, like a car started with the stereo on full blast. System overload.

Pain slammed my frontal lobe, dissolved. I breathed a barely audible whimper. Sweat glistened on my skin.

My heart rate quadrupled.

Terrified of discovery, I slammed my sunglasses into place. Golden eyes hidden, I checked for open mouths and pointing fingers. Listened for frightened screams.

No one so much as glanced at me.

A waiter passed, hoisting a platter of veggies. Two tents away, the lacrosse guys were discussing a prize wheel. Nearby, a gaggle of blue-haired ladies compared hats while sipping from champagne flutes.

The party rolled on, oblivious.

Hands shaking, I smoothed my hair and resumed my circuit

around the yard.

They can't see your eyes. No one can tell.

This hadn't happened before. I'd never burned in the open. Hell, in a freaking *crowd*. Madness. Suicide.

To flare so easily, without a spark? Triggered by nothing more than a bump and a few snickers? Why here, why now?

This was incredibly dangerous. From now on, I'd carry sunglasses everywhere, day and night. What if I hadn't brought them today? What would have happened?

My haphazard wandering brought me to the clubhouse entrance at the end of the lawn. To my left, a garden bench was tucked among a stand of dogwoods. I hurried to it and sat. Perhaps alone, in the shade, I could pull myself together.

Calm. Breathe.

Data bombarded from all directions, demanding attention. The world was etched in crystalline detail. Slowly, carefully, I sifted through the sensory muddle.

I could see individual blades of grass, the stitching on my classmates' clothing. Could smell a perfume of oleanders, human sweat, iced shellfish, and bruschetta. Could hear whispers, the clink of silverware, the crunch of gravel underfoot. Could taste ocean spray on the wind. Could feel the gentle weight of the sliver necklace hanging from my neck.

It was incredible.

For the first time that day, I didn't feel overwhelmed by insecurity. These snobs couldn't do what I could. Couldn't even fathom the experience.

Confidence restored, I decided to take another spin around the yard.

Without straining, my ears teased snippets of conversation from the general din. Had anyone noticed my fit? Was anyone watching my movements?

No and yes. Though my flare had gone undetected, plenty was being said about me. Classmates spoke behind their hands. The words weren't pleasant.

My good mood evaporated.

To be fair, I've never been part of the "in" crowd. No Viral is. Bolton preppies mock us relentlessly. They call us things like peasants, or island refugees. They know we aren't rich, and never let us forget it.

Tuning in that afternoon, I discovered that recent events had made me even *less* popular, which I hadn't thought possible.

To many Bolton students, I was "that girl." As in, "that girl who broke into Claybourne Manor." Or "that girl who got Chance arrested." But I had other titles as well. "The young girl" or "the little kid." Or my favorite: "the science weirdo."

From what I could eavesdrop, I was practically a villain. The blue bloods were horrified that a boat kid from Morris had taken down members of their circle.

Stories reached me, burned my ears. Wild tales straying *far* from the truth. I couldn't believe some of the rumors. Everyone had an opinion, none complimentary.

Disheartened, I tried to shut out the whispers.

Focus on another sense. Try your nose.

I drew air through my nostrils, careful not to snort. Usually I could ferret a few scents from the breeze. Fresh-cut grass. A cloying perfume. *Creed?* Sweaty underarms. Melting butter.

Good. Safe, familiar scents.

Then the odors changed. New smells entered my perception. Trace odors, lurking just below the top layer. Undefined and faint, the aromas were difficult to pin down. Yet recognition danced on the tip of my consciousness.

My mind tried to dissect the new olfactory input. Failed. To put it more clearly: my nose stopped making sense.

That sour tang wafting from the red-dressed debutante talking with her boyfriend. Was that . . . *nervousness?*

And the dull vinegary smell oozing from the toddler by the koi pond, the one randomly dropping pebbles into the water. If forced to pick a label, I'd go with . . . *boredom.*

I couldn't explain it, but I smelled . . . something. And my brain was insisting on the connections. I dug deeper.

A door banged open in my brain. Thousands of trace scents poured through.

Dropping to a knee, I grabbed my head with both hands. The torrent of information was more than I could bear. Straining and quivering, I tried to shake off my flare. I had to make it stop.

SNUP.

The power receded. My senses normalized. It was over.

I pulled off my sunglasses and rubbed my eyes, feeling like I'd been through a ringer. When my lids opened, the Tripod of Skank was three feet away.

CRAP CRAP CRAP.

Courtney Holt. Ashley Bodford. Madison Dunkle.

Three spoiled brats playing at princess. My personal nightmare.

They didn't like me, and I *loathed* them. These girls were the last people on earth I wanted to see.

"What are *you* doing here?" Courtney seemed genuinely astonished. Which, with her intellect, was routine. "Surely you can't debut now? Not after what you did to Hannah."

"After what *I* did?" I spoke without thought. "To *her*? Seriously?"

Courtney nodded, wide-eyed, blonde curls bouncing. Her microscopic blue dress struggled hard to cover a perfect figure. Sapphire jewelry sparkled in the afternoon sunshine.

"You're a criminal," she said, dead serious. "You make people go crazy!"

The Tripod stood shoulder to shoulder before me. I felt trapped.

"I don't know *how* you stayed active." Ashley brushed glossy black hair from her eyes. "But what I can't get is *why*. No one wants you here. You must know that."

Okay. That hurt.

Madison giggled. She was the nastiest—the Tripod's front foot. Hair, nails, and makeup flawless, she practically glowed with expensive excess.

Madison also had a crush on Jason. His fascination with me did not go over well.

Where *was* he? I could've used his attention right then.

"The word's out, Tory," Madison said cruelly. "Everyone knows you're a freak. Whose house do you plan to rob next?"

Enough. Three against one, and they weren't pulling punches. Time to retreat.

To my left was a clubhouse door. I strode over and tried to shoulder it open. It didn't budge.

Laughter erupted behind me.

"Try pulling, sweetie." Madison.

"And don't muss your rented clothing," Ashley added.

"That *is* a nice dress," Courtney said, oblivious as always. "I wonder how she got it? Is there, like, a Goodwill thing for debs or something?"

Our face-off had begun to draw a crowd. I hated the attention.

Madison, however, relished an audience. She moved in for the kill.

"Maybe you should find another activity, Tory." Chilly smile. "One more suited for someone like you."

Ashley and Courtney nodded.

Humiliated, I yanked the door open and fled inside.

"So long!" Madison called. "We'll be here all season!"

Spiteful giggles followed me into the air-conditioned darkness.

CHAPTER 9

The doors banged shut behind me.

I sped down a red-carpeted hall, past trophy cases, model ships, and massive murals depicting ancient ocean voyages.

The setting barely registered. My emotions were on tilt.

Get away. Get calm.

The cowardly mantra kept looping inside my head.

Get away. Get calm.

Eventually the hallway dumped me into a lavish dining hall. A gigantic mahogany table occupied the center of the room, surrounded by chairs adorned with embroidered cushions. On the far wall, sunlight poured through huge windows overlooking the harbor. The air reeked of wood polish and fresh linen.

The grandeur of the chamber stopped me in my tracks.

"Swank." The empty room swallowed my whispered comment.

Hands on hips, I breathed deep, trying to regroup mentally. Slowly, my shaking legs steadied.

I considered my options. Return to the party? No chance. I was done with awkward circling for the day.

Bail? Sure, but how? My ride wasn't due for an hour.

As I dithered, undecided, a painting caught my eye. Bold and colorful, it stood out from all others decorating the walls.

I stepped closer for a better look.

Oil on canvas. Cedar frame. Old, more weathered than the surrounding paintings, but somehow more vibrant as well. All blues and reds and splashes of yellow. Eye-catching, but clearly not a masterpiece.

Unlike the dour males staring down around me, the subject of this portrait was a woman—a lady swashbuckler dressed in men's clothing. She stood on the deck of a ship at sea, auburn hair streaming, a pistol in one hand and a dagger in the other.

Captivated, I tried to make out the vessel's name. No go. I checked the portrait's curved wooden frame for a nameplate, title, artist, anything.

"Admiring young Bonny, eh?"

I started at the voice. Turned.

A man dressed in a butler's uniform stood behind me. He was wearing black pants and a white shirt, coat, and vest. A ridiculous white bowtie topped off the outfit. He'd entered so silently I hadn't heard a sound. *Weird.*

"You have a good eye." The man drew close, nodding toward the painting. I guessed his age at somewhere north of seventy. He had a full head of white hair and thick, bushy eyebrows. My mind sent up an image of Colonel Sanders.

Bushy Brows smiled, eyes locked on the canvas. "It's not the priciest picture in the collection, but it has the most *character*." He clenched a fist for emphasis.

I stared, at a loss for words. The old coot seemed to have sprung straight from the carpet.

"Sorry, my manners aren't what they should be." Bushy Brows extended a hand. "Rodney Brincefield. Caterer. Bartender. Amateur historian. Jack of many trades."

I reflexively took his hand, but my guard stayed up. Way up.

"I work part-time for the Palmetto Club." Brincefield winked. "I love to sneak in here and see my girl."

Excuse me?

Slight step backward.

Brincefield jabbed a gnarled thumb at the painting. "Anne Bonny. You've heard of her, of course?"

Ah. The codger was an art lover. Fair enough.

I shook my head. "I just moved to Charleston a few months ago. Was she local?"

"Some might argue. Others would strongly disagree. No one can say for sure."

Um, what?

"Anne Bonny was a fearsome pirate. Practically a legend." Brincefield frowned to himself. "They need to teach these things in school."

"Pirate?" I couldn't keep the skepticism from my voice. "I thought that was a boys' club."

"Mostly, but Bonny was special. An original feminist, if you will. Centuries ahead of her time. But I won't bore you with the details." He sighed. "Today's youth have no interest in history. It's all video games and the Internets, or whatever you call them."

"No, no. Please go on. I'm interested." I was.

Brincefield gave me an appraising look.

"You know, you look a bit like Bonny," he remarked. "And not just the red hair."

I said nothing. The intensity of his gaze was making me slightly uncomfortable.

Brincefield rubbed his chin. "Where to start?"

I waited, feeling awkward.

Admittedly, I *did* look a bit like the woman in the picture. Red hair. Tall, slender build. And she was pretty, thank you very much.

I liked Bonny's eyes the best. Emerald green, like mine. The artist had given them a mischievous glint, as though their owner was challenging the world. As if Bonny knew a joke the rest of us didn't.

I could see why the old guy admired the painting so much.

"Bonny worked the Atlantic during the early 1700s," Brincefield began abruptly. "Sometimes she dressed like a man, sometimes she didn't. In this portrait Bonny is on the deck of *Revenge*, a ship she crewed under a pirate named Calico Jack."

Brincefield tapped the side of his nose. "Rumor has it, they had a thing. And he was *not* her husband."

I nodded. What else was I supposed to do?

"*Revenge* terrorized a swath of ocean from the Caribbean to the North Carolina coast. Her crew liked to hijack vessels entering or exiting Charleston Harbor. Easy pickings . . . for a while."

Another pause.

"A while?" I prodded. I suspected Brincefield's mind had a tendency to wander.

"By the 1720s, colonial authorities were cracking down on pirates. The predators became the prey. Eventually, Calico Jack and his band were caught and put on trial. All were hanged."

"Hanged?" I was shocked. "Bonny was hanged?"

My eyes flicked to the canvas. This devil-may-care woman died at the end of a rope?

Brincefield chuckled at my dismay.

"No one knows," he said. "After the trial, Bonny disappeared from her prison cell."

"Disappeared?"

"Poof." He curled then splayed his fingers. "Gone."

"So it's not *certain* she was hanged."

Brincefield shrugged. "Who knows? Some say Bonny escaped, dug up her treasure, and lived out her life in luxury. Maybe right here in Charleston."

"Treasure?"

"I had a feeling that might interest you." Brincefield's lips turned up in a grin. "The other part of Bonny's legend is her buried riches. A fortune. *Never* found."

"Really?"

"*Really*. Hundreds have searched, but without success. Some never returned." Brincefield's eyes drifted to a point somewhere between us. "My older brother Jonathan was one," he said softly.

Though curious, I didn't want to pry. "I'm sorry to hear that."

Brincefield snapped back into focus. "That was a long, long time ago, in the forties. Jonathan was almost twenty years my senior. I rarely saw him."

The old man strode to the windows and gazed at the harbor. Boats glided past. Gulls dove and splashed. It was a gorgeous afternoon.

But I hardly noticed.

An idea was taking shape in my mind. A crazy one.

I wanted to grill Brincefield on Bonny's legend. Extract every detail. I had one thought, and one thought only.

I could really, *really* use a pirate treasure.

But Brincefield seemed to have closed down. Not wanting to unearth painful memories, I remained mute. But I made a mental note to research, to tap other sources.

Finally, the old man stirred.

"Jonathan fixated on Bonny's treasure," he said. "Talked about it incessantly. The adults all thought he was cracked. Eventually, he shared only with me." Brincefield looked down at his hands, chewing the corner of his lower lip. "Then one day he vanished. I never saw him again."

"I'm sorry."

Lame. But I meant it. I understood how it felt to lose family. To miss someone. Daily. Terribly. To have a hole in your life.

"Enough about that." Brincefield's smile snapped back into place. "The treasure! It's said to be worth millions! And it's rumored to be right here in Charleston."

Okay. Seriously? Was this a cosmic joke?

Lost treasure. Worth a fortune. Possibly in Charleston.

Against all reason, I found myself growing excited.

"Where in Charleston?" I asked, casual as possible.

"Oh ho!" Brincefield laughed. "A kid actually caring about history!"

"Someone should find that treasure," I said. "Why not me? If it's out there, it's a free fortune. And historically important," I added quickly.

"Well, yes. I suppose someone should find it. Of course."

"Where can I learn more? Are there books? Clues to the treasure's location?"

"I assume so." A bit less jovial. "Probably useless. Remember, in all these years, no one's discovered *anything*."

"But you said there were rumors," I pressed. "Legends. Where can I get more information on them?"

"Oh, here and there." Brincefield's hands dropped into his pockets. "Around."

Odd. He'd been so excited before.

Whatever. I wouldn't hound the old guy. If there's one thing I'm good at, it's digging up dirt. I was eager to get started.

For the first time since Kit's news dropped, I had a glimmer of hope.

Okay, barely a flicker. Pirate treasure? Even I couldn't take it seriously. It was ridiculous. Comical. A story for moon-eyed five-year-olds.

But at least now I had a purpose. Any plan, however far-fetched, was better than no plan at all. Right?

Step 1: learn everything I could about Anne Bonny.

"Thanks for the history lesson, Mr. Brincefield. First chance, I'm going to read up on Miss Bonny. She sounds like an interesting lady."

"Truly?" Brincefield looked startled. "What's your name? I'm sorry, I never caught it."

"Tory Brennan. Pleased to meet you, sir. And thanks again."

"Yes of course," he said distractedly.

Anxious to get started, I snapped a pic of the painting with my iPhone and headed out the door.

CHAPTER 10

For long moments, Rodney Brincefield stared at nothing.

The girl was gone.

He feared he'd made a big mistake.

Why did I tell her about Jonathan's treasure?

That's how Brincefield thought of it, even after so many years. Even though Jonathan had never once mentioned sharing.

Brincefield stood still as a statue. But his mind circled back to his youth.

Poor Jonathan.

Today they'd call it a disability. Clubfoot. Not severe enough to prevent him from walking, but sufficient for rejection from the army.

Jonathan had been devastated. He'd wanted to fight Nazis, had gone to enlist with the other able-bodied men. Brincefield remembered his brother's torment when told he couldn't serve. When left behind.

The army's decision had eaten at Jonathan. Made him feel like a failure. Less a man. Ashamed.

For weeks, Jonathan had refused to leave the farmhouse. Bottle after bottle disappeared down his throat. Brincefield had feared for his brother's life.

Until the day they heard the legend of Anne Bonny. Then everything changed.

"Obsession," Brincefield whispered.

Jonathan caught pirate-treasure fever. Became fixated, to the exclusion of all else. No one understood it.

None but Rodney Brincefield. He knew his brother was haunted, that Jonathan needed to find Bonny's treasure to expunge his disgrace. To show everyone the army was wrong.

For months, Jonathan spoke of nothing else. He ranged far and wide seeking stories, rumors, anything pointing to the treasure's location.

The world thought he'd lost his mind.

I was the only one who listened, Brincefield thought. *I was his sounding board. His confidant. Eight years old, and just as hooked. The treasure came to dominate* my *thoughts, too.*

Brincefield saw the images clear as day. The little boy plotting with his adored older brother. The excited chats in the old barn behind the farmhouse. Bonny's lost horde was the topic that bridged the age difference. That connected them more powerfully than their shared blood.

Those were the happiest days of Brincefield's childhood.

Then, one day, Jonathan vanished.

He'd gone to chase down a lead. A real scorcher, he'd said. He'd left no clue about his destination, only hinted that he was closer than ever before.

Brincefield never saw him again.

No one did. Everyone assumed the Mad Clubfoot had finally despaired and taken his own life. They'd muttered condolences, held a Mass, and gotten on with things.

Not Brincefield. He knew better. The treasure had become too important to Jonathan. He'd never have stopped until it was his.

Brincefield felt his chest heave. The ache was still there, as strong as half a century before. Not knowing. It was terrible. He squeezed his eyes shut.

"Jonathan's treasure." Brincefield spoke to the empty dining room.

The old man turned from the windows.

"Jonathan's treasure," he repeated. Quiet, but firm.

"*My* treasure."

Straightening his tie, Brincefield strode from the chamber.

CHAPTER 11

"Man, Charleston was just silly with pirates."

Coop cocked an ear, but quickly returned to chewing his rawhide.

"Well it's true," I said.

This time, not even a glance from the pup. Coop rolled onto his side, toppling a stack of reference books piled beside my desk.

"Watch it!" I scolded. "I'm not done with those yet."

Since catching the altered parvovirus, I'd been researching like crazy. Behavioral studies of wolves. Canine anatomy and physiology. Viral epidemiology. I needed to learn everything I could about my new DNA.

The sudden flare at the yacht club had only increased my anxiety.

I'd decided to keep what happened to me a secret for the moment—the other Virals were worried enough already—but I had to find answers, and soon.

But that project had to take a backseat.

"Listen, dog-face, this stuff is interesting." I tapped the computer screen. "Back when this city was known as Charles Town, it was a pirate magnet. They practically owned the place."

Coop righted himself and, less than riveted, switched to gnawing the leg of my desk chair.

I swatted. Missed. Coop yipped once, then sauntered from my bedroom.

"Ungrateful mongrel," I called after his retreating tail.

Safely back in my townhouse, I'd scoured the Internet for mentions of Anne Bonny. In the process, I'd unearthed a mountain of info on local buccaneers. Hundreds of links.

"This calls for backup," I told the empty room.

Opening iChat, I checked to see who was available. Clicked Hi's icon.

He'd recently switched avatars and was now the Green Lantern. I was still the Gray Wolf. Classics never die.

Wolf: Got a minute? I have a . . . plan? An idea. Sort of.

Green Lantern: Do I need life insurance?

Wolf: Haha. Come over now. Grab Shelton if you can.

Green Lantern: Boo. I thought you were hitting on me.

Wolf: Nope. Still intimidated by your good looks.

Green Lantern: Understandable.

Wolf: Try to grab Ben too.

Green Lantern: Will do.

◯   ◯   ◯

Five minutes later, in strolled Shelton and Hi. Hi wore an eye-jarring orange Kool-Aid Man T-shirt, paired with khaki shorts. Shelton was sporting his favorite—a brown tee with "n00b" printed on it. Together, they looked like a Reese's peanut butter cup.

Hi flopped on my bed and kicked off his shoes.

"Ahh! Lady pillows. So much fluffier than mine." He took a giant whiff. "Why does everything girlie smell so delightful?"

"Because we acknowledge the importance of basic hygiene. And periodically clean our bathrooms."

"Brilliant. I should write that down. After all, it takes a village."

Shelton shook his head. "I'd never let him roll in *my* bed. I've seen *his*. Not pretty."

"Believe me, I'm not thrilled." I noticed Coop was missing. "Have you seen the dog?"

"On the prowl," Shelton said. "He ran right by us."

"Great." Coop had snuck outside. Again.

"You try stopping that mutt when he wants to go somewhere," Hi said. "I don't get between wolves and their goals. Safer that way."

"No biggie."

Charleston has a leash law, but on Morris Island, what's the point? Isolation is the one advantage to living so far out. Collared, tagged, and chipped, Coop wouldn't be mistaken for a stray.

And by whom? The neighbors all knew Coop and had accepted him as my pet. To varying degrees.

The dog would return when hungry. Count on that.

"Ben's on the dock changing an oil filter." Mercifully, Hi abandoned my coverlet and moved to the ottoman. "I just shot him a text."

"What'd you find, anyway?" Shelton slouched on my daybed by the window. Outside, the ocean steadily lapped the shore. "Hi said something about selling junk bonds?"

"Hilarious." I hesitated. Was my idea any less crazy? But four eyes watched me expectantly.

"Have either of you ever heard of Anne Bonny?"

"Of course." Shelton.

"Aye, matey! I knowest that foul female brigand!" Hi.

"Oh, good. I just found out about her." I hedged. "Her story sounds fascinating."

"She was awesome," Shelton agreed. "There used to be lots of pirates around here. From, like, 1600 to 1750, this area was swarming with them."

"The golden age of piracy!" Hi spread his hands wide. "Now you have to go to Somalia, and they use rocket launchers. That's no fun."

"I found a ton of stuff." I chin-cocked the computer. "And was hoping you guys could help me sift through it."

"Sure," Shelton said automatically. "But why? Some kind of paper?"

"Did you know that Blackbeard himself was killed off the coast of Ocracoke, *right here* in the Carolinas?" Hi continued with his documentary shtick. "Ambushed, he fought valiantly, absorbing twenty sword wounds and five pistol shots." Dramatic tonal shift. "When Blackbeard finally fell, the British navy hung his severed head from a bowsprit to prove that he was really dead."

"Nice," I said. "We didn't study that in central Massachusetts."

"Blackbeard was a master showman," Hi added. "Long hair. Wild beard. He wore six pistols, a bunch of knives, and a cutlass. He'd work himself into a frenzy before battle to scare the crap out of his opponents."

"Tricky, too," Shelton added. "I read that he'd burn hemp rope under his hat to create a smoke cloud. When he attacked, his victims thought he was the real devil. Sailors would surrender at the sight of him. He wrecked shop all around here."

"Don't forget the siege," Hi said. "In 1718, Blackbeard and another pirate named Stede Bonnet attacked so many ships around Charleston Harbor that the city closed down the port. Nobody got in or out for months."

"Yikes," I said. "Did Blackbeard kill everyone? Sink the ships?"

"Naw, but he took a lot of prisoners," Shelton said. "He'd snag the bigwigs and hold them for ransom. Usually freed them unharmed if the bounty was paid."

"Why is so much known about him?"

"Blackbeard was pardoned for a while," Hi said. "Used his real name: Edward Teach. But the straight life didn't take. You know what they say: *once* a hijacking, murdering, high-seas gangster . . ."

"That's great," I said, "but what about Anne Bonny?"

"Bonny?" Shelton's face scrunched in thought. "She came from Ireland, I think. Rolled with Calico Jack, the pirate who stole Bonnet's ship, *Revenge*."

Hi resumed his TV-host baritone. "Master of both sword and pistol, Anne Bonny was a deadly fighter with a *nasty* temper. As a teenager, Bonny stabbed her serving maid." Eyebrow flare. "As a pirate, she once undressed a fencing instructor using only her sword!"

Shelton broke in. "Anne Bonny pummeled any fool who hit on her without permission. She was definitely a badass."

Inside, I smiled. I liked that.

"But that's all small potatoes," Shelton said. "She's famous, *really* famous, because . . ." He stopped dead. "Wait."

I met his gaze levelly. No point in being discrete now.

"No." Shelton shook his head. "You can't be serious. *That's* your plan?"

"What plan?" Hi asked.

"You have a better idea?" I crossed my arms. Defiant. And a little self-conscious.

"But that's not even a real plan. It's a joke." Shelton's fingers found his left ear. Tugged. "Why not just chase rainbows looking for lucky charms?"

"What plan?" Hi repeated.

"I'm not claiming it's a slam dunk," I said.

"It's not even a full-court shot," Shelton said. "Blindfolded. Underhand. With a bowling ball."

"We have to try *something*."

"WHAT. PLAN?" Hi. Exasperated.

Ben walked in and popped the back of Hi's head. "WHY. ARE. YOU. YELLING?"

"Wonderful." Hi slid to the floor and rolled to his back. "First ignored, then attacked. I need new friends. And a lawyer."

"You'll survive." Ben dropped into my lounger and crossed sneakered feet. His black T-shirt was stained with grease and oil. "Now answer the question."

Sighing theatrically, Hi spoke to the ceiling. "Tory came up with one of her special schemes. Shelton thinks it's insane, big shock there. Neither will tell me what they're talking about. Then you came in and assaulted me. That's all I got."

"Brennan here thinks she's found a way to solve our fiscal problem." Shelton laid it on thick. "Easy! All we have to do is find Anne Bonny's lost pirate treasure."

Ben snorted.

Hi's giggles rose from the floor. "Okay, *that's* pretty nuts."

My face burned, but I didn't back down.

"Why is it so crazy? No one has ever found it, right? We need tons of cash, and we need it *now*. I'm open to other suggestions." I cupped a palm to the side of my head. "All ears."

Ben's forehead crinkled. "You're talking about finding buried treasure. You realize how absurd that is, right?"

"I do."

"No one's sure the treasure even exists," Shelton said. "It could be an empty legend."

Hi sat up. "Hundreds of people have searched. Experts.

Geniuses. Dudes with elephant guns and funny hats." He waved a hand. "It's a myth."

"Fine. Prove it. Help me research. Show me how foolish I'm being."

Groans. Head shakes. The idea wasn't a crowd pleaser.

"You've got better things to do?" I wheedled.

"I don't," Hi admitted. "I'm in."

Ben rolled his eyes.

"Damn it, Hi." Shelton sighed. "Now we're all doomed."

"Hey, pirates are awesome." Hi shrugged. "I don't mind reading up on them. I thirst for knowledge."

"There's an old Sewee legend about Bonny's treasure," Ben said.

"*All* Sewee legends are old," Hi quipped.

Ben crooked two fingers, daring him to say more. Hi wisely refused the bait.

"Supposedly," Ben continued, "Bonny stashed her loot around the time my ancestors were forced into the Catawba tribe. I've only heard a little of the story."

"That's great," I said. "Tell us."

"I don't know it by heart. Something about the devil and red fire. I could ask my great uncle."

"Please do," I said. "You never know what might help."

"I can do you one better," Shelton said. "I read there's a map."

"A treasure map!" Hi rubbed his hands together. "Now we're talking. This'll be easier than a trip to the ATM."

"So where is it?" I asked.

Two googles later, we had the answer.

CHAPTER 12

Foregoing our usual route, Ben motored *Sewee* up the east side of the peninsula to the docks beside the South Carolina Aquarium. Charleston University reserves a slip there for the use of LIRI's staff. It was empty, so we helped ourselves.

No, we didn't have permission. But it was late afternoon, crazy hot, and docking there made for a much shorter walk. It's not like CU had an armada of boats. The time saved was worth the slight risk.

We walked through the garden district, one of Charleston's most picturesque neighborhoods. The street-corner parks were a riot of camellias, azaleas, and crepe myrtles. Ancient magnolias shaded the sidewalks, tempering the worst of the day's heat.

On Charlotte Street we passed the famous Joseph Aiken Mansion, a nineteenth-century carriage house converted to an upscale tourist hotel. At Marion Square we took a right and reached our destination in a few short blocks.

"There," I said. "The ugly one."

Founded in 1773, the Charleston Museum was America's first. Located on Meeting Street, it anchors the northern end of Museum Mile, a historic district of parks, churches, museums, notable homes, the old market, and City Hall.

"Not much to look at," Ben commented at the museum's front entrance.

Ben was right. The two-story edifice is not Charleston's finest architectural moment. Bland, late-seventies drab, where dull brick meets plain brown paint. The place looks more public high school than historic landmark.

"The exhibits are pretty good," Shelton said. "I went with my mom. Lots of natural history displays and Lowcountry stuff."

"Check that out." Hi pointed.

Just before the doors, an enormous iron tube gleamed in the sunlight. Thirty feet long and coal-black, the cylinder was covered in huge metal rivets. Two hatches protruded from its top. A thick wooden shaft jutted from its front end with a metal ball affixed to its tip.

A red-faced man in an aloha shirt motioned his wife into position beside the monstrosity and began snapping pictures. We approached after they'd completed their Kodak moment.

"What is that?" I asked.

"A replica of the *H. L. Hunley*." Of course Shelton would know. "A Confederate submarine from the Civil War."

"Men got inside that thing? Underwater? In the 1860s?" Hi shivered. "No thanks, pal. I'll pass."

"Good call, since the sub didn't work out," Ben said. "They found the real *Hunley* in 1995."

"Where?"

"At the bottom of the harbor. Crew still inside."

"But *Hunley* got her target." Shelton read the sign next to the replica. "First sub in history to sink a ship. So she's got that going for her."

A nearby stand held an assortment of museum handouts. Hi grabbed one and began flipping pages.

"Oh!" he squealed. "The museum has the largest silver collection in Charleston! And a section dedicated to eighteenth-century women's clothing!" He mock-sprinted to the doors. "I hope those exhibits aren't sold out!"

"There's a pirate collection, too!" I called after him. "Smart-ass."

Inside, a blast of AC triggered goose bumps on my arms and legs. I'd forgotten the absurdity of museum thermostat settings. It felt like I'd entered an industrial freezer.

Enormous bones loomed to our left. "What the what?"

"The full skeleton of a right whale, one of nature's goofiest-looking seafarers." Shelton paraphrased from the placard. "This dude swam into Charleston Harbor in 1880 and never swam out. Tough break."

"Somewhere in here are the remains of an extinct crocodile over twenty-five million years old." Hi gestured vaguely past the whalebones. Then he turned, eyes wide, hands clamped together before him. "Can I go see it, Mommy? *Please please please?*"

"Fine." I waved, magnanimous. "Have fun. But no talking to strangers."

Hi winked, then set off in pursuit of his fossil. Ben, Shelton, and I proceeded to a brightly lit info desk.

"Can I help you?" A plastic name tag identified the young woman as Assistant Curator Sallie Fletcher.

Sallie definitely dressed the part. Black cardigan. White turtleneck. Gray tweed skirt. Beyond the clothing, however, nothing was dowdy.

Sallie was pretty, with elfin features and close-cropped black hair, stylishly mussed. A tiny thing, she couldn't have weighed much more than a hundred pounds. There were rides at Six Flags for which she might've failed the yardstick test.

"You guys here for the knitting exhibition?" Sallie's caramel eyes twinkled with good humor.

Okay, did I say she was pretty? Striking was more accurate. Even stunning.

Ben flushed, straightened. Shelton focused on his shoes.

Boys. I took the lead.

"We're looking for the exhibit on Anne Bonny." I didn't mention the map. No need to seem foolish right off the bat. "We understand the museum has a pirate collection?"

"That we do. Unfortunately, the display is closed for renovation right now."

Damn.

"Any chance we could get a look anyway?" I asked. "We came such a long way."

Sallie tapped her lips with one manicured nail. An emerald-cut diamond sparkled on her petite third finger.

"I think we can pull that off." She beamed a mile of teeth, devastating my male companions. "Franco's on security today, and he never leaves the booth. Bad hip. And I know the other curator fairly well, since he's my husband."

I could sense Ben and Shelton deflate.

Tough break guys. Otherwise, you totally *had a chance.*

Doofuses.

"Follow me." Sallie popped up from her chair. "No one else is here, so I can give you a quick peek."

We wound through the museum, collecting Hi along the way.

Sallie led us up two sets of stairs and down a long hall to a room closed off by thick black curtains.

"I'll text Chris," Sallie said. "He'd hate to miss a chance to pontificate about Anne Bonny. He's infatuated."

I hid my impatience. I just wanted access to the damn exhibit.

"He'll be right up." Sallie closed her phone and stretched both arms above her head. "I'm *so* tired of manning that desk."

In my periphery, the Three Stooges followed her every movement. Elbow-jabbing each other in the ribs.

Good Lord.

Seconds passed. Became minutes.

Sallie broke the silence. "What got you interested in our female pirate?"

"I just learned about her," I said. "I didn't grow up around here. She sounds incredible."

"Oh, she was," a voice called from behind me. I turned. A smiling young man was striding toward us.

"Franco?" he asked Sallie.

"In his cubby. The Braves are up in the fourth, so he won't be out for a while."

Chris wasn't bad looking either. Pale blue eyes, collared shirt, weathered jeans, red hair curling from under a beat-up Mets cap. Though a bit soft at the belt line, the guy radiated a sense of ease.

Chris stepped past me, arm-wrapped Sallie, then introduced himself with a round of handshakes. "It's great to welcome Anne Bonny fans. I meet very few people your age who know of her."

"We're very advanced," Hi said earnestly. "I can even zip my own pants. Most times, anyway."

"Thank you *so much* for letting us steal a peek at the collection," I said quickly. "We really appreciate it."

"My pleasure." Chris pulled back the curtain and waved us through. "But let's not mention this visit in the comment box." He fired a shooter at Hi. "And nice going on that pants zipping. That's sophisticated work."

Hi snorted, shot him a thumbs-up.

Eyes rolling, I slipped through the drapes into darkness.

CHAPTER 13

I heard Chris pass me on the right.

Fiddling sounds. Then a floor lamp ignited, followed by another. Chris moved to the opposite side of the room and powered a third.

"Sorry for the gloom." He foot-shoved an extension cord toward the wall. "The power is disconnected in this area. We're re-jiggering the wiring."

The lighting was soft and yellow, perhaps fifty percent of normal. The room's corners remained deep in shadow. I wished I could flare to see better, but I wasn't crazy.

We were standing in a windowless chamber about thirty feet square. Display cases lined the walls, each stuffed with antique pirate paraphernalia. Tattered banners. Replica ships. Gold coins. Daggers.

Beside each cabinet, a sign explained the contents in flowing, antiquated script. The room had a jumbled, eclectic feel.

I was captivated. Pirate gear is just too cool for words.

The room's center held a small assemblage of dummies, each costumed in authentic pirate regalia. Foremost among them was a woman wearing a white linen shirt, a red and purple velvet vest, men's breeches, wool stockings, and a mottled waistcoat. Gold hoop earrings, a silver pendant, a pearl necklace, a wide leather belt, ribbons, brass buckles, and sturdy black boots completed the ensemble.

The lady had flair.

She also had a wicked iron cutlass, three knives in leather sheaths, and a pair of pistols strapped to her chest.

"Meet Anne." Chris gestured to the lady buccaneer.

"Amazing." I crossed to study the mannequin. "Where was she from, exactly?"

"Her early history is hard to pin down," Chris said. "The most widely accepted story places her birth in County Cork, Ireland, sometime before 1700."

"Her father was a Kinsale lawyer named William Cormac." Sallie had been so quiet I'd forgotten she was there. "He was quite prominent, but had an affair with his serving woman and got caught."

"*Playa's gotta play*," Hi muttered under his breath. "Oof!"

My elbow, his gut.

Chris picked up the story. "When his wife exposed the adultery, Cormac was publically shamed and driven out of business. His reputation was shattered, so he fled to the New World with his mistress and their newborn daughter. That would be Anne."

"Where'd they end up?" Shelton asked, voice neutral. I suspected he knew the answer and was testing.

"Right here in Charles Town," Chris replied. "Cormac soon had a thriving legal practice, and he and his family became part of the city's upper crust. Anne grew up rich on a Lowcountry plantation."

"So why'd she turn pirate?" This time, Shelton's curiosity sounded genuine.

"By all accounts, Anne was a wild child," Sallie answered. "Her father constantly griped about her tomboy ways, but she was stubborn. And he worked too much to keep close watch over her."

"Anne's mother died when she was a teenager," Chris added. "Having no siblings, Anne spent a lot of time alone, and eventually fell in with the 'wrong crowd.'"

My breath caught. My eyelids burned.

Oh God. Don't fall apart.

Sometimes it happened like that. The slightest connection to my mother and, without warning, I'd go to pieces. I always tried to hide my sadness. Mostly, I succeeded.

It'd been less than a year since the accident. Though duller now, at times the pain still cut like a knife.

Anne lost her mother. You lost your mother. Shake it off.

I refocused on Sallie's words.

"—stabbed him with her dagger! Young Mr. Grabby-Hands was hospitalized for weeks. After that, nobody made unwanted passes at Anne. And she was only fourteen!"

Like ping-pong, the tale bounced back to Chris. "At sixteen, Anne fell for a drifter named James Bonny. Most think he was simply after her inheritance. When they married, her father was furious."

Ping. Sallie's turn.

"Cormac had always wanted Anne to be a lady of importance," she said. "He planned to marry his daughter into a respectable Charles Town family, through a man of his choosing. She was supposed to be an aristocrat. A plantation owner's wife."

Pong. Chris took over.

"When Anne refused to renounce her no-account, sea captain husband, Daddy Cormac gave her the boot. So the couple moved to New Providence, a pirate hotbed in the Bahamas."

"She was married?" That surprised me. "Even as an outlaw?"

"Not for long," Sallie said. "Anne got cozy with the local pirates, then found out James had turned informant. She left him for a flashy swashbuckler named Calico Jack Rackham."

"This part I know," Shelton said. "Calico Jack offered to buy Anne, but her husband wouldn't have it. So they ran off together."

"Buy her?" I couldn't keep the irritation from my voice. "He tried to purchase Anne like cattle?"

Shelton shrugged and grinned. "It was a simpler time."

"And that was before Anne's 'lady friend' entered the picture." Hi's leer aimed for lecherous, nailed it. "You know Bonny swung both ways, right?"

My look conveyed that I did not.

"He's telling the truth," Shelton chuckled.

My eyes swung to Chris, who nodded with a grin.

Why do boys find this topic so thrilling?

"The Neanderthals are referring to Mary Read, another female pirate." Sallie rolled her eyes at Chris, whose palms rose in innocence. "Read joined Calico Jack's ship, *Revenge*, also dressed like a man. Anne took a shine to the 'new guy,' but eventually discovered Read's deception. Nothing changed. From then on, Read and Bonny had a *special* relationship of an *undisclosed* nature."

"*Pillow fights*," Hi fake sneezed, then danced away from my elbow.

"Mary and Anne were two of the toughest sailors on board," Sallie said. "The crew all knew their secrets but accepted them as equals."

"Pirate ships were very liberal, almost complete meritocracies," Chris said. "Bonny and Read could sail, fight, and handle themselves, same as the men. Nobody messed with them."

"Tell the capture story," Shelton urged. "Didn't they shoot up their own guys?"

"Only because the men wimped out." Sallie looped my arm as if we were confidantes. "In 1720, Captain Jonathan Barnet, a pirate turned pirate hunter, attacked *Revenge* while she was anchored. The crew was passed out, having celebrated the capture of a Spanish trading ship the previous night by getting bombed."

"Barnet sailed close and blasted *Revenge* with cannon fire. Badly hungover, Calico Jack and his men refused to fight. Only Anne and Mary resisted."

Sallie threw a classic "men stink" look at Chris. I was starting to like her.

"Legend goes, Anne screamed, 'If there's a man among ye, ye'll come out and fight!'" Sallie snorted derisively. "The men cowered in the hold like beggars. The two ladies were so incensed they began shooting at *them*, killing one and wounding several others, including Calico Jack."

Chris grinned at his wife. "In the end, only Bonny and Read stood their ground against Barnet's crew. Though they fought like hellcats, everyone was captured. Eventually, the whole crew was hanged."

"But not Anne." I remembered Rodney Brincefield's story. "She may have escaped."

"So you *do* know a little." Chris looked impressed. "Back in Port Royal there was a trial, sensational because two of the accused were women. Read and Bonny were reviled for rejecting polite society and defying traditional female conventions."

"Polite society?" Sallie scoffed. "More like uptight prigs."

"When found guilty of piracy," Chris continued, "the ladies played their trump card."

"Which was?" I asked.

"They pled their bellies."

"Come again?" Hi said.

"Each claimed to be pregnant," Sallie clarified. "English law forbade the hanging of a woman with child, so Anne and Mary couldn't be executed. While the others swung, they were spared."

"Calico Jack was hanged, then disemboweled," Shelton said. "The governor propped his body in a cage at the port's entrance, where every ship could see. Nasty."

That stopped conversation for a moment.

"And?" Ben's first words since entering the building.

"That's the mystery," Chris said. "Mary Read succumbed to a fever in prison. No one knows what happened to Bonny."

"Some say she died in jail. Some say she was hanged after giving birth the following year." Sallie shrugged. "Others insist her father paid a ransom and brought her back home to Charles Town. Still others argue that Bonny escaped altogether, and went on pirating. No one knows for sure."

"One crackpot book claimed that Bonny became a nun," Shelton said. "Another swore she got back with her husband. It's all bunk. Straight-up guessing."

I glanced at Bonny. The fine clothes. The jewels. The braided hair.

What happened to you? I wondered. *Was yours a happy end, or a terrible one?* "So where's her loot?" Hi blurted out. "Bonny was a badass, kick-you-in-the-mouth boat jacker. What happened to all that cheddar?"

Chris grinned. "I figured you'd get around to that."

"Buried. Somewhere. If it ever really existed." Sallie smoothed her hair with both hands. "For years, everyone thought her treasure was on Seabrook Island, but that was a hoax. Then the popular choice became Johns Island, because certain features match up with the map."

"Map?" I said, innocent.

"Yes, map." Chris checked his watch, then strode to a dark wooden bureau on the far side of the room. "Over here."

I tried not to sprint.

"We've got only a few minutes, but you have to see it." Chris tugged keys from his pocket. "It's amazing."

Behind the heavy doors were rows of drawers. Chris worked a second lock, then pulled the bottom one out as far as it would go.

Jackpot.

CHAPTER 14

The document looked ancient.

A glass barrier covered the cabinet drawer, making it hard to read details. But what I could see piqued my imagination. And then some.

The map was sketched on a square foot of crinkly brown paper, now pinned at the corners to a cloth backboard. Squiggly lines formed a central image that appeared to be an island.

Script ran across the top of the page, but in the dim light I couldn't read the words. The bottom left-hand corner had an odd illustration of some kind. A skull and crossbones adorned the bottom right.

No problem interpreting that one. Danger. Stay away.

"This is made of hemp." Shelton was reading the brass placard affixed to the case. "The whole map is pure dope."

"You guys are storing illegal drugs in here?" Hi shook his head. "It's my civic duty to turn you in."

"Too true," Chris said. "But you may want to call Washington. The Declaration of Independence is written on the same stuff."

I ignored the banter. Though tantalizingly close, the map was still obscured and unreadable.

"Is there any way to . . . you know . . . remove it?" I asked.

"Sorry." Sallie pointed to bulbs set inside the casing. "Usually the drawer light comes on, and we have overheads. But without power, this is the best we can do."

"It'll still be here in the spring," Chris said lightly. "Gives you a reason to come back."

"But I need to see it *now*." Sharp. I immediately regretted my tone.

"Why now?" Chris's eyebrows rose. "You plan on tracking down the treasure this weekend?"

"Who says we couldn't?" Ben snapped.

Chris raised a hand in a placating gesture. "I'm sure you could. But it's been almost three hundred years. What's the rush?"

Patronizing? Ben's face said that was his take.

"No rush." I chuckled for effect. "I'm just the impatient type."

"We're big history buffs." Shelton stepped in front of Ben. "Solving mysteries is our hobby. We're good at it." Big toothy grin.

"Let me know when you find it," Sallie said dryly.

"If you guys like history, Sallie and I run a ghost tour downtown." Chris pulled a flyer from his back pocket. "*Lots* of mysteries along our route. Pirate stuff, too."

"Cool." I accepted the handout. "We'll have to check it out sometime."

"Weeknights at seven sharp," Sallie said, "Saturdays at eight and ten. All tours subject to having enough people to make the trip worth going."

Chris's phone beeped sharply. Repeated.

"That's my cue," Chris said. "Cole and I are reorganizing the colonial ceramics. He must think I skipped town. Nice to meet you guys."

"Thank you!" I called to his retreating back.

Sallie closed the drawer, then the bureau doors.

"And *I've* left the front desk unmanned for too long." Sallie clasped her palms together. "Anything else I can direct you fine folks to today?"

Bye-bye treasure map. I hardly knew ye.

"No, you've been great." I was reluctant to leave, but couldn't think of an excuse to linger. "We'll get out of your hair."

"No, no!" Sallie waved both hands. "Stay. No one else is here. Just please unplug that extension cord when you leave."

"Oh my gosh, thanks! We won't be long."

"No problem. I know what it's like when you want to scope something with your friends, and the lame employee won't leave you alone."

The boys made protest noises.

"Sure, sure." Sallie pulled at the curtains until a gap appeared. "Just don't steal any artifacts. Or burn the place down."

"Thanks again!" I repeated.

Sallie's heels clicked down the hallway.

"And like that," Hi snapped his fingers, "she left me. My life is so tragic."

"My heart bleeds for you," Shelton said. "But she was way more into me."

"That guy was an ass," Ben grumbled.

"She didn't lock up," I whispered.

They all looked at me. So?

"The bureau door." I pointed. "The drawer. She didn't lock them. Chris left first, and he has the keys."

No change. So?

"We can examine the treasure map." I gestured with annoyance. "The glass case is unlocked!"

"Yes." Hi didn't move.

"We can *examine* it," Shelton said carefully. "In the case."

Ben looked beyond dubious.

"What?" I may have sounded a wee bit petulant.

"I know what you're thinking," Hi said.

"Oh? Do you?"

"No." Ben shook his head. "Not a chance."

"No *what*? I just want to study the map."

"We are *not* stealing that thing!" Shelton hissed.

"No way!" Hi echoed. "*Nyet. Nein. Non.*"

"Oh *come on*. I just want to look at it! Quit being so dramatic."

Ignoring their disapproval, I opened the bureau, pulled out the drawer, and leaned close.

No good. Too dark. I needed better light and more time.

I glanced over my shoulder. Ben, Shelton, and Hi stood behind me, shoulder to shoulder. Scowling. A solid wall of opposition.

Deep breath.

"Guys . . ."

"Absolutely not!"

"Crazy woman!"

"I just got *out* of trouble!"

Okay. Bad start.

Hi ran a hand through his hair. "Look, I'm as excited about some girl-on-girl pirate action as anyone could be—"

"Oh, real nice!" I cut in, but Hi rolled right over me.

"—and would *love* to go treasure hunting all day, but you've officially lost it. *This is not a realistic idea!*"

"You're talking about stealing an artifact from the Charleston Museum!" Shelton's eyes darted to the curtains. "There must be alarms, cameras, motion sensors. We won't get ten feet!"

"Look around." I dropped all pretense of not plotting a robbery. "There's no power in here! Just extension cords. No electricity, no security."

It was true. The wall cameras were clearly down. Inside the glass case, the sensor lights were inactive.

"No one's been in this room in months." I ran a finger through the layer of dust coating a nearby case. "You heard Chris. This exhibit won't reopen until *spring*. We'll return the map before anyone notices it's missing."

"Chris will notice when he comes back to lock the bureau," Hi said.

"Shelton can use one of his pick thingies and secure the drawer behind us," I countered. "We only need the map long enough to copy it, or make some sense of it. Plus, Chris might not even remember."

"No." Ben stepped forward. "Too much risk, and for what? This isn't a freaking Disney movie. We aren't really going to find buried treasure. Grow up."

"Then let's all say our good-byes now, because I am out of ideas!"

Tears threatened, but I fought them back.

Right now, I needed to bully.

"This is it, guys." One by one, I met their eyes. "Our parents can't fix it. Money won't fall from the sky. We either give this a shot, or call it a life. We'll each have to deal with the flares on our own."

Dead silence. Seconds. Minutes. Hours?

"Crap." Shelton rubbed his forehead with one hand.

"Victoria Brennan, you are the worst influence in the history of high school friends." Hi covered his face with both hands. "How many felonies are we up to now? Three? Six? Ten?"

Ben locked his eyes on mine for a long moment. Then, "How?"

"How do you think?"

I smiled, then slapped him full across the face.

"Ow!" Ben's eyes blazed in the gloom. "Warn me next time!" he said with an inhaled breath.

"Then it wouldn't work." Hi's irises flashed to yellow. "You're not skilled like me." But a sheen of sweat betrayed Hi's bravado. He knew how unstable the powers could be. How easily one could lose control.

"*Stupid, stupid, stupid!*" Shelton trembled as the flare fired through him. "Fear still gets it done. Got plenty of that right now."

I blocked the others out. Reaching deep, I tried to tap into my canine DNA.

Nothing.

Then . . .

SNAP.

Heat coursed through my body. My skin roiled with the torture of a thousand bee stings. Sweat burst from my pores. Teeth clenched, I grimaced as the wolf came out.

"You okay?" Hi asked.

"Fine," I panted. "It was worse this time."

"We shouldn't be doing this!" Shelton whined. "It's playing with fire!"

"More like Russian roulette." Hi shuddered. "I'll watch the door."

"I'll join you," Ben said.

I quickly scanned the room, my gaze lasering through the shadows. The exhibit now seemed lit up like a Broadway show.

"Help me with the drawer case," I said to Shelton.

"It's a very simple lock," Shelton tapped the side. "The key would go here. They must rely on high-tech sensors."

"Let's hope I'm right about the electricity. Open."

Shelton popped the case with preternatural speed.

We froze. No screaming alarm.

I lifted the glass and removed the pins. Still nothing. Rolling the map as tightly as I dared, I reached to slide it under the back of my shirt.

Ben strode over and held out a hand. "Give it to me."

"Why?"

He snatched the map from my grip. "No point in *you* getting busted if this fiasco falls apart." Ben jabbed a finger at Shelton. "Bolt this thing up and we're out of here."

"All clear," Hi whispered from beside the curtains. His voice boomed in my supersonic ears. "But hurry, my head is spinning!"

"Done." Shelton pocketed his lock-pick set and rushed next to Hi. We waited as he cocked his head toward the hallway. Best ears.

"Okay," he said. "Let's bounce."

We hurried down the hall, trying to look natural.

My flare raged like a caged animal, barely in check. Was it adrenaline? Or was the virus wreaking havoc inside me? My steps quickened.

"Sunglasses," I whisper-barked.

Four sets of shades went on. Screw how we'd look to anyone inside.

Luck was with us. We encountered no one. No guards. No gawking tourists. No Sallie manning the desk by the doors.

"Almost there," I hissed.

Like theatergoers leaving a movie, we strolled into the fading afternoon light. Rounded a corner. Cool as cucumbers. Casual as Friday.

I'm not sure who broke first, but my money's on Shelton.

We ran. It started slow, then spread like wildfire. A light trot became a full-on sprint. Pent-up energy surged through my muscles as I tore down the sidewalk.

SNUP.

We didn't slow until we reached the dock, breathless, our flares extinguished. Together we flopped to the wooden planks.

"I had a future once." Hi's color was an alarming scarlet. "College. Ph.D. Nobel Prize. World's Sexiest Man." He waved one hand aimlessly. "Now I'm just a thief. A good one, at least. Thank God."

"And a dog-boy." Shelton used his shirt to wipe sweat from his glasses. "Don't forget that."

"Right. Genetic freak. Can't leave that off the list."

Ben popped both their heads. "Dorks."

I ignored them. One thought ricocheted through my mind.

We have the map. We have the map. We have the map.

I didn't know what tomorrow would bring, but today was progress.

Right?

Toward the west, the sun was sliding into the murky orange depths of the inland marshes. Lights were flickering on. Around us, insects were beginning their evening symphony.

Peaceful. Quiet. Calm made whole.

Baby steps. Keep moving forward.

Tomorrow we'd take my reckless scheme to the next level.

Somehow, make it work.

We *had* to.

We had no other choice.

PART TWO:

BUCCANEER

CHAPTER 15

I didn't unroll the map that evening.

Too wiped out. After the day's drama, treasure hunting went on hold. I conked out minutes after unlocking my front door.

We gathered the next morning in Shelton's garage. Nelson Devers, LIRI's tech director, had converted the small space into a computer repair station. Metal shelves lined the walls, jammed with plastic containers full of bolts, screws, circuit boards, and other mechanical bits. Fluorescent lights hung from the ceiling. A large drafting table, the primary workspace, occupied the center of the floor.

"Time to work." Switching on a handheld magnifier, I unfurled our stolen prize.

The treasure map was weathered and cracked, but well preserved. The paper had dulled to the color of Dijon mustard, and smelled of dust, must, and age.

Faded script flowed across the document's top and bottom. At center, intersecting lines formed a vague image of some sort.

"Huh." Hi scratched his chubby chin. "Hmmm."

"What the frick?" I'd expected mountains, valleys, maybe a shoreline or rock formation. *Some* identifiable feature. Instead, I was seeing a confounding muddle of straight and squiggly lines, surrounded by a simple black border.

"Who drew this?" Shelton complained. "Monet? Picasso?"

"Three vertical lines, and seven or eight horizontal." I frowned. "Then you've got this thick streak running from top to bottom, beneath the jumble."

There was no recognizable topography or geography. Not even a directional indicator. The sketch looked like a child's drawing, or superimposed games of tic-tac-toe.

"That's a map?" Ben scowled. "Looks like a scribble of random lines."

"Underwhelming," I admitted.

"Focus on the writing," Hi said. "The words might explain the drawing."

A two-line stanza crossed the top of the map in bold, graceful calligraphy. Focusing the magnifier, I read aloud:

Down, down from Lady Peregrine's roost,
Begin thy winding to the dark chamber's sluice.

"A riddle?" I couldn't believe it. "Seriously?"

The cryptic verse shed no light on the chicken-scratch design.

"Read the bottom," Hi said. "Maybe the poem makes sense in combination."

I ran the lens over the second verse. Same aggressive handwriting. New unfathomable message:

> Spin Savior's Loop in chasm's open niche,
> Choose thy faithful servant to release correct bridge.

"Not very helpful." A classic Hi understatement.

"Is that supposed to rhyme?" Shelton sounded unimpressed.

He got no answer.

I searched, but found no more writing.

No wonder museum security was lax, I thought. Without context, the map was useless.

"This could be a diagram of underground tunnels," I said, gesturing at the mishmash in the center, "or possibly caves."

"Maybe a coastline?" Hi ventured. "But it doesn't say what island."

"That mess could be anything," Shelton muttered. "We don't even know this *is* an island."

"All the rumors point to an island." Hi yanked a wad of folded papers from the back pocket of his shorts. "I spent hours online. Seabrook. Johns. Fripp. Some fishermen think the references point to Kiawah. But *everyone* agrees—Bonny buried her treasure on a barrier isle."

"No one's found it," Ben countered. "So the popular theories must be wrong."

"Don't shoot the messenger," Hi replied. "Other than those theories and this map, we've got squadoosh."

Having nothing to add, I kept scouring the map for further clues.

A symbol decorated the lower left corner. I leaned closer to inspect it.

It was a green and silver cross. Tall. Thin. Oddly shaped, with the upper tine curving sharply to the right. A circle ringed the intersection of the vertical and horizontal arms.

The odd little emblem held my eye. I'd never seen anything like it. The cross was beautiful, and drawn with care. But it told me nothing.

"Let's brainstorm," I said. "What do we know about Anne Bonny?"

"She was ballsy," Shelton said. "She liked to disguise herself as a man and slip into Charles Town. Even with a bounty on her head."

"Women be shoppin'," Hi said matter-of-factly. "Can't stop 'em."

I ignored him. "So Anne would just stroll around downtown? In the open?"

Shelton nodded. "My pirate book says Bonny owned a small boat. She kept it outside the harbor and used it to sneak ashore."

"A fellow skipper," Ben said. "I like her more already. What'd she name her vessel?"

"Hold on." Shelton disappeared into his house, returned

shortly with a battered hardback. "Her boat was named *Duck Hawk*."

Something clicked. "*Duck Hawk*?"

Shelton nodded.

I reread the map's first line. "Down, down from Lady Peregrine's roost."

"I think this sentence tells you where to start." Excited, I tapped the words. "Directions to the tunnel entrance, or whatever the thick streak on the map is. We should be looking for Lady Peregrine's roost."

"Old news," Hi said. "That's why people suspected the islands I mentioned. In the early 1700s, both Seabrook and Kiawah had peregrine falcon colonies."

"Treasure hunters dug beneath every falcon nest in the state," Ben added. "Found jack squat."

I ignored them. My mind was connecting dots. "Isn't 'duck hawk' another name for falcon?"

"That's true." Shelton pursed his lips in thought. "You think the poem's talking about her boat? But where would Anne Bonny's boat go to roost?"

"No." I held up a hand. "You missed a link. The rhyme mentions a 'Lady Peregrine.' That could mean 'girl falcon.' *The* girl falcon, actually, since the words are capitalized."

Shelton squinted. "I don't follow."

"Anne Bonny named her boat *Duck Hawk*. *She* could be the girl falcon. Anne Bonny might be Lady Peregrine!"

"So we should be looking for Anne Bonny's roost." Hi got it.

"Which makes no sense," said Ben.

"Wait," I said. "Give me a second to think."

They did.

"When Bonny snuck into town," I asked, "where did she park *Duck Hawk*? Didn't the town watch patrol the docks?"

"Not all of them," Shelton said. "There must've been a few piers she could've used to stay under the radar."

"Can we find out?"

"Sure." Shelton began flipping pages in his book.

"What are you thinking?" Ben asked.

"Bonny liked to hide in plain sight, right?"

"Right."

"Why not bury your treasure in plain sight as well?"

Hi's brow furrowed. "You think she stashed her loot somewhere downtown? Inside old Charles Town? That's new, I'll give you that much."

"So," Ben said slowly, "you're saying that 'Lady Peregrine's roost' could describe where Anne Bonny would dock *Duck Hawk*?"

"It's just a theory."

"Got it!" Shelton's finger jabbed a page. "According to the author, Bonny used the docks on East Bay Street. They allowed for a quick getaway if needed."

"Huh." Hi rolled back on his heels, examined the ceiling.

"What, Hi?" I hated having to drag things out of him.

"Well . . ." Hi hesitated. "Sea caves."

Impatient, I almost tapped a foot. "Care to elaborate?"

Hi turned to Shelton. "Does this room get Wi-Fi?"

"Yeah, why?"

"Back in a jiff."

Hi headed toward his townhouse.

Several minutes passed.

"If he's making a burrito," Ben growled, "I'll pound him."

"Now, now." Hi walked in carrying his laptop. "Patience! Dr. Hiram is going to blow your mind."

"Get on with it," Shelton grumbled.

"East Bay Street runs along the eastern edge of the peninsula, yes?" Hi adopted a professorial tone. "That shoreline is riddled with sea caves, some leading under the city streets."

"How would you know that?" Ben. Skeptical.

"Because I do," Hi said primly. "My uncle's a city planner, and *I* like maps."

Hi tapped a few keys, then flipped his laptop around, displaying a geological map of Charleston. The left side of the peninsula was dotted with tiny indentations.

Another mental click. "Oh my."

Six eyes rolled to me.

"Peregrine falcons nest in sea caves," I said. "In other words, they *roost* in them."

"So?" Ben said.

"Anne Bonny would dock *Duck Hawk* near the East Bay sea caves."

"Ah." Shelton said. Ben still looked lost.

"Bonny's falcon-named boat would 'roost'—" air quotes, "—

on East Bay Street." I let the idea sink in. "We should be looking downtown."

"Which is why I got my computer," Hi said. "Watch."

Whipping out his iPhone, Hi snapped a shot of the treasure map. "Step one."

He downloaded the image to his laptop.

"Step two."

"You're such a dork," Shelton snickered.

Hi waggled a finger. "Do not interrupt a master at work. Step three."

Opening Firefox, Hi pulled up a satellite map of Charleston. Then he double-clicked the treasure-map image and set them side by side.

"I see." Shelton adjusted his glasses. "I can do better, if you let me."

"I was wondering how long it'd take you." Hi stepped aside. "Have at, hack master."

My gaze flicked between the two. "*I* still don't have a clue what you're doing."

"Hi had a good idea," Shelton said. "For once. I'm gonna wash out the treasure map image so only the lines remain. Then we can superimpose it over the satellite photo and see if the configuration matches anything."

Clickity click. "The straight lines on the map. Could they be streets?"

"Nice!" Shelton opened a new browser. "Let's check them against a map of old Charles Town."

A million cyber loops later, Shelton had located a city diagram dated 1756.

"Close enough," he said.

For the next few minutes we looked for corresponding patterns. It was like searching for a needle in a stack of needles.

Finally, Hi spotted a semi-match.

"Check that out!" His voice cracked. "These two straight lines track pretty well over East Bay and Church streets. I think we may have something!"

"That's straight CSI right there." Shelton fist-bumped Hi, and both exploded it backward. Tools.

Ben snorted. "There's no way pirate treasure is buried under East freakin' Bay Street. That's the middle of town. It would've been discovered decades ago."

"There's not much infrastructure underground in that area," Hi said, "because of the caves. Not even sewer lines."

"And that's where the East Bay docks used to be." Shelton's voice was suddenly energized. "The ones Bonny used!"

My mind charged ahead, plugging in the pieces. "If our theory's right, the tunnel entrance should be close to those docks."

"We need to inspect all the low places," Hi's face had reddened with excitement. "Cellars, basements, crypts, anything underground."

"Can't we check from the shoreline?" I asked, a bit dubious.

Hi shook his head. "The Battery seawall blocks off the caves. You can't see anything without scuba gear."

I snapped my fingers. "I've got it."

Now it was my turn to run home. Twenty steps to the door, straight up the stairs to my bedroom, a bit of pocket rifling, then a dash back down. The roundtrip took less than two minutes.

"Impressive," Hi said. "But I was carrying hardware."

"I know how we can get into some downtown basements." I held out a crumpled flyer. "Anyone up for a ghost tour?"

CHAPTER 16

The spirits would have to wait.

Kit axed my proposal the moment I presented it.

"Not a chance," he said. "You're still on probation. That means no Wednesday-night trips downtown. Period."

No matter how much I argued, he wouldn't budge.

A flurry of texts followed. The other parents were on the same page. We'd have to go another time.

I tried not to sulk. I needed to get back on Kit's good side. So, Tory the Obedient Daughter spent the afternoon cleaning out her closet, then joined Kit on the couch for some evening network TV.

Yippee.

After circling three times, Coop flopped on his mat. Satisfied that Kit and I were settled, he got down to some serious napping.

I didn't mention my recent activities. The yacht club. The museum. The pirates of Chuck Town. The last thing I wanted was Kit shining a light on my day-to-day. Each attempt at small talk received a vague, innocuous reply. Eventually he lost interest.

Above all, I didn't mention Anne Bonny. Until a certain stolen document was returned, I was at risk. Both curators could ID me. The less people thought about pirate treasure, the better.

And there was another reason for my evasiveness: Kit would think I was nuts. Or worse, childish.

Frankly, I might have agreed with him. Buried treasure was the most ridiculous solution imaginable for our problem. But we had nothing else.

A ridiculous plan was better than none.

"*Bones* okay?" Kit slouched, feet propped on the coffee table.

"That's fine."

We watched in silence, side by side, occasionally chuckling at some of the jokes. I relaxed. Spending time with Kit wasn't so bad. I vowed to do it more often.

But then he decided to chat.

"I talked to a guy in Minnesota today."

"About?"

"A job with the Forest Service. Near Lake Winnibigoshish. Could be fun."

"Winni-what?"

"In the Chippewa National Forest." Kit sat forward. "It's gorgeous, all lakes and woodlands. *Tons* to do. Kayaking. Hiking. Ice fishing and sledding. You could ski every day."

"I don't know *how* to ski, Kit."

"You could take lessons. Or ski cross-country; that's more

popular there anyway. We could live in Cohasset, which isn't that much—"

"Enough!"

Coop's head popped up.

Kit flinched.

"God, you just don't get it!" I knew I was losing it. Couldn't help myself. "I don't want to move *anywhere*. I want to stay here!"

"I have to find work, Tory." Kit spoke carefully. "I don't want the institute to close any more than you do, but it's not up to me. And I have to take care of you."

"Bang-up job so far."

Unfair. Didn't care. The words flew out.

"You move me down here, I finally get settled, and then, *boom*, it's all over? Just like that? And I'm supposed to just nod and accept it?"

"I'm trying to find something you'll like."

"That's crap! Thirty seconds ago you were hard-selling the Great White North. Ice fishing? What a joke."

"What am I supposed to do?" he shot back. "You tell me."

"Fix it! Make it so we can stay!"

Kit's mouth opened, heated words at the ready. But they didn't come. Instead, he closed his eyes, took a deep breath, and rubbed his face. When he finally spoke, the anger was gone.

"I wish I could, Tory. I really do. But some things are beyond my control."

"That's not good enough!"

"No. It's not. I feel terrible about the prospect of uprooting you again, so soon after . . ." Kit trailed off. Nine months in, yet he was still uncomfortable speaking about my mother. Then, finally, "I don't know what else to say."

Coop came over and shoved his snout in my lap. Watery blue eyes met mine. Called me out.

"I know it's not your fault," I said. "It's just . . ."

The words wouldn't form. I was being selfish and immature, acting like a spoiled child. How could I blame him? But I was still too angry to apologize.

"I'm taking Coop for a walk."

I crossed the room and grabbed the leash from its peg. Kit didn't try to stop me.

"Be careful. It's late."

Coop scampered to the door, eager at the prospect of a nighttime jaunt. I carried the leash and let him run free.

Outside, the moon was a bright lunar spotlight. A breeze tousled my hair. The air felt warm and moist, but not un-pleasantly so.

Walking in the dark, a feeling of shame overwhelmed me. Once again, I'd wrongly blasted Kit. My father. The person who wanted the best for me, and loved me above all others. Why did I use him as a punching bag? What good did it do?

Coop ran ahead down the beach, chasing crabs and the occasional night bird.

My pocket beeped and vibrated. Incoming text.

I almost ignored it, certain Kit was sending a heartfelt request for forgiveness. The last thing I wanted was more guilt.

But curiosity got the best of me.

Digging out my iPhone, I tapped the screen.

Jason Taylor.

Great.

I pulled up the message.

Jason apologized for abandoning me at the yacht club. He'd just heard, felt terrible. Blah blah blah. Could I please write him back?

Delete.

The *last* thing I wanted to deal with right then. And for some reason, his message pissed me off. Where *had* Jason been? Five minutes after hitting the dock, he was gone. So much for showing me around.

And why the apology? Jason hadn't caused the Tripod attack. He owed me nothing. It wasn't his job to defend my honor.

His attitude annoyed me. I could take care of myself.

"Why does everything happen at once?" I asked the Big Dipper overhead.

Coop glanced up from a pile of reeds, trotted over, and licked my hand.

"Thanks, boy." I stroked his back. "You're the number one man in my life."

I felt Coop tense. His head whipped toward the townhouses.

"Something wrong?" I whispered.

Coop stepped forward, braced his legs, and growled. Hackles up, his eyes focused on something in the darkness.

It occurred to me that I was alone at night, on a dark beach, in the middle of nowhere.

I froze, listening.

The swish of shifting sand. The snap of flapping nylon.

My eyes strained. A shadow took shape, denser than the surrounding blackness.

It loomed directly between me and my home.

CHAPTER 17

"Chill out, Coop!"

Tension drained from me. I knew that voice.

Shelton approached, careful to let the wolfdog recognize him. Though still a puppy, at sixty pounds Coop could do serious damage.

"Easy, boy." I scratched doggy ears. "He's one of us."

Coop finally caught Shelton's scent, yapped, and wagged his tail.

"He's becoming quite the guard dog," Shelton said. "Good thing we're tight."

Coop rushed forward and planted his forepaws on Shelton's chest.

"Okay, okay!" Shelton struggled to keep his balance. "I missed you, too!" I clicked my tongue. Coop spun back to my side, then scuttled off in search of more crabs.

"What's happening?" Me. False cheerful.

"Something wrong?" Shelton. Not buying it.

"I had a fight with Kit. And *yes*, it was my fault."

"It's eggshells at my house, too. My parents are so stressed, barely anyone talks."

"Is that why you're out here?"

"Naw, I came to find you. Your dad said you'd taken Coop for a walk."

"Well, here I am."

Coop's route took us back toward the docks. We trailed along, letting the wolfdog set the pace.

"What'd you and Kit fight about?" Shelton asked.

"Moving." I sighed. "He keeps mentioning job offers in different places. I know it's not true, but sometimes it feels like Kit doesn't even care about my feelings. So I lost my temper and blasted him. I won't be winning Daughter of the Year this time around."

We walked a few more yards in silence.

"I can't stop worrying about Whisper and the other Loggerhead animals. That island is a special place. Selling it to developers would be criminal."

"Remember when Hi sat on that anthill near Dead Cat Beach?" Shelton chuckled. "Sucked to be him. The welts didn't go down for a week."

I giggled. "Almost as funny as Ben getting chased by those monkeys."

"Good times," Shelton said. "Good times." His voice was softer this time.

More quiet paces. Thoughts of Loggerhead saddened me now. I changed the subject. "What did you want to tell me?"

"Oh, right! I found something online," Shelton said. "Anne Bonny–wise."

"Super." Stuck in a funk, I couldn't get excited. After my argument with Kit, searching for treasure seemed so juvenile.

But Shelton was pumped enough for both of us.

"I was bored, so I started googling names and phrases. *Anne Bonny*, *treasure maps*, whatever I could think of. For an hour, nothing but wasted time. Then I scored *this* baby!"

Shelton held up what I guessed was a printout.

"It's too dark," I said. "What is it?"

"An ad. A pawnbroker in North Charleston is selling a box of pirate artifacts."

"That's it?" Shelton's naïveté surprised me. A pawnshop listing?

"Of course not. This seller claims the collection includes papers belonging to Anne Bonny!"

"And you believe it?"

Shelton nodded. I think.

"Wait a second. Where in North Charleston are we talking about?"

"Well, not the best part," Shelton admitted. "Myers."

"Myers." One of the roughest neighborhoods in the area. Maybe the country.

"It can't be *that* bad," Shelton muttered. "We can go during the day."

"Let me get this straight." I stopped walking. "You want to visit a Myers pawnshop because of an ad for 'pirate artifacts' that mentions Anne Bonny? Seriously?"

"I haven't told you everything."

"All ears."

"Come over by the light." Shelton hurried toward the dock with me trailing behind.

"Notice anything?" Shelton shoved the paper into my hand.

I skimmed. The print was hard to make out in the dim glow. The listing looked like any other classified ad. Authentic pirate collection. Rare papers. Anne Bonny. Priceless. Historical. Yadda yadda yadda.

I was about to quit when I caught it.

"*Oh.*"

"Oh is right," Shelton said. "Think maybe we should check that out?"

"Yes. Yes I do."

A rectangular border surrounded the ad, each corner embellished with a corny illustration. Skull and crossbones. Dagger. Treasure chest. Standard stuff.

Except for the image in the lower right.

That corner was decorated with a cross. Tall and thin, ringed, and oddly shaped, with the upper tine curving to the right.

"Where have we seen *that* before?" Shelton crowed.

Our high five echoed far out over the water.

CHAPTER 18

"How do we get there?" Hi wiped perspiration from his brow.

We were on the blacktop behind our townhomes. The sun was already beating down, the morning a scorcher.

Shelton was entering the pawnshop's address into his cell phone's GPS program. He wore a white polo and beige cargo shorts. Silent as usual, Ben stood beside him in his black tee and jeans. The heat never seemed to touch him.

"Ben will drive," I said.

"I will?"

"We'll take Kit's car. He's at work."

"Kit said we could take his 4Runner?" Shelton sounded skeptical.

"He never said we couldn't. That gives me a get-out-of-jail-free card."

"How do you figure?" Hi asked.

"If Kit gets mad, I'll play dumb and apologize. He'll let it go the first time."

"I'm not stealing your dad's car." Ben was firm. "Call him."

"Trust me, he'll never know." I checked my watch. "We have *six hours* to get there and back. We could make five round trips!"

Time for an ego tweaking. "You *can* drive, right?"

"Of course I can!" Last month, with everyone grounded, Ben had finally gotten a driver's license. "That's not the point."

"There's no other way," Shelton said. "We can't sail to North Charleston."

Ben said nothing.

"Come on!" Sweat rings had formed around the pits of Hi's sky-blue Hawaiian shirt. "We're standing in the hottest spot on planet Earth. Let's just go!"

"Fine. Everyone wears seatbelts. No radio. No distractions." Ben shot Hi a stern look. "No running commentary."

"Your loss," Hi said. "To the pimp ride!"

Five minutes later, we were cruising the unmarked, one-lane blacktop that connects Morris to Folly Island. After passing through Folly Beach, we picked up State Highway 171 and cut north toward James Island.

I'd cranked the AC to maximum for Hi's benefit, but I was only wearing a tank top, shorts, and sandals. The arctic blast immediately covered me in goose bumps.

Honoring Ben's request, we rode in silence. It was strange for us, traveling alone by car. A first for the Virals. Outside, Lowcountry marshland slipped by on both sides. Here and there an egret or crane rose from the still water on long stick legs.

Turning right on the James Island Expressway, Ben crossed to the downtown peninsula and continued on Calhoun Street. A right on King took us north, away from the touristy, historic districts we usually frequented.

We drove past the Cooper River Bridge, a dividing line between blue blood and blue collar. A few miles farther and we crossed into North Charleston.

Myers is a tough district, filled with seedy houses, cheap high-rise apartments, liquor stores, and pawnshops. It's one of the poorest locales in America—few residents finish high school, and even fewer attend college. Crime is common and frequently violent.

Those lucky enough to have jobs are mostly factory workers or day laborers. The homeless and unemployed gather on street corners, shooting up and drinking to escape the reality of their lives.

Myers was not a neighborhood to visit on a lark.

Hi reached over and hit the door locks.

"Next right," Shelton said. Then, "There, on the left. Bates Pawn-and-Trade."

"Are we one hundred percent sure about exiting the vehicle?" Hi's voice was a bit high. "It might not be here when we get back."

"I'll park right in front." Ben also sounded tense.

"We'll be fine," I said. "In and out."

"That's what she said," Hi mumbled, hauling himself from the car.

Bates Pawn-and-Trade was the last unit in a dilapidated strip mall composed of a Laundromat, a nail salon, a pool hall, and a Baptist church.

A red banner proclaimed the shop's name in bold letters. Barred windows displayed an array of dusty offerings. Nine-millimeter cameras. A drum set. A sad little collection of gold watches.

And guns. Lots of guns.

Ben shouldered the solid steel door. Nothing.

"Hit the buzzer," Shelton suggested.

We waited a few moments, idly staring at a security camera set inside a metal cage. A buzzer sounded, the locks clicked, and we pushed through.

Inside, naked bulbs hung from the ceiling, barely lighting the cloudy glass cases lining the concrete walls. Even by pawnshop standards, this store was dreary.

A thick wooden counter ran the length of the rear wall. Behind it sat an immense black man counting a wad of bills. I put his weight at over three hundred pounds. Short and balding, he wore faded black pants, a UPS work polo, and red and white throwback Jordans.

An unlit cigar jutted from a corner of the man's mouth. The stool supporting his enormous derriere appeared on the verge of giving up.

"Ya'll need something?" The man didn't glance in our direction.

"Just looking, thanks!" Reveal our target and he'd jack up the price.

"Umm hmm." His eyes never rose. "The bongs are in the corner, FYI."

Great. He thought we were stoners.

"Spread out," I whispered. "Scratch your head if you spot the collection."

We all moved in separate directions, which caught the man's eye.

"Don't even *think* about pulling a stunt." A thumb jabbed his chest. "This here is *my* shop. Lonnie Bates. I don't tolerate foolishness."

"No sir," Shelton squeaked. "No stunts."

"Damn right." Again the thumb. "Don't forget I've got to buzz ya'll back out."

Bates went back to counting.

Noticing movement, I glanced to my right. Hi was rubbing his dome with both hands. Not exactly subtle. We all closed in.

Hi pointed to a crate on a wall-bolted shelf. We scanned the jumbled contents. Dusty papers. A souvenir eye patch from the Pirate Aquarium. Costume jewelry. Two three-corner hats. Replica flintlock pistols. A torn Jolly Roger flag, made in China.

"Garbage," Ben whispered. "Useless crap."

"I see you've located some of my valuable antiques." Bates slipped from his stool and waddled toward us. "Priceless heirlooms."

Shelton snorted. "You could buy this junk at Party City. In better condition."

"Not true." Bates yanked the box from the shelf. "Some crap was added later, but this crate is full of historical documents. Blackbeard's personal shit. Some Anne Bonny stuff, too."

Beefy hands eased a stack of papers from underneath the kitsch.

My pulse cranked. Bates was right. The documents were either very old or very good fakes. If the former, they might actually be worth something.

"I'd need to have these appraised," I said. "Verify they're real."

"Sorry, paying customers only." Bates held the papers to his chest. "I can't risk ya'll damaging historical treasures."

Crap! I needed to check for the symbol. To be sure. That meant haggling with this greasy con man.

A crazy idea crossed my mind. Dangerous. Irresponsible.

It worked before. Let's put my nose to the test.

I'd promised not to do it, but desperate times call for desperate measures. We needed an edge. I spoke before I could chicken out.

"Do you have a bathroom?"

"What am I? A spa?" Bates cocked his head. "Use the Laundromat next door."

"All by myself? Can't I please use yours?"

"Unbelievable." Eyes rolling, he pointed. "Through the beads."

"Thank you!"

"Don't touch nothing! I got cameras back there, too."

My eyes widened.

"No, I don't mean—not in the damn bathroom!" Bates

rubbed his forehead. "Just keep your hands in your pockets, you hear?"

I hurried through the curtain, then listened to make sure Bates hadn't followed. No way. He was busy pumping up the collection's inestimable value. I locked myself in the bathroom.

Ready? Not really.

I shook out my limbs. Took several deep breaths. Closed my eyes. Reached.

SNAP.

The flare came easily, as if the wolf had been lurking just beneath the surface.

But not without pain.

My arms and legs quivered as the fire flowed through me. Lights strobed behind my eyeballs. I wanted to whimper, but clamped my jaw shut.

In silence I rode the wave of primal energy. Suffered the transformation.

My eyes snapped into hyperfocus. My body burned with visceral force. My ears hummed like a tuning fork.

Ready to rock.

Slipping on my sunglasses, I flushed the toilet and strode back through the beads. Nonchalant, but my heart was racing.

Bates was still working the boys. They seemed overwhelmed by the onslaught.

Seeing my shades, Shelton frowned. Then his eyes went saucer. He elbowed Hi, who elbowed Ben.

They knew.

"It's way too bright in here," I said.

Bates looked at me funny. His shop was lit like a cave.

Now! Before you lose control.

"Mr. Bates, I don't think these are authentic," I said. "Interesting, sure, but not worth much."

"Child, please. These are rare, precious artifacts," Bates insisted. "Extremely valuable. I bought 'em from a *serious* collector."

"Really? Who? I think you got taken."

"That's *my* business, not yours." He crossed arms the size of telephone poles. "Five hundred bones. Not a penny less."

Bates's poker face was impressive. I couldn't get a read.

Luckily, I had other tools.

As discreetly as possible, I drew air through my nose. Sniffed. Sifted. When I found his scent, I nearly staggered backward.

Onions. Coffee. Garlic. Sweat trapped inside rolls of flesh. Cheap drugstore aftershave.

I coughed, violently, nearly losing my eyewear.

"You sick, girl?" Bates squinted.

Hi provided a distraction.

"Can you prove these papers are real?" he asked. "Show us some evidence? You keep documentation, right?"

"I don't have to *prove* nothing, boy." Impatient. "Buy 'em or not. If ya'll don't, somebody else will."

Bracing myself, I inhaled again. The funk sickened me anew, but I kept control this time. My nose sorted, divided, categorized.

From beneath the stench, earthier scents emerged. One odor

outweighed the others, salty and acrid, like a towel soaked in cat urine.

I named the smell, though I couldn't say how.

Deception. Bates was lying.

"You believe this box is valuable?" I asked.

"Young lady, I *know* it."

The acid reek increased.

Lie.

And now, another smell. Rank. Sickly. A little sweet.

Worry.

Bates was anxious we'd call his bluff.

Which is exactly what I did.

"No thanks, we'll pass. You guys ready to go?"

"Wait now, hold on! I didn't say we couldn't work something out." Bates ran a hand over his jaw. "Two-fifty."

"Twenty bucks," Hi hard-balled. "For everything."

"Twenty dollars!?! That's robbery!" Bates's eyes narrowed to slits. "One-fifty."

The twin odors rolled in waves.

"Thanks for your time." I jerked my head toward the door. "Let's bail."

"Fine. One hundo. Final offer."

A new scent appeared. Metallic. Hard. Like iron shavings.

Resolve. Bates wouldn't go lower.

"Deal," I said. "Shelton, pay the man."

Shelton counted five twenties, about half of our available funds. Bates scribbled a receipt and handed the crate to Ben.

"Good luck with those 'artifacts,'" Bates chuckled. "That box ain't nothing but garbage. I paid twenty for the whole lot!"

"Think again," Shelton shot back. "We already *know* the papers are real. Pretty dumb to put the map symbol right in your ad."

Ben cuffed Shelton, but the damage was done.

"Say what?"

"Nothing," Shelton mumbled. "I was just joking."

"Map symbol?" Bates's left eyebrow rose. "What chu' mean, map?"

Nice job, Shelton!

I searched for a credible answer. Blanked. My blood pressure spiked.

SNUP.

The power dissolved. I swayed, but managed to keep my feet. Hi caught my arm.

"Clear?" Hi whispered.

Shaky nod.

"Steady. Don't pass out."

"I just need a sec." My head spun like the teacups ride.

Bates's face pinched in confusion. "How'd ya'll know about my ad?" Then, with realization, came anger.

"Ya'll played me!" he fumed. "Acting the fool, like ya didn't know what ya came for! *Bull*-crap! Ya'll wanted that box the whole time!"

Bates stormed over to Ben. "Forget this! No sale."

"Too late." Ben put a hand on the crate. "Deal's a deal. You took the money. We have a receipt. Done."

"Is that a fact?"

Ben didn't blink.

"Fine!" Bates's eyes were bulging like golf balls. "Get out my shop! And watch yourselves, this neighborhood ain't safe. I'd run back home, if I was you."

I was down with that. We hustled to the door.

"Wait!" Bates pointed at me. "Sign the receipt. Otherwise, the deal ain't official."

I hurried to the counter, jotted as fast as possible.

"Who sold you this box, anyway?" I asked.

"Piss off."

"Hey!" Ben shouted. "Watch your mouth."

Ben stepped toward the counter. Hi grabbed his arm as Shelton placed a restraining hand on his shoulder. Though furious, Ben allowed himself to be halted.

I joined the boys. "Let it go. We got what we came for."

The others followed me toward the door.

"Can we get some buzz-out music, please?" Hi's smile looked forced. Shelton's hands were shaking. Time to bolt.

Bates watched us for a very long moment. Finally, his hand moved below the counter.

Buzz!

"Ya'll don't come back here. Ever."

Not a problem.

CHAPTER 19

Lonnie Bates was furious.

Worse, his pride was stinging.

He'd run Bates Pawn-and-Trade since age seventeen, first for his uncle and now for himself.

Buy for a dollar, sell for two. That was his mantra. It worked. He was rarely taken for a fool.

Except today.

Those downtown brats had swindled him. He felt it in his bones. The punk kids had seen the ad and come for the pirate junk. They'd driven all the way from under their mommy's skirts, walked into his shop, and swindled him good.

Bates couldn't calm himself. Anger burned like an ember in his gut.

The black kid had blurted something about a map. He'd tried to cover his slip, but Lonnie Bates was no fool.

Why would rich kids come all the way to the projects for a box of pirate junk?

They wouldn't. Unless they knew the stuff had value.

Bates thought back. Two years earlier he'd bought the crate from a strange old cracker. Weird dude, obsessed with pirates. Wouldn't stop running his mouth about Anne Bonny.

Bates should've suspected something—dude wore a white tuxedo. In Myers! He'd written the guy off as a lunatic.

Twenty bucks for some fake pirate crap. No big deal.

The geezer had whined, but accepted the price. They always do. No one leaves without selling. Hard cash talks when you've got none.

A hundred bucks. Those kids knew something in the box was worth more, had come specifically for it. The papers? Had he been sitting on a gold mine and blown it? That possibility burned the worst.

Don't sit here feeling sorry, played, and stupid. Do something!

The map. Those papers. Find out.

Bates prided himself on his ability to sniff out money. To know when there was coin to be made. He was feeling that itch now. Full tilt.

He'd screwed up, but wouldn't just roll over. Not in this lifetime.

Bates reached for his cordless phone. Fat fingers punched the keys.

Two rings, then a groggy voice answered.

"Wake up, slack ass! It's your pops. Got a job for you boys."

CHAPTER 20

The placemats were neatly pressed.

Linen napkins. China plates. A full battery of utensils. Crystal stemware.

The table was set for three. Kit. Me. And the Blonde Bimbo.

Picnic lunch. No possibility of escape.

Whitney had selected the roof deck for a surprise meal. The weather was her accomplice, with low humidity and cloudy skies keeping the mercury down.

Whitney arranged her bounty with precision, everything just so. She'd made potato salad, cornbread, fish tacos, and wild rice. Her culinary skill was perhaps her only saving grace.

Coop sat to one side, eyes and ears alert. Any scraps would have a short stay on the tiles.

Throughout the meal, Kit *ooh*ed and *ahh*ed like a bumpkin, praising everything from the salad to dessert.

Blech.

I ate in silence, bored silly, counting the minutes.

When Coop nudged my knee, I absently scratched his ears.

"Shoo!" Whitney flicked her napkin at the wolfdog. "Get back!"

"Tory, don't feed Coop at the table," Kit said. "Whitney worked hard to make us a nice lunch."

"He's not bothering anyone." I gently pushed away his snout.

Coop whined and backed up a step, his eyes never leaving my face.

"Can we please put the animal inside?" Whitney never referred to Coop by name. It was always, "that beast," "the animal," or "that mongrel." Drove me bonkers.

Did she not understand that her attitude bothered me? Or did she just not care?

Kit looked uncomfortable, stuck in his usual spot between daughter and ditz. Sometimes I really did pity him.

"If we put *Cooper* inside, he'll just whimper at the door," I said. "He'll be fine. So will you."

Whitney bristled but let it go. Lunch proceeded in silence.

"How was the yacht club?" Whitney asked. "Did you have the *best* time? I know you looked *adorable* in that dress! Celia says that style is *très* popular this season." The attempt at French was jarring in her thicker-than-Dixie drawl.

"It was fine."

The idiot woman was born without tact. Like I wanted to discuss the merits of my borrowed dress.

"Did you meet that friend of yours?" Kit thought a moment.

"Jason? Jackson?"

"Jason Taylor?" Whitney beamed. "Oh my! That boy is from a *fine* family. I'm well acquainted with his mother. And such a handsome young man!"

Gross. Whitney knowing my friends made me ill. Completely unfair, but this was a strike against Jason.

And I did *not* want to discuss the party.

"We talked a bit. The whole thing was a bore."

"Well, darlin', that won't be true of the debutante ball. A young lady in Charleston cannot find a better time."

"Oh, indeed."

Whitney smiled, surprised. Sarcasm was not her strong suit.

Kit caught it, however.

"Tory, clean your plate," he ordered, drilling me with eye contact. "Now."

I downed the last of my taco.

Whitney began collecting dirty dishes in a way-too-cute wicker basket. Realizing it was crunch time, Coop inched close. Unaware, Whitney grazed his tail.

Coop growled.

Whitney gasped and skittered backward, nearly dropping the basket.

"Cooper!" Kit clapped twice. "No!"

Coop scampered to the corner, tail tucked.

"He tried to bite me!" Whitney wailed.

"No he didn't!" I snapped. "You startled him. Don't be so dramatic."

"Put Coop inside," Kit ordered. "He's lost his deck privileges for the day."

Jaws clamped, I complied. Coop scooted out of sight down the stairs.

"I swear." Whitney's hand fluttered to her chest. "That dog hates me."

"Try being nicer to him. Canines are very perceptive."

Kit tried to change the subject. "You mentioned dessert?"

"Well, of course!" Whitney's beaming smile returned. "Would I do otherwise?"

The blueberry pie was still warm from the oven. Fantastic. I was finishing my second slice when Kit casually dropped the bomb.

"Whitney, we need to talk." I could hear dread in his voice.

"Yes, sweetheart?" Eyelashes fluttering.

"I'm sure you've heard about CU's money problems. The budget shortfalls."

Flutter flutter flutter.

"The cuts are going to hit hard." Kit swallowed. "LIRI may not survive."

The lashes froze. "What does that mean?"

"It means I need to find a new job. Tory and I may have to move."

For several seconds, nothing. Then the floodgates opened.

"Move?" Tears moistened the Chanel mascara, creating black trails across her face. "You're—" choked sob, "—leaving me?"

"Nothing is decided." Kit handed Whitney his napkin. "We're

considering all options. Today I heard about a position in Scotland that sounds fascinating, and—"

My turn to overreact.

"Scotland? What?"

"We'll talk later," he said. "It's a two-year gig in the Hebrides, the islands off Scotland's north coast. The work sounds . . . interesting."

Whitney's shoulders and chest heaved. The expensive makeup was now an impressionist painting.

"Hey now, come on." Kit was at a loss. "We can talk this out."

"Was—" *gasp*, "—it—" *gasp*, "—something—" *gasp*, "—*I* did?"

I slipped inside as fast as my legs could carry me.

CHAPTER 21

We clustered around the bunker's only table.

It would've been more clinical to inspect the crate in Shelton's garage, but we opted for secrecy. Plus, the bunker was a better venue for chewing me out.

"Flaring in public is *dangerous*!" Shelton sounded outraged. "You don't know what could happen. What if you'd lost control in front of Bates? What if the virus had suddenly caused a new side effect? We don't know enough to roll the dice like that!"

"You put us all at risk." Ben's finger stabbed in my direction. "*You* get caught, *we* get caught. You want to end up in a cage? Become a lab rat, like Coop was?"

Hi glared, arms crossed, content to let the others do the scolding.

I'd offered apologies on the car ride home, but no one was buying. Then or now. Finally, I'd had it.

"Enough! We've been over this. My actions were impulsive

and risky. For that, I'm sorry. But we needed an edge against Bates, and it worked. Now can we please inspect our purchase?"

I didn't tell them about my sniffing ability. Now was *not* the time. If the boys found out I'd also flared at a yacht club party, they'd flip out.

Scowls still in place, the boys let it go. They knew how stubborn I could be.

"Most of this stuff is junk." Shelton shoved several items aside, including the eye patch, the hats, and the replica guns. Working quickly, we removed other worthless filler probably added by Bates to increase the price.

When we'd finished, what remained was a scroll of papers tied by a scruffy leather cord. Wrinkled and frayed, the documents had definitely seen better days.

"Hell-o!" Hi pointed.

The strange little cross decorated the very first page.

"Booyah!" Shelton unwound the cord.

"Don't get too excited," Hi cautioned. "Bonny's treasure map is well known. A clever counterfeiter might've copied that symbol to dupe people like us."

"True," I said. "Let's not lose our scientific objectivity."

Nodding enthusiastically, Shelton moved aside for Hi, considered by all to have the best "science" hands.

"Which one of you is my assistant?" Hi raised both forearms, fingers splayed.

Ben shoved him a box of latex gloves. Properly garbed, Hi lifted the top sheet of parchment.

"It's the first page of a letter," Hi said.

I scanned the first few lines. "Addressed to Anne Bonny! Find out who wrote it."

Hi checked the next sheet. I noted that both pages contained the strange cross.

The letter signed off with a bold set of initials.

"Somebody named M. R." Shelton said. "Who could that be?"

"Mary Read." I couldn't believe it. "The letter is from Mary Read to Anne Bonny!"

"*I kissed a girl, and I liked it!*" Hi sang.

Shelton chuckled. "There's no proof they had that kind of relationship."

But even I laughed. Whatever. If the documents were genuine, we'd hit the jackpot. That letter alone could be worth thousands.

Moving gingerly, Hi leafed through the remaining pages.

"Three letters," he said. "Two from Read to Bonny, and one back from Bonny to Read. All dated early 1721."

"How did Bates get letters going both ways?" Ben asked. No one could answer.

"When was *Revenge* captured?" I asked.

"Calico Jack was hanged in 1720," Shelton replied. "So these were written after they'd been caught."

"While in prison," I said. "But why write each other letters? Weren't their cells in the same jail?"

"How about we read and find out?" Hi said.

Good point.

Back to page 1. We studied the document in silence.

The language was antiquated, the script faded and hard to decipher. Still, it was English. Eventually the odd prose started making sense.

"There!" My finger shot toward the page. "Read says that she's 'bored to tears' now that Bonny 'has gone so far away.'"

"Gone?" Shelton ear-tugged. "Where'd she go?"

"Shhh!" Ben hissed. "Some of us don't read as fast."

We waited.

"Next." Ben glanced my way. "And no spoilers this time."

Hi flipped the page. My greedy eyes devoured the archaic text. *Wow!*

I waited, hands clasped in impatience. Finally they saw it.

"Holy smokes!" Hi.

"My God!" Shelton.

Ben looked up, eyebrows high on his forehead.

"Congrats guys," I breathed. "We just discovered what really happened to Anne Bonny. The truth."

Hi read aloud. "'Thank goodness your worthy father saw fit to claim you home.'"

"Worthy father?" Ben asked. "Like God? She died?"

"No! No! *Her* father. William Cormac! He *did* ransom her!" Shelton clapped his hands once. "Bonny went back to Charles Town."

"You sure?" Ben sounded unconvinced.

"Yes." My lips spread into a dopey grin. "She wasn't hanged."

"Letter two," Hi said with a flourish.

We crowded together again.

"This one's from Bonny to Read," Hi said. "A month later, in February 1721."

"Not dead," Shelton noted. Ben shrugged in agreement.

The handwriting was stronger, the language more sophisticated, reflecting a better education. The correspondence consisted of two pages, the second largely covered by an enormous signature.

Anne Bonny. Clear as daylight.

Even better, Bonny had sketched the bent cross in the corner of both pages. "That symbol must mean something," Hi said.

"Decorative?" Shelton mused. "Like handmade stationary?"

"I'm thinking something practical," I said. "Like a calling card."

"Watermark." Ben stated it as fact.

I looked a question at him.

"It's a security feature." He pointed to the image. "Not a typical cross, but one that's slightly flawed, so the reader knows *exactly* who drew it."

"Of course!" I said. "Read and Bonny both sketched the symbol on every page, like an authentication: *I really wrote this.*"

"Let's *read* the bloody thing," Hi suggested again. "Sound good?"

He set the pages side by side so we could see the whole letter.

I read both pages quickly.

"Oh!" My disappointment was obvious.

"I see." Ben frowned.

"Ah." Shelton ear-tugged.

"That blows!" Hi crossed chubby arms. "They didn't let her go?"

"Not according to this." Shelton reread the passage. "Bonny wrote that colonial authorities only transferred her to Charles Town to face more piracy charges."

"What is Half-Moon Battery?" Hi asked. "That's where she said she was being held."

No one knew.

My heart sank. Bonny had still faced execution. And given her notoriety in the Carolinas, her chances might've actually been worse.

"This is exciting!" Shelton wasn't feeling my empathy. "We may rewrite the history books!"

I considered the new facts in Bonny's letter. "Bonny was transferred to Half-Moon Battery at Charles Town. Subsequently, her father's petition for release failed."

"Scheduled to be hanged," Shelton added. "They were really gonna do it."

"Last correspondence," Hi said. "Read to Bonny. March 1721."

This letter was longer, stretching five pages. When we'd finished, everyone spoke at once.

"She's talking about the treasure map!" Shelton squealed.

"Escape attempt?" Hi began to pace. "Wow!"

"We were right," Ben said. "It's all about the docks!"

"Hold on!" I raised two palms. "Organize. What do we know?"

Shelton pointed to the second page. "Mary wrote, 'the sketch is safe, as is the subject.' She must be talking about the treasure map. And the treasure! What else?"

"Could be," I allowed. "Or she could be talking about someone's portrait."

Shelton looked at me as though I'd lost my mind.

"I'm only saying it's not *certain*," I said. "I tend to agree with you."

"'Keep faith and wits about ye.'" Hi read aloud. "'Even the darkest holes may be breached, the stoutest locks tickled.'" He slapped a thigh. "Tell me she's not hinting at escape!"

"Again, I agree. But we should avoid unfounded assumptions."

Ben tapped the second-to-last page. "Read mentions a place called Merchant's Wharf, and describes it as 'thy favorite landing.'"

"We know Bonny used the East Bay docks," I said. "Merchant's Wharf must've been one of them."

"I still can't believe she'd tie up in the center of town," Shelton chortled. "That's beast!"

When Ben cleared his throat, we all went quiet.

"Bonny wrote she was being held at Half-Moon Battery. Then, in this last letter, Read said the dungeon was close to 'both favored wharf and recent earthen works, a happy chance of fortune.'"

"And?" Shelton didn't get it.

"'Recent earthen works,'" Ben repeated.

"That could be a reference to where they buried the treasure," I said.

"Of course!" Hi's face was flushed with excitement. "Mary is telling Anne that her prison cell is close to the treasure tunnel!"

Clickity click! "Maybe they used the tunnel to bust Bonny out?"

"Son of a gun." Shelton stared, thunderstruck. "Tory, you're a genius."

"These letters confirm everything!" Hi broke out a dance move—the Cabbage Patch. "Bonny's treasure is buried beneath East Bay Street, somewhere near the old docks!"

"And we should look for the tunnels near that dungeon, Half-Moon Battery." Shelton joined Hi by doing the Soulja Boy.

"We did it!" Hi crowed. "We figured out where Anne Bonny buried her treasure! Holy shnikies!"

"Just a second!" Ben's voice halted the dance party. "Those are *huge* assumptions you're making."

"Ben's right," I said. "We don't even know what Half-Moon Battery is. But first things first—we need to authenticate these letters."

"Thank you," Ben said. "Let's not embarrass ourselves again."

"How?" Shelton asked. "You got a rare document expert on speed dial?"

"The treasure map." Hi unrolled our stolen booty. "Let's compare the handwriting in these letters to the verses on the map."

"Good idea." I placed a page on either side of the map, one penned by Bonny, the other by Read.

Mary's block-letter style was clearly not a match.

But Anne Bonny's bold, curling script, sweeping the page in aggressive, slashing strokes . . .

"The writing looks an *awful* lot alike," Shelton said.

"Yep," Hi agreed.

Ben nodded.

"We may be onto something," I said. "But we need to be *absolutely* sure."

"How?" Shelton asked.

"Leave that to me!" Hi beamed. "I know just the man for the job."

CHAPTER 22

"How'd you find this place?" I asked.

Before us, eight stone columns flanked the entrance to a massive stone building. The roof was at least forty feet above our heads.

"And who's responsible for this behemoth?" Shelton's head was craned back as he spoke. "It's ginormous."

"Methodists." Hi scrolled on his iPhone. "Pre–Civil War. The website says, 'The Karpeles Manuscript Museum is housed in a grand and bold Greek Revival structure of the Corinthian order, styled after the Temple of Jupiter in Rome.'"

"Okay," Ben said. "That fits."

The colossal edifice was definitely shooting for the Greek-temple look.

"Are we set?" I asked. "This guy will help us?"

Hi nodded. "He's a document whiz. My mother had him trace our family tree."

"Remember, no one utters the phrase 'treasure map.' We're only showing him the two lines we photocopied."

The main doors led into a cavernous chamber resembling a courtroom. White columns lined walls edged with decorative friezes. Corner windows stretched from floor to ceiling. Rows of pews marched from the entrance to an open central area, where glass display cases surrounded a long wooden table. Beyond, against the rear wall, a low wooden divider encircled a stone pulpit.

The room was outsized and majestic, reflecting its past as a congregational hall. It made me feel very, very small.

"Mr. Stolowitski?" a prim voice called. "Is that you?"

"Yes, Dr. Short. Thanks for agreeing to see me on such short notice."

A compact man, Short wore tweed pants and a blue wool sweater. Tiny round glasses rested halfway down his nose. Snaggletoothed, with thinning brown hair, the guy was no beauty.

Short's lips twitched in what might've been a half smile. "To be honest, Hiram, I'm not sure I *did* agree. But, here you are."

"Yes, well," Hi stammered, "I'm sure you'll find this interesting. Thanks again. Sir."

"These are your friends?" Short dipped his shoulders in a slight bow. "Dr. Nigel Short. Assistant director, museum historian, and resident forensic document examiner."

"Tory Brennan."

"Shelton Devers."

"Ben."

"Shall we get to it?" Short gestured with perfectly manicured fingers. "Place the documents on the table, then please stand aside. I'll be with you in a moment." Turning on a heel, he strode in the opposite direction and disappeared through a doorway.

"He's prickly, but everyone swears he's the best," Hi whispered. "Trust me."

I laid out Bonny's two-page letter, then a photocopy of a pair of lines from the treasure map:

Down, down from Lady Peregrine's roost,
Begin thy winding to the dark chamber's sluice.

"Anyone have a clue what 'the dark chamber's sluice' might be?" Hi asked.

"One thing at a time," I said. "Here comes your guy."

Short was wearing white linen gloves and carrying a small bundle. Noting the photocopy, he frowned.

"What's this? A *reproduction*? You said the articles were originals."

"We don't have the second document," Hi lied. "We had to print it off the net."

Short peered over the rim of his spectacles.

"I don't work with copies." Curt. "Fine points can be missed. I won't be able to authenticate."

"We only need to establish the *letter's* authenticity," Hi said. "Not the copy. We brought that solely as a handwriting sample."

We were pretty confident the map was real. After all, we'd stolen it from the Charleston Museum ourselves.

Short's eyes narrowed. I worried he suspected deception.

Careful. This guy is sharp.

"Very well." Short slipped a jeweler's loupe from his bundle. "I may require more details in a moment. For now, please have a seat in the gallery. I'll be with you as soon as I've reached a conclusion."

We scurried to the pews as Short began poring over Bonny's letter, nose inches from the parchment. For a full twenty minutes he ignored us completely.

A case of the yawns circulated. My mind was drifting when Short's voice snapped me back to attention.

"Please return to the table." Short scrutinized us, fingers steepled. "Where did you get this letter?"

"A pawnshop," I replied. On this point, why not be honest?

"A *pawnshop*?" Short looked offended. "Are you having fun with me?"

"No, sir. The letter was in a box of pirate junk at a store in North Charleston."

"This correspondence is signed by Anne Bonny." Short's eyes gleamed. "Do you know who she was?"

Nods.

"I believe the document to be authentic," Short said. "If so, this is an *extraordinary* find! To think where this letter has been, how it made its way to you."

My stomach did a backflip. If the letters were genuine, the clues might be too!

"Bonny writes that she's imprisoned in a Charles Town dungeon," Short went on. "That fact has never been proven before. Remarkable!"

"We know," Ben said.

"Why were you rooting through pirate paraphernalia in a North Charleston pawn—" Short changed gears. "These lines you photocopied. What are they from?"

"Something we found online." Back to lying. "Her diary, I think."

"You are *certain* Anne Bonny wrote this?"

"The, uh, website said so."

"Because if that verse *was* written by Anne Bonny, then the letter is almost assuredly genuine."

"How can you be sure?" I asked.

"The penmanship." Short adopted a lecturing tone. "A person's handwriting is as unique as his or her fingerprints. Experts such as I can compare features on different samples to match or exclude a suspected author, even if that author tries to disguise his or her hand."

"So Bonny wrote both?" Hi asked.

"Let me clarify," Short said. "These items were penned by the same hand. The letter is signed, 'Anne Bonny.' You've assured me the verse was written by Ms. Bonny as well."

"The letter's *not* a fake?" Ben's shock was obvious.

"If it's fake, it's a masterpiece. The paper, ink, and style are all appropriate for the era. Without scientific testing, I can't be one hundred percent certain, but I'm reasonably confident the letter is authentic."

"Can you explain how you determined that the handwriting matches?" I asked.

"Very well." Short pointed to the letter's first page. "Antiquated cursive, typical of the early seventeenth century. That is clear right off. I compared individual letters—and *connections* of letters—to those in the copy. There were notable similarities."

"Do you need the exact same words?" Hi asked.

"That's helpful, but not required. Examining single letters, letter groupings, or even mere capitalization works almost as easily."

"Here." Short scribbled on a notepad, then handed it to me. "Write this sentence."

I did. Read the words aloud. *"The quick brown fox jumps over the lazy dog."*

"That inane little sentence uses every letter in the English alphabet," he explained. "It's the perfect control."

"Control?"

"For comparison. For example, if the police can persuade a suspect to write those words, I can compare them to, say, a ransom note, or a shopping list. If the same person wrote both, I'll know."

"That's what I did today." He turned to the documents. "First, I examined vowels such as *o*, *a*, and *e*." Checked whether the loops are open or closed. See how the letter *o* has a minor swirl at the top in both writing samples?"

"Yes," I said. "Neat."

"Next, I compared characters like *f*, *b*, and *l*, which extend upward. Conversely, letters such as *p* and *q* extend downward."

"Sounds difficult," Hi said.

Short looked pleased. "Sometimes other features are more informative, such as whether the author points or rounds off letters like *s*, *n*, or *m*. I also gauge the *slant* of the writing."

"And the letter and poem match?" I wanted to be perfectly clear on this point.

"Absolutely," Short said. "Look at the capital *L*, both here in *Lady*, and here, with *Last*. The author uses a rare formulation."

"You mean the large circle at the apex?"

"Precisely. And, even more oddly, the author combines *t* and *h* when grouped together, as with the word *the*. To me, that might as well be DNA."

"Hey Tor." Hi was holding *my* writing sample. "You've got the same quirk."

"Huh?"

Short laid my sentence beside Bonny's poem and letter. "Well, Miss. How about that."

Hi was right. I'd never noticed before, but I combined *th* into a single character, almost like a Chinese symbol.

"That's a strange idiosyncrasy to share." Short looked at me oddly. "Normally, I'd consider such a peculiarity a fairly strong identifier."

"That's why I never write anything longhand," I joked. "Too hard."

"No one does anymore." Short *tsk*ed in disapproval. "Cursive is a dying art. But. That aside." His voice grew serious. "This letter is a historic treasure. We need to validate it scientifically, then discuss preservation."

"And we will," I hedged. "But for now, we'll hang on to it."

Short scowled. "Young lady, I have no intention of interfering with your ownership of this document. You can sell it for whatever you like. But we need to assure its safety until—"

"Dr. Short, you misunderstand. I don't plan to hawk the letter on eBay. But we need it for the time being. Sorry."

"Very well." Cold. "Please wait."

Lips tight, Short disappeared through the same doorway as before.

"Why are you pissing him off?" Hi whispered.

"We have to keep the letter. It might help us locate the treasure."

Short returned with a notebook-sized metal case.

"At least use this container for transport." Without asking for permission, he inserted the letter. "Take *extreme* care when handling these pages. They are irreplaceable."

"Understood. Thank you."

"You can thank me by returning the letter undamaged."

"We will," Hi promised.

"Then be off. I have work."

Needing no urging, we headed for the exit.

Sudden thought. I hit the brakes. Turned.

"One last thing, Dr. Short."

"Yes?"

"Have you ever heard of something called Half-Moon Battery?"

Short hesitated. "Why?"

"I'm curious about the original Charles Town dungeons."

Short seemed to debate with himself. Then, "In 1771, the Exchange Building was constructed on the site of an older fortification known as Half-Moon Battery. A decade later, during the Revolution, the British converted the cellars into the Provost Dungeon. Seems Charleston's darkest cells have always occupied the same space."

"Thanks!"

Short watched us hustle from the chamber.

○   ○   ○

"Did you hear?" I practically skipped. "The Provost Dungeon was built on the ruins of Half-Moon Battery. Bonny's original cell may still exist!"

"That's the right area," Shelton said. "The Exchange Building is on lower East Bay Street."

"Why do we care about the dungeon?" Ben asked. "Aren't we looking for some kind of tunnel?"

"Mary Read's letter," I reminded him. "Read said the 'recent earthen works' were close to Bonny's cell. 'Earthen works' must refer to the tunnels depicted on the treasure map. I think the pirates used those tunnels to break Bonny out of Half-Moon Battery."

"*If* they broke her out," Shelton said. "We don't know for sure that Bonny was rescued. She could've been hanged."

"She must've escaped! Otherwise, there'd be a record of her execution."

Data bytes coalesced in my brain. "We just learned that Half-Moon Battery—the place Bonny was held—was located close to the East Bay docks," I said. "That confirms we're looking in the right place!"

"Stop." Hi literally quit walking. "Let's spell it out."

We circled up on a street corner, one of our habits.

"Fact one," I said. "Anne Bonny drew a treasure map, which hints that her fortune was buried in downtown Charles Town, somewhere close to the East Bay docks."

"Some *huge* leaps there," Ben said, "but go on."

"Fact two," Shelton said. "We found letters between Anne Bonny and Mary Read stating that Bonny was transferred to Half-Moon Battery, a Charles Town dungeon."

Hi picked up the thread. "Fact three: Read's letter hints at a possible breakout attempt. Fact four: the letter also suggests that the treasure tunnels lie close to Bonny's dungeon at Half-Moon Battery."

"Fact five," Shelton added. "The dungeon was close to the docks."

"Which leads to my deduction," I said. "Because the treasure tunnels were close to Bonny's prison cell, they might've factored into her rescue."

We all paused to digest.

"Flash forward fifty years," Hi said suddenly. "The Exchange Building is constructed over the remains of Half-Moon Battery.

Its cellars are later converted into the new Provost Dungeon."

"Okay," Ben said. "Let's assume the map's treasure tunnels are somewhere near where the Provost Dungeon is today. What next?"

"We get inside," I said. "Poke around."

"And how do we do that?" Ben asked.

We shouted the answer as one.

"Ghost tour!"

CHAPTER 23

I upended a bulging Hefty bag and disgorged the contents. Crumpled clothes tumbled to the paving stones. My fifth heap so far. Once again, I began sorting mismatched garments into smaller piles.

Friday morning. Seven a.m. Saint Michael's on Broad Street.

My cotillion group was providing manpower for a winter clothing drive, and I'd been tasked with organizing donated articles. A mountain of black plastic bags loomed on my right, proof that parishioners had heeded the call.

Community service is fundamental to the debutante system, providing cover for the excess and redefining snobbery as "charitable work." We participated in at least one major project per month.

Not that I'm complaining. Charity is the upside to an otherwise vapid tradition. Helping the less fortunate is the only part of cotillion I actually enjoyed.

I tossed a musty flannel shirt onto a stack, nose wrinkling at the smells of sweat and moldy tobacco.

Okay, maybe not "*enjoyed*." More like "*appreciated*."

While my hands worked on autopilot, my head moved ahead to the evening. We Virals would be taking the Fletchers' ghost tour that night. Since it was the weekend, Kit had relented and given me a pass until ten o'clock.

I'd almost forgotten to show up this morning. Yesterday's craziness had driven the cotillion event from my mind. Whitney remembered, however, and had texted a reminder thirty minutes before I was due.

Which explained my current look: an Outward Bound T-shirt, running shorts, sandals, greasy ponytail, and a double layer of Lady Speed Stick.

I'd volunteered to work outside. Alone. No one had objected.

Saint Michael's is the oldest church in Charleston. Its famous spire rose two hundred feet behind me, gleaming white, an eight-foot iron weathervane crowning its apex.

The courtyard was pleasantly cool. White brick buildings formed the sides, shading a grassy enclosure bordered by a trestle-covered cobblestone walk. In the center, flagstones paved a circular space set with four curved benches, each now serving as one of my garment sections.

I was subdividing clothing by gender, then separating youth sizes from adult. Grabbing a pair of raunchy bell-bottoms, I tossed them on the proper stack. A college kid might buy them for a seventies party. Or maybe the style would come back. Who knew?

Jason appeared, lugging three more trash bags.

"They found these in a crawl space under the rectory." Dropping the newcomers with a grunt. "Enjoy."

"Fabulous."

"Any interesting styles? I bet you could craft a wicked retro look."

There's a Brett Favre Jets jersey," I said. "XXL. That's worth what, two, maybe three bucks?"

"I've got my eye on that kilt."

"Shrewd."

Jason finger tapped his temple. "Always thinking." Then, after a pause, "How are you getting home? I could drive you. I don't mind."

"Thanks, but Ben is picking me up."

"Ben." Jason shook his head. "I guess you're taking community service to heart," he quipped.

"Out of bounds," I warned. "Ben's a good friend."

"He's a prince. Enchanting. Tell him I miss him."

I let the dig slide. I couldn't force people to like each other. No point trying.

"If you change your mind, my truck's out front."

"Thanks," I said. "Now get back to work. God is watching."

"Adios."

I worked through two more Hefties, then turned to the first sack from the rectory basement. It was old and grimy, the plastic dried and brittle. Without Jason's explanation, I'd have assumed the bag held actual garbage.

Great.

The first sack contained several dozen ragged and stained towels. The second held an assortment of moth-eaten ceremonial robes.

The third sack knocked me silly.

Cutting the tie unleashed a noxious stench. Whatever lurked within smelled like dirty diapers covered in mildew, or fetid meat left too long in the sun.

I dropped to a knee, certain I'd retch.

Instead, *it* happened.

SNAP.

Lightning struck. My blood boiled. Sweat pumped from my pores. My senses flickered, exploded. Colors, sounds, and smells slammed into my brain.

The flare traveled my veins and nerves, unbidden, unstable. For the second time that week, my powers had ignited without being called. Hair-trigger sensitive.

Reaching blindly, I found and jammed on my sunglasses.

Breathe. Relax. Breathe. Relax.

Calm returned. Slowly, my pulse descended.

I checked for spying eyes. The courtyard was empty. I slumped onto a bench and repeated a soothing mantra.

You're okay. You're okay. You're okay.

Then my ears detected trouble.

Voices. Close by.

Ashley, Courtney, and Madison. The Tripod of Skank was coming my way.

FRICK!

A fourth voice joined the babble.

"You girls are angels for stuffing all those envelopes." Adult. Tenor. "Our mailings are vital to keeping the soup kitchens running."

"No," Madison cooed, "thank *you*, Pastor Carroll. It's an honor to assist with your selfless efforts. If only we could focus on the Lord's work every day."

"Amen!" Ashley gushed. "Praised be his name."

"Charity is hard." Courtney. Moron.

"God bless you!" Pride swelled Pastor Carroll's voice. "Enjoy the sweet tea and shade in the courtyard."

Double frick! Incoming.

A set of footsteps receded. Safely alone, the Tripod abandoned their pretenses.

"Thought he'd *never* leave," Madison said. "I'm sick of wasting my mornings in crappy churches. I should be sleeping right now."

"These hands weren't made for office work," Ashley griped. "My manicure is ruined. I should send the bill to Pastor Creepy Eyes."

"Blech!" Courtney made a dramatic gagging sound. "This tea was made with real sugar!"

"Gross." I heard three separate splashes on the pavement.

"Why can't my driver do these events?" Ashley whined. "He

could represent me. What's the difference?"

Expensive perfume wafted around the building's edge. I braced for impact, flare senses humming.

They saw me at once. Triplet smiles revealed sets of perfect teeth.

"Boat girl!" Madison noticed my carefully sorted piles. "Collecting new outfits?"

"She's stealing clothes?" Courtney, wide-eyed. "They shouldn't let her work unsupervised."

"Nice sunglasses, Ray Charles." A sneer twisted Ashley's beautiful face. "And it's rude to mock the poor by dressing like them. Shame."

A three-pronged attack is impossible to defend. I was about to retreat when Jason appeared, his jaw clamped in determination.

"What's going on?" Looking hard at the Tripod. "Everyone being pleasant?"

"Just chatting." Madison's half smile never wavered. "Tory was explaining her trash-sorting system."

Suddenly, my nose took in something beneath the perfume, a layer lower. An odor was seeping from Madison, acrid and biting, like the sourness of dried sweat.

Anxiety. She was nervous. *Very* nervous.

I searched Madison's face, found nothing. Outwardly, she was her usual smug, condescending self. As if to mock my observation, she yawned.

But my nose was sure. Her cool was an act. Jason's appearance had ruffled her feathers.

Curious, I tried to catch Jason's underscent. It was brittle, like ashes mixed with hot cement. *Anger.*

My apprehension began to subside. Why should these tramps intimidate me? They were spoiled princesses, nothing more. I had abilities they couldn't fathom. Could bite back just as hard.

Time to test my instincts.

"Jason?" I smiled wide. "Does your offer still stand?"

"Huh?" Jason. Blank-faced.

"Can I still get a ride home?" I added quickly. If his answer was no, I was about to look like a jackass.

I needn't have worried.

"Yeah, of course!" Jason's face brightened. "Maybe we can grab lunch on the way?"

"I'd love that." I batted my eyelashes. Wasted behind the shades.

The nervous scent poured from Madison, intertwined with sour ropes of anger. Then a thorny new aroma entered the mix. Harsh. Slimy. Like crushed poison ivy mixed with mud.

Envy. Madison reeked of jealousy.

But the façade never cracked. Madison cupped a hand to her mouth, whispered to Ashley, then giggled at her own wit.

Am I imagining these things? Is this how you go crazy, by thinking you can smell other people's emotions?

I could feel my flare burning. Hidden behind dark lenses, I quickly tested my other hypersenses.

I could see a mistake in the cross-stitching of Courtney's miniskirt, hear the tick of Jason's wristwatch, feel grains of sand in my tennis shoes, taste molecules of grime floating from the trash bags.

Amazing. A vicious superbug might've mangled my chromosomes, but the side effects still blew me away.

And the powers *never* lied.

Trusting my instincts, I pushed forward with my ploy.

"I need to get these piles to the laundry," I said to Jason, "but they're way too heavy. I could use a little muscle."

Jason straightened, masculinity at the ready. "No problem. We'll knock this out in a flash." He gathered a heap of pants. "Feel free to lend a hand, ladies."

The Tripod stood frozen. Taking another deep whiff, I picked up new elements. Snow. Refrigerated orchids. Dead leaves.

Imperfect descriptions, but the emotions seemed clear.

Dismay. Disappointment.

The girls hated that Jason was helping me. Worse, he'd blown them off.

Tough luck.

Gathering a pile of sweatshirts, I moved toward the church without a backward glance. The Tripod ignored me, but the smell of disappointment cloaked them like a second skin.

Jason waited at the courtyard wall, a too-large bundle locked between his straining arms. Knowing he'd never make it, he wore a goofy grin.

"After you," he panted.

SNUP.

Blood rushed to my head, nearly causing me to faint. My legs wobbled, but held. The world crashed back to its normal sensory backdrop. I instantly felt weakened. Diminished.

I pretended to struggle under the weight of my load, determined not to spoil a rare moment of triumph. Jason noticed my discomfort. "You okay? I can carry that pile next."

"Fine. I just haven't eaten in a while."

"I'll fix that." Big smile. "Count on it."

The Tripod didn't bother with good-byes. Banking as one, they headed toward the chapel.

"Good-bye ladies!" I couldn't help myself. "See you soon!"

CHAPTER 24

B en didn't answer my call.

I left a message, uneasy, feeling genuinely sorry. Ben could nurse a grudge. I knew my doghouse stay might be an extended one.

I'd texted him before leaving Saint Michael's. Unfortunately, Ben had been halfway across the harbor, already on his way to pick me up. When informed that Jason would drive me home, he'd stopped responding.

Not good. Ben was clearly taking this personally.

What is it with those two?

Jason had insisted we eat at The Wreck of the Richard and Charlene, a ramshackle seafood joint overlooking Shem Creek. Mount Pleasant was the wrong direction from Morris Island, but Jason had been adamant.

And he'd been right. The restaurant was shabby-quaint, the food delicious. We'd gorged on fried shrimp and scallops. Two hours later, Jason finally dropped me at my townhouse.

With no afternoon plans, I decided to do some research. My newfound olfactory perception had somewhat unnerved me.

Could I really smell emotions? Motivations? I thought so, but wasn't sure. Was such a thing possible, or was it the first sign of a brain tumor? Or dementia?

Google wasn't immediately helpful. Dozens of articles linked smell and emotion, but none described anything similar to my experience.

Frustrated, I sought backup. With Ben pissed off, that left Hi and Shelton.

Hi arrived with his laptop in minutes.

I told him what happened at the church. Then, after a moment's hesitation, about the yacht club episode a few days before.

"Stop it with the public flaring!" he snapped. "You're gambling with *all* our lives. I'm not spending my teenage years on a hamster wheel, dancing for the Dharma Initiative."

"They weren't intentional. Lately my flares come too easily, out of nowhere."

"You can't let that happen," Hi said. "Someone spots your eyes, just once, and you're toast. We don't know enough about the virus to take those kinds of risks."

"Then help me get answers!"

His eyes narrowed. "The pawnshop. You were sniffing out Bates, weren't you? Or was that flare an 'accident'—" air quotes, "—too?"

"Well . . . no. I told you, we needed an edge."

Dramatic sigh. "This is how it ends."

I ignored him. "Let's start with this emotional sensory thingy. It's creeping me out, big time."

Search after search led nowhere. Switching to more complicated strings, we added new terms and finally got some hits.

"Here." I tapped the monitor. "A Rice University study found that certain couples can correctly identify their partner's emotions by smell."

"Gross." Hi was sprawled on my bed. Naturally.

He tapped his laptop's screen. "Some Ph.D. in San Diego claims that body odors can convey emotional states. Even to strangers."

"So maybe I'm *not* crazy."

"The guy works at Sea World."

"Oh."

Thirty minutes later, still nothing.

"I'm adding 'canine' to my searches," I said. "And 'instinct.'"

"Whatever. I'm adding 'lunatic.'"

Suddenly, I hit pay dirt. An Alaskan study. On point.

"Here we go. Hi, check this out!"

He rolled from my bed and dropped into the chair beside me.

"This guy claims that Arctic wolves can detect changes in human emotion, using only their sense of smell." Excitement rode my voice. "That must be it!"

"How can he prove that? Wolves can't exactly fill out questionnaires."

I shrugged. "This journal calls the evidence 'compelling.'"

"He sounds like a crank," Hi said.

Coop nosed into my room, yapped, and sat.

"Quiet, dog breath." I scanned the article. "Olfactory receptors—that means your nose—connect to the limbic system, the primordial core of the human brain. That's where emotions originate."

Hi chortled. "So funky stank hits your primitive mind first?"

"Exactly," I said. "Smells only get to the cerebral cortex—the cognitive center—*after* touring the deeper parts of the brain."

Coop whined, danced a circle. I ignored him.

"By the time you can name a scent," I said, "that odor has already activated the limbic system and triggered your deep-seated instincts."

The wolfdog barked one last time, gave up, and rocketed down the stairs.

"Coop?"

"The limbic system," Hi repeated. "Wait a sec. Remember what Dr. Karsten said about the virus?"

I thought back. Karsten believed that his mutated parvovirus rewrote our DNA, inserting canine snippets into our genetic blueprint.

"Karsten thought the changes might be rooted in the hypothalamus," I said.

Hi nodded. "The quarterback gland of the limbic system."

I paused, trying to process. "Karsten thought that a flare triggered when our hormone production spiked, because our nervous and limbic systems had incorporated canine genetics."

"Our senses become wolflike," Hi agreed. "Maybe even sharper than wolves, who's to say?"

"The point is," I said, "our powers emerge when something stimulates the limbic portion of our brains. Stress. Emotion. Strong sensory input."

"If the limbic system is the brain's emotional seat," Hi said, "and our noses are hardwired directly to it . . ."

I nodded rapidly. "Then my ability makes sense. An ultra-sensitive nose could conceivably detect emotions."

Hi grinned. "And your schnoz is the king."

"Thanks."

I finished reading the article, found something near the bottom. "Pheromones?"

"I'll run the term."

"Interesting," Hi said. "Pheromones are chemical factors secreted by the body to trigger social responses in members of the same species."

"I know you'll explain that."

"They're scents. Pheromones act outside the body of the secreting individual by impacting the behavior of the receiving individual." He thought a moment. "Smell instructions. Bizarre."

"What do they do?"

"There are alarm pheromones, sex pheromones, lots of others. Insects use them."

"How so?"

"Here's an example." Hi clicked the mouse. "If an ant finds

lunch, it secretes a smell trail for his bros to follow to the food source. When certain animals are looking to mate, they do the same."

"Humans?"

"Not so much, unless you believe Axe Body Spray commercials."

"Not so much."

Hi checked his watch. "Snacky time?"

"Ugh, I'm still stuffed. But help yourself."

We headed for the kitchen. Hi located a pair of Hot Pockets. Ham and cheddar.

"Awesome." He popped them in the microwave. "We never have anything good in our kitchen."

"Your mom would kill me for corrupting your diet. Consider this a bribe to keep quiet about my nose."

Hi's brows rose. "Even with Ben and Shelton?"

"For now." I wasn't sure why, but I didn't want to share just yet.

We waited while the microwave counted down.

Hi spoke abruptly. "Do you ever wonder why our powers aren't the same?"

"What do you mean?"

"Yesterday, Shelton and I compared what our flares feel like," Hi said. "His experience is different from mine. And our strengths aren't the same either. Shelton can hear better than me, and my eyesight easily beats his. But we all caught the same virus."

"I wish I knew. My guess is that since everyone has a distinct genetic code, the canine DNA affects each of us differently."

The microwave beeped. Hi deftly scooped his snack onto a paper towel.

"Do you think our powers will ever go away?"

"What?" A shocking thought.

"The flare ability. Think it's permanent?"

"I . . . I don't know." The thought had never occurred to me.

To my surprise, I wasn't sure what I wanted. My powers would forever brand me as an outcast, but they also made me special.

Coop barged between my legs. Cocking his head, he let out a yip that morphed into a growl.

"What's with you today?"

I reached down to stroke his head, but he danced away. Barked twice.

"Suit yourself. Hi, watch him. I need to grab the mail."

"Get over here, mutt!" Hi ordered. "You can lick my toasting sleeves."

Grabbing my keys, I bounced down the steps, through the garage, and outside. The mailbox stood twenty feet away. All junk, except for a letter to Kit with a Buffalo return address. I debated tossing it out with the credit card offers.

Suddenly, I had the sensation of being watched. Stiff neck hairs. Ice on the spine. You know the one.

I waited, but it didn't pass.

My feet spun a quick three-sixty. Nothing.

Coop was at the kitchen window, barking frantically.

Freaky.

Reverse spin. There was no one in sight. Nothing moved.

"Shake it off, Brennan."

I hurried back inside. Foolish perhaps, but so what?

I hate that feeling, like being a bug in a jar.

The creepy tickle of eyes on my back.

Feeling like a target.

CHAPTER 25

We arrived on Market Street fifteen minutes early.

The tour was scheduled for eight, but we couldn't risk being tardy. The flyer warned that cancellation was possible if there weren't enough guests.

"There they are." I pointed.

Sallie and Chris Fletcher stood on a street corner across from the market entrance, a clapboard sign propped between them. The heavy wood was painted black. Garish red letters screamed out their offering:

> CHARLESTON GHOST TOURS
> Meet local ghouls on the scariest walk
> in downtown Charleston!
> All tours include exclusive access
> to the Provost Dungeon.
> $10.00. Not for the faint of heart!

"What's that supposed to mean?" Shelton tugged an earlobe. "I thought the tour was informational. I don't like people trying to scare me."

"Quit being a wuss," Hi said. "This is the easiest way into the Provost Dungeon."

"It's a freaking ghost tour." Ben snorted. "What'd you expect?"

"Exactly." I shot Ben a get-a-load-of-this-guy look.

Ben pointedly turned away.

Still not forgiven. Fine. Rome wasn't built in a day.

"The hottie just spotted us," Hi said. "She's waving."

When we joined the Fletchers, they both smiled warmly.

"Hey guys!" Sallie gestured to the clapboard. "Here for the show?"

"You bet," I said. "It sounded too good to miss."

"Fantastic!" Sallie's eyes glittered in the lamplight. "I promise you won't be disappointed."

"I better get to work," Chris said. "We need at least one more person."

"We'll take you guys regardless," Sallie confided. "But let's wait a few more minutes. I'm feeling lucky, maybe we can get a big group tonight."

"No rush," I said. "Please, do your thing."

"Chris can handle sales," Sallie said. "It's his turn anyway."

We waited on the corner as Chris worked the crowd. A pair of seniors laughed at his jokes, but ultimately passed. The clock ticked closer to eight.

I chatted with Sallie. The boys ogled her, pretending not to.

"How'd you get into the ghost business?" I asked.

"Bills," Sallie laughed. "Chris and I are grad students in archaeology. The Charleston Museum is great, but it doesn't pay much. So we work the streets."

"This makes money?" Shelton glanced around. "We're the only ones here."

"Hey, don't jinx it," Sallie joked. "There's still time."

We smiled politely.

"Seriously! On a good summer night, we make a killing. The rest of the year can be hit or miss, but overall, we do pretty well. Tourists love ghosts."

As if on cue, a hefty couple approached wearing matching Packers jerseys and munching waffle cones. Chris's pitch hit the mark. The couple bought tickets, then wandered into the market.

"It's a great idea," I said. "How'd you get permission to visit the Provost Dungeon?"

"That's our ace," Sallie said. "The director is a CU alum. Chris schmoozed him and got us access in exchange for cross-promotion at the museum."

Two more couples approached. The men wore polos and linen shorts, the women sundresses and strappy little sandals. Chris beamed as he doled out four tickets.

"See?" Sallie winked. "Money in the bank."

"You'll be rocking a penthouse soon," Hi quipped. "Platinum watches."

"Not likely. Every extra dollar goes to our expedition fund."

She read the question on my face.

"Egypt. Next summer. Chris and I plan to join a new excavation at Deir el-Bahri, unearthing a temple complex built by the pharaoh Hatshepsut in the fifteenth century BC."

"Sounds wonderful." I felt some hero worship kick in.

"We're super excited," Sallie said. "The temple sits among the cliffs at the entrance to the Valley of Kings, on the west bank of the Nile. There's nowhere more beautiful in the world."

"I'm officially jealous." I was.

"We have to foot the bill first," she said. "It's a two-year commitment, so that means hawking a whole lot of ghost stories on Market Street."

Over Sallie's shoulder, I noticed two young African American men amble toward Chris.

The first was maybe eighteen, with a shaved head, deep-set eyes, and a Z-shaped scar cutting across his left check. His oversized white tee and weathered jeans hung loose on his slender frame.

The second guy was older, perhaps twenty-five, and larger. Much larger. Well over six feet, he towered over his companion. Muscles bulged beneath his authentic Kobe Bryant Lakers jersey.

Shelton whistled softly. "Look at the *size* of that guy."

Baggy Jeans handed Chris a bill. Chris said something. Baggy Jeans shook his head. Nodding quickly, Chris signaled to Sallie. She joined the pair, then hustled back to us.

"Can you guys pay now?" she asked. "That kid only has a hundred dollar bill, and Chris is short on change."

"No problem." Hi produced two twenties. "It's all about the Benjamins."

"Thanks." Sallie scurried back to Chris. Transaction complete, the newcomers strolled to a nearby wall, leaned back, and waited.

The next customer was a shocker.

Rodney Brincefield. Minus his yacht club butler's uniform.

Today Brincefield wore a khaki shirt-and-shorts combo with a matching Bushmaster hat. Tan socks, brown sandals. No kidding.

Shifting a sixty-ounce lemonade, Brincefield shook hands with Chris and bought a ticket. Below the bushy white brows, his bright eyes roved to our little troop.

And lit on me. A toothy grin spread Brincefield's face.

"Miss Brennan, what a delight!" Closing in like a charging rhino.

"Who's Father Time?" Shelton spoke sideways to me. "He looks crazy."

"He's fine," I whispered. "Harmless."

But Brincefield worried me. The old guy was charming, but a chatterbox. Once inside the Provost Dungeon, we Virals planned to snoop around. Alone. We had to locate the older, deeper places where Bonny might've been imprisoned. Brincefield's presence could complicate things.

"Good to see you, sir." I gestured to the others. "These are my friends. Ben, Shelton, and Hiram."

"A pleasure." Firm handshakes, then a mischievous rubbing of hands. "So we're all off in search of spirits?"

I nodded. "Sounds like fun."

"It's an extraordinary program!" Brincefield exclaimed. "This is my second time."

"Can I have everyone's attention?" Sallie had climbed onto a plastic crate, which brought her to about eye level.

"Hello to everyone!" she shouted. "Welcome to the world-famous Fletcher Ghost Tour!"

There was a smattering of applause.

"We'll begin in a few minutes," Chris said. "Please take a moment to introduce yourselves. We'll be spending the next ninety minutes together, communing with restless ghouls and dangerous specters. So remember—" dramatic voice quaver, "—there's safety in numbers!"

Laughter. Chris was a born showman.

Brincefield began pressing palms, making introductions. Not my style, so I slipped outside his orbit.

And bumped square into Baggy Jeans's chest.

The young man glared at me, clearly irritated. His tree-sized buddy smirked.

"Sorry," I said. "Didn't see you there."

Without a word, Baggy Jeans stepped aside. Feeling awkward, I introduced myself.

"I'm Tory." I held out a hand. Neither took it.

"Marlo," said the smaller guy. Tree Trunk remained mute. Without another word, the pair turned and walked away.

"Al-righty then."

"Making friends?" Hi asked.

"Shut it."

"It's amazing how so many folks *instantly* dislike you," Hi continued. "You have a gift."

"It's amazing that any—"

"Everybody ready?" Sallie cut short my clever retort. "Here we go!"

CHAPTER 26

The first hour was fantastic.

Sallie and Chris led us along dark streets, dispensing trivia and funny bits of city lore. The group would stop and gather close while the duo spun tales of famous hauntings, poltergeists, and unexplained occurrences.

We learned about the Lowcountry's notorious pantheon of spirits. Haints—dead souls who take the form of ghosts or people. Boo-hags—beings who shed their skins and roam the marshes by moonlight. Plat-eyes—one-eyed phantoms who creep inside houses on hot summer evenings.

Sallie talked of the protective powers of boo-daddies, tiny figures made of marsh mud, Spanish moss, sweet grass, and salt water, then incubated inside large marsh oysters.

"If you fear the local baddies," Sallie warned, "keep a boo-daddy in your pocket."

She waggled her personal model above her head. "A good

boo-daddy protects you from night creatures. The more boo-daddies, the better."

Our route hit several well-known spectral hot spots. South End Brewery. The Rutledge Victorian Guest House. Circular Congregational Church.

Passing the Dock Street Theatre, we craned for a glimpse of Junius Brutus Booth, father of the man who killed Abe Lincoln. No luck. Then we cruised by Battery Carriage House Inn, where a male presence is said to slip into the beds of female guests.

Our path traversed an ancient graveyard, where the ghost of Sue Howard Hardy has been photographed weeping beside her child's grave. Our snack break was at Poogan's Porch, where Zoe St. Amand, a one-time resident, is occasionally spotted waving from a second-floor window.

Finally, the tour reached the old Exchange Building at the intersection of East Bay and Broad.

Stone steps ascended to a porch where porticos adorned three sets of white double doors. Above, imposing two-story windows were flanked by large arching casements. The building's exterior was faced with gray-and-white stone, once dull with age, now restored to its colonial glory.

The group gathered at the base of the steps.

"In 1771," Chris explained, "with trade booming, Charles Town's elite decided their city needed a modern customs house. The new Exchange would stand for more than mere economic prosperity. It would symbolize optimism for a glorious future.

"The city fathers chose a site on the Broad Street waterfront, where the biggest docks and streets converged," Chris continued. "Construction took two years. When completed, the Exchange was one of the first landmark buildings constructed in colonial America.

"But that's not why we're here, is it?" Smiling wickedly, Chris pointed to steps descending the building's side. "*We* came to see . . . the dungeons."

Sallie lit and distributed candles, then, single file, we trooped down the narrow staircase. At the bottom, a door led into a gloomy basement with a low ceiling constructed of barrel-vaulted brick. Archways divided the space into murky, shadow-filled alcoves.

The sundress ladies tittered as their husbands exchanged jokes. The Packers couple snapped shots with their Nikons. Brincefield scouted the room, excited, a kid at Disneyland. Marlo and Tree Trunk stood at the back of the group, silent and still.

Sallie spoke in hushed tones, candlelight dancing shadows across her features. "The Provost Dungeon served a sinister function during the Revolutionary War. Beneath the beautiful façade of the Exchange above lurked this nightmare." Sallie swept her free hand in a wide arc.

"Cruel men converted these cellars into a ghastly prison." Sallie's whisper forced us to draw close. "Dark. Dank. Without heat or light. Those caged within these walls faced sickness, despair, even death. The British used this hole to jail American patriots." The flickering light distorted her face, Halloween style. "Brave Charlestonians were clapped in irons, locked underground, and forgotten."

Chris's voice sounded dull in the subterranean gloom. "Deserters. Women. Slaves. Highborn sons. All those suspected of aiding the rebel patriots were crowded into cages and left to die."

Chris told the story of Isaac Hayne, an American war hero captured and hanged by the British.

"Hayne refused to surrender," he whispered. "His ghost now haunts these dungeons, searching for enemy redcoats, even in death unable to lay down his arms.

"So." Chris smiled. "Shall we proceed?"

Huddled close, our little band tiptoed through the cellar and eventually descended a second staircase, steeper than the first.

At the bottom was a wide, dark chamber, older than the room above. Clammy, bare-earth floor. Low, claustrophobic ceiling. Stale, fetid air.

Shelton fiddled an earlobe, face tense in the glow of his candle. I placed a reassuring hand on his shoulder, knowing how much he hated tight spaces.

"We've traveled further back in history," Sallie whispered, "to a time before the Exchange existed."

My heart threw in a few extra beats. This was what we wanted.

"For you see," Sallie intoned, "the Exchange was constructed atop an even older fortification, one dating to the town's founding." She paused for effect. "That bastion, too, had a dungeon."

Chris picked up the narrative. "Half-Moon Battery."

My elbow found Hi. Just as his found me. We listened intently.

"You are standing in the linchpin of Charles Town's original defense system," Chris said. "Half-Moon Battery was so named because it jutted into the harbor in a half circle. This vault was discovered during a renovation in 1965. Rumors persist of older, deeper spaces yet to be discovered.

"Every town needs a prison. Long before the Provost Dungeon was established, dangerous criminals harried the streets and waters of old Charles Town."

"Pirates," Sallie whispered.

"From its founding, pirates plagued the city," Chris said. "Blackbeard. Stede Bonnet. Ruthless marauders captured dozens of Charles Town vessels and held their occupants for ransom.

"At the urging of terrified merchants, the colonial governor finally commissioned privateers to end the reign of terror. In October of 1718, Stede Bonnet was captured."

"And brought here." Sallie's flame spluttered as she arced her candle in the blackness. "The dungeons of Half-Moon Battery became Captain Bonnet's new home."

He's not the only one.

"Bonnet and his crew were tried and sentenced to death," she continued. "On December 10, 1718, they were hanged at White Point on the Battery."

Theatrical pause, then the Fletchers led the group back to the staircase. I hung to the rear. Tried to melt into the shadows. The other Virals did the same.

I blocked my candle by cupping the flame with one hand. As the others clomped up the stairs, the chamber went darker and darker, eventually black. We were alone.

Now or never. If Bonny was down here, we have to find some evidence.

We'd agreed. To search the dungeon, we needed our abilities unleashed. It was time to test what our powers could do.

"Burn," I whispered.

In the darkness, four gleaming orbs suddenly appeared. Eyes of golden fire.

Hi, always quickest. And Shelton, tapping his fear of the dark.

SNAP.

Almost instantly, the flare tore through me, washing my innards with ice and fire.

From deep within, my powers emerged and stretched their legs.

Beside me, Ben cursed. Then, "No go. I'll watch the stairs."

I heard rubber soles on hard-packed earth as he headed to the door.

"Spread out," I hissed. "We only have seconds."

Hi and Shelton nodded, their faces distinct. With my hypervision unleashed, the candle lit the room like a bonfire.

Seeing a wall a dozen yards ahead, I fired in that direction, senses casting a wide net. Searching.

Shelton's voice stopped me short. "Hear that?"

The tour group was gone. Even flaring, I heard nothing but the sounds of our own breathing and movement.

"There." Shelton crossed to the rear wall, crouched, and tapped the stones. "Listen. Hear that trickling?"

I hurried to his side. Yes! My wolf-ears pulled in a faint whistling, underscored by a soft murmur. "Incredible."

"Moving air." Shelton squeezed his eyes shut. "Or maybe running water?"

"Let me look," Hi urged.

The wall was constructed of roughly shaped stone sealed with crumbling mortar. Ancient, but solid looking.

"Bottom row," Hi pointed downward. "At your feet. The mortar looks different."

I squatted and peered at the base of the wall.

"Hi's right," I said. "This stone has darker mortar, with more cracks. Like it was sealed at a different time."

Ben's whisper cut through the darkness. "Hurry."

Something velvet brushed my face. The slightest touch.

I froze.

My glowing irises spotted a dancing wisp of light. A silvery curl that reached out and stroked my cheek, then drifted away.

Ghost stories flashed through my mind. My breath caught. I was about to scream when my higher centers reengaged.

Spiderweb. One single strand. I watched the tendril puff away from the stones, relax, then settle back into place.

A draft! Air was circulating from somewhere *behind* the wall. Without my powers, I'd never have noticed.

"It's here!" I said. "There must be open space behind these stones!"

"Someone's coming!" Ben hissed. "Move!"

I jumped to my feet and shot to the stairs. Marlo's feet were descending the steps.

Averting my eyes, I tried to douse my flare. For a panicky moment, the power wouldn't fade. Then the sensory doors slammed shut.

SNUP.

I stumbled into Shelton, who steadied me. Spittle clung to the corner of his mouth, but his pupils were human. A quick look confirmed that Hi had also shut down.

"What's going on in here?" In the light of his small flame, I could see Marlo's frown. "Ya'll getting high or something?"

The charge was so absurd, I laughed out loud.

"Sorry," Hi stuttered. "We, uh, dropped our candles and couldn't see."

"All of 'em?"

Hi shrugged. "We're extremely clumsy."

"How come that one's lit?"

"There you are!" A yellow glow preceded Brincefield down the steps. "Everyone's waiting outside. Sadly, I think the tour is over."

"On our way." Slipping by Marlo and Brincefield, we raced up both sets of stairs, passing Tree Trunk on the way out.

"That way guys." Chris pointed to the exit. "We ran a little long. Time to call it a night."

"It was great." Thrown over my shoulder. "Thanks so much!"

Outside, I gulped fresh air. Divine.

The others emerged quickly, and we hustled across East Bay.

"Don't be a stranger!" Sallie called.

I gave her a five-finger wave good-bye. Chris was padlocking a sliding iron gate while chatting with Brincefield. Beyond them, Marlo and Tree Trunk were shuffling away down the sidewalk.

"Man, I *hate* basements," Shelton whined as we hoofed it up the block. "Nasty, stinking graves."

I checked my watch. Five past ten. Five minutes past curfew.

"Crap! I'm late."

"Me too," Hi said. "My mom's gonna rip me a new one."

"I found something right before—"

Ben cut me off. "Let's talk aboard *Sewee*. For now, we haul ass."

As we hurried to the marina, my mind was already testing excuses.

CHAPTER 27

G rounded.

Kit bought none of my explanations.

"I said ten." He pointed to the mantel clock. "What does that say?"

"Ten forty. But the tour ran long!"

"Did you call?"

"I couldn't interrupt the guides."

"Text?"

"They, um, had a no cell phone policy. Plus, we were underground."

"Not good enough," Kit said. "Two weeks. Lockdown. End of story."

I groaned. Kit arched a brow, daring me to continue. Defeated, I stomped to my room, Coop on my heels.

"You gave me no choice," Kit called after me.

"We'll see about that," I muttered.

⬡   ⬡   ⬡

"Change of plans," I said. "We go tonight."

"It's always midnight break-ins with you!" Hi pulled his hair in frustration. "You're like a Colombian drug lord!"

I'd called an iFollow conference. The boys were not cooperating.

On the ride home, I'd told them about my air-behind-the-wall discovery. Everyone got excited. Nevertheless, we'd decided on a cautious plan of attack. No big risks.

Yet there I was, not thirty minutes later, pushing for another high-stakes gamble.

"Why not just visit the dungeon again?" Shelton whined. "Take the official tour. See if we can sneak away like earlier tonight."

"That *was* the plan," Hi tapped finger to palm. "The plan to which you agreed."

"Won't work," I said. "I'm grounded now."

"How long?" Ben asked.

"Two weeks. We can't afford to wait."

"Bonny's treasure has been missing for three hundred years," Hi said. "It can sit tight another fortnight."

"Fine." Not a care in the world.

Hi leaned close to his screen. "What do you mean, 'fine'?"

"Don't come with me," I said. "I'll go by myself."

The boys all spoke at once.

"Don't be a drama queen." Hi.

"You can't go alone." Ben.

"*Somebody* has to watch your back." Shelton.

I bulled ahead. Crazed idea or not, I was tired of arguing. I could sense Bonny's treasure was tantalizingly close. No chance I'd wait another night.

"The only way through that wall is to move the stones," I said. "And we can't dismantle masonry on a guided tour."

Sullen looks, but no contradictions.

"We either finish the job, or give up." I crossed my arms. "I've made my call. Make yours."

◇   ◇   ◇

"I go first." Ben pointed with his bolt cutters. "Ten seconds, then Shelton. After him, you two count to thirty, then come as fast as you can."

"Everyone off the street ASAP," I added.

We were huddled behind a jewelry store, one block south of the Exchange Building. Dressed in black. Just past three in the morning.

I carried only my backpack. Inside were a pen, four flashlights, bottled water, an electric lantern, and Bonny's map.

"If Shelton can't pick the door quickly, we bail." Ben looked hard at me. "Right away. No exceptions."

"Agreed."

"If I see a car, my ass is hauling," Hi said. "Usain Bolt style. I'll swim home if necessary."

"I'll pop the lock," Shelton promised. "But if the building has an alarm . . ."

He didn't finish. No point. We had to pray for low-tech security.

"The rally point is Washington Park," Ben said. "Miss that, meet back at *Sewee*."

"Of everything we've done," Hi said, "this is by far the stupidest. Just wanted to get that on record."

Ben closed his eyes, inhaled, then charged around the corner.

"One one thousand . . . two one thousand . . ."

At ten, Shelton took off like a shot.

As I counted to thirty, Hi did little toe jumps at my side. Finally, after an eternity, we hit our mark.

"Go!"

We sprinted the short block to the building.

Success! The gate was open. Hi and I slid through and pulled it shut.

I turned and scanned the street. No movement, no signs of life.

"Keep going," Hi said.

We streaked down the staircase. The door at the bottom swung open. Ben waved us through, then closed it behind us.

I clapped Shelton's back. "Nice work!"

"No sweat." Shelton's face was drenched. "Okay, a *lot* of sweat, but that lock was a joke."

We thumbed on our flashlights.

"This place is scarier at three a.m." Hi whispered.

"A tad." Shelton's voice quavered.

I didn't disagree.

We crossed the basement and descended the second set of steps. At the bottom we paused to regroup.

"Flare time." As usual, three of us had no problem.

SNAP.

"*Damn damn damn!*" Ben. Struggling.

"Try to relax," Hi suggested. "Let it come to you."

"Relax?" Ben hissed. "What are you, an idiot? That never works."

"Over here." I'd already located the oddly mortared stone.

Shelton and Hi hurried to my side, leaving Ben to stew alone.

"The air seems to flow from behind," I said. "Help me push."

Shelton dropped to a knee beside me. Together we pushed with all the flare strength we could muster.

Nothing. The rock didn't budge. A sick feeling formed in my stomach.

Hi added his back to the mix. We gave it everything. The stone refused to give.

The sick feeling grew.

"It's no good," Shelton panted. "This bastard's not moving."

"Let's take off," Hi pleaded. "We'll try something else."

"No," I said. "We need Ben."

"Ben can't play right now!" Shelton yelped. "And we don't have time to wait."

I grabbed Hi's shoulder. "Go! Do your thing!"

"You're pretty casual with my life, you know."

"Go!"

Groaning, Hi got to his feet, considered a moment, then crossed to Ben.

"Still failing?" Hi asked. Casual.

"I almost had it!" Ben barked.

"Maybe it's your Native American blood," Hi offered. "Perhaps conquered peoples can't tap superpowers?"

Ben stilled. "What did you say?"

"Weakness," Hi mused. "Inferior races might lack the genetics for flaring."

Ben grabbed Hi by the shirt, pulled his face close.

"You wanna see an inferior race, you—"

Ben shuddered as the power scorched through him. Hi scooted backward, just in case.

"God, you're easy!" Hi chuckled.

Ben's eyes burned a deep amber-gold. "You're getting a little *too* good at pushing my buttons, Stolowitski."

Hi bowed. "Practice makes perfect."

"Ben!" I called out. "Move this fricking rock, already!"

Ben's eyes swiveled to me. Without a word, he charged across the dungeon, dropped to his back, and slammed his boots into the stone.

A ghastly creaking filled the dank chamber. Fragments of mortar cascaded to the floor. Slowly the stone moved backward from the rest of the wall.

Ben paused, panting. Then he slammed again, legs driving. Two more thrusts drove the stone into open space.

"You did it!" Hi said.

Ben's efforts had created an opening just large enough to wriggle through. Heads close, we peered through it. Nothing but darkness. A chilly breeze caressed the skin on our faces.

I pointed my flashlight. The beam probed the blackness beyond, revealing a narrow tunnel approximately three feet in diameter.

Shelton spoke first. "No way I'm going in there."

"This must be how Bonny escaped," I said. "The treasure could be—"

"Look at that!" Near hysteria coated Shelton's words. "We have *no idea* where this pit leads! We could get trapped and never get out!"

Ben squared Shelton's shoulders and looked him in the eye.

"I'll be with you the whole way," he promised. "You can do this. Any problems, we turn around."

Shelton let out a strangled cry. Wiped his glasses. Nodded.

"Ready?" I asked.

"We're ready," Ben said.

Dropping to all fours, I crawled into the hole.

CHAPTER 28

Silence filled the dungeon in the ruins of Half-Moon Battery. Deathly. Foreboding.

Dust particles danced in the air oozing from the fresh wound in the rear wall.

Absolute blackness blanketed the chamber.

Then, a noise.

Overhead, wood creaked.

A faint glow appeared at the top of the stairs, slowly worked its way downward.

Moving shadows shot the walls at sharp angles.

The glow reached ground level.

Gravel crunched.

The flickering light crossed toward the back of the chamber. Paused.

Seconds ticked by.

Shadows spun the walls.

The light reversed and bobbed back up the steps.

Darkness returned.

Moments later, footsteps again broke the silence. Descending with purpose.

This time, the light was stronger, white and penetrating.

Without hesitation, the radiance moved into the exposed gap and was gone.

CHAPTER 29

Claustrophobia threatened to overwhelm me.

The tunnel was rough-edged, low, and seemingly endless. My flashlight beam dissolved into darkness two yards out.

As I inched forward, the walls tightened like a fist. Within twenty feet I couldn't rise to my knees. I dropped and dragged myself with my elbows.

My body scraped over gravel, sharp rocks, and things I tried not to imagine. Progress was agonizingly slow. In my mind's eye I saw us—a line of ants creeping through a narrow straw.

Shelton's whimpers told me he was barely holding it together. Without Ben's prodding, I'm not sure he would've kept going.

At one point I glanced back. Hi's glowing eyes were right behind me. And looking petrified.

"You okay?"

He gave a shaky thumbs-up. "Just keep moving. And please

yell if you see an exit sign. I feel like I'm crawling down a monster's throat."

Swallowing hard, I dragged myself another few yards. The skin on my elbows was growing raw.

Hi was right. Things got worse if you stopped. The walls closed in. My brain reminded me of the crushing weight hanging over my head.

"You see anything?" Shelton yelled from down the line. "Tell me this leads somewhere! I'm buggin' out!"

I aimed my flashlight dead ahead. Still the blackness ate the beam. Even flaring, I couldn't see more than six feet.

"Not yet," I said. "But the air is still moving. It has to come from somewhere!"

"Don't stop!" Shelton pleaded. "It's not like we can turn around."

He was right. The passage was way too tight for a U-turn. If we hit a dead end, we'd have to back our way out.

My mind shied from that terrifying possibility.

Reach. Drag. Pull.

Reach. Drag. Pull.

The passing minutes seemed like hours. Without my extra flare strength, I'd have collapsed.

Questions hounded me. Did this hole lead anywhere? Was it tilting downward? How far below ground were we? Was I dragging myself to hell?

It was then that my flashlight died.

Nightmare.

Heart hammering, I snaked ahead faster, yanking forward with ragged, frantic lunges. The rough ground tore at my skin. I felt blood on my elbows and knees.

Adrenaline raced through me. My breath came in great, heaving gulps.

"Tory?" Hi called. "Is this your flashlight?"

I didn't answer. Didn't slow. Just squirmed forward, desperate to reach the end of this pressing, suffocating, horrifying subterranean crack.

Tears streaked the grime coating my face.

I was wrong! my brain screamed. *I've led us into a grave.*

"Who's bleeding?" Ben shouted. "Is everyone alright?"

"Blood!?!" Shelton shrieked. "Where!?!"

Then my outthrust hand hit something solid. A wall. Fingers trembling, I traced its surface, looking for a way through or around.

No deal. The rock face was solid.

I nearly screamed. We'd reached a dead end. We were trapped.

"Why are we stopped?" Hi sounded nearly as frightened as Shelton.

Moments from despair, my wits returned.

The breeze is still there!

My hands shot left, right. Struck solid earth.

Near panic, I rolled to my back and reached for the roof. My hand encountered nothing but open air.

Tucking in my limbs, I rotated and got to my knees. Holding one arm above my head, I carefully rose to my feet.

"I can stand!" I shouted.

"Seriously!?!" Shelton sobbed. "Here I come!"

"Hold on!" Hi yelped. "Tory, is there room for the rest of us?"

I spread my arms, took two steps forward, two backward. The opening was at least two yards wide.

"Yes! We can all fit!"

Hi belly-crawled forward, flashlight bobbing. I grabbed his shoulders and pulled him to his feet. Together we helped Shelton and Ben.

Packed in tight, we panted in unison. Then the boys aimed their beams into the gloom.

"Wow," I said.

Our heads were poking through the floor of a cavern measuring about twenty feet square. Wooden beams supported a fifteen-foot ceiling. Straight ahead—in the general direction we'd been crawling—a low passageway wound from sight.

No one needed an invitation. We scrambled from our hole like escaped convicts.

Hugs. Backslaps. We'd have lit cigars. Right then, open space—*any* space—was the most wonderful thing in the world.

"Thank the Lord," Shelton breathed. "I couldn't take much more!"

Got that right. Everyone had been close to the edge.

"Let's see those elbows," Ben demanded. "You left a bloody streak in the shaft."

I let him inspect my wounds, glad he'd forgotten to be mad at me.

"Not too bad. Next time wear long sleeves."

"Yikes!" I winced. "Know your own flare strength, buddy."

"This chamber is man-made," Shelton said excitedly.

"What tipped you off?" Hi joked. "The ceiling, or the tunnel?"

I pulled the lantern from my backpack and powered it on. Light filled the room, more than enough for canine eyes.

"Look!"

Hi pointed to a line of narrow wedges cut into one wall. Arrayed vertically, the indentations marched upward toward a hole in the ceiling.

"Steps," Ben guessed. "This must be how the builders entered and left."

"Out we go!" Shelton said. "Follow my lead!"

"Hold on!" I grabbed his arm. "We must be standing in Anne Bonny's treasure tunnel. We *found* it! We need to go that way!" I pointed to the opening on the chamber's far side.

Shelton looked like I'd offered a swim in a shark tank. "We don't know this was Bonny's tunnel. Or where it leads."

"We're in the right place," Ben said. "This cavern must be directly under East Bay Street."

"See how smooth these walls are?" Hi said. "Water did that. At some point, this chamber was completely submerged."

"Sea cave?" I asked.

Hi nodded. "I think this is it. There might be chests of diamonds right down that passage! We're all gonna own private islands!"

"Okay!" Shelton surrendered. "We'll keep going. For a bit, anyway."

"What's that?" Ben trained his light halfway up the primitive ladder.

A horizontal wooden beam crossed the ladder's path, its far end attached to a rusty iron hinge. Three feet to the beam's left was a massive iron spring. Above the spring hung a frayed rope.

Using the foothold indentations, Ben climbed up and gave the beam a tentative tug. The hinge screeched as the timber swung out from the wall.

"God in heaven." Ben's eyes went round as golden soccer balls.

Attached to the beam's wall-facing side was a three-foot metal blade.

"Booby trap," I whispered.

"Had to be." Shelton's brow glistened. "Pirates don't give up their treasure without a fight."

"That's some serious *Goonies* action right there." Hi whistled. "Trip that spring release and the blade cuts you in *half*. Bad day."

"Ben, please come down from there," I said.

He dropped to floor level.

"The mechanism was triggered but never reset," Ben said. "Maybe the other traps are disarmed, too."

"Others?" Hi said.

"You think that's the only one?" Shelton's voice was back in the stratosphere. "That whole passage is probably a death trap."

"Keep your flares lit," Ben ordered, "no matter what."

"We'll proceed slow and steady, like the turtle." I sounded like a high school coach prepping his team. "Our senses will detect the traps before they activate."

Would they? They had to. No way I was quitting. These pirates weren't going to outsmart me.

"You *still* want to go in there?" Shelton. Incredulous.

"Of course," I said. "If something's hidden in that tunnel, I intend to find it."

"Treasure," Hi said. "Mucho dinero. I'm *so* in."

"Then we better hustle," Ben said. "It'll be dawn in a few hours."

At the mouth of the passage, cool air washed over me. I sniffed, straining for clues of what lay beyond.

Stone. Mildew. Salt water. No help there.

The others gathered behind me.

Deep breath.

I stepped into darkness.

CHAPTER 30

The second tunnel was wide enough for two to walk side by side.

Well constructed, the passage had semi-smooth walls and a level floor. Stout oak crossbeams braced the ceiling at regular intervals.

Yet the passage was clearly ancient. Despite air movement, the atmosphere was musty and sour. Slimy mud coated the ground.

Slowly, we edged forward, clumped close, our flare senses on high alert.

Hi was beside me, holding the lantern. Its halogen bulb illuminated a ten-foot radius, allowing my pupils to register details with remarkable clarity.

As we crept along, the beam-and-blade trap dominated my thoughts.

I remembered the verse on the treasure map. Not the first line. I was sure we'd bypassed the tunnel entrance, making "Lady

Peregrine's roost" a moot point. My focus was on the second line.

"Begin thy winding to the dark chamber's sluice."

Dark chamber's sluice? What could that be?

My mind sifted possibilities. Came up empty. I was forced to admit that, without more, the rhyme was too vague to be useful.

And the map's other stanza? What did those words mean?

I felt Hi grab my arm. My head turned. He was staring at the ground.

"Don't. Move."

Ever so slowly, Hi knelt, then lay flat on his belly, eyes glued to a spot at my feet.

"What is it?" Shelton's face had drawn level with my ear.

Hi's gaze rolled to the ceiling. Gingerly, he eased back to his feet.

"No one move. There's a tripwire ahead, and it might not be alone."

"Tripwire?" Shelton quavered. "For what?"

"For whatever's above our heads. Snap the wire and something nasty's coming down."

My eyes darted upward. Hi was right. Three vertical slots split the ceiling, spaced at one-yard intervals.

Ben's flashlight probed the far left opening.

"Metal grates, hanging by ropes." His beam worked its way right. "Spikes along the bottom."

Gulp.

"Everyone stay still," Hi said. "I'll check for other wires."

"Go slowly," I warned. "Please be careful."

Hi studied the ground, rotating the lantern in a circular pattern. Finally, he began inching forward.

Step. Pause. Step. Pause. Then he lifted his knee in a long stride.

I stared at the space Hi had high-stepped, stretching my flare vision to its limit.

And saw it.

A strand no thicker than fishing line. The filament crossed the passage at knee level, virtually invisible in the murky light.

Without Hi's sharper eyes, we'd have tripped it. A chill passed through me.

So close.

"There's only one wire." Hi was barely breathing. "I'm straddling the sucker to show where it is."

Sweat dripped from Ben's chin. "Don't screw up."

Legs spread, Hi gestured us forward.

It was almost comical. A mime's game. Hi squatted over nothing, poised in a shaky basketball defensive stance.

"Come on," he urged. "I can't stay like this all day."

I went first, eyes never straying from the wire. Once over, I scurried from the danger zone.

Shelton came next, moving slower, face a mask of concentration. Ben traversed the obstacle nimbly, then offered a hand back to Hi.

Shaking him off, Hi swung his back leg over the wire, ballet style. He turned in a pirouette, grin already forming. Then his plant foot slipped on the slick floor. As he fell, his back leg slashed the tripwire.

Something groaned and shifted overhead. Pebbles rained from the slots in the roof.

Ben moved quick as a bullet.

Grabbing Hi with both hands, he backpedaled with a powerful lunge. The two slammed into Shelton and me, bowling us over.

Objects fell from the ceiling with a terrible shriek. Dust billowed in clouds.

Then the clamor ceased. The dirt began to settle.

Coughing and spitting, we picked ourselves up and inventoried the damage.

"Anyone hurt?" I asked, wiping grit from my eyes.

"No."

"Not really."

"Holy crap."

Back down the passage, three massive iron sheets lay jumbled on the floor. Right where we'd been standing.

"Hi," Shelton panted. "I love you, man."

"Back at you." Hi spat gobs of filth. "I'm going to kiss Ben now, in case some of you don't want to watch."

"I'll pass." Ben ruffled Hi's hair. "Next time, show a little coordination."

"Stupid Nikes. Next time, I'm buying Adidas."

"Everyone still flaring?" I asked.

Three affirmatives.

"Then we need to keep moving."

All smiles faded.

Who knew what other traps lay ahead?

○   ○   ○

"Wait." Shelton raised both hands. "Quiet."

Everyone froze.

"Something's changed. The wind sounds . . . different."

We held our breath. When it came to sonic hearing, Shelton was the undisputed champ.

"Does anything look wrong?" Shelton was tilting his head from side to side, like a parakeet assessing a new cage. "Out of place?"

"Holes in the wall!" Hi's finger shot out. "Both sides."

Three yards ahead I could see four circles, two on each side. Shoulder high, each was roughly six inches wide.

"That's the noise!" Shelton exclaimed. "Air flowing over the gaps. Can't you hear the whine?"

I shook my head. "I'm glad *you* did."

"The ground," Ben hissed. "The center of the passage humps up slightly."

"He's right," I said. "Looks like another trap. But what kind?"

Ben withdrew a water bottle from my pack.

"Head's up!" He tossed it directly onto the mound.

Click.

Spears shot from each side, crossed, and slammed into the opposite wall. Wooden shafts snapped and clattered to the ground like pick-up sticks.

"Whoa," Hi said.

Agreed.

We picked our way through the debris, carefully avoiding the hump. Who knew if the trap could reload?

We'd gone another thirty yards when I noticed a glint in the distance.

"Stop!" I raised the flashlight as high as I could. "Something's reflecting."

"Great," Shelton muttered. "Probably machine guns."

As one, we crept forward, senses firing. Sweat slicked my palms, soaked my shirt, and drenched my face.

Ten yards. Fifteen. Twenty.

A starburst of light danced around us.

"Oh my God!" Hi dropped the lantern in shock. The light tilted, casting ghastly shadows across the passageway.

Before us lay another trap, already tripped.

Twin metal spikes had swung down from the ceiling, one in front, the other from behind, their deadly points meeting like monstrous pinchers.

An object was caught between them.

Shelton screamed.

Ben cursed.

Hi puked on his Nikes.

I stood, speechless.

Eyes glued to an impaled corpse.

CHAPTER 31

The dead man dangled, arms outstretched, jaws wide, as though frozen by the horror of his fate.

Iron talons pierced his chest front and back. The guy hadn't stood a chance.

Never forget. Pirates are merciless.

It took a few moments to calm ourselves.

"Poor bastard," Hi said. "Dodged the first three traps, but not this nightmare."

"Don't touch anything," Ben warned. "We don't know if it's safe."

"How long?"

I knew what Shelton was asking, but had no answer. Though the body was mummified, it was clear that the man's death hadn't been recent.

"Not centuries," I said. "The clothes are modern, and haven't completely rotted. The skin has gone leathery. No animals or insects down here, and the cool temperatures would've helped with preservation."

"Check for a wallet?" Hi suggested.

No one moved.

Fine.

Stepping forward, I delicately poked through the man's pockets. Jacket. Shirt. Pants.

"Nothing. He's not carrying any personal items."

"What's below him?" Ben asked.

Lying beneath the body was a grimy canvas sack. Upending it, I shook out the contents. Canteen. Rotting Archie comic. Wax paper wrapping something that might once have been food. And a polished stone disk the size of a hamburger.

The disk was an inch thick, with four holes running vertically and three more crossing its face. A tiny triangle protruded from the center.

"What the hell?" Shelton sounded puzzled.

"No idea." I shoved the thing in my backpack. "No ID on the body, either."

As I stood, my elbow accidentally grazed a shriveled leg. The body shifted, then one black boot dropped to the earth.

I danced back, heart pounding.

Nothing happened. My pulse returned to a normal pace.

The boot set a bell dinging inside my skull. Curious, I dropped to examine the desiccated foot. The bell dinged louder as I peeled off the sock.

The boys sounded their disgust. Ignoring them, I prodded the hard, leathery skin. Traced the ankle with one finger.

"I know who this is!" I said.

"Not a chance," Ben scoffed.

"See how this foot angles medially at the ankle? There's inversion at the subtalar joint, adduction at the talonavicular joint, and ankle joint equinus."

Blank stares.

"Maybe try English?" Hi suggested.

"Clubfoot! A common, correctable birth defect. But this person never had treatment or surgery." I tossed the boot to Hi. "Notice the sole. It was custom made to reduce pressure on the ankle."

"Okay, clubfoot," Shelton said. "But how does that tell you who this guy is?"

"Because I know of a missing clubfooted man who obsessed over Anne Bonny. This must be Jonathan Brincefield."

"Who?" Three voices.

"Remember the old man from our ghost tour?" I told them about my chat with Rodney Brincefield at the yacht club. "He said his brother Jonathan disappeared while searching for Bonny's treasure. That was sometime in the forties."

"So this stiff is Brincefield's brother?" Hi asked. "That's one hell of a coincidence."

"Not to mention that geezer being on our tour in the first place," Shelton said.

"Maybe he followed me." I didn't really think so.

"Unreal." Hi leaned against the wall. "You attract weirdos like—"

Click.

Ben yanked Hi sideways as spikes snapped from the walls, slamming into the sides of Jonathan Brincefield's rib cage.

Hi panted like a greyhound. Once again, only Ben's reflexes had saved him.

"Please stop doing that!" Ben barked.

"Please keep doing that!" Hi warbled.

Smashed segments of the cadaver's upper body littered the tunnel. The legs and pelvis remained intact, now fastened in place by two pairs of pincers.

"Let's keep moving," I said. "We're running out of time."

"You guys hear that?" Shelton's voice was hushed.

Everyone went rigid. I closed my eyes and listened, hypersonic ears on max. Heard nothing.

Shelton broke the silence. "Thought I heard shifting, or crunching. Like movement."

"The trap probably dislodged some dirt," Ben said. "It must be centuries old."

"Could be." Shelton glanced back the way we'd come.

"Keep moving," I repeated, picking up the lantern. "We've got to be close."

"Stay alert," Ben said. "I don't want some douche finding *our* bodies sixty years from now."

I seconded that.

More careful than ever, we picked our way forward.

CHAPTER 32

Something echoed in the distance.

A gurgle. Soft swishing. My ears identified percolating liquid.

"Water," I whispered. "Not far ahead."

Just then, the ceiling rose sharply, disappeared into inky black.

Holding the lantern before me, I led the group into a small cave. Tiny waterfalls trickled the walls. Moonlight oozed down from above. A mound of boulders and stones spilled across the floor, evidence of a long-ago rockfall.

The passage we'd been following exited through an opening at the chamber's far end. I could see the tunnel veer sharply before continuing out of sight.

"See that?" Hi pointed skyward.

Even my enhanced vision couldn't penetrate the murk.

"There's a fissure!" Hi was excited. "Maybe forty feet up. That's how the light is coming through!"

"We could climb up!" Shelton crowed. "It's a way out!"

True. The rockfall was steep, but nothing we couldn't handle.

"The tunnel keeps going," I pointed out. "This isn't the end."

Hi rubbed his face.

Ben and Shelton just stared.

"We've nearly been killed," Shelton said. "Twice."

"But we escaped."

"You think the way will be easier ahead?" Hi said. "As we get closer to the prize?"

Ben strode forward to examine the stones. "Move aside in case anything tumbles."

Vaulting onto the pile, Ben clambered from boulder to boulder, moving higher with every step. In seconds he was swallowed by shadows.

Silence. Hi and Shelton avoided my eye. If Ben found a way out, I doubted they'd continue.

"There's a metal screen covering the opening," Ben called down.

A lot of banging and clanging followed.

"It's bolted in place. I think this fissure opens into a sewer."

"Ha!" Shelton elbowed Hi. "There *are* sewers under East Bay."

Hi ignored him. "How big is the gap? Could we fit?"

"Probably, but it's locked. We'd need the bolt cutters, but I left them back in the dungeon."

"Shoot!" Shelton began pacing. "Can you see anything else?"

"The chamber overlying this one is still below ground level," Ben answered, "but I can see something through what looks like a sewer grate."

"What?" Hi asked.

"Yellow monkey bars."

"Monkey bars?" Shelton stopped in his tracks. "You sure?"

Hi snapped his fingers. "The East Bay playgrounds! They're a few blocks south of the Exchange."

"Make noise!" Shelton urged. "Attract attention! This is our way out!"

Watch check: three fifty-eight a.m. Had we really been underground only an hour?

I barely remember my life before these freaking tunnels.

"No one will be on the streets this early," Hi said.

"Then we can wait!" Shelton snapped. "Someone will rescue us eventually."

Air drifted from the tunnel ahead. Curious, I stepped to the opening and peered in. The air was gusting, blowing gently, then going still. The cave's waterfalls formed a creek that ran along one side of the passageway.

Every fiber of my being yearned to explore.

"If we quit now, they'll split us apart." I addressed the boys gently, no bullying this time. "All of us will move, probably far away. Permanently." No one answered.

"We'll call each other, and text," I said. "Maybe chat every day. But we won't live in the same neighborhood. We'll never hang out at the bunker, or take *Sewee* to chill on Loggerhead."

Still no responses.

"If we give up, we can't protect each other. Can't watch each other's backs. We'll never figure out what's happened to our bodies. Each of us will be stuck dealing with the flares alone."

They'd heard it before, but I had to try one last time.

"We either see this through, or abandon our pack forever. No more Virals."

My hand found Shelton's shoulder. He didn't pull away.

"I'm going ahead. I can't force you to follow, but I'd appreciate the company."

Ben dropped from above. "I'm in."

Hi's head flopped backward, revealing dirt in the creases circling his neck.

"Blaaeeaaah," he groaned. Then his head came up. "In."

Shelton merely nodded.

Words of gratitude were forming when a soft whooshing floated from the tunnel behind us. Our heads whipped around. The sound was faint, but unmistakable to our enhanced ears.

Footfalls.

Someone was approaching from the direction we'd just come.

What should we do? I mouthed.

Shelton and Hi looked uncertain. Not Ben. Hurrying to the tunnel mouth, he aimed his flashlight into the gloom.

"Who's there? Show yourself!"

All noise ceased abruptly.

But no. I could still hear *something*. Breathing. Just outside the range of Ben's beam.

Ben stepped back, turned, and raised both hands in silent question.

Crack! Crack!

Bullets ripped the airspace Ben had vacated.

"Run!" he bellowed.

As one, we fired into the tunnel ahead, fleeing for our lives.

CHAPTER 33

I ran panting, then skidded to a stop.

The Virals slammed into me from behind.

"Stop!" I ordered. "We can't just run blindly!"

"Gun gun gun!" Shelton yelped.

"Why do people always try to shoot us?" Hi whimpered. "We have the worst freaking luck!"

"Quiet!" Ben alone sounded calm. "Kill the lights. We have an advantage in the dark."

The beams cut off, followed by the lantern. We crouched in silence, breathing hard, listening for sounds of pursuit.

"Wait here." Ben disappeared down the passage, then hurried back. "Someone's in the cavern."

"Could you tell who?" I asked.

I sensed Ben's head shake. "Too dark. The person's not using a light."

"Keep moving," I whispered. "Everyone still flaring?"

"Yes."

"Yeah."

"Yes."

"Then let's hustle. Hi, you're in front with me; you've got the best eyes. One flashlight only."

"Awesome."

"Shelton, hang back and listen for signs of someone following. Ben, stick close to Shelton. If someone catches up, you know what to do."

"No problem."

We moved as quickly as possible in the tomblike dark, senses probing for the slightest whiff of danger. My pulse raced. Sweat coated my skin.

Please, no more traps!

Twenty yards. Thirty. Fifty.

With each step, the tension mounted. Water murmured in the creek at my side, kicking my nerves into even higher gear. I begged various deities for the passage to lead us to safety.

"Wall dead ahead," Hi whispered.

The murmur became a rush of falling water as the passage hair-pinned left and narrowed to a crack.

We shifted to single file and scraped through, one by one.

The darkness on the other side was denser, the air colder. A strong breeze stroked my damp skin.

"Lights," I ordered.

Shelton powered the lantern.

"Whoa!" Knees shaking, I shrank backward until my back struck solid rock.

We were on a five-foot-wide stone ledge overhanging a deep, black chasm. The tunnel creek was now a waterfall, cascading to an unseen bottom. The shelf stretched forward ten yards before ending at the cavern wall.

Across the abyss jutted another outcrop similar to the one on which we stood. From it, a passage led into the wall behind. The gap between the ledges was at least twenty feet. Infinite.

Dead end. Trapped. There was no way to cross.

"How do we get over there?" Shelton whined.

"Jump?" Ben suggested without enthusiasm.

Hi's head wagged emphatically. "No chance I make that, not even flaring! Try again!"

"Then I'll toss you," Ben growled. "We can't stay here!"

"Everyone calm down," I said. "Look around. What do you see?"

Flashlight beams searched the darkness. I examined the far ledge, but could see no way to get there.

"Up," Hi squeaked. "Giant stone platform, dead overhead."

My eyes shot skyward.

Hi wasn't kidding.

Fifteen feet above us, a slab of rock dangled on rusty iron chains. One end overhung us directly. The other hung above the opposite ledge.

"Why's that monster up there?" Shelton groaned. "How do we reach it?"

"Impossible." Ben was eyeing the wall at our back. "This cliff face slopes outward. No chance without professional equipment."

"Then we bring the rock thingy down to us," Hi said.

Synapses fired in my brain.

Bridge. Chasm. Bridge.

"The treasure map!" I shouted. "The second verse!"

My fingers tore at my backpack.

I grabbed the parchment, unrolled it, and hit the words with a flashlight. The Virals huddled close as I read the first two lines aloud:

> Down, down from Lady Peregrine's roost,
> Begin thy winding to the dark chamber's sluice.

"The first line is done with," I said. "And we've certainly been winding, but what is 'the dark chamber's sluice'?"

"Skip to the bottom," Hi urged.

I did.

> Spin Savior's Loop in chasm's open niche,
> Choose thy faithful servant to release correct bridge.

A tingle traveled my spine. "This riddle has to contain the answer!"

"But it makes no sense," Hi said.

"Correct bridge." Ben frowned. "I don't like the sound of that."

"If this really is giving us directions," I said, "we've got to identify 'Savior's Loop' and locate the 'chasm's open niche.'"

For a moment no one spoke.

Then Shelton gasped.

"Could it be that? That hole?"

Shelton's trembling finger pointed at a moss-covered alcove cut into the rock wall at our backs. Bread-box-sized, the tiny cubby was barely visible.

I scraped away the moss with my fingernails and peered inside. The nook contained a single object—a flat, circular stone the size of a small pizza. Seven nodules formed a T on its face. The center was notched. The object was clearly the work of human hands.

"Shelton's right!" I said. "This must be the niche!"

"Now we need 'Savior's Loop.'" Hi said. "But what could that be?"

I worked the phrase in my mind.

Spin Savior's Loop. Spin the loop. Savior's Loop.

"Anne Bonny was Christian," I said. "Jesus would be her 'Savior,' right?"

"So maybe we spin *Jesus's* loop?" Shelton asked. "Like a circle? Spin Jesus in a circle?"

Click.

"Say that again."

"What? Spin Jesus in a circle? How would we do that?"

"What represents Jesus?" I squealed. "A cross! And look!"

I pointed inside the niche.

"The bumps form a cross!" Hi exclaimed. "Spin that sucker!"

"Do it!" Shelton was right with us.

I reached in and tried to rotate the stone clockwise. Nothing. I tried counter-clockwise. No go.

"Let me." Ben strained, muscles bulging. No movement in either direction. "It's too wide. I can't get a proper grip."

"We're missing something," Shelton pounded his forehead.

A new synapse fired in my brain. "Bonny capitalized 'Savior's Loop.' Like a proper name."

"So we need a real object?" Hi scanned the rock wall. "I don't see anything."

The answer came in a flash. "I've got it!"

Riffling through my backpack, I pulled out the object I'd found on poor Jonathan Brincefield. A circular stone disk. Seven holes.

The gaps formed a T. A sort of cross.

Savior's Loop.

"This is it! The holes should match the bumps!"

I fitted the disk over the carved stone and pressed firmly.

Chunk.

The holes and bumps aligned perfectly, and the wedge on the disk fit smoothly into the notch in the stone.

I rotated the pattern clockwise. The stone circle turned easily.

In the darkness, something rumbled.

Crash!

A chunk of wall tumbled free, tipped forward, and dropped off the edge. Seconds later we heard it strike far below.

A new niche had been revealed in the wall behind our ledge. Inside were seven dusty levers.

"What now?" Hi sounded nearly spent. "Another fricking choice?"

I nodded grimly.

"Oh no." Ben was flat on his belly, peering down into the void.

"What?" Hi asked.

Ben hesitated.

"What is 'oh no' down there?" Hi insisted.

"I know what the poem means about releasing the correct bridge."

"Yes?" My mouth went dry.

"We're standing on the *incorrect* one."

CHAPTER 34

"We're on a ledge," Ben said. "Connected to the rock face by wooden beams."

"So?" Shelton toe-tested the ground with one foot. "Seems solid."

"Ropes run alongside the timbers," Ben continued. "If we choose Bonny's 'faithful servant' incorrectly, I think *this* bridge will release."

I heard Hi swallow. Shelton's mouth opened, but nothing came out.

Ben looked at me.

I was about to respond when noises from behind us cut me off. We all turned, startled. Ben reacted first.

Springing to the opening, he craned his neck around the corner and peered back into the passageway.

Two slugs slammed the tunnel's rear wall, sending Ben reeling backward.

"You've got to come through here!" Ben shouted. "I'll be waiting!"

His eye darted to mine. I read their message. *Hurry!*

"Shelton! Hi! Help me decide!"

Terrified, we examined the levers.

"'Choose thy faithful servant to release correct bridge,'" I repeated.

"But which one?" Hi said.

"Five of the handles are crossed!" Shelton exclaimed.

"Good!" I said. "'Thy faithful servant' must be another Christian reference."

I stared at the five candidates, willing the correct choice to announce itself.

None did.

"Check the proportions," Hi said. "The horizontal bar on this lever is too low for a traditional cross."

I froze. Why did that seem important?

"Same with those two!" Shelton squeaked. "And that one's too high!"

"This one!"

My mind spun. What? What?

Hi pointed to a central handle. Even in the dim light of our lantern, it was clear that better care had gone into its carving. The lever formed a perfect cross in exact, eye-pleasing proportions.

Still I hesitated. Something in my lower centers was clamoring for attention.

"Tory!" Hi exclaimed, "It must be the center one!"

"Footsteps!" Ben hissed.

"Pull it!" Shelton urged.

I locked up. Something was terribly wrong.

"I'll get it!" Shelton reached for the knob.

What? What?

Shelton's fingers curled around the handle.

"NO!"

My hand shot forward and slapped Shelton's away. He jerked backward, startled by my sudden move.

"Bonny called it 'thy faithful servant!'" I rushed. "'*Thy!*' Hers! We need to look for Anne Bonny's cross!"

"The symbol from the map!" Hi was with me.

I grabbed the treasure map, held it before the levers.

At first, nothing was obvious.

Then I saw.

The rightmost lever had a high crosspiece, making it tall and skinny, just like the curious little illustrations. I shoved my nose close. Details zoomed in with laserlike clarity.

There. The upper tine curved *ever so slightly* to the right. Nearly imperceptible, unless one was looking for it.

Bonny's bent cross. Her calling card. *Thy faithful servant.*

I pointed.

"Together?"

Hi and Shelton nodded excitedly, then reached for the dusty stone handle.

I called a heads up to Ben. "One! Two! Three!"

The cross arced down slowly, groaning after centuries of disuse. Finally, it could descend no further.

Fearfully, we pressed our backs to the cavern wall.

Boom! Boom! Boom!

Ropes snapped. Pullies creaked. Iron chains screeched as they released their centuries-old payload.

Overhead, the massive stone slab began to descend.

Clink. Clink. Clink.

The rock suddenly halted. A rumbling sounded behind the wall at our backs.

I tensed. Something was wrong.

Crack! Boom!

The slab above us shivered, then dropped in an avalanche of dirt, pebbles, and mouth-coating grit. It struck with the power of a train crash.

The noise thundered in my canine ears. I covered them, yelping in agony.

SNUP.

For seconds, all was chaos. I couldn't see or think. Choking and gasping, I tried to breathe through my shirt.

After what seemed an eternity, the dust storm settled.

I surveyed the scene.

"Oh no." Ben pointed across the abyss, his eyes their normal black-brown.

Upon impact, the stone slab had shifted sideways, leaving only one corner on the opposite ledge. It teetered, threatening to slip into the chasm at any moment.

"We have to go now!" I jammed our lantern and the map into my pack. "Before it falls!"

"I can't cross that!" Shelton was almost crying. "I lost my flare!"

"You have to!" I hand-cupped his cheeks. "Remember, you're a Viral. You can do anything."

Screwing his face into a determined mask, Shelton spun and shot over the bridge, never slowing until he slammed into the opposite wall.

"Ooof!"

Hiram and I inhaled sharply. Shelton crumpled, but gave a woozy thumbs-up.

"Unreal!" Hi croaked. "Here goes nothing!"

Hi stormed forward, wailing the entire way. Then he collapsed next to Shelton. The two exchanged a shaky fist bump.

"Go!" I said to Ben.

"You next. I'm heaviest."

I squeezed Ben's arm, then fired across.

The platform wobbled wildly as I dismounted. A low grinding filled the cavern.

"Now Ben!" I screamed. "Hurry!"

As Ben raced for the bridge, a shadow appeared in the opening behind him. I barely noticed. My eyes were locked onto Ben, who seemed to move in slow motion.

The grinding amplified.

Crrrreeeeeeeaaaaaaaaak!

Ben pounded across. With each step, the bridge wobbled

more. Then the end slipped from the ledge and the slab plunged downward.

"*BEN!*"

I watched in horror as the bridge dropped from beneath his feet.

Ben threw himself forward, arms out-thrust.

Time froze. My heart stopped.

Ben's forearms caught the cliff's edge. His fingers clawed for purchase. Then his body slammed the rock face, causing his grip to falter.

Six hands shot out and seized Ben's arms, hair, shirt, and neck. As one, we pulled him to safety.

"Thanks," he wheezed. "I was a little short."

"Anytime." Shelton. Doubled over.

"I still owe you one," Hi panted. "And that's just tonight."

Crack! Crack!

Bullets smashed the rocks above our heads.

"Move!" I shouted.

We charged into yet another black passage.

CHAPTER 35

We tumbled down a ramp and landed in a tangle of arms and legs.

Everyone lay still, too overwhelmed to move. My thoughts were firing in short jagged clips.

We're alive. Unharmed. The shooter can't follow.

Slowly, my panting subsided and my pulse decelerated. Disengaging myself from the others, I rose and looked around.

The current chamber was circular, the size of a classroom. A waterfall poured from a hole in the roof to a pool in the center of the floor. I guessed the pool's diameter and depth at about ten feet each. The water swirled, eventually draining through a chute at the bottom.

The effect was beautiful, like a graceful garden fountain. The rest of the room was empty.

"This must be 'the dark chamber's sluice,'" I said. "We made it!"

My gaze scoured the walls, snagged on a platform jutting from the rock. Roughly a yard square, the platform held nothing. Deep gouges marred its otherwise smooth stone surface.

My shoulders slumped in dismay.

Something heavy had once rested there.

Like a chest.

No.

"What's that gibberish?" Shelton pointed to black letters chiseled into the wall directly above the platform.

"Another riddle?" I said. "But that's definitely not English."

The characters were recognizable, but I couldn't place the language. Beside the lettering was the now-familiar symbol. Bonny's signature bent cross.

My heart sank into my socks.

She took it. The treasure isn't here.

"No!" Hi slapped his forehead. "Tell me this isn't where the treasure's supposed to be. Please."

I couldn't meet his eye.

"It's *gone*?" Shelton wailed. "How? Nobody's been in here before us! Those tunnels would've been front-page news. And the skybridge! That never came down until tonight!"

I shook my head. I couldn't agree more.

Then the pieces fell together. I'd been a fool.

Hi must've read my expression.

"What?"

"They moved it."

"Who?"

"Anne Bonny. Her people." I punched the air in frustration. "*Why* didn't I think of this before?"

Shelton waved his arms. "Explain! Right now!"

"Bonny's crew busted her out of the dungeon, right?"

"Yep," Shelton said. "We crawled down that god-awful hole ourselves."

"She must've worried the Brits would discover her escape route."

"But they didn't," Hi argued. "If they had, everyone would know about these tunnels. Her crew must have resealed the dungeon like we found it."

"But Bonny couldn't be sure that would work," I said. "She *had* to worry that the tunnels could be compromised."

Hi and Shelton groaned.

"So she and her crew removed the treasure themselves," Hi said, "reset the booby traps, and took off. Mother—"

"Come *on*!" Ben's bellow echoed loudly in the small space. "Why can't we catch one stinking break!"

My eyebrows rocketed up in surprise. "What?"

"What do you mean, *what*?" Ben spread his hands. "Look around, Victoria! There's no way out of here!"

I spun a three-sixty. Ben was right.

No doors, no tunnels, no cracks, no fissures. We were stuck in a subterranean aerie with no outlet.

"So no treasure?" Hi whined. "I thought we had it!"

"It's gone," I said. "Bonny moved it somewhere else."

Hi sat and dropped his head between his knees. Shelton slumped beside him and grabbed one ear.

Ben started tapping the walls, searching for an exit. Clueless what else to do, I removed the treasure map and my pen. As Ben circled the room, I copied the foreign words from the wall onto the back of the map.

Ben and I finished at the same time.

"Nothing," he said. "The only way out is how we came in."

"That won't work," I said.

"Maybe the waterfall?" Ben levered himself up on the empty platform and stepped toward the wall.

Click.

Ben froze. Pulled his foot back. Looked down at the platform. Swore.

Rumble. Pop! Pop!

Shelton and Hi sprang to their feet.

"It's a pressure switch!" Ben shouted. "I tripped it!"

Somewhere close, water gurgled, like a giant flushing toilet.

The chamber shook, then went deathly still.

"I think we might—"

"Look!" Hi pointed frantically at the ramp we'd tumbled down moments before.

An enormous boulder now blocked the opening.

"Oh no!" Ben gestured at the roof.

A sluice gate opened overhead. The waterfall surged.

The room began to flood.

Fast.

CHAPTER 36

Water started overflowing the basin.

My eyes darted, searching for escape. Found nothing but solid stone walls.

"What should we do!?" Shelton yelled.

"Stay together!" I said. "We may have to swim out!"

"How!?" Hi shouted. "Where!?"

I tried to concentrate. There *had* to be a way!

Ben leaped from the platform, hands outstretched, and caught the waterfall's edge. Incredibly, though pummeled by the flow, he held and tried to pull himself up.

No good. The deluge loosened his grip and washed him to the floor. Ben popped to his feet and yelled in frustration.

We weren't getting out that way.

"I don't wanna drown!" Shelton wailed.

I looked down. Water swirled like a vortex inside the pool. If the roof was impossible, that left the floor.

Maybe.

I jumped into the pool and fought my way to the bottom. Water was draining through an opening no wider than a Hula-Hoop. Just not fast enough.

We could squeeze through, but there's no turning around.

I kicked to the surface and crawled out of the basin.

"What are you doing!?" Shelton screamed.

"I have a plan." As calm as possible.

The boys gathered close, eager for something, anything.

"We swim out through the bottom of the pool," I said.

"What!?" Shelton was nearing full-blown panic.

Hi looked at me as if I'd proposed we grow wings and fly.

Ben stood motionless, dripping, neck veins bulging.

"It's our only chance. The drain must lead somewhere."

"What if there's no air?" Hi yelped. "We could drown!"

"The pool might empty into the chasm," Ben warned. "Straight shot, right into the abyss."

I blinked back tears. "I don't have another idea."

The group stood, paralyzed by indecision. The water was up to our shins, heading for our knees.

"We can't just wait here to die," I said.

"Fine," Ben said. "Let's go for it."

"Just like a waterslide." Hi. Shaky.

"Don't put me last." Shelton's voice cracked. "I won't be able to do it."

Ben tapped us, one by one, then himself. "Tory. Shelton. Hi. Then me."

"I took skin-diving lessons," Hi said. "Well, one. To maximize oxygen intake you take two deep breaths, then hold the third and go."

Ben nodded. "Don't exhale until you have to, then release the air slowly. And don't panic. Just keep swimming no matter what."

Inside my backpack was a Ziploc bag. I folded the treasure map, zipped it tight, and crammed the baggie in a pocket.

"Our flashlights are supposedly waterproof." I didn't say more. No point.

"I'll take the lantern," Ben said.

We'd come down to it. No one wanted to move, but we'd run out of time. The water was at waist level.

I hugged each of them. "I'll see you in a few seconds!"

Grim faces.

I couldn't hesitate any longer. If I did, we'd all lose our nerve. Maybe our lives.

I stepped to the pool's edge and whispered a prayer.

Inhale. Exhale.

Inhale. Exhale.

Long inhale.

Splash.

I dove, kicked hard for the bottom, and fired through the hole. Beyond was an underwater tunnel. I dolphin kicked, hauling with my hands. The flashlight slowed me, but I had no choice. Without it I'd be in total darkness.

Seconds ticked by in my head.

Eight . . .

Nine . . .

Ten . . .

The tunnel veered left, then angled downward. My beam barely dented the inky black. I dragged myself forward, arms aching. To my horror, another flooded channel stretched before me.

Fifteen . . .

Sixteen . . .

Seventeen . . .

Panic threatened, but I shoved it aside. Dribbling air from my lips, I struggled on. Ahead, the channel descended even more sharply.

Twenty-two . . .

Twenty-three . . .

Twenty-four . . .

Desperate, I kicked harder, arcing the light wildly. Ten feet ahead lay another bend.

My lungs burned. I was out of time.

Primal terrors howled full throat in my brain.

SNAP.

The flare blasted through me.

I coughed out my last remaining oxygen. Gagged on seawater.

The walls closed in.

I was done.

Then I saw it.

Just around the bend, the roof of the tunnel bubbled upward. Dropping my flashlight, I thrust with both arms. When I broke the surface, my head nearly slammed into the low ceiling.

Air pocket!

Thank God!

I gulped greedy mouthfuls of air.

Inside, my powers raged. Images flashed from some hidden corner of my psyche. Thoughts burned in my skull.

Somewhere, I knew Coop howled.

More images formed. Shelton. Hi. Ben.

Underwater. Gripped with panic. Losing faith.

As I gasped and sputtered, my brain fired a message.

Air pocket at the third bend! Don't give up!

I could feel the thought knife into each of them. Their minds latched on and their limbs paddled madly.

Shelton's head broke the surface. I dragged him to me with one hand. Hi appeared next, hacking and spitting. Then Ben's face erupted from the liquid.

"Everyone okay?" I yelled.

The boys were too shell-shocked to answer. Only Hi still held his flashlight.

We treaded water, clinging to projections from the tunnel wall.

I noticed that none of the boys were flaring.

"What'd you do?" Hi backhanded water from his eyes. "I heard you inside my head!"

"You saved me!" Shelton said. "I was all turned around!"

"Later." Ben was still breathing hard. "We have to get out of here."

"Follow me," I said.

We swam down the tunnel, using a stone outcropping to pull ourselves along. I thanked the heavens for our last remaining flashlight, and prayed it wouldn't fail.

Then we hit another dead end.

"Oh no!" Shelton wailed.

"Shh!"

My ears picked up a familiar sound. My nose identified a familiar scent.

Waves crashing. Sand.

"We're near a beach!" I said. "I can hear the surf!"

"Promise?" Shelton sniffled in the darkness.

"Promise." I glanced down. The water seemed deeper, but I couldn't tell how much. "Wait here a sec."

Holding my breath, I sank to the bottom of the channel. Through the murk, my glowing eyes detected a diffuse light. An opening, several yards ahead. I rose to the surface.

"We're going to have to dive again," I said. "Follow my light. I won't let you down."

"Just get us out of here, Tory." Hi was near his breaking point. "Now, if you don't mind."

"Will do. Ready?"

"Ready." Times three.

Inhale. Exhale.

Inhale. Exhale.

Long inhale.

Splash.

I kicked forward, then through the gap into a murky sea cave.

The others were right behind.

The surface was twenty feet above. Beyond it, moonlight.

Treading in place underwater, I pushed Hi and Shelton past me. Ben was just behind. We fired to the surface as one.

My head struck something hard. Light exploded between my eyes. I sank, stunned. The flashlight slipped from my fingers.

SNUP.

The power fizzled.

My mind drifted. The world grew fuzzy.

A hand grabbed my arm, yanked hard, dragging me upward. Lightheaded, I allowed myself to be pulled.

My head broke the surface. I took a giant breath.

"Tory!" Ben's face was inches from mine. "You okay?"

"Fine," I said. "Dandy. I bonked my head."

Ben looked at me oddly. "Let's get to shore."

"Shore?"

Ben smiled for the first time. "Look around."

I did. Knew the place.

We were floating just off the Battery, at the very tip of the downtown peninsula. We'd traveled roughly seven blocks underground.

Hi and Shelton waved from a staircase embedded in the seawall.

"An easy way up for once!" Shelton sounded ecstatic.

Ben and I paddled to the steps and slip-slid up to street level. The four of us crossed into White Point Gardens, found a park bench, and collapsed.

My watch was missing. I had no idea of the time.

But dawn was purpling the eastern sky.

Beside me, Hi broke into laughter, sides shaking with spasms of uncontrolled amusement.

"What?" The sound was infectious. I felt a smile tickle my lips.

"Say hi to our buddies." Hi jabbed a thumb over his shoulder.

I turned, came face-to-face with a monument dedicated to Stede Bonnet and his pirate cronies. I nearly busted a gut.

Cackling, Shelton stumbled to the big hunk of granite. Kicked it twice. Hard.

"Thanks for nothing, you jerks! Tell your buddy Anne we don't accept IOUs."

Ben guffawed, reigniting the rest of us. We let the giggles flow, taking the tension with them.

"Do you guys have any idea how screwed I am?" Hi moaned. "My mother gets up in ten minutes."

"I feel you," Shelton said. "I'm just as toast."

"No point worrying about it now," Ben said. "We survived. We can take whatever comes next."

Definitely. Kit was going to filet me, but at the moment, that seemed trivial.

"Let's enjoy the fresh air for a while," I said.

So we sat, side by side, and watched the sunrise.

PART THREE:
BULL

CHAPTER 37

"Miracles can happen," I joked. "You just have to believe!"

Noon. Bunker. We lounged in our clubhouse, still beat from the previous night's insanity.

The boys were sprawled about the room, idly tossing a tennis ball. I was on the bench. Coop was gnawing a Frisbee at my feet.

Impossibly, no one had been caught.

Five hours earlier, I'd tiptoed through my front door, prepared for the worst. Already grounded, I had no idea how Kit would react to my sneaking out until dawn. For all I knew, a cop could be sitting in our living room.

So I'd slipped inside, nervous that Coop would blow my cover. Instead, much to my surprise, I'd found a Post-It stuck to the banister.

Early trip to LIRI. Back by dinner. Don't leave the house. Kit.

He had no idea.

After executing a few of Hi's best dance moves, I'd collapsed on the couch. I was exhausted, emotionally drained, and smelled like sewage and sea scum.

Coop had hit me like a Patriot missile, tail thumping, his pink sandpaper tongue slathering my face.

"It's okay, boy. Mommy's fine. Just had a little scare, that's all."

Coop continued bathing my face. From that moment, he hadn't let me out of his sight.

A foghorn sounded in the harbor, scattering the seagulls roosting outside the bunker's window slit. Cruise ship, headed to the peninsula.

Sunlight glinted off the tranquil ocean. The temperature was well past ninety.

"My mom caught me downstairs, but she thought I was going *out*." Hi laughed. "Like I'm getting up that early on a Saturday. Thank God she's groggy before her first three cups of coffee."

"My parents were still in bed." Shelton lobbed the tennis ball toward Ben. "They *never* sleep past six. I must have a guardian angel."

"Will your Dad get after you?" I asked Ben.

Tom Blue's workday began well before sunup, even on weekends. By the time we'd docked *Sewee* that morning, his ferry had already set sail.

"I'll say I went fishing." Ben caught the ball and flipped it to Hi. "He won't ask a lot of questions."

The tennis ball arced across the room, was caught, arced back.

Then Hi voiced the question on everyone's mind. "*So* . . . any guesses at who tried to kill us?"

"Honestly, I have no idea," I said. "None."

"It makes no sense!" Shelton spread his hands. "Who could've known we planned to break into the Provost Dungeon last night?"

"We didn't know *ourselves* until a few hours before," Hi said. "And what sane person would follow us down the rat hole we uncovered?"

"iFollow?" Ben ear-tucked his hair. "Maybe someone hacked our videoconference."

"Is that possible?" The idea disturbed me.

Shelton shook his head. "We formed a new group with a new password. That program has tough encryption. Believe me, I checked. It's extremely unlikely."

"And why bother?" I said. "Who'd want to spy on us?"

"*Kill* us," Hi corrected. "Whoever followed us underground was willing to create a pile of dead bodies. Chew on *that* for a second."

"We sure know how to attract psychopaths," Shelton muttered.

"It's connected to Bonny's treasure somehow," Ben said. "That's the only logical explanation."

"There's another possibility." Hi sat forward, face tight with concern. "What if someone else knows about our flares?"

"What?" Shelton pulled his earlobe. "How?"

"I don't know, but we can't just discount it." Hi avoided my eyes. "Not every move we've made has been private."

I opened my mouth, but Shelton spoke first.

"You did the mind thing again, Tory." Fingers tugging double time. "In the tunnels, underwater, I heard your voice inside my head."

"Me too," Hi said.

Ben hesitated, then nodded. "You flared a second time, too. How?"

"I don't know." Thinking back, I shuddered. "I was panicking. Couldn't find air. Then something twitched in my brain and the flare exploded through me. It was more unconscious than anything."

"How come only you can touch minds?" Shelton asked.

I shrugged. Of course I had no answers.

The room fell silent.

"Well, you saved our lives," Ben finally said. "That's all that matters."

"Excellent point." Hi shuffled over, grasped my hand, and deposited a sloppy kiss. "I'm in your debt, milady."

"Quit being a spaz." Shelton's eyes met mine. "Thanks, Tor. Just keep doing what you're doing."

"Done." I smiled. "Should be easy, since I have no idea what I did."

Tensions eased slightly, but the good vibes didn't last.

"Now what? Should we call the cops?" Shelton sounded unhappy with his own suggestion.

"With our track record?" Ben scoffed. "We can't report *another* ancient skeleton and *another* mysterious gunman. After the monkey-bones fiasco on Loggerhead last May, we've got zero credibility with the police."

"Hello Officer Hates-Our-Guts," Hi mimicked. "You remember us! Last night we used a stolen artifact to break into a historic city landmark. Which cell will be mine?"

"Hi and Ben are right," I said. "We'd be arrested, then committed."

"Someone's gonna find that gap in the dungeon wall." Shelton tapped his watch. "It's a matter of hours."

"Then we need to hurry," I said. "The Exchange is closed on weekends, so that buys us some time."

The boys glanced at each other, but not at me.

"What?"

"Tory, it's over." Ben's voice was firm.

"Over?" I was caught by surprise. "Of course it's not *over*. We have the next clue!"

"Shelton's right," Ben said. "On Monday, someone will notice the stone we dislodged. By lunchtime, everyone in America will know about Charleston's secret tunnels."

"Crap!" Shelton sat upright. "We still have the treasure map!"

Bonny's drawing lay upside down on the table. A little worse for wear, but nothing too dramatic. Amazingly, the Ziploc kept it dry during our aquatic escape. The foreign words I'd copied onto its back were still visible in bright blue ink.

Hi rubbed his forehead. "We have to return that, pronto. It's about to be *very* popular, and it won't take the Fletchers five seconds to figure out who stole it."

"We're screwed anyway," Shelton griped. "Tory wrote on it."

"I was a little short on options."

"When the news breaks," Ben said, "treasure hunters will flock to Charleston from all over the world. One of them will find the stash."

"No!" I said sharply. "Think! The pool chamber flooded. No one else will have Bonny's last poem."

"Which we can't read," Hi mumbled.

"I'm working on that!" Their constant resistance was starting to irk me. "Quitting is *not* an option. Don't you see? We're the only ones with the final clue to the treasure's location. We can find where Bonny moved it!"

"What makes you think it's still there?" Ben asked. "Maybe the pirates divided up the loot and skipped town."

"Then why leave a clue at all?" Snap decision. I'd share my pet theory. "I think Bonny left the poem for Mary Read."

"But Read was dead by then," Shelton said. "She died of fever in a Jamaican prison."

"Maybe Anne didn't know that. Or maybe Mary survived."

"That's a lot of maybes," Hi said.

"Anne drew her signature cross next to the poem. I think she was letting Mary know the clue was genuine, like she did in her letter."

The boys remained mute, but I sensed a slight softening. I scratched Coop's belly, allowing my argument time to sink in.

Then I pressed forward. "The treasure wasn't discovered, guys, it was *moved*. And we hold the *only* clue to the new location."

Nothing.

"We can still win. We can still save Loggerhead."

Shelton rubbed his chin. Ben seemed skeptical. Hi had a speculative look.

"It's out there," I insisted. "Waiting for us. All we need are the guts to take it."

Shelton and Hi nodded, the former reluctant, the latter suddenly eager.

"Fine." Ben picked up the tennis ball and lobbed it my way. "Where do we start?"

I made the catch without looking. "We find out everything there is to know about Anne Bonny."

CHAPTER 38

I scanned the handout and dialed the number at the bottom.

A female voice answered after two rings.

"Charleston Ghost Tours."

"Sallie? This is Tory Brennan. My friends and I took your tour last night?"

"Hi Tory, how can I help you? Did you lose something?"

"No, nothing like that." Breezy. Casual. "I actually have a question, if you've got a minute."

"Shoot."

Careful. Don't remind her about the treasure map.

"I was thinking about our conversation at the Charleston Museum."

"I'm manning the info desk as we speak," Sallie said. "This is my cell number."

"Oh! Then I'll be quick. I was just wondering where I could find more info on Anne Bonny."

"Hmm." Brief pause. "There's a bit online, and some decent books I could recommend, but so little is truly known about Bonny that most sources are repetitive, even contradictory."

"That's been the problem."

"What exactly are you looking for?"

"I have a school project," I lied. "We're supposed to trace the background of a Lowcountry historical figure, and I figured Anne Bonny would be fun."

"Did you try the Karpeles Manuscript Library? It has genealogies dating back to the first settlers. Their document guy is a bit pretentious, but he really knows his stuff. Sorry, his name escapes me."

"Thanks, Sallie. I think I know who you're talking about."

◇   ◇   ◇

"We appreciate your assistance, Dr. Short." I flashed my most charming smile. "Especially on a Saturday."

"And *I* expect you to honor our bargain, Miss Brennan." Short led us down a hallway exiting the library's main gallery. "Anne Bonny's letter will join the Karpeles collection after being properly appraised and registered. Agreed?"

"Agreed."

Short had driven a hard bargain, but we'd had little choice. The clock was ticking.

"Then I'm happy to be of service." Short even smiled. "I've set you up in viewing room A. I was able to locate several documents I believe will be of interest."

We entered a brightly lit chamber housing four chairs and a long wooden table. Three carts lined the rear wall, each topped by a large metal container.

"This area is temperature and humidity controlled." Short was handing out pairs of linen gloves. "Please do not touch any documents with your bare hands. The oils on your skin can damage the parchment."

He gave us a sharp look. "You're not chewing gum, are you? I know children like to do that."

Head shakes.

Short clasped his hands before his chest. "On the first cart is a genealogy of the Cormac family, from their arrival in Charles Town in the late 1600s to the present."

I nodded, if only because he seemed to expect it.

Short moved to the center cart. "Here are documents pertaining to William Cormac himself. Letters, estate records, wills, anything we could collect."

Excellent. Exactly what I wanted.

"And finally we have documents relating to Anne Bonny." Short gestured to the third cart. "Not much, I admit, but there are a few items of note."

"Thank you," I said. "We're extremely grateful for your thoroughness."

"I will return in one hour. If you need anything before then, or have additional requests, simply press the call button. And be aware." Short pointed to a shiny black orb positioned in the center of the ceiling. "*That* device is a security camera." He headed for the door.

"Quick question before you leave . . ." I handed Short a slip of paper. "Can you identify this language?"

Short glanced at the page, which contained a few words from Bonny's poem.

"Gaelic. Original dialect, not the offshoot Scottish idiom. The language is often referred to simply as 'Irish.' Anything else?"

"Not right now, thank you."

As the door closed, Shelton snorted. "Of course he's happy to help. We struck the worst bargain in history."

Hi shrugged. "It was the only way to get access. He had all the leverage."

"Let's go one cart at a time," I suggested. "Then we won't miss anything."

We gave the first box a cursory examination. Cormac family history *after* Anne Bonny was of little interest.

Moving to the middle cart, we inspected William Cormac's private papers. Most were legal tracts, or reports on the productivity of his plantation. I began to worry we'd find nothing of use.

"Nice!" Shelton had taken a handful of pages to the table. "Check this out!"

I dropped into the chair beside him. "What've you got?"

"A letter to Cormac from the father of his wife."

"His wife?" Hi asked. "You mean Anne Bonny's mom?"

"No, his *real* wife. The one Cormac cheated on in Ireland."

"Ouch!" Hi leaned over Shelton's shoulder. "What did her father write? Is it a challenge to a duel?"

"The language is pretty old school," Shelton said, "but this is *not* complimentary. He's railing Cormac for 'lecherous behavior' and things like that. Calls him a 'paunchy, beetle-headed foot-licker.'"

Hi smirked. "Why would anyone keep this letter? Cormac must've been a glutton for punishment."

"Well, well." Shelton had reached the end. "How about that!"

"What?" I asked.

"We know Anne's father was named William Cormac," he said. "And when she married, Anne took the last name of her loser husband, James Bonny."

"Yeah. So?"

"Guess what her *mother's* name was? The serving woman Cormac ran on with."

Shelton waited, enjoying center stage.

"Come on!" Hi said. "You don't really expect us to guess names do you?"

"It's *go-od*!" Shelton promised in a singsong voice.

"Out with it." My patience was wearing thin.

"Anne Bonny's mother was named—" Shelton drum-rolled the table, "—Mary *Brennan*."

My eyes went squinty. "Seriously?"

"See for yourself." Shelton handed me the page. "Daddy is furious because Mary Brennan was his daughter's personal servant. He wrote her full name twice."

"Shelton's right." Ben placed another document on the table. "This is an expense report from the Cormac estate in County Cork, Ireland. Dated 1697. It notes that a serving woman named Mary Brennan gave birth to a daughter, Anne."

"How about that?" Hi joked. "Anne Bonny could be your super-great-grandma. Must be the source of your charm."

"Very funny."

But a shiver flashed through me. The yacht club painting. The shared handwriting quirk. Now this. Was it possible? Could I be *related* to Anne Bonny?

Nonsense.

"There must be a thousand Brennans in North America," I said.

"How many in Massachusetts?" Hi was flipping through the last papers in the William Cormac box. "Here's a letter written by Mary Brennan herself. 1707. Never posted, but addressed to a cousin in 'the colony of Massachusetts Bay.'"

Second chill. This was definitely getting weird.

"That's it for Big Willy Cormac." Hi returned the sheet to its container.

"Say hello to Anne Bonny." Shelton moved to the third cart, then handed Ben a small collection of musty documents. "Enjoy!"

"Not much to see." Ben placed the papers on the table. "Let's examine them one by one."

"Tory?" Shelton was studying the side of the last document box. "You don't believe in coincidence, right?"

"No," I said. "Sharing a surname hardly proves—"

"Not that. Guess who was the last person to review this stuff before us?"

"Enough guessing games," Ben growled. "Make your point."

"Check the signature." Shelton passed me a smeary sign-out card. "None other than your boy, Rodney Brincefield."

"The old fogey again?" Hi arched one brow. "What gives?"

I shrugged. "He really likes Anne Bonny. No big deal."

But part of me wondered. Brincefield kept popping up like a whack-a-mole. He seemed harmless, but I'd learned the hard way not to underestimate people.

Was Brincefield involved in our attack?

Shelton interrupted my thoughts. "You guys were talking about Massachusetts a minute ago, right?"

Nods.

"I never mentioned it before," Shelton said, "but my pirate book includes a rumor that Bonny fled north."

"When?" Ben asked.

"After her trial in Jamaica. One theory holds that Bonny sailed to Massachusetts Bay Colony and settled in New England. Nothing more specific than that."

This time the chill ran both my arms and legs. Things were getting freakier and freakier. I felt like I was being punked.

Sudden pang. Mom would've *loved* the intrigue.

I shoved the painful thought aside.

"But that's wrong," Hi countered. "Bonny was transferred to Charles Town."

"Maybe she fled north after escaping Half-Moon Battery,"

Shelton suggested. "I'm just telling you what's in the book."

"Can we please get through this last set?" Ben said. "I'm losing steam here."

The remaining papers provided no spoilers. Most were contemporary descriptions of Bonny's sea conquests. A few were reports on her trial. Interesting, but not useful.

I scanned the last page with a sigh. "We done here?"

"Completely." Hi yawned. "I'm still gassed from last night."

I pressed the call button. When Short arrived I thanked him, and we headed for the door.

"I'll expect Bonny's letter in a timely fashion."

"Yes sir." I followed the others outside.

The sun was a brilliant white disc high in the sky. It was hard to believe that, just a few hours earlier, I'd swum from a submerged sea cave into Charleston Harbor.

Though dog-tired, we weren't done yet.

"So what'd we learn?" Ben asked.

"Not much," I admitted. "Short said the poem is written in Gaelic. We need a translation."

"We learned Tory descended from a filthy, murdering, hot-tempered lady-pirate."

"Shut it, Hiram."

We trooped down the front steps and started back toward the marina.

Stopped.

Marlo and Tree Trunk were leaning against a fence halfway up the block.

Marlo again wore a long white tee and black jeans. A white iPod was strapped to his belt, earphones snaking up to his head. Tree Trunk rocked another NBA jersey, this one a Charles Barkley Sixers throwback.

There was no way to avoid them without turning around.

"Ideas?" Hi asked sideways.

"Walk right by," I whispered. "They don't intimidate us."

"Speak for yourself," Shelton muttered.

As we drew close I smiled and flicked a wave. Marlo's face remained stone, but his eyes followed our progress. One hand rubbed the Zorro scar on his cheek. Tree Trunk ignored us completely.

Shelton's comment about coincidence replayed in my head.

A few steps more, and we rounded a corner.

"Gheeeyaaaah!" Hi scrunched his shoulders. "Those guys give me the creeps!"

"What's their deal?" Shelton glanced behind us, but the pair hadn't followed. "You think they're the ones that stalked us in the tunnels?"

"Look at my arms," Hi said. "Goose bumps everywhere."

"Forget them," Ben said. "Let's focus on the Gaelic poem."

"How do we get it translated?" Shelton asked.

"We're in luck," I said. "I know a languages ace. Time to bring in a heavy hitter."

"Who?" Hi sounded wary.

"My great-aunt Tempe."

CHAPTER 39

Marlo Bates watched the nerdy kids disappear around the corner.

He didn't move to follow. Didn't move at all.

Instead, he kicked back against the fence and bobbed to the Lil Wayne track blaring through his earphones.

Moments later, a giant hand tapped his shoulder.

His brother, Duncan, looked a question at him.

With a sigh, Marlo paused his iPod and removed the buds from his ears.

"What, yo?" Marlo had to crane his neck upward to see his brother's face.

Duncan said nothing. No surprise there. But Marlo understood.

"*I* don't know, man." Frustrated. "I ain't never been down here, neither."

Duncan frowned—which, for the big man, was practically a shout.

"What is this place, anyway?" Marlo turned to scrutinize the large stone building at their backs. "Some kinda white people church?"

Duncan folded his arms in a clear expression of impatience.

"You heard Pops." Marlo spat in disgust. "Ain't like this was *my* idea."

Marlo stroked the Z-shaped scar on his cheek, an unconscious tell that he was considering something.

Finally, he pushed off the fence.

"Let's see what's inside real quick." Marlo hitched his pants, then brushed pollen from his plain white tee. "I ain't spending my whole damn afternoon on this shit."

Wordlessly, Duncan followed Marlo up the steps.

"These youngins sure be pissing me off," Marlo grumbled. "I should be tending my *business*, not wasting time down here with the damn tourists."

Duncan didn't comment, a moving, breathing statue come to life.

At the entrance Marlo tugged a door open. Paused. Peered into the lobby.

"Pops better know what he's talking about."

Marlo hated big buildings like this. Imposing. Official looking. They reminded him of the schools he'd attended before finally dropping out. Of the failed expectations, the humiliation of needing help but being too proud to ask.

"Better be right," Marlo muttered before stepping inside, the giant shadow of his brother looming on his heels.

CHAPTER 40

B ack home, I made my second call of the day.

A familiar voice answered. "Temperance Brennan."

"Aunt Tempe? Hi, it's Tory." Then I quickly added, "Kit's daughter."

"That was my guess," Tempe quipped, "since I've only got one grandniece. How are you, sweetie?"

"I'm good. You?"

"Swamped. I've got three cases in the lab, and a fourth on its way. The price I pay for the glamorous life." Her voice grew softer. "I heard about LIRI. I'm so sorry, Tory. Tell Kit I'll be happy to help in any way I can."

"Thanks," I said, slightly embarrassed. "I'm sure he'll appreciate your offer."

Perhaps sensing my discomfort, Tempe changed the subject. "To what do I owe this pleasure? Not that I'm complaining, since we rarely get a chance to chat." Her voice became mock stern. "You must call more often."

"I will, promise. But I *do* have a specific question, if you've got a moment."

"Fire away. Your timing is perfect. I'm grabbing a late lunch."

"Are you sure? I know how busy you are."

I was finding it hard to get to the point. Aunt Tempe is my hero. She's the *last* person I want to view me as foolish.

"Never too busy for you," Tempe chided. "Let's hear it."

"You once told me your family came from Ireland."

"*Our* family," Tempe corrected. "Kinsale, in County Cork. My grandfather was born there."

"You wouldn't happen to speak Gaelic would you?"

"*Níl agam ach beagáinín Gaeilge,*" Tempe replied. "That means, 'I only speak a little Irish.' At least, I think that's what it means."

"So you know the language?"

"*Níl agam ach beagáinín Gaeilge,*" Tempe repeated with a laugh. "I've conquered French, can get by with Spanish, even a little German. But Gaelic is tough stuff."

"There aren't any Gaelic translator programs online," I said. "Only chat rooms."

"I'm not surprised. It's a beautiful language that was spoken for centuries, but Gaelic declined sharply under British rule. Then the Great Famine of 1845 devastated rural Ireland, where Gaelic was most prevalent. The language never really recovered."

"So no one speaks it anymore?"

"Less than fifteen percent of the Irish population, though the current government is working hard to preserve it. Gaelic speakers are fairly rare here in the States."

"Oh." My spirits sank.

"I can give it a shot." I heard static as Tempe adjusted the phone. "When I was a kid, a second cousin lived with my family briefly. She spoke Gaelic fluently, so I learned the language to keep her company."

"And you still remember it?"

"We'll see. Do you need something translated?"

"I've got a . . . poem."

"From a book?"

"No," I said. "Some pottery washed up on the beach near my house. A few lines are visible on the inside."

I hated lying to my idol, but what choice did I have?

"A mystery! Awesome! Email me the poem and I'll take a run at it."

"That'd be great! Thank you so much."

"Stop," Tempe chuckled. "After what I've been slogging through today, poetry will be a welcome change of pace."

There was an awkward pause while I debated with myself.

"Was there something else, Tory?"

Snap decision.

"Do you know anything about Anne Bonny, the female pirate?"

"I've heard of her, of course. But I'm a little light on specifics. Why?"

Throwing caution to the wind, I told Tempe my suspicions. Mary Brennan. The painting. Bonny's Massachusetts rumors. Our shared handwriting trait.

When I'd finished, the line was quiet for a very long time.

Great. She thinks I'm a moron.

"Wow. Who knows? It could be true."

I realized I'd been holding my breath. "It's wacky, granted. But I can't shake the feeling there's a connection."

"I understand," Tempe said. "I'm a Brennan too, remember? Though *I'm* definitely not related to Anne Bonny. My grandparents didn't leave the Emerald Isle until after World War I."

"It's crazy we share the Brennan name, even though I grew up in another family. But I'm glad we do."

"It shows we were meant to connect," Tempe said. "I just wish it had been under happier circumstances."

Tempe went silent, possibly regretting the reference to my mother's death.

"I'll send the poem to your Gmail," I said. "It was great chatting."

"Don't give up on the pirate connection. I expect a *full* report, matey."

"Aye aye, captain. And thanks again."

"*Slán agus beannacht leat.*"

"What does that mean?" I asked.

"'Good-bye and blessings upon you.'" Tempe chuckled. "I hope."

CHAPTER 41

I felt better after hanging up.

Talking with Aunt Tempe always recharged my batteries.

Watch check. Four p.m. Kit wasn't due home for a few more hours.

After emailing the poem, I texted the Virals. We assembled in my living room ten minutes later.

The boys were running on fumes.

Shelton and Hi slumped on the couch while Ben fiddled with the remote, trying to locate a baseball game. Coop lay curled in his doggie bed, paws outstretched, content to merely observe.

"I sent the Gaelic stuff to my aunt," I said. "She'll take a crack at translating and get back to me."

I didn't mention the Anne Bonny portion of our conversation. I'd been teased enough for one day.

"How long will it take?" Shelton asked.

"No idea."

"Seven to one?" Ben had finally found a game. "Man, the Cubs stink."

"Yep." Hi yawned. Then, "Oh! I almost forgot. My mother said something odd."

"I'm sorry, but it's true." Shelton placed a hand on Hi's shoulder. "You're *not* the most handsome boy in school. Oh, burnsauce!"

"Hilarious. No, she said a strange car drove by the complex this afternoon."

"You can't *drive by*," I said. "This is the end of the world."

"No argument here," Hi replied. "But according to mommy dearest, a vehicle cruised up the driveway, idled a few minutes, then left. She almost called the cops."

Ben fought a smirk. "Why?"

"You know Ruth," Hi answered with a sigh. "She probably thinks the car was full of Al Qaeda operatives sent to exterminate the neighborhood watch."

I didn't like it. "Can you guys recall a car ever showing up out here by mistake?"

No one could.

"You can't get *that* lost," said Shelton. "Our townhomes are fifteen minutes from the last state road."

"Most people don't know anything is back here at all," Ben agreed. "And a lost motorist would turn around long before crossing to Morris Island."

"A delivery guy?" Hi offered. "Or someone's guest? They could've called up, gotten no answer, then left."

"Maybe it was local kids thinking they could drive all the way to the Morris beach," Shelton offered.

"What type of car was it?" I asked.

"That's the craziest part." Hi sat forward, elbows on knees. "My mother is dead certain the car was a 1960 Studebaker Lark station wagon. Cherry red. She hadn't seen one in decades. My grandfather apparently drove the same model."

"That's not a delivery vehicle," Ben said.

I thought a moment. "What about the driver?"

"She didn't get a good look. But whoever it was wore a fedora."

"Stylin'," Shelton cracked.

I didn't like it. After dodging bullets in the tunnels last night, I felt as paranoid as Ruth. A strange car in the neighborhood was definitely cause for concern.

"Old-man car. Fedora." Shelton tapped the side of his nose. "Sounds like Tory's buddy Brincefield."

"The thought crossed my mind," I admitted. "But why would he come way out here?"

"Who knows?" Shelton said. "Why'd he show up for our ghost tour? Maybe he's senile. Or a pervert."

"That Marlo guy and his ogre buddy are just as creepy," Hi said. "And they were stalking us today."

"We don't know they were following us," Ben said. "Being downtown could've been a coincidence."

Coincidences seemed to be piling up.

"What about Lonnie Bates?" Shelton asked.

"The pawnshop guy?" Ben seemed to consider the idea. "He *was* pretty pissed that we outmaneuvered him."

Hi's palms rose in a "who knows?" gesture.

Ben clicked off the baseball game. "If it's sharing time, I've got news, too."

We all looked appropriately interested.

"I talked to my uncle Bill about the Sewee legend regarding Anne Bonny."

"Fantastic." I'd completely forgotten. "Anything useful?"

"Depends on your definition of 'useful.'" Ben shifted his feet, as if suddenly uncomfortable. "Uncle Bill couldn't recall the actual wording, but this was the general idea. It's a chant."

"A chant?" Hi asked innocently.

I narrowed my eyes in warning. No cheap shots.

With obvious reluctance, Ben recited, "When the night sky burned as daytime, a flaming brand mounted the field of bones, and staked the devil's hand."

"Umm." Hi.

"Okay." Shelton. Puzzled.

"I told you." Ben sounded defensive. "It's a Sewee story about Anne Bonny. And no, I don't have a clue what it means."

"I can't handle any more brainteasers," Hi grumbled. "I'm riddled out."

"Then don't," Ben snapped. "Forget I said anything."

"Thanks for running it down," I said diplomatically. "Maybe it will prove useful later, when we have more insight."

"I *have* a theory," Ben said. "If anyone's interested."

"Please." Carefully hiding my skepticism.

"I've heard the phrase 'when the night sky burned as daytime' in other Sewee stories. It refers to a full moon."

"And the rest?" Shelton asked.

"No idea. But I think the full moon bit is important somehow. Otherwise, why include it?"

"You're in luck." Hi was tapping his iPhone. "The next full moon is in . . . three days. Ask your spirit guide for more specific instructions by Tuesday."

"I'll give you—"

Shelton cut Ben off. "So what's our next move?"

"Maybe we should research Bonny's favorite symbol," I said. "We can't work the poem yet. Why not try our luck with the cross?"

"We could run an image comparison," Shelton suggested. "Online."

"Worth a shot."

I unfurled the treasure map on the coffee table, snapped a pic of the illustration, then downloaded the image to my laptop.

"Your move." I stepped aside so Shelton could man the keys.

"I know a website that lets you upload images and search for matches online." Shelton's fingers were already flying.

In moments, a grid of crosses filled the screen. Shelton clicked one that linked to an online encyclopedia.

"It's called a Celtic cross," Shelton said. "The central ring is the defining feature."

I nudged Shelton's shoulder. "My turn to drive."

"Every time." Shelton slid right so I could take his spot.

"According to this entry, the Celtic cross was introduced by Saint Patrick while converting the pagan Irish," I said. "It combines the traditional Christian cross with a circular emblem representing the sun. Some argue it originated from the ancient custom of wreathing a cross after a victorious battle."

I navigated back to the pictorial grid. "Some of these crosses are tall and skinny, like the one Bonny sketched."

I eyeballed the results, selected a design closely resembling Bonny's sketch.

"This is called a high cross." I clicked the brief description attached to the image. "A favorite of the Irish church, it was used in monuments as far back as the eighth century. Mostly headstones."

"Ugh." Hi was reading from his iPhone again. "The Celtic cross is now popular among white supremacy groups. The symbol has actually been banned in Germany."

"Great job, Germans," Shelton deadpanned. "Another ancient religious symbol ruined for all time. Shelve this one next to the swastika."

"The top tine of Bonny's cross always curves right," I reminded them. "That must mean something, don't you think?"

"It's certainly distinctive," Shelton said. "May I resume my work, madam?"

I yielded.

"I'll keep looking." Shelton was punching keys like mad. "But that might simply be Bonny's thing."

Fifteen minutes passed. Shelton ran through search screens faster than I could follow.

Then, "Oh no!" He slapped my laptop shut.

"What?" I asked. "Did you find something?"

"Nope!" Shelton's left hand rose to his earlobe. "Hey, did anyone get a Mets score? My dad's a big fan."

"The Mets?" That didn't make sense. "What's going on?"

Shelton refused to meet my eye. "Your computer crashed."

"No it didn't. You closed it."

"Spyware. Malware. I think you've got a virus."

"It's a Mac."

His voice dropped to a mumble. "The battery died."

"Shelton!" I'd had enough. "You're lying. And you're tugging your ear."

"No I'm not." The hand dropped.

That did it. "Stand aside, Devers."

"No!" Shelton covered the laptop with both arms. "You're gonna make a bad decision."

"What's wrong with you?" Ben barked. "Get out of the way!"

Shelton started to protest once more, then the fight drained out of him.

"Mistake," Shelton muttered to Ben as he trudged to my couch. "You should've trusted me."

I opened the screen and reloaded the last page.

And understood in seconds.

"Well?" Hi said. "Why did Shelton go nuts?"

"He located Bonny's bent cross," I said. "It's real."

"That's great!" Hi exclaimed.

"No it isn't," Shelton moaned.

"Explain," Ben said.

"A Celtic cross *identical* to one Anne Bonny liked to sketch was sold at auction fifteen years ago." I couldn't help but smile. "Right here in Charleston."

"Even better," Hi said. "I'm failing to see the downside."

"Wait for it." Shelton.

"Uh-oh." A frown creased Ben's brow. "Please tell me I can't guess the buyer's name."

"You most certainly can," Shelton said. "But now it's too late."

Hi's gaze bounced from Ben to Shelton to me. "Out with it."

I turned the screen to face him. "The winning bidder was Hollis Claybourne."

"Oh," Hi said. Then, "Crap."

"I told ya'll." Shelton shook his head. "You should've let me erase the whole flipping hard drive."

The boys glanced at me, knowing.

I didn't disappoint.

"It's time for a visit with Chance."

CHAPTER 42

Kit's text message sealed the deal.

Behind schedule. Home late. Feed self.

"We're going today," I said firmly. "No arguments."

The other Virals groaned, but fell in line without much fight. Perhaps they were too tired to protest.

"Told you," Shelton muttered. "Once she found out Hollis bought the cross, our tickets were booked."

Hi hauled himself from the couch and stretched. "Are we stealing Kit's 4Runner again?"

"We're borrowing it," I amended. "We'll be back before seven if we hurry."

I knew where to find Chance. Everyone did. His current address was an open secret.

It's not every day that Bolton Prep's most illustrious student is committed to a mental institution.

Psychiatric care facility, I should say. Chance had been a

patient at Marsh Point Hospital since the shootout at Claybourne Manor three months earlier.

"Will he agree to see us?" Ben asked.

"Leave that to me."

○   ○   ○

Nestled within a tangle of creeks, ponds, and meandering swampland, Wadmalaw Island is one of Charleston's most bucolic districts. Quiet, pristine, and intensely rural, its acreage is some of the least developed in the Lowcountry.

Winding country roads criss-cross the landscape, which is lined with family farms and roadside produce stands. The local population is sparse: most residents are farmers, fishermen, and employees of America's only active tea plantation.

With only a single bridge connecting Wadmalaw to the outside world, conditions were perfect for the island's most discrete tenant.

We drove north to the Maybank Highway, then headed southeast across Johns Island. Minutes later we crossed to Wadmalaw and followed signs toward Rockville. Several miles before the small village, Ben turned right onto a narrow private drive.

"Guardhouse," he warned. "Dead ahead."

Three officers sat inside a roadside booth, each wearing a firearm, their attention focused on a small TV. We stopped at the gate and waited.

Finally, a guard peeled his eyes from the screen, emerged, and walked to the driver's-side window. Bald, paunchy, and well past forty, the guy's name tag announced him as Officer Mike Brodhag.

"Name?" Bored, and slightly annoyed.

"Tory Brennan," I answered from the passenger seat.

"ID?"

I handed over my Bolton Prep library card.

Brodhag's gaze shifted to Hi and Shelton in the backseat before returning to me. Everyone was wearing a Bolton Prep uniform.

"State your business."

"We represent the Bolton Academy student council," I said cheerily. "We're here to present Chance Claybourne with this year's Human Spirit Award."

Brodhag appeared unimpressed. "Do you have an appointment with someone on the medical staff?"

"I spoke to a—" quick glance at my notes, "—Dr. Javier Guzman. He's expecting us."

Brodhag retreated to the guardhouse and picked up a telephone.

"Human Spirit Award?" Hi whispered. "That's the dumbest thing I've ever heard. And why would we give it to a lunatic?"

"Shhh." My eyes stayed on Brodhag. "I thought something official-sounding would be more likely to get us inside."

Brodhag cradled the receiver and returned with a yellow guest pass.

"Proceed directly to the building and park in a visitor's spot." Monotone. "Do not stop along the way. Display this tag in your vehicle at all times."

We rolled forward through dense swampland. Massive ferns and droopy willow trees crowded the driveway, creating a natural tunnel. The air was thick with the smell of stagnant water and the buzz of flying insects.

Twenty yards down the blacktop the shoulders dropped away and the road became a bridge across a shallow tidal lake. Reeds and bulrushes rose from the water. Tricolored herons searched for food on long, spindly legs.

"Prime gator country," Ben said. "Look at those sandbars."

Dry land reappeared a few hundred yards ahead. Stretched across it, on the crest of a small rise, was a massive building that looked like a medieval nightmare.

"The grounds are an island within an island," Shelton said. "Creepy."

"You couldn't design better security," said Hi. "This road must be the only way in or out."

Another quarter mile brought us to the hospital itself. Three stories tall and built completely of stone, the brooding monstrosity was a moat and drawbridge short of being a full-blown castle.

Ben parked in a gravel lot beside the main entrance. A smiling dark-haired man stood before the front doors. I guessed his age at maybe thirty-five.

"Let me do the talking," I whispered.

"No problem," Hi said. "I couldn't sell this Human Spirit garbage if I tried."

Dr. Javier Guzman was a compact man with bronze skin and a neatly trimmed black goatee. Old-fashioned spectacles sat high on a thin nose. Behind them was a pair of intelligent brown eyes.

"Miss Brennan?" Spoken with a slight Spanish accent.

"A pleasure to meet you, Dr. Guzman."

Guzman's smile revealed dazzling white teeth. "The pleasure is mine. Welcome to Marsh Point Psychiatric Hospital. I can't tell you how much I appreciate this."

"You're welcome." I had no idea what he was talking about, but didn't let that stop me. "The council is excited to bestow its award upon such a worthy recipient."

Guzman nodded seriously. "For a while I worried that Bolton Prep would sweep Mr. Claybourne under the carpet, so to speak. I'm pleased to learn I was wrong."

Totally lost. But I bounced Guzman's smile right back at him.

"We are thinking of allowing him regular visitors soon," Guzman said. "I think a school delegation such as yours is an excellent starting point. Please come inside."

"Chance hasn't had any visitors?" I asked as we passed through the main lobby.

"None. His father is in prison, and, frankly, a major cause of Mr. Claybourne's psychological rift to begin with. He has no other family to speak of."

Despite all he'd done, I could empathize with Chance. I know what it's like to feel completely alone.

"There's a long road ahead," Guzman continued. "Of course, professional ethics prohibit me from discussing the particulars of Mr. Claybourne's condition, but I've grown convinced that he's neither suicidal nor a danger to others. His main issues appear to be ones of trust."

"That's good to hear," I said.

"Mr. Claybourne has been largely isolated since his breakdown." Guzman led us up a flight of marble steps. "The catatonia subsided some time ago, but he only recently resumed speaking. I'm hoping some friendly faces will spur him to seek more human interaction."

Friendly faces? I had no clue how Chance would react to our visit. He'd been humiliated and locked away as a direct result of my actions. He might flip the frick out.

My pulse quickened. Too late for second thoughts now.

We entered a bright, airy room with pastel walls. Art supplies filled one corner. Easels. Paints. Stacks of blank canvas. Circular tables sat in casual disarray beneath a row of large bay windows. The space had a happy, optimistic feel.

"This is our artist's retreat," Guzman said. "Mr. Claybourne spends a great deal of his time here, so I thought it would be a comfortable meeting place."

"Sounds perfect."

I began to sweat. Awesome.

"I can only allow two of you to meet with the patient." Guzman wore a pained expression. "I'm terribly sorry, but he's not ready for a larger group at this time. There's a bench in the hallway where the others can wait."

"We understand completely." Shelton.

"I wouldn't dream of endangering a patient's recovery." Hi.

The two beelined back out of the room.

I glanced at Ben, who nodded.

"Ben and I will handle the presentation."

"Wonderful." Guzman gestured to one of the tables. "Please have a seat. Mr. Claybourne will arrive in a moment."

"You're not staying?"

Though it caught me off guard, this was a lucky break. I hadn't worked out how to question Chance in front of his doctor.

"I think it best if you talk unaccompanied by medical staff." Guzman's face went serious. "Mr. Claybourne is highly suspicious. I'm hoping time alone with friends will be beneficial."

Friends. That word again. I swallowed hard.

"I hope so, too."

"I'll return in five minutes." Guzman's heels clicked sharply as he strode from the room and down the main hallway.

Seconds later, Chance ambled in through a rear door. He was wearing navy sweatpants and a gray Bolton lacrosse tee. Dark crescents hung below his piercing, deep brown eyes. A scraggily beard clung to his chin.

No matter. Even in nuthouse garb, the guy was freaking gorgeous.

Chance was grinning as if remembering a joke and trying not to laugh. He made it two steps before seeing me.

He froze. His eyes locked on mine. Then his head moved slowly from side to side.

Chance's gaze flicked to Ben. Returned. Crossing to the table, he sat, leaned back in his chair, and regarded me.

An awkward silence ensued.

Eventually, I had to break it.

"On behalf of the students of Bolton Academy," I began, "we are honored to present you with this year's—"

"Stop." Never taking his eyes from me, Chance pointed at Ben. "Leave."

Ben snorted. "Piss off, Claybourne."

Chance's jaw tightened. "Leave. Now."

"Go, Ben," I whispered. "We don't have much time."

Ben hesitated, then stood and strode from the room. Chance never glanced in his direction.

I started again. "On behalf of the students—"

"Give it a rest," Chance said. "The Human Spirit Award? I only agreed to this farce because I wanted to see who was yanking Guzman's chain. I'll admit, you surprised me."

"I needed to talk. It worked."

"Like my new home?" Chance waved an arm. "I always wanted to live in a castle. Does it count if I'm a prisoner?"

"You're not a prisoner," I said. "You're a patient."

"I can't leave, so what's the difference?" He winked. "But at least I dodged jail."

"Don't worry, charges will be waiting when you're deemed mentally fit."

"You think so? I doubt the DA will bother pursuing a few petty misdemeanors. They already got the big fish." Chance smirked. "Otherwise, I could be looking at six whole months of probation. Not sure I could bear it."

"So this is all a big act? You've got them all fooled?"

"Of course." The dark eyes narrowed. "I'm not crazy. I was stressed for a bit, I admit, but I'm much better now. Sound as a pound."

Despite the bravado, Chance seemed edgy. His hands darted from place to place. One foot tapped incessantly, as if on its own accord.

"Take advantage of the rest," I said diplomatically. "I remember that night. After what Hannah—"

Chance slammed the table with both fists.

"*Do NOT mention that name!*"

I jumped back, astonished by the outburst. Ben charged back into the room.

"It's okay!" I waved Ben away. "Watch the hall."

Ben looked hard at Chance, withdrew.

"Why are you here, anyway?" Chance was examining his nails. I noticed the cuticles were red and raw.

"Fifteen years ago, Hollis Claybourne bought an artifact at auction." I chose my words carefully. "I thought you might know something about it."

"My father buys lots of artifacts. I can't possibly recall every one."

"He purchased a rare Celtic cross. It's distinctive. The top portion curves to the right."

Chance paused, as if weighing possible answers. "Why do you want it?"

"So you do remember the cross?" I pressed.

Chance folded his arms. "Why should I help you? I'm *in here* because of you."

"That's not true, Chance." I spoke quietly, but firmly. "Think what you like of me personally, but you know I'm not responsible for . . . this."

Chance opened his mouth, seemed to change his mind.

"This cross," he said. "You need it for some reason?"

"Yes." No point being coy.

"I remember it. Even better, I know where it is."

"Will you tell me?"

"So you can steal it?" He chuckled. "No Tory, I've seen firsthand your lack of respect for Claybourne family property."

Chance leaned forward. "But I'll do you one better. I'll *take* you to it."

"Take me?" I didn't like where this was going. "How can you do that?"

"Because I'm leaving." A wicked gleam danced in his eyes. "You and your pals are going to help me escape."

CHAPTER 43

Debate raged on our drive home.

"No way." Ben passed the guardhouse and turned onto the highway. "Chance is a total ass-clown. Why should we help him?"

"Because he can deliver Bonny's cross," I said. "He can actually take us to it."

"Chance isn't a map you can stuff down your pants," Shelton argued from the backseat. "How would we spring him? That place is a fortress."

"In the middle of a lake," Ben added.

Hi poked his head between the front seats. "The staff will notice the minute he's gone. Then Guzman will put two and two together and call Bolton. And the police."

"We aren't student council," Ben said. "And you used your real name."

No reminder necessary. If we helped Chance, I was almost certain to get caught. It was a desperation move.

"Why can't Chance just run away?" Shelton asked.

"The only road out leads past that guardhouse," I said. "Not that it matters, because he doesn't have a car."

"He'd be legitimately crazy to try the marshes on foot." Hi shuddered. "They must be crawling with alligators. Might as well wrap yourself in bacon."

"A fortress," Shelton repeated. "We can't get a car past the guardhouse, either."

"Plus, how can we trust him?" Ben aimed the question at me. "He's a whacko."

"We *did* just leave an insane asylum," Hi agreed. "For all we know, Chance spends his nights dancing naked with sock puppets, plotting to invade Canada."

"I don't think so." I raised a hand to forestall Hi's reply. "Chance is emotional, and *definitely* has issues, but he isn't nuts. Just . . . upset. And maybe a little scared. You heard Guzman say he's not a danger to anyone."

"Then Chance is playing us." Shelton changed tack. "He's probably never even seen Bonny's cross. Did you ask him to describe it?"

"There was no time." *Shoot.*

"Guzman said we're his first visitors." Shelton wouldn't let it go. "Chance would've said anything to get our help."

We rode several miles in silence, reached James Island, and turned south onto Folly Road. Twenty-five minutes from home.

I made my choice. "Until we translate Bonny's poem, the cross is our only lead. Chance holds all the cards. I'm willing to risk it."

At first, no one responded.

"Suppose we decided to help Chance," Ben said slowly. "How would we do it?"

It was the opening I needed.

"We do it our way," I said. "No guardhouse, no bulky SUV."

"Crap!" Hi was peering out the back window. "Crap crap crap!"

"What?" Hi's melon head blocked my sight line. "Was there a wreck?"

"Red Studebaker! Three cars back."

"Are you sure?" Ben punched the accelerator. "Is it following?"

As I turned, a red wagon darted into the left lane, passed two vehicles, and swerved back to avoid an oncoming truck. Horns blared in protest.

"It's keeping pace!" Shelton was staring out the back window. "Not good!"

"How long has it been there?" Ben's eyes shifted between his mirrors and the road. "Since the hospital?"

"No idea," Hi said. "I just noticed."

We crossed the Intracoastal Waterway and entered Folly Beach, then turned left on Ashley. Ben slowed as we passed through the busy residential area.

"The wagon's following!" Shelton exclaimed.

Traffic thinned as we neared the northern edge of town. Ahead lay nothing but a long strip of beach houses and the crossing to Morris Island.

"Still there." Hi's voice was up an octave. "The windows are tinted. I can't see inside."

"There's *zero* chance that car just happened to be headed this way," Shelton said. "None."

Water now bordered both sides of the narrow street. There were fewer than a dozen beach homes ahead, and beyond them only the unmarked pavement to our little enclave.

"Summer Place Lane is the last turnoff," Ben said, as we drove past it.

I held my breath.

The Studebaker stuck to our tail.

Everyone groaned.

Ben pulled into the cul-de-sac at the end of the state road. The unlined blacktop leading to Morris Island began just ahead. A yellow sign warned: *Private Property—No Outlet.*

If the Studebaker followed, it could have only one destination.

Ben pulled onto Morris Island's private drive, rolled a dozen yards, and stopped. "I want the driver to know we see him."

Four sets of eyes watched the Studebaker roll into the cul-de-sac. Stop. Idle. Rev its engine.

Seconds ticked by. We hardly dared breathe.

Then the Studebaker circled back the way it came.

Sighs of relief filled the 4Runner.

"Did anyone get a look at the driver?" I asked.

Head shakes. The windows were too dark.

We drove the last mile in hushed uneasiness. Had the wagon been stalking us? My brain was too exhausted to focus.

At dawn, I'd dragged myself out of Charleston Harbor. Then I'd visited the bunker, haggled with Dr. Short, talked to Aunt

Tempe, and faced Chance in a mental hospital. All on less than two hours' sleep.

"Guys," I yawned. "It's time to call it a day."

○   ○   ○

Coop greeted me at the door.

My luck was holding—Kit wasn't home. Thank the Lord for small favors.

Collapsing into bed, I nearly whimpered with pleasure. I planned to sleep forever.

Then my cell exploded. I ignored the first three rings, pretended it wasn't happening.

"Blaaaaargh!"

Reaching blindly, I scooped up the phone. Too late. The call rolled to voice mail. Shortly after, the message icon appeared: Aunt Tempe.

"Sorry I missed you, Tory. *Ta suil agam go bhfuil tu i mbarr na slainte.* That means, 'I hope you're in the best of health!' I've actually been enjoying my assignment. After a rough start, vocabulary started coming back. I'm emailing you my translation now. Let me know if you need anything else, and please call more often. *Oíche mhaith.* Good night!"

As the message ended, an email appeared in my inbox.

I fully intended to open it.

My eyes just needed a short rest.

CHAPTER 44

The knocking finally roused me.

"I'll be at work all day," Kit called through the door. "I know you're angry at being grounded, but get moving. Too much sleep is as bad as too little."

"Wha?" Best I could manage.

Kit's footsteps retreated. I glanced at the clock. Sunday. Ten forty-five.

"Frick!"

I'd overslept. For my idea to work, we had to go today.

I rushed to my computer, tracked down the Virals, and handed out assignments. The boys grumbled but agreed. As I knew they would. We had no other choice.

Logging off, I couldn't shake the feeling I'd forgotten something.

I reviewed the plan in my head. There were holes, sure, and a few shaky assumptions, but the concept felt sound. Yet the nagging wouldn't let up.

What?

Coop pushed into my room, tail wagging like a windshield wiper.

"Come on, boy."

I trudged downstairs to see if Kit had left any coffee.

It was going to be another killer day.

○   ○   ○

"Eyes peeled," Ben warned. "We don't want to run aground."

Mid-afternoon. We were aboard *Sewee*, carefully picking our way through the snarl of overgrown swampland surrounding Wadmalaw Island.

It had taken hours, but Shelton finally scored the intel we needed.

Then a sprint to the boat.

Sailing south past Folly and Kiawah, Ben steered into the mouth of the Edisto River, heading inland to the warren of marshes and tidal pools surrounding Wadmalaw Sound.

The channel narrowed as *Sewee* nosed through tall reeds and thick stands of cordgrass. Blackbirds circled, feasting on insects made drowsy by the afternoon heat. Egrets perched on dry mud banks, alert for movement in the still, brackish water.

My plan was simple.

Escape by car was impossible. Marsh Point had a single access road straddled by a well-manned guardhouse. No driving around it.

Flight on foot was equally unrealistic. The hospital grounds occupied a tiny islet surrounded by muck and open water. The only walking path paralleled the road, and was completely exposed.

That left a waterborne getaway.

By worming through swampland to the lake surrounding the hospital, we could bypass the guardhouse and access the grounds from their unprotected rear.

Ben's face was tense as he maneuvered the tricky passages. For good reason. If we bottomed out in the shallow swamp, *Sewee* could be mired for hours.

Ben's gaze flicked left. His body stiffened.

"Nobody freak," he said quietly, "but there's a monster gator ten yards to port."

Heads whipped sideways.

An eight-foot alligator was lounging on a sandbar, its gray-green scales caked with dried mud. Reptilian eyes opened, regarded us dispassionately, then slowly slid shut again.

"That's right," Shelton said in a shaky voice. "Nappy time. We're not worth your trouble."

Ben motored down a channel, hit a dead end, reversed, chose a new route. Sweat dripped from his temples as he struggled to navigate the stifling green maze.

Hi slapped his neck. "These mosquitoes are eating me alive."

"Me too." Shelton tossed Hi the bug spray. "We must be delicious."

"Buckeye!" Ben eased *Sewee* between a pair of grassy humps.

"Lunatic Island, twelve o'clock."

Fifty yards of open water separated us from Marsh Point Hospital and solid ground.

"There." Ben pointed to a knot of weeping willows growing hard against the water. "Those trees should screen us from view."

"Everyone knows his job?" I spoke to cover my pregame jitters. "Let's review one more time."

"I dump you guys on shore," Ben said, "then pull back and hide *Sewee* in the rushes. Wait for the signal."

Shelton spoke next. "We sneak to a door at the left rear corner of the building. I unlock it and stand guard."

Shelton had found and downloaded the hospital blueprints earlier that afternoon. After studying the layout, we had a pretty good feel for our target.

"The door shouldn't be alarmed," I reminded.

We were counting on that.

The Marsh Point Hospital website emphasized the open, unrestrained character of their treatment facility. Residents were never locked in their rooms, and were generally free to roam the grounds at their leisure.

Small wonder. Given the Alcatraz setup, there was nowhere for a patient to go.

If only I could get a message to Chance. He could walk out to meet us.

Impossible. Patients weren't allowed unsupervised phone calls. Chance had no idea we were coming.

But we couldn't wait. Sunday meant less staff, less opportunity to get caught. I'd just have to find him myself.

Hi picked up his part of the sequence. "Once inside, Tory and I climb to the fourth floor, where I keep watch in the stairwell."

My turn. "I search the guest rooms, find Chance, and we rejoin Hiram."

"Back down the stairs," Hi continued. "Link up with Shelton."

"I text Ben," Shelton said. "Then we haul ass back to the drop zone."

"Where I'll be waiting," Ben finished. "We disappear into the swamp. Done."

Our strategy was solid. But so much could go wrong.

What if someone noticed *Sewee*? How many guards were in the building? How would I locate Chance's room?

I shoved my doubts aside. No plan could account for the unknown. We'd adjust on the fly.

Deep breath. Go time. "Take us in."

"Roger that." Ben gunned the engine and we fired across the lake.

Reaching the cover of the willow trees, Shelton, Hi, and I jumped from the bow and waded ashore. Ben reversed *Sewee* and retreated into the marsh.

"Now?" Hi asked.

"Yes." Steeling myself. "Do it."

SNAP.

The power tore through me. Lightning. Fire. I closed my eyes and waited for the tremors to subside.

My senses came alive. The world shifted into laser clarity.

"Ready?" I panted.

The boys nodded, golden eyes hidden behind dark lenses. Positioning my own sunglasses, I headed up the hill.

The low-hanging sun at our backs helped obscure our approach. We scurried into the yard and ducked behind a hedgerow. Lucky break. The suffocating heat had kept everyone inside.

I assessed our target in silence. The castle-like structure was equally menacing from this angle, but the entry was there as expected.

"Here goes." Shelton streaked to the door, pulled, and nearly fell flat as it swung open, unlocked. He held it ajar for Hi and me.

"Good luck." Shelton melted into the nearby bushes.

Inside was a wide stairwell. I paused to get my bearings.

Muffled voices came through a door to our right.

Lobby, Hi mouthed.

Keys jingled. A shoe squeaked. Someone laughed gruffly.

Hi and I fired up the steps.

Fourth floor. Double doors separated the stairwell from a long corridor beyond. I strained my ears.

Nothing. Even flaring, the only sound I detected was a ticking clock.

Where is everyone?

"Wait here," I whispered.

I slipped into a white-tiled hallway lined with steel doors. A metal clipboard hung beside each one. At the far end sat an empty chair.

I dashed from clipboard to clipboard, checking names, certain I'd be caught, one eye watching the elevator beyond the nurse's station.

Chance Claybourne's was the fifth room down.

I didn't hesitate.

Heart in my throat, I stepped inside.

The space was cozy, with a single bed and a small wooden desk. Soft blue walls, bare. The sole window overlooked a Japanese rock garden.

Chance was propped in bed, reading a book. Even wearing raggedy gym clothes, he looked like a fashion model. How could I still find him so attractive?

Remember what he did. What he tried to cover up.

Chance's yelp brought me back to earth.

"Tory?" Eyes popping. "What in God's name are you doing here?"

"You said you needed rescuing. I haven't slain any dragons yet, but the day is young."

"Now?" Chance was too shocked to play it cool. "You have a way out? Why are you wearing sunglasses?"

"No questions. Unless you have other plans?"

"None whatsoever." He began stuffing items into a duffel bag. "I take it you have a way off the grounds?"

"Naturally."

"How'd you get up here without being noticed?" Chance glanced at his desk clock. "Nap time! Of course. That was clever. At this hour, the orderlies all play cards in the lobby."

"That was the idea." Talk about dumb luck.

Chance frowned. "But we'll never get past them to the parking lot."

"We don't need to. Will you please kick it up a notch?"

I cracked the door and peered down the hall. Empty.

"Come on."

Chance was hot on my heels as I raced toward the stairwell.

Suddenly, an elevator opened.

A doughy derriere backed into the hallway, followed by a rattling medicine cart.

I yanked open the closest door and shouldered Chance inside. The latch clicked just as the orderly turned around.

"We should've run for it!" Chance hissed. "That's the med cart. We'll be stuck in here for at least ten minutes. By then the halls will be crawling with people."

"Let me think."

I looked around. We stood inside a linen closet. Shelves filled with blankets and towels lined one wall. A chest-high metal rectangle was cut into the other, with a handle attached dead center. Next to the handle was a shiny black button.

"What is that?" Chance whispered.

"No clue."

I pressed the button. Something thunked inside the wall.

"Are you crazy? We don't know what that does!"

With a loud whir, the metal rectangle began to vibrate.

In for a penny . . .

I flipped the handle. A steel sheet slid upward, revealing a compartment the size of an oversized pizza oven.

"It's a dumbwaiter!" I whisper-shrieked, probably too loud.

Instant change of plan. I yanked out my cell and texted Shelton and Hi.

"Get in," I said.

"You're nuts."

"It's the only way out undetected. They must use this to send dirty linens down to the laundry."

Chance didn't move. "It's a metal coffin."

"We'll be fine." I couldn't let him see my own nerves. "Once we shut the door, this thing will head straight to the ground floor."

He still didn't budge.

"Look." I crawled inside the narrow compartment. "Ladies first."

Chance shook his head. "If we get stuck, you're my next meal." Wedging himself beside me, he tugged the door shut.

Nothing happened.

My mind fired terrifying images. Me, trapped inside this box. Struggling to move, to breathe. My heart rate went gangbusters. Sweat slicked my palms.

Then the engine cut on and we began to descend.

Chance lay beside me, panting, clearly unsettled by the confining space. My back rested against his chest. His knees pressed the back of my thighs.

I was very, very aware of how close we were.

SNUP.

My flare died, leaving me momentarily drained. A tremor traveled my body. I slipped off my shades and rubbed my eyes. Slowly, the disorientation passed.

The dumbwaiter stopped with a jerk. I thought of how it would appear if someone found us.

Please, I prayed. *No audience.*

The door rose.

Chance practically leaped to the floor. I scrambled out behind him, trying to look everywhere at once.

We'd landed in the corner of a large laundry facility. Granite counters lined the walls, interspersed with sinks and industrial-sized washers and dryers. Thankfully, the room was empty.

"We're in the basement," Chance whispered, eyes darting. "What next?"

"We need a way out the *back* of the building."

"There's a rear staircase used for deliveries."

"How do you know that?"

"I pay attention. I've been contemplating escape since the moment I arrived."

Chance was right. A narrow flight rose from the laundry room to a small patch of pavement behind the hospital.

"Can we get to the water without being seen?" I asked.

"Follow me."

Chance led me along the rear of the building, past the doorway through which I'd entered. I desperately hoped my texts had been received.

Chance darted into a maze of hedges. I was right behind.

"What's this?" I hissed.

"The meditation garden. It provides cover to the dogwood grove, which stretches out of sight from the hospital."

"You really *have* thought about this."

He smiled for the first time. "You've no idea."

In minutes we reached the weeping willows. Ben had *Sewee* idling. Hi and Shelton were already aboard. I can't say who among us was most relieved.

"Come on, come on, come on!" Hi squeaked. "Let's bail."

"You did it." Ben sounded mildly surprised. "Did anyone see you?"

"Don't think so," I said as we clambered into the boat. "But let's not tempt fate. Hit the gas!"

⬡　　⬡　　⬡

Chance chuckled. "You four are not to be underestimated."

"Remember that," I said. "We have a deal."

We were ten minutes beyond the swamp. *Sewee* was rounding Seabrook Island, skirting the coast in a northeasterly direction. Homeward bound.

"The Celtic cross." I had no intention of wasting time. "Where is it?"

Chance considered before he spoke. "The cross has been at my father's fishing camp since its purchase. Hollis and his buddies would go there to drink and avoid their wives." The ghost of a smile teased Chance's mouth. "Father often joked that the cabin needed a little holiness to offset the debauchery."

Adrenaline rushed through me. I could feel Bonny's cross in my hands.

"Where is this camp?" Ben asked.

"*Tut tut.*" Chance leaned back and stretched. "I'm not revealing all my secrets at once."

"What the hell?" I jabbed a finger at his face. "You promised."

"And I'll deliver." Gently brushing aside my hand. "First I need a place to crash until I figure out my next move. Food. A shower."

Chance sent a meaningful look my way.

"You can't stay with me." What was he thinking?

"I'm short on options at the moment." His tone hardened. "You need the cross. I need temporary lodgings. That makes us partners a bit longer."

He had me. But how could I hide him from Kit?

"Tomorrow night," Chance promised. "You have my word. Until then, you're blessed with the pleasure of my company."

I could think of nothing to say.

Chance smiled beatifically. "So. What's for dinner?"

CHAPTER 45

We beat Kit home by five minutes.

Hi and Shelton took off the moment *Sewee* nosed up to the dock, claiming dinner responsibilities. They'd had their fill for one day.

Glaring at Chance, Ben asked if I needed anything. I assured him things were under control. A tremendous but necessary lie.

"Please show me to my quarters," Chance said flippantly.

"Cause any problems," I warned, "and you sleep on that boat."

Once inside the townhouse, Coop circled our guest, snuffling, opinion uncertain. I was settling Chance in my bedroom when the front door opened.

"Stay here and be quiet," I ordered. "If you hear someone coming, hide."

"I'm hungry. Tell Daddy a friend came for dinner."

"Don't be an idiot."

I ran a brush through my hair and hand-smoothed my

clothes, trying to calm my tattered nerves. Could I really pull this off?

"Kit would recognize you," I said. "The night you met wasn't exactly forgettable. Besides, you're basically a fugitive."

"I've grown a beard." Chance stroked his chin. "And I can do a mean British accent. *'Ello Govna! May I 'ave some more gruel?*"

He clearly wasn't taking the situation seriously.

"I'm also grounded and not allowed visitors," I said. "It won't work."

"What am I supposed to eat?"

"Dinner usually takes ten minutes. I'll bring you something."

"Won't he check on you later?"

"He thinks I'm still angry. He won't be suspicious if I lock myself in here."

"Tory!" Kit called. "Whitney's here. Please come down for dinner."

"Frick!" Of all the timing. "You've got to be kidding me!"

"Whitney Dubois?" Chance grinned. "That pretentious nitwit from the cotillion committee?"

I nodded miserably. "Why do you think I'm making my debut?"

"The question had occurred to me."

Kit could be such a jerk sometimes. He'd given me no warning. My *one* rule.

"Sit tight." I motioned for Coop to stay. "Any noise and my wolfdog will maul you."

I slipped out, leaving Chance nervously eyeing my pet.

Kit was setting the table as Whitney moved about the kitchen. Two bags from Palmetto Pig rested on the counter.

"Whitney. What a surprise." I scowled at Kit. "I had *no idea* you were stopping by."

Kit remained focused on flatware.

Whitney looked pleased. "When your father answered his work phone, I just *knew* that no proper dinner had been planned. I took it as a call to action."

Kit smiled at me weakly. "Isn't that nice, Tor?"

"Mmm-hmm."

Whitney set out plastic containers of pulled pork barbeque and baked beans. "And we have so much to discuss."

"Discuss?" That sounded bad.

"Tory, you're in charge of drinks," Kit said. "We'll talk after we eat."

Warning bells dinged.

Kit fidgeted throughout the meal, laughed too hard at my lame jokes. Whitney's good mood was unshakable—my snidest comments sailed over the top of her carefully coiffed head.

The dinging escalated to clanging. This was starting to feel like a setup.

Whitney was spooning banana pudding into bowls when Kit cleared his throat.

"I've made a few decisions. About our future."

"Have you." I put down my fork.

Kit's foot began tapping. Whitney placed a reassuring hand on his shoulder.

Great. Whatever was coming, I wasn't going to like it.

"I've been offered a job." He swallowed. "I'm going to accept."

"What!?" I studied his face. "Just like that?"

"Your daddy thought long and hard," Whitney began. "It wasn't easy to—"

"Excuse me." My words were ice. "I'm having a private discussion with my father."

Whitney inhaled sharply.

Kit placed his hand on hers.

"I understand you're upset," Kit said. "But sometimes a parent has to make unpopular decisions. This is the best opportunity I've come across. It's a down economy. Frankly, I'm lucky to have an offer at all."

My hands reached for each other in my lap. Clamped so tightly I could feel the bones in my fingers. "What is this wonderful opportunity?"

"Seven Mile Island Wildlife Park has an opening for an environmental specialist." Kit spoke softly. "Professionally, I'm a perfect fit. The pay is excellent. I know you'd prefer to remain in Charleston, but I can't pass on this one."

"Where is Seven Mile Island?" Barely audible.

"Alabama," Kit said. "Near a town called Muscle Shoals."

"Roll Tide!" Whitney piped.

Kit cringed, fearful of another outburst from me. His instincts were good.

"Alabama? We're moving next door to Forrest Gump?"

"My back is against the wall, Tory. This job is a way out."

"You'll adore Alabama," Whitney said. "You just have to give it a chance."

"What do you care?" I turned on her, furious. "Anxious for some personal space?"

Kit shifted. Cleared his throat. "Whitney's decided to come with us."

The shock rocked me to my core. My eyes began to burn.

Don't cry. Don't you dare cry.

"Coming with?" Oh, so very calm. "For a visit? To help us move?"

"Your father is my world," Whitney gushed. "I can't bear to lose him."

"Whitney is moving, too." Kit watched me intently. "We hope she can live with us, but only with your permission of course. If that makes you uncomfortable, she'll find an apartment close by."

A headache formed. Pounded my frontal lobe. I felt dizzy, like the room was spinning.

Alabama? Whitney? Kit had pummeled me with a deadly one-two.

"Don't worry, darling." Whitney, Queen of Saying the Wrong Thing. "You still have time to finish your debut. With a little luck, we can advance you to *this* season's cohort."

"This season?" I could barely form words.

"I'll handle everything," she chirped. "I'll speak to the women's committee after tomorrow's gala. Remember, you have a brunch in the morning."

"Tomorrow," I stammered, my mind numb. The idea of living with Whitney was beyond horrifying. "Brunch. Yes."

"Good." Kit tried for levity. "You can remind your friends that you're still grounded."

"I don't have friends at cotillion."

"Tell that to whoever keeps ringing the house phone."

His comment puzzled me. "No one calls me on the landline."

"There are three new entries on the caller ID. Someone named Marlo Bates. I never said you couldn't use the phone, but remember, you're *supposed* to be under house arrest."

The name jolted me fully alert. Marlo had gotten our phone number. How? Why? Yesterday's encounter at the manuscript library had clearly been no fluke.

Those guys were tracking me.

"I'll tell him," I said, hiding my alarm.

"Don't worry, sugar." Whitney's face was scrunched in earnestness. "This move will be good for all of us. You'll see that one day."

You are not my mother!

I pushed back from the table.

"May I be excused?" Glacial.

Screw permission. I bolted up the stairs.

CHAPTER 46

"The nerve of that bitch!"

My hand still gripped the doorknob. "What's *best* for me? Piss off!"

"She walked all over you," Chance said matter-of-factly. "Stop being such a pushover."

"Be quiet." I snapped the lock on my bedroom door. "What would you know?"

"I was bored. I eavesdropped. Dinner sounded delightful." Checking my hands. "No plate for me, it seems."

Chance was stretched out on my bed, idly thumbing through an old *US Weekly*. Coop was snoring at his feet.

Turncoat.

"There's a box of granola bars on my dresser," I huffed. "Go nuts."

"Stick up for yourself." Chance continued with the unsolicited advice. "It's the same with Madison and her clique."

"Who are *you* to instruct me? You're an escaped mental patient."

Chance's mouth tightened into a thin line. "I know what I'm talking about. And even as a wanted lunatic, I'm still more popular than you."

Sad but true. I'd learned that much at the yacht club.

"Mind your own business." I walked to my bathroom and grabbed my toothbrush. "I'm doing fine, thanks."

But I wasn't.

As I brushed, my anxiety level remained sky-high.

Why was Marlo calling? Was he the one stalking us in the Studebaker?

And don't forget my personal problems. Alabama. Cohabitating with Whitney. And, of course, the Tripod. I really needed Chance bringing *that* up.

"You're worried." Chance swung his legs over the side of the bed. "But I can help you handle the spoiled brats."

I finished flossing and grabbed my facial scrub. "They don't intimidate me."

They did.

By flirting with Jason, I'd tweaked Madison in front of her lackeys. Next time, she'd be out for blood.

Chance watched me from the bedroom. "If you remain an easy target, they'll keep coming at you."

I splashed water on my face. "Maybe I'll just blow the whole thing off."

Right.

If I hoped to fight Kit's proposed relocation, now wasn't the time to make waves. Severing ties to Charleston was a bad idea. Plus, I needed reasons to get out of the house, and cotillion was a can't-miss excuse.

Ugh.

"Skipping events is not a solution." Chance tracked me with his eyes as I moved to my desk. "Those girls won't disappear."

"Maybe I will," I muttered. "You heard Kit."

On impulse, I googled the town of Muscle Shoals, Alabama. The results did nothing to improve my mood.

"You've got to be kidding."

"What?" Chance hopped from the bed to read over my shoulder.

"Worse and worse," I moaned. "I can't buy a break."

"Yikes. There was a chemical weapons facility there?" Chance chuckled. "At least they closed it. I'm sure most of the nerve gas has gone inert. Almost all."

The humor escaped me.

I crossed to my closet, closed the door, and grabbed a tank top and shorts. Thinking better of it, I changed into sweats.

Chance whistled when I reemerged. "Nice swag. But perhaps too much ankle?"

"Sleeping on my floor is a privilege, you know. There's space in the garage."

Chance raised both hands in mock surrender. "Just point me to my patch."

"Over there." I indicated a gap between my bed and the far wall. "You won't be visible from the doorway."

Chance saluted.

"If Kit sees you," I said sweetly as I handed him a pillow, "you broke through the window and attacked me."

"Nice." Chance slithered into the tight space. "No one can fault your graciousness."

I turned off the lamp and crawled into bed. Then I lay still, listening in the dark.

Chance was three feet away. I couldn't believe how surreal events had become. Ridiculously, I regretted choosing to wear sweats to bed.

Get a grip, Tory. This is no time for puppy love.

But it wasn't that easy. I'd crushed on Chance all last year, and feelings like that are hard to squash. They tended to pop up at inconvenient times. Like now.

Despite my best efforts, I couldn't stop thinking about how close Chance was. How easy it would be to get a lot closer.

Fantasies began cycling in my head, each more scandalous than the one before.

My cheeks burned.

Disturbed by how shallow I was being, I reminded myself of his many betrayals. Chance had toyed with my emotions, playing head games to throw me off track. He'd lied to my face repeatedly, had even pointed a gun at my head.

His mind fractured that night. Don't forget he's not well.

Yet, even damaged, Chance had a magnetism that no one else could match. Lying in my bed, listening to him breathe, I could feel the pull.

Chance's voice broke the silence. "You can't dodge Madison forever."

"Watch me."

"Interesting. I never pegged you for a coward."

That touched a nerve. "If you're such an *expert*, tell me what you'd do."

I heard fumbling at my bedside, then the lamp flicked on.

"There's only one way to deal with a bully." Chance was sitting up, looking right at me, his dark eyes reflecting the lamplight. "No fear."

"No fear?" I cocked my head. "That's it? That's your big advice?"

Mocking phrases popped to mind, but I held my tongue. Once more, I wondered at the absurdity of the escaped mental patient Chance Claybourne crashing on my bedroom floor, giving me life advice. What a world.

"Bullies are inherently insecure," Chance continued. "They attack those they perceive as weak, so that by humiliating them they can feel better about themselves. But bullies always run from a fair fight."

"Okay, Dr. Phil. So what am I supposed to do?"

"You want those bitches off your back?" Chance fist-slammed his palm. "Give as good as you get. Don't retreat. Attack."

He was right. I couldn't avoid the Tripod forever. And even if I did, someday other tormenters would take their place.

I had to get tough. Stand up for myself.

"No fear, huh?"

Chance nodded. "No fear."

CHAPTER 47

Charleston Country Club occupies the northern tip of James Island, just across the harbor from downtown.

Elegant and exclusive, the club provides its members with easy access to tennis courts, swimming pools, and eighteen manicured holes.

At ten o'clock the next morning, Kit dropped me at the elegant wood-and-stucco clubhouse.

I wore a strapless Nicole Miller cocktail dress. Mocha. Sleek and form fitting. And borrowed, of course.

By silent agreement, we'd avoided conversation the entire drive.

"Two hours?" Kit finger-tapped the wheel, anxious about last night's bombshells.

"One," I replied.

He nodded. "Have fun."

I stumbled while stepping to the curb. I'd barely slept. Hiding

Chance had frazzled my nerves. As had the prospect of a new encounter with the Tripod.

Taking a moment to gather myself, I repeated Chance's advice in my head.

Stand your ground. Fight back. No fear.

Shoulders squared, I strode into the foyer.

Expensive Persian rugs covered a dark hardwood floor overhung by a massive crystal chandelier. Twin grand staircases curved upward along each wall.

A regency table held a flower-filled vase and a silver-framed placard announcing that brunch would be served outside by the putting green.

Standing next to the table was Rodney Brincefield.

Dear God. What was *he* doing here?

"Tory." Brincefield smiled broadly. "What a pleasant surprise!"

"Hello." Startled, I said nothing more.

"I didn't know you frequented the club." Brincefield wore a charcoal suit and black wingtip shoes. I was unsure if he was an employee, guest, or member.

"I'm here for the garden brunch," I said. "For cotillion."

"Wonderful. How goes the treasure hunt?" He lowered his voice. "Any clues?"

Flashbulb image. An antique red station wagon weaving through traffic, tracking the Virals to Morris Island.

I opted for directness. "Mr. Brincefield, have you been following me?"

"Following you?" The bright blue eyes bored into me. "Why on earth would I do that?"

"It's just, I keep running into you."

"I've been walking the same treads for decades." Brincefield chuckled. "It's *you* that recently appeared in my world."

Fair point. I'd only seen Brincefield at places I'd never been before.

Maybe *I* was following *him*.

I didn't notice Brincefield inching closer. When he next spoke, the snowy eyebrows nearly brushed mine.

"Have you found it?" he whispered. "Do you know the volume?"

I hopped backward. "What are you talking about?"

Footsteps sounded behind me. "Tory?"

I turned to see Jason bang into the room, a pair of wooden folding chairs tucked under each arm.

"Did you just get here?" Jason shifted his weight, searching for a comfortable grip. "Everyone's out on the lawn. I got stuck hauling things again."

"On my way." I turned back to Brincefield. "Sorry, gotta run!"

I hurried to the rear doors. In the mirror, I saw Brincefield watch me exit.

Outside, I suppressed a shudder.

Had Brincefield been waiting for me? His last question had been intense, almost manic. What did he mean? Perhaps the old man wasn't harmless after all.

Focus. You're exposed.

I stepped behind a stand of trees just as Jason emerged. After glancing around, he lugged his payload over to a white pavilion.

Screened from view, I surveyed the scene.

Most of the cotillion crowd had arrived. Blue bloods milled, chatting, wearing their newest finery. Women in bright sundresses held tiny plates heaped with sliced cantaloupe, honeydew, strawberries, and cheese. Fake laughter floated on the air.

Impulsive decision: no more surprises.

If an attack was coming, I wanted *all* my powers in place.

SNAP.

The transformation came swiftly, leaving me trembling and gasping as usual. I held position, willing the burning in my limbs to cease.

My receptors kicked into high-definition.

Slipping on my shades, I stepped from the trees and joined the party.

The adults had congregated by buffet tables under the pavilion. My classmates strolled the putting green a few dozen yards away.

Jason spotted me and waved.

Swallowing my apprehension, I walked to his side.

"There you are." His tie was loose, his top button undone. "You disappeared."

"Bathroom break. Still on setup crew?"

"Indentured servitude. The geniuses only set out fifty chairs."

Eyes hidden, I covertly searched for the Tripod. Nowhere in sight.

Then a deeply southern voice called Jason's name.

"Again?" He groaned. "This woman is a grade-A dingbat. Back in a minute."

Jason followed an elderly woman inside the clubhouse.

I was alone.

Determined to make the best of my situation, I mingled, hanging on the fringes of a few group conversations. No one spoke to me, but no one chased me away, either. Progress.

Then my finely tuned ears caught the sound I dreaded.

Madison. Somewhere behind me.

I flexed my sonic ability, trying to tease her voice from the cacophony of gossip and giggles.

". . . be sorry this time. Someone has to teach her . . ."

"Now." Ashley. "Jason's gone inside."

Fabric swished in my direction.

I took a deep breath. *No fear.*

"Boat girl."

I ignored the taunt.

"Boat. Girl."

Slowly, I turned.

Madison stood a few feet from me, arms crossed, flanked by her sycophant flunkies. She'd spoken loudly, intending her performance to be *very* public.

My pulse raced. I didn't trust myself to speak.

Madison arranged her features in a puzzled expression. "I thought we made it clear you weren't welcome here?"

Conversations halted. A loose circle formed. Feral excitement gleamed in the onlookers' eyes. The crowd smelled blood.

"You shouldn't be here," Courtney parroted.

"Nope." Ashley flashed a predatory smile. "This isn't for you."

"It's a free country." But my voice was shaky.

"Actually, it's not." Madison giggled. "It's quite pricey. But I imagine you *wish* that were true, since you can't afford places like this."

Scattered chuckles. I could sense the crowd holding its collective breath. Not a voice spoke in my defense.

The silence lengthened, but I was determined not to break it. This was Madison's show. If she wanted drama, she'd have to carry the performance.

Then a familiar scent drifted my way.

Beneath the Dior perfume and La Mer body lotion, Madison emitted the aroma of nervousness.

Outwardly, she *looked* relaxed. But my enhanced vision noted her tense muscles, saw the tightness to her jaw. The vein in her neck was pumping mile-a-minute.

The confident pose was an act. Madison Dunkle was wound tighter than a snare drum.

"You're out of your depth, Tory." Madison pitched her voice to carry. "And not just here. Bolton Prep is *far* too prestigious to accept riffraff out of misguided pity."

"Pity?" My face was burning, but I kept my tone calm.

Ashley laughed. "Everyone knows you can't afford the tuition. They only let your pathetic group attend because some lame administrator needed a good deed for PR."

"But we're the ones who suffer." Madison shook her head in solemn distress. "Deserving students, forced to share classrooms with a band of island hicks. It's a wonder we learn anything at all."

Enough. Chance said to attack? Done and done.

"*I'm* not deserving?" I rolled my eyes. "Last I checked, I outscored you in every class we shared. You know, the sophomore courses I took as a freshman?"

Madison's eyes widened. She covered her anxiety with a smirk, but the nervous smell ripened.

I didn't let up. "Unlike you, I bust my ass every day. That's why I'm a Bolton Scholar and you're not. We'll *both* be taking the AP schedule next year. If you ask nicely, maybe I'll agree to tutor you."

Madison's smirk wavered. Another scent flooded my nose.

Embarrassment.

I'd hit a nerve.

The answer dawned on me.

"You *were* accepted into the AP program, right?" My face was the model of sincerity. "I know you applied."

Madison stiffened. "You don't know *anything*."

My nose told me otherwise.

"Wow." I shook my head. "Awkward. That's not going to help those college applications. But maybe your parents' money can buy you in somewhere."

Snickers, hastily covered by hands. But the target was different this time. Eyes had shifted to Madison.

She started to speak, but I cut her off.

"Honestly, it's pathetic how you continually follow me around. Don't you have *anything* else to do? Get a freaking hobby."

The snickers became chuckles. Fickle as ever, the crowd had turned. Watching Madison squirm was even better entertainment.

"We do *not* follow you," Ashley snapped. "You're a loser!"

"Could've fooled me. Everywhere I go, you guys trail along like lost puppies. When I look out my bedroom window, I expect to see you three rooting through my trash."

"Hold on!" Courtney looked stunned. "You can't talk to us like this!"

"I'm sorry, are my words too big for you? Need make more simple?"

Laughter swelled. I was on a roll. Why had I ever let these bimbos get to me?

"You're a *nobody*." Madison's cheeks were scarlet. "Not one person here wants to see your face again."

"Don't worry about me, Maddy. I'll be fine. If people dislike me for no reason, that's their problem."

Game. Set. Match. Ashley whispered into Madison's ear. I overheard easily.

"She's making you look stupid. And Jason's coming back."

Embarrassment overpowered all Madison's other scents. She'd also started to sweat. Surprisingly, I hadn't.

I stood calmly, waiting for her to lob me the next volley.

Madison licked her lips, desperate for a clever exit line.

"Yes?" I tipped my head. "Some final witty comment before you run along?"

"*You're* the one who needs . . . witty comments. Bitch."

"Brilliant." I nodded in appreciation. "Well played."

Cackles sounded from all sides.

Madison elbowed through the encircling debs and their dates, not bothering to hide her fury. Ashley and Courtney scurried in her wake.

The crowd fragmented into smaller groups to rehash the showdown. Eyes darted in my direction, a few carrying respect.

Suddenly, I felt exhausted.

Almost no sleep and nothing to eat. Still flaring. I stared longingly at the buffet, but the Tripod had stormed in that direction. No way would I reenter their orbit.

I needed a moment alone. Careful to maintain my composure, I slipped into the clubhouse and found the ladies room.

I was splashing water on my face when the Tripod walked in.

Ashley and Courtney blocked the door. Madison stormed to me, seething.

Keeping my eyes lowered, I reached for a towel, dried my face, then shoved my shades into place.

"No one talks to me like that!" Madison radiated indignation. "Especially not some poser charity case from the sticks!"

I looked at her, no longer scared in the slightest.

"Excuse me." Calm. "You're in my way."

"So?" Madison sneered. "What are you going to do about it?"

"If you don't move?"

"Yeah."

I closed the gap until we stood nose to nose. "I'll knock you on your spoiled little ass."

I heard Madison's heart pound. Saw her hands tremble. Smelled sweat on her skin.

"You wouldn't dare." A quiver in her voice betrayed the bravado.

"Try me," I said.

My hand rose, causing her to flinch.

Leaning close, I raised my glasses and drilled her with my glowing, golden irises.

"Boo."

Madison yelped, then fled in panic. Ashley and Courtney glanced at me, puzzled, before rushing after their queen bee.

"Bye ladies!" I called. "Have a good one!"

The feeling of triumph was short-lived.

Ohmygod!

My stomach churned as I realized the magnitude of my mistake.

Madison saw my eyes.

"Stupid stupid stupid!" I said to the empty bathroom.

I squeezed my lids shut, wishing I could undo the last five minutes.

SNUP.

My head spun.

The room wobbled.

I ran to a stall and vomited into the toilet.

Then I lowered the seat, dropped, and berated myself. I'd committed a terrible blunder.

Go home. Worry later.

Legs shaking, I stood, straightened my dress, washed out my mouth, and exited the bathroom.

Jason was waiting outside the door.

"Tory, are you—"

"I'm not feeling great. I'm heading home."

"I saw what happened." Jason wore an astonished smile. "I don't know who *that* Tory was, but she's a badass!"

"All I did was stoop to their level."

"Not true! You had every right to stick up for yourself."

Not wanting to argue, I simply nodded.

"Anyway, I heard you're moving into this year's cohort."

"What? Who told you that?" *Goddamn Whitney!*

"My mother, a few minutes ago. If that's true, you're going to need an escort. I just so happen to be available."

My disgust for the whole scene boiled over. Suddenly it was all too much. Madison. Whitney. My own loss of control.

Jason was closest, so he took the hit.

"Why would I choose you?" I snapped. "So you can disappear when someone attacks me?"

Jason recoiled in surprise. "I didn't know! That crazy woman had me hauling—"

My hand shot up, cutting him short.

Too much for one day.

Too many boys in my life.

"I have to go."

Before Jason could respond, I rushed out the door.

CHAPTER 48

"You're sure everything's okay?"

Kit stood in the kitchen, a concerned look on his face. "I'm supposed to meet Whitney for a movie, but I could cancel."

"I'm fine." Rattled or not, I couldn't waste an opportunity. Kit being gone freed my entire evening.

He seemed unconvinced. "Do you want to talk about last night? I know you were upset. I could hear you muttering in your room."

"Kit, I'm okay. Just let me process for a while."

"That I can do." Goofy smile. "Gather your thoughts. That way you can yell at me with more focus."

"Exactly. I should write down all the ways you're a doofus."

"Excellent plan."

Kit grabbed his workbag and headed down to the garage.

I was dialing before the door closed.

○   ○   ○

My living room was divided into uneasy camps.

Chance and I were on one side. Ben, Hi, and Shelton formed the opposition.

The mood was distinctly chilly.

I wanted to tell the Virals about my mistake with Madison, but Chance's presence made that impossible. I'd wait until we were alone.

"We're supposed to trust this whack job?" Ben refused to address Chance directly.

"We're talking in circles," I said. "He can take us to the cross."

"And I will." Chance leaned forward. "But first tell me what's going on. Why did you risk breaking me out?"

"Not part of the deal." Hi folded his arms. "We sprang you in exchange for the cross. You're not entitled to our life stories."

Chance was undeterred. "Why do you want it? You saw the auction listing. The cross isn't particularly valuable."

"*Our* business," Shelton said. "Just take us to your father's fishing camp."

"No." Chance calmly intertwined his fingers. "If I have to take you somewhere the authorities might look for me, I want to know more."

"You don't get to dictate new terms," Ben said. "Tell us where. Now."

"You think you can force me, boy?"

Ben fired to his feet.

"Wait!" I shouted. "Everyone chill. Let me think."

Seconds of tense silence.

"How about this?" I turned to Chance. "Take us to your father's fishing camp. Produce the cross. *Then* we'll tell you what's going on."

Shelton *tsk*ed. "We don't have to—"

"He's not going to help us otherwise."

Chance nodded his head as he weighed options. "Agreed."

Shelton puffed air through his lips. Ben stormed from the room cursing under his breath. Only Hi seemed satisfied.

Whatever. Under the circumstances, it was the best I could do.

"It's settled," I said. "So. Car or boat?"

Chance answered without hesitation. "Boat."

○   ○   ○

Ben eased *Sewee* from the dock. "Well?"

Chance pointed north. "Sullivan's Island."

"At least it's close," Hi said. "We could practically swim."

Hi's joke did nothing to ease the tension. Ben barely held his temper in check, and Chance seemed to enjoy goading him. It was a recipe for trouble.

Ben motored across the harbor mouth, passing the tiny island of Fort Sumter, site of the opening shots of the Civil War. The sun was setting. Sullivan's Island lay dead ahead.

"Head west past Fort Moultrie," Chance instructed. "Then swing into The Cove. The camp is five hundred yards up the waterway."

Sullivan's Island is largely residential. No hotels, waterslides, or mini-golf. The lots are big and so are the homes. The coastline is surprisingly undeveloped, with much of it held in trust by the town itself. Much like Morris, the island has a rich military history, and many dwellings are old fortifications or barracks converted to modern use.

"There." Chance pointed to a wooden pier jutting from the shoreline into the sheltered bay. "The cabin is back in those trees."

"This is the 'fishing camp' you've been talking about?" Hi employed air quotes. "That's a million-dollar house, easy."

"I never claimed it was a canvas tent. We Claybournes like our comfort."

Chance jumped to the dock and tied the bowline to a heavy metal cleat. "Come along."

The dock bridged an acre of shallow, brackish water before entering a two-story boathouse. Inside, small watercraft occupied alcoves on each side, several accessible only by hydraulic lifts.

Chance crossed to a Jet Ski, dug a key from under the seat, then strode from the shed's rear door into the yard beyond.

A gravel path wound up to a large log cabin. Chance unlocked the door and stepped back, gesturing us inside with a bow. "Make yourselves at home."

We trooped through a gourmet kitchen into a massive great room. Chance walked a circuit, powering an array of antique lamps.

An enormous brick fireplace took up most of one wall, the mantel carved with the foxes-and-vines motif of the Claybourne family crest. Stuffed birds, rodents, and other small mammals crowded every inch. Leather couches faced the giant hearth, surrounding a rustic wagon-wheel coffee table. Deer heads stared glassy-eyed from all four walls.

"Who decorated this place?" Hi said. "The Crocodile Hunter?"

"Has a woman ever set foot in here?" I asked.

"Only the cleaning lady," Chance said. "Hollis kept his clubhouse private."

Shelton and Hi flopped onto a couch and began checking their iPhones.

Ben stepped face-to-face with Chance. "The cross."

Chance smirked, about to argue for the sport of it.

"We had a deal." I shot Chance a warning look.

Chance sighed dramatically, then pointed to an antique safe in one corner.

The safe was a black cast-iron cube the size of a washing machine. Stamped with the official seal of the United States Postal Service, the thing must've weighed a thousand pounds.

"It's a collector's item." Chance rapped the side with his knuckles. "Constructed in 1880. My father's servants store valuables inside when closing the cabin for the season."

Chance moved backward.

Ben stopped him with an outstretched hand. "Combination?"

Chance shrugged free. "I'm not divulging family secrets. Step away."

Ben and I complied. Hunching his back to block our view, Chance spun the dial. Forward. Back. Forward. Then he twisted the handle and pulled.

The door didn't budge.

A look of surprise crossed Chance's face. He tried the combination a second time. No luck. The surprise morphed to irritation. Chance turned the dial a third time, slowly, making sure to align the numbers exactly.

The door refused to yield.

"What the hell?" Chance kicked the safe in frustration. "It won't open."

"Problem?" Shelton asked.

"The combination isn't working," Chance said. "8-16-24. Try it yourself."

Shelton knelt before the safe. Three attempts produced the same result.

"The mechanism seems okay." Shelton scratched his head. "Either the combination was changed, or you've got the numbers wrong."

"I don't have them wrong," Chance snapped. "It's multiples of eight."

"Then we're sunk." Shelton almost sounded relieved.

My mind raced, but couldn't devise a way into a locked safe. We'd have to try something else.

Hi caught my attention, tipped his head toward the kitchen door.

I took the hint. "Is there anything to drink in this house?"

"Try the refrigerator." Chance was focused on the safe and didn't bother to look up. "But I'd check expiration dates if I were you."

Hi followed me. We huddled and spoke quickly.

"My grandfather had a safe just like that," Hi said.

"Could you crack it?"

"I know how it works. The locking mechanism consists of three notched discs that hold the bolt in place. The door opens when the correct combination aligns the notches, allowing the bolt to slide free."

"How is that useful?"

"Just listen! If you rotate the knob three hundred and sixty degrees, you'll hit the first correct number at some point. When you do, the bolt will tap the notch on the first disc."

"So?"

"That contact makes a soft click, usually inaudible to human ears."

"Oh." I saw where Hi was going.

Hi swept on. "Center the dial back to zero, then work left until you hear a second click. Jog a little farther left, and then repeat to find the last digit. Boom! Three. Done."

"Will the clicks occur in the correct order?"

"Not necessarily. But when you have all three numbers, you can test different sequences until the right one opens the safe."

"You're a genius!" I said excitedly. "Did you bring your shades?"

"Not me. I'd soil myself if I flared in front of Chance." Hi squeezed both my shoulders. "But you, my dear, have experience with such adventures."

"Fabulous."

CHAPTER 49

I reentered the room carrying a glass of water. Hi trailed stiffly behind me.

Ben was standing by the fireplace, while Chance and Shelton knelt on the floor by the safe.

Chance noticed me first. "Nice shades. Trying to keep up with the Kardashians?"

Ben and Shelton tensed. Realizing.

"Headache." I saw Chance in razor-sharp detail, could make out a single bead of perspiration on his left temple. "I'm very light sensitive."

"Let's search the house," Hi said too loudly. "If someone changed the combination, maybe they wrote it down."

"And left it lying around?" Chance scoffed. "That'd be incredibly stupid."

"It's worth a look." Shelton hopped to his feet.

"Okay." Ben was looking at Hi, but his words were directed at me. "I hope you know what you're doing."

"I do." Hi over-nodded. "Trust me."

"You guys are *way* too serious," Chance said. "I'll check the master bedroom."

"I'll hang here." I tried to sound spur-of-the-moment, but I'm the worst actress on earth. "Maybe try my luck with the safe."

"Don't waste your time," Chance said. "That demon isn't opening without dynamite."

The boys dispersed, pretending to scour the cabin. I sat cross-legged in front of the safe, honed my ears to block out distractions, and rotated the dial a full circuit.

Not a sound.

On impulse, I chugged my water and placed the rim of the glass against the safe's door. Pressing an ear against its bottom, I closed my eyes and gave the knob a second go.

This time, I heard a very faint ticking. I nudged the dial, straining to pick up the slightest variation.

Tick. Tick. Tick. Tick.

Clink.

My eyes darted to the dial. 24. Okay. Score one for Chance.

I reset the wheel to zero. Moving counterclockwise, I repeated the painstaking process.

Tick. Tick.

Clink.

12! Two-thirds of the combination was mine.

I was jogging the dial back to zero when Chance emerged from the hallway.

"Pointless, as I knew—" He halted at the sight of me. "You're listening through a drinking glass? What are you, nine years old?"

"Give me a minute before you scoff." Barely breathing, I worked back across the wheel.

My straining ears registered air moving in and out of Chance's nose, my own heartbeat, waves lapping outside the cabin. But the lock remained silent.

Tick. Tick. Tick.

I sensed the other Virals drift back into the room.

I'd almost completed the final circuit when I heard it.

Clink.

Yes! 36. I had all three.

Time to close shop.

SNUP.

The power drained way. Thankfully, I was already seated. When the weakness subsided, I removed my sunglasses and rubbed my eyes.

"I have it," I said. "The numbers are 24-12-36."

"But 12 and 36 aren't multiples of 8. It doesn't fit the—" Chance stopped, went squinty eyed in thought. "Shoot. Maybe it was multiples of *twelve*."

"You've *got* to be kidding!" Ben snorted. "Thanks for nothing."

"Like you've never forgotten anything," Chance shot back. "I'm on medication!"

I tried the digits in numerical order. The handle turned and the door swung open.

The safe's interior was divided into levels.

Our prize rested on a red velvet cloth on the top shelf.

Anne Bonny's cross was slender and delicate, beautifully carved from a single piece of cherry wood. The upright was two feet long, with the horizontal bar crossing six inches below the apex. The central ring formed a perfect circle at the point where the two parts intersected. A clear crystalline substance filled the space between arms and ring, causing the cross's heart to sparkle in the lamplight.

Gracefully, uniquely, and perplexingly, the top tine curved gently to the right.

"That's it," Shelton breathed. "That's the symbol on the treasure map."

"Treasure map?" Chance didn't miss it.

"Shelton, I swear, you'd make the *worst* secret agent in history." Hi smacked his forehead. "Dead within hours. I'd probably off you myself."

"Talk about this map," Chance pressed.

No one spoke.

"Hey! I did my part. You promised to explain if I produced the cross." Chance waved a hand at the safe. "Voilà! There it is!"

"This cross may be tied to Anne Bonny's lost treasure," I said.

Choosing my words carefully, I gave Chance a sanitized version of the events of the last few days. The other Virals listened in perturbed silence. But a deal is a deal.

"Wow. I didn't see *that* coming," Chance said when I'd finished. "Where'd you find the map?"

"On eBay," Ben said. "Treasure map section. We paid the Buy It Now price."

Chance ignored him. "And there was nothing at the end of the tunnels?"

"Only a goofy poem," Shelton said. "Tory's getting it translated."

Wince. Cursing a blue streak, I reached for my iPhone.

"What?" Hi said.

"I'm such a dope." I scrolled through my unread email. "Aunt Tempe sent me her translation two days ago. I fell asleep and forgot all about it."

Finding the message, I read aloud:

On the moon's high day, seek Island People.
Stand the high watch, hold to thy faith, and look to the sea.
Let a clear heart guide you through the field of bones.

"Great." Shelton tugged an earlobe. "Now what the frig does *that* mean?"

"It says 'island people'?" Ben sounded excited. For Ben.

"Yep." I double-checked. "Both words capitalized. 'On the moon's high day, seek Island People.'"

"Moon's high day!" Ben's eyes gleamed. "That must be another full moon reference, like in the Sewee legend. 'When the night sky burned as daytime.'"

"Sounds reasonable," I agreed. "But how does that help?"

"And who are the island people?" Hi asked.

"I don't think it's a *who*." Too agitated to stay still, Ben began pacing. "When I was a kid, my grandfather would take me fishing. Wherever we stopped, he'd teach me the old Sewee name for the place. He never accepted European changes."

"Progressive," Chance muttered.

Ben was too absorbed to notice. "One I remember—an island named Oneiscau."

"Wonderful," Chance said. "Let's plan a cruise."

"I think we should." Ben stopped pacing. "In Sewee, Oneiscau translates to 'Island People.'"

We all stared in shock.

I recovered first. "Which island?"

"No idea." Ben shook his head in frustration. "My grandfather died when I was eight. But I remember seeing it once in a book about Charleston's barrier islands."

Hands fumbled for smartphones and began tapping furiously.

"How do you spell that?" Hi asked. "Sounds like a lot of vowels."

"Got it!" Shelton won. "It's Bull Island!"

"That's close!" Ben exclaimed. "Just two islands north of here."

"Oneiscau was renamed Bull after a colonial leader," Shelton read. "Right about the time Bonny was hijacking ships in the area. She'd have known *both* names."

"Bull Island borders Sewee Bay," Ben added. "Smack in the heart of ancestral Sewee territory. Most of the tribe lived near there."

"If Bonny operated that close to Sewee villages," Shelton said, "a tribal legend would make sense. Ben's story could be dead on."

"Both poem and legend mention a field of bones," I said. "I don't know what that means, but the similarity lends credit to each reference."

Hi pocketed his phone. "FYI, the full moon is tomorrow night."

"Then we need to be there," Chance said firmly. "Could be our only shot."

No one responded.

Chance glanced from face to face. "What?"

"You're not coming," Ben said. "Not in this lifetime."

"Of course I am." Chance reached into the safe and removed the cross. "This is mine. If you need it to find buried treasure, I'm in."

"We don't need the cross," Shelton said. "Not for sure."

Chance's smile held zero warmth. "I'll call the police the moment you walk out that door."

"They'll haul you right back to the Crazy Town Inn," Hi pointed out. "The cops must be looking for you right now."

And me, I thought glumly.

Marsh Point would be frantic to find Chance. Who had they already contacted? The police? Bolton Prep? Kit? The awful possibilities tightened my gut.

Chance shrugged. "This lovely jaunt won't last anyway. Do you think I plan to live as a fugitive forever?" He snorted. "I'm a Claybourne. I was bored, but I'm not stupid."

"What you *are* is delusional." Ben fumed. "The treasure belongs to us."

Chance's hands found his hips. "Cut me out, and I'll make sure you get nothing."

Unexpectedly, twin yellow beams flashed across the room.

"Headlights," Chance warned. "In the driveway."

"Kill the lamps!" Ben ordered.

Shelton and Hi did. Then we huddled in total darkness.

"Who uses this place?" I whispered.

"No one. My father's in prison, as you well know. And the servants don't come after dark."

The front doorknob jiggled.

Chance rose. "If some lowlife thinks he can rob me, he's about to learn a harsh lesson."

I grabbed his arm. "We didn't tell you everything! Someone's been following us. And whoever it is fired shots down in the tunnels."

Chance dropped back into a crouch. "Guns? Seriously?"

"Yes. So let's sneak out the way we came."

"Someone's at the back door!" Shelton hissed from behind me. "We're trapped!"

Glass shattered in the kitchen.

My heart pounded. "Is there another way?"

"The basement." Chance tucked the cross under his belt. "Follow me!"

We raced down a hallway to a steep, narrow staircase. Descending at full speed, we reached a dark earth-floored cellar.

"This way." Snatching a flashlight from a shelf, Chance hurried to a pair of wooden doors on the back wall.

"Tunnel." Chance yanked one side open. "This cabin was originally part of the Underground Railroad for escaped slaves."

"Where does it lead?" Shelton asked. He'd clearly had enough of tunnels.

"The boathouse. Fifty feet."

Something rattled at the top of the stairs.

"Go!" I whispered.

We slipped into the passage, and Chance pulled the door shut. Scurrying like rats, we quickly reached the tunnel's end.

Chance palm-pushed a trapdoor above our heads. Hinges groaned. The wooden panel swung open and flopped to the floorboards.

Cupping his hands for my foot, Chance boosted me up through the opening.

All was quiet in the boathouse.

I turned to help Shelton and Hi. Ben came next. Then he reached back and pulled Chance after him.

We sprinted down the dock and jumped aboard *Sewee*. Ben fired the engine and slammed the boat into gear.

Feet pounded down the planks behind us.

"Too late," I whispered.

Sewee sped out into the cove.

CHAPTER 50

We broke for dinner.

Chance was restless, full of questions, but no one else felt like talking.

For the Virals, getting chased by thugs was becoming routine.

After a quick check of the premises, I smuggled Chance into the townhouse and scrounged up some mac and cheese.

"Don't think I'm cooking for you." The water was taking forever to boil. "This box just happens to be family size."

"If you're grounded, where's your father?" Chance was idly spinning a quarter on the countertop. "He's not exactly running a supermax prison here."

"He's at a movie with Whitney." I snorted. "He just texted a reminder for me to record *Deadliest Catch*. Sometimes I'm awed by his cluelessness."

"*My* father is serving life in prison. I've got you beat."

Chance's attempt at humor fell flat.

We ate our pasta in silence.

○　　○　　○

"Whaddyagot?" I said.

Videoconference. Chance and I sat side by side before my computer screen.

"Plenty." Shelton flipped the pages of his notepad. "Bull Island is the perfect place to stash something you don't want found."

"Oneiscau," Ben corrected. "That's the true name."

"I'm sticking with words I can pronounce," Shelton said. "Take it up with Google Maps."

"Shelton's right." Hi was munching on a french bread pizza. It wasn't pretty. "Historically, there haven't been many people or structures on the island since the Sewee disappeared."

"Pirates loved it," Shelton added. "Bull was so popular with bandits that colonial authorities built a watchtower there."

"How big is the island?" Chance asked.

"Five thousand acres." Hi read something off screen. "Bull is the largest barrier island within the Cape Romain National Wildlife Refuge. It's all forests, swamps, dunes, and beaches."

"Who lived there?" I asked.

Ben chimed in. "The Sewee until the early 1700s. The English landed in 1670, on their way to settle Charles Town. One was Stephen Bull, and somehow he got the island named after him. Jerk."

"No one lived there after the Sewee?"

"Very few," Shelton said. "In 1925, a Senator Dominick purchased the island and built a manor house. The Refuge was established in '32, and Dominick sold to the Fish and Wildlife Service in '36. The manor house operated as an inn until the 1960s, when the whole shebang was declared off-limits for development."

Chance leaned in front of my webcam. "So you're saying Bull Island has been essentially unoccupied since Bonny escaped in 1720?"

"Yes," Hi answered. "Bull Island is a class-one remote wilderness area, which means it's basically untouched. The manor house is still used by Refuge employees, but nothing else was ever built out there."

"That's not to say no one visits," Shelton said. "There's a daily ferry. The bird watching is supposed to be top notch, and the island is criss-crossed with trails. But Bull is closed to the public after dark."

"Perfect," I said. "That's when we'll go."

"Tomorrow night," Hi reminded. "Full moon."

"Five *thousand* acres." Chance scratched at his thin beard, puzzled. "How will we know where to look?"

"I've got an idea about that," Shelton said. "The second line of Bonny's poem reads, 'stand the high watch, hold to thy faith, and look to the sea.'"

"So we'll be looking east," I said.

"Remember the watchtower?" Shelton glanced at his notepad. "In 1707, the South Carolina General Assembly authorized lookouts on six coastal islands, each to be built on a hill or high dune."

"Bull got one," Hi guessed.

"Yep. It was called a Martello tower, and would've been manned by a white dude and a couple of Sewee, for the sole purpose of watching for pirate ships. If they saw one, they'd fire a cannon three times, then run like hell."

"Heroes," Hi said. "What happened to the thing?"

"The Union blew it up during the Civil War."

I saw where Shelton was headed. "You think the tower is the 'high watch' mentioned in Bonny's poem?"

"Makes sense, doesn't it?"

"It does." I smiled. "Good job. We have a place to start."

"Any thoughts on the field of bones?" Ben asked.

"No," Hi admitted.

"Not yet," said Shelton.

"Keep looking." I yawned, exhausted by another long day. "Let's talk again in the morning."

"Wait!" Chance glanced at me in surprise. "We aren't going to discuss what happened at the cabin?"

"What's the point?" Ben said. "We don't know who was out there."

"You're hanging with us now, bro." Hi flicked imaginary dust from his shoulder. "Don't worry so much."

"Truth." Shelton fist-pounded his chest. "We'll keep you safe."

"Good night, tough guys." I logged off.

Chance propped his feet on my ottoman. "What now?"

"We lay low until tomorrow night. *You* hide up here."

"But I'm bored. Don't you have a Wii or something?"

The front door opened. Keys hit the hall table.

"Tory, I'm home!" Kit's voice carried up the stairs. "Wanna watch some *30 Rock* reruns?"

"Coming!" I turned and whispered to Chance. "Read a book. *Bridget Jones's Diary* is on my shelf. You'll *love* it."

I shut the door on his groan.

CHAPTER 51

We left just after midnight the following night.

Quiet as a whisper, Chance and I crept downstairs. Kit had gone to bed early and was usually a heavy sleeper. Nonetheless, my heart raced with every creak of the floorboards.

In the living room, Coop padded over and whined softly.

"Stay, boy." I led him back to his doggie bed, praying he'd cooperate. Then Chance and I slipped through the front door and raced to the dock.

Ben was already aboard *Sewee*, double-checking the gear we'd assembled that afternoon. Shelton and Hi arrived moments later. We eased from the pier and motored north toward Bull Island.

A full moon hung low on the western horizon. Bright. Timely. It glowed like a giant white eye, alleviating the need for battery-powered light.

We rode in silence, each wrapped in our own thoughts. The only words spoken were occasional navigational commands.

Ben crossed the harbor mouth, rounded Sullivan's Island, and headed back into The Cove. We'd decided to take the Intracoastal Waterway—a combo natural and man-made canal running between the barrier islands and the mainland. Traveling the open sea after sunset was too risky.

Before long we reached the Claybourne cabin we'd fled the previous night. The property was dark and quiet. Continuing north, *Sewee* passed island after island on our right. Sullivan's. Isle of Palms. Dewees.

Then the waterway narrowed. Signs of human influence fell away as we crossed into thick, undisturbed swampland. The only sounds were the hoots and peeps of nocturnal birds and an occasional muffled splash.

We huddled close together aboard our little craft, keenly aware that humans were interlopers in such wild, primal Lowcountry.

After what seemed a lifetime, Ben pointed to a black shape on our right.

"That's the southern edge of Bull Island," he said. "Most of the high ground is on the northern side."

"Should we anchor here?" I asked.

"We need to go farther up the waterway," Ben said. "The next stretch is pretty raw, but leads into Sewee Bay. From there we can cut through the swamp and come ashore on one of the beaches."

"Let's hustle." Hi gestured at the gloom around us. "This place feels like Jurassic Park on crack. I don't wanna get chomped by a velociraptor."

We entered a narrow channel overhung with trees that

blocked the moonlight and wrapped our vessel in shadow. As our progress slowed, my anxiety increased.

Finally, the canal opened into a wide tidal lake. Scattered docks appeared. Ben skirted the shoreline, then turned into a network of narrow creeks. Shelton sat next to him, relaying GPS directions stored on his iPhone.

After a zigzag course we pulled into Bull Harbor. I could hear the Atlantic surf not far off.

"There she blows." Ben pointed to the landmass looming ahead. "Oneiscau. Bull Island." To Hi, "You have that map handy?"

"Yep." Hi tapped his smartphone.

"Which way?" Ben asked. "The island has only one dock."

"We should anchor near the watchtower," Shelton blurted. "Keep the boat close."

"Why?" Hi asked.

Shelton's teeth glinted in the moonlight. "Call it a hunch."

"Care to share more?" I said. "We're on a tight timetable."

"Not just yet. But I've got an idea. Humor me."

"Humoring you means getting in the water," Hi grumbled. "It better be worth it."

Shelton slapped Hi's shoulder. "Seeing you in a wet tee is reward enough."

"Which way to the fort?" Ben asked.

"Hard to starboard." Hi's features glowed blue in the light of his phone's display. "The watchtower is near Bull's northeastern point."

Ben skimmed past dense forest growing tight to the water's edge. Live oaks and palmetto palms jockeyed with cedars, loblolly pines, and sprawling magnolias. The tangled understory blocked all view of the island's interior. *Like Loggerhead*, I thought.

As *Sewee* crept forward the woodland gave way to marsh. The water grew shallow. Reeds and spartina grass poked from its surface. Frogs croaked. Insects hummed and whined all around us.

"Bull Island has an enormous alligator population," Ben whispered. "So . . . uh . . . keep your head on a swivel."

"Swamps suck donkey balls," Shelton muttered. "Seriously."

"There." Hi pointed inland, where, roughly a quarter mile distant, a steep hill rose in the moonlight. A jagged silhouette crowned the hilltop.

"It's too boggy to go ashore here," Ben said.

"Continue north a bit." Hi was peering at his iPhone. "There's a beach."

Shelton nodded with feeling. "I'm not swimming here. This place looks like a gator's kitchen."

Five minutes motoring brought us to a white beach running the island's northern rim. Twenty yards inland, a row of head-high dunes marched to a grassy plain. The moonlit hill was a vague cutout in the darkness beyond.

Ben coaxed *Sewee* as close to shore as possible.

"There's a trail from the beach." Hi pocketed his phone. "The tower's about a half mile away."

Chance was watching the beach. "What lives out here?"

"Animals," Ben said.

"Care to be more specific?"

"The Refuge website listed deer, raccoons, gators, and some smaller guys like fox squirrels and lizards." Shelton was untying his tennis shoes. "But Bull is really about the birds. Over two hundred species."

"Ducks, mallards, pintails." Ben cut the engine and tossed the anchor overboard. "Sandpipers, yellowlegs, warblers, sparrows, woodpeckers. Not that you'd know the difference."

"Keep talking," Chance warned. "But don't act surprised when I clock you."

"Enough!" I said. "Let's get to the beach."

We divided the gear. Then, Nikes strung around my neck, excavation tools strapped to my back, I lowered into the surf and waded ashore. The boys followed close behind.

Once on dry land, I set down my tool kit and pulled on my socks. The others gathered in a semicircle to re-shoe. The huge moon lit the landscape with an eerie blue radiance. We kept our flashlights off.

"Where exactly is the tower?" Ben.

"In those hills." Hi pointed south over the dunes. "Past the beach is a long grassy field. From there, a trail leads into the woods. The tower should be along it somewhere."

"I'll scout ahead." Ben shouldered my tool bag. "If I'm not back in ten minutes, follow me south." With that, he disappeared over the nearest dune.

"Is he always like that?" Chance asked.

No one bothered to answer.

I had one sneaker laced when I heard a soft rustling off to my left.

I peered down the beach.

Nothing but moonlit sand.

My second shoe was half-tied when sand swished somewhere among the dunes. My eyes darted, searching for the source of the noise.

"Ben?" Shelton called hesitantly.

Two points of yellow flashed in the night. Disappeared.

"What was that?" Hi whispered.

"Shh!" My eyes strained to pierce the gloom ahead.

Two shadows streaked from a stand of sea oats. Four amber dots flashed, closer this time. Shot sideways. Vanished.

My mind filled in the blanks.

Eyes. Circling.

I began to hiss a warning, but a growl stilled my tongue.

More snarls joined the first, creating an eerie, keening chorus.

Chance dropped to a crouch. "Whatever's out there doesn't sound happy."

"I forgot to mention something." Moonlight reflected off Shelton's glasses. "Next year, the Wildlife Refuge plans to reintroduce red wolves to Bull Island."

"Sounds like they stepped up their timetable," Hi whispered.

Three silhouettes loped across the dunes. Sleek. Four-legged.

"There!" Hi pointed to our right. "Wolves! Big ones."

Chance gestured left. "Over here, too."

As I stared in terror, a shape took form directly before me. My mind logged details. Large, triangular head. Massive forepaws. Powerful, muscular trunk.

Wolf. Male. Enormous.

I could make out some of his coloring in the pale moonlight. Cinnamon-brown belly and pelt. Charcoal back and tail. White muzzle.

My brain estimated stats. Length: five feet. Weight: eighty pounds.

Almond-shaped eyes studied me.

"Easy big fella." I took a small step backward, arms straight down at my sides. "We're all friends here."

A second wolf appeared, then a third, each resembling the leader, but smaller.

I stood facing the wolves, Hi and Shelton flanking me, Chance a step behind. Where was Ben?

"Another on our right," Hi whispered.

"And left," Shelton said. "Pacing."

Five in all. A decent-sized pack.

"We can swim to the boat," Chance hissed. "They hate water, right?"

"What about Ben?" Hi's voice cracked.

"Everyone relax," I said. "Red wolves don't attack people."

"You sure?" Hi croaked. "This one's staring like I'm Lean Cuisine."

The wolves *did* seem agitated. Though White Muzzle sat calmly on his haunches, the others circled, growling and sniffing, tossing glances at the night sky.

Suddenly it dawned on me.

"The full moon," I whispered. "It's freaking them out."

"Great," Shelton whimpered. "We're dog food."

White Muzzle abruptly stood. Hackles up. Ears flattened. Tail horizontal.

Uh oh.

The rest of the pack froze.

"Not good," Hi said. "Where do I kick an attacking wolf?"

Shelton tugged my arm. "Talk to them, dog whisperer. Calm them down."

"What are you babbling about?" Chance's face glistened with sweat.

But I understood what Shelton meant.

Keeping Chance at my back, I stilled my thoughts and closed off sensory input.

SNAP.

My canine DNA fired into action. As the flare ripped through me, the world cranked into focus.

But something was different.

Though always a struggle, this time the transformation was wilder and more chaotic. Raw-edged.

My body pulsed with more power than ever before. My brain flooded with too much data. I nearly lost control.

White Muzzle tensed, barked twice, and lunged in my direction.

"I'm there." Shelton's voice sounded strangled. "But amped too high."

"Plenty of *flare* over here," Hi spluttered. "Overload. What's going on?"

Watching the skittish wolves, the answer suddenly dawned.

"The full moon," I whispered. "It must be affecting our flares. Riling the wolf DNA inside us."

"What are you babbling about?" From behind, Chance couldn't see our eyes. "We should retreat to the boat!"

White Muzzle's lips drew back. Predatory teeth gleamed in the moonlight. He growled, fur bristling.

Tread carefully.

White Muzzle viewed us as a rival pack invading *his* turf. He was alpha. I was alpha. This wasn't Whisper, an animal accustomed to human interaction. This was a wild creature, feeling threatened, instinctually defending his family.

Inching forward, I willed the wolf to understand.

We mean you no harm.

My mind probed, found the invisible barrier blocking my thoughts from the rest of the world. I pushed.

Hi and Shelton hovered close. I strained. Reached. Failed. No matter my effort, the wall separating our psyches wouldn't yield. I couldn't connect my brain to theirs.

Frustrated, I fired my message outward, toward White Muzzle.

A primal consciousness brushed against mine. Contact.

An electric shiver coursed through me as our thoughts melded.

We mean you no harm.

White Muzzle started, stepped backward, raised his snout and howled. The rest of the pack joined his keening wail.

We mean you no harm.

SNUP.

I fell to my knees. Beside me, Shelton trembled. Hiram wheezed and spat.

"What's happening!?" Chance sounded near panic. "Are you guys okay!?"

I wobbled to my feet, eyes never leaving our four-legged hosts.

White Muzzle eyed me a moment longer, then turned and trotted over the dunes. The other wolves followed single file.

"They left." Chance barked a nervous laugh. "Just like that. They left."

"Yeah," I panted. "Just like that."

Head spinning, I turned and puked on the sand.

CHAPTER 52

W e'd just crossed the dunes when I spotted Ben pounding down the trail.

"What happened!?" Concern crimped his features. "Is everyone okay?"

"Fine," I said. "We met a wolf pack, but they left in peace. I got sick."

Ben looked a question at me, but because of Chance, didn't press. He gestured back the way he'd come. "I found the watchtower."

I noticed Ben was empty-handed. "Where are my tools?"

"By the fort. I had a sudden . . . feeling you guys needed help."

"Psychic?" Chance needled. "Who ya got in the Super Bowl?"

Ben's jaw tensed. "Forget it. Let's go."

We followed the moonlit trail downward into swampier terrain. Ravenous insects began to feast, sent invitations to all their friends and relatives. More than once we paused to slather on bug spray.

As we walked, Ben whistled "I've Been Working on the Railroad."

"You forget about our stalker?" Shelton complained.

"There must be a thousand gators on this island," Ben said. "I'd rather not surprise any that might be snoozing on this path."

Ten more paces. Shelton began humming "Who Let the Dogs Out?"

A stream took shape alongside the trail, eventually dumping into a large pond. Rising from the pond's shoreline was the steep wooded hill we'd seen from the boat.

"The watchtower must be up there." Ben pointed to the crest. "Highest point for miles around."

Hi squinted. "Could be. I see some broken stones littering the hilltop."

"There's a marker here." Shelton rubbed at the plaque, then read aloud. "'Near this site the first permanent European settlers of South Carolina landed on March 17, 1670, on their way to establish the settlement of Charles Town.' Man, that's *old*."

"This way." Ben led us along a narrower side path branching toward the water's edge. Shelton's humming grew louder. And shakier.

In twenty yards we reached the base of the hill. Grabbing my tool kit from where he'd left it, Ben started up a broken track barely visible in the moonlight.

As we climbed, questions lined up for attention.

Bonny's poem was cryptic and vague. Did we have the correct translation? The right location? What were we supposed to do next?

Bull Island is immense. We could spend years digging in random spots and still find nothing. To have any hope, we had to solve the clues.

At the summit, we stopped to catch our breath and look around. A ring of stones circled the tiny hilltop. From this vantage, I could see the whole island.

"Look at this." Shelton had dropped to a knee beside one of the rocks. "These were cut and fitted in place. This must've been the tower's foundation."

"So." Hi walked a circuit. "We're supposed to do what, exactly?"

"Focus on the poem," I said. "The first line said, 'On the moon's high day, seek Island People.'"

"Full moon on Bull Island," Shelton said. "Check and check."

"Then we move to line two," I said. "'Stand the high watch, hold to thy faith, and look to the sea.'"

"Hopefully we're standing the high watch right now," said Hi. "So we need to 'hold to thy faith and look to the sea.' Whatever that means."

"The last part is easy." Chance pointed. "There's the Atlantic."

Everyone gazed at the iridescent black ocean stretching endlessly eastward.

Across the pond, beyond a low wooded ridge, I could just make out a jumble of debris on the seaward shore.

We surveyed the eastern landscape for long minutes, seeking inspiration. Found none.

"Um." Hi shuffled his feet. "Okay."

"We skipped the middle part," Shelton said. "We're supposed to 'hold to thy faith' somehow."

"Which means?" Chance crossed his arms.

"Bonny's clues have been literal," I said. "What could we hold?"

Hi sucked in his breath, then scurried to my backpack. "The second rhyme from Bonny's treasure map had similar wording."

Of course! I felt like a dunce. "The riddle about the bridge!"

"Exactly." Hi withdrew and scanned the map. "Here, Bonny used the phrase 'thy faithful servant' to describe the correct lever to pull."

"The lever shaped like Bonny's Celtic cross!" Shelton was working his earlobe double-time.

"And we *have* Bonny's cross," Ben said. "A tangible thing."

"That makes sense." Chance pulled the cross from his pack and handed it to me.

"This cross has been the key," I said. "Bonny's touchstone. The symbolic expression of her faith."

"Don't just stand there!" Shelton was on fire.

"Do what, exactly?"

No one could answer.

"Talk the instructions through," Ben said. "Step by step."

Worth a shot.

"Stand the high watch."

I moved to the center of the hill.

"Hold to thy faith."

Grasping the cross with both hands, I held it aloft before me.

"Look to the sea."

I turned due east and faced the Atlantic Ocean.

Holding that position, I peered across the moonlit island. Searched. My arms soon grew heavy.

"Now what?" I said finally.

"See anything unusual?" Hi stepped up beside me. "If the treasure is hidden below, there must be some indication from this spot."

"Unless it's gone," Ben said. "That poem was written three hundred years ago."

"But nothing's changed!" Shelton whined. "There's been no development here. No houses. No sewers. No Time Warner Cable."

I studied the panorama below. "Hi, what am I seeing?"

"Jack's Creek. It's kind of a swampy lake that spreads out like an amoeba with tentacles. Shallow water riddled with sandbars and small islets."

"That's probably where the gators live," Chance said.

"A terrible place to bury valuables," Ben said. "You'd never get them back."

"What's beyond Jack's Creek?" I asked. "Straight east."

Hi checked his phone. "There's a ridge, then a wide beach."

"Hold up!" Shelton piped. "I forgot to tell you my hunch."

"Anytime you're ready," I said.

"We've followed Bonny's poem so far, but there's one line remaining."

"You're right." I recited the last part of Aunt Tempe's translation. "'Let a clear heart guide you through the field of bones.'"

"That stretch down there?" Shelton pointed to the debris-littered beach bordering the Atlantic. "It's called the Boneyard."

An electric sizzle traveled through me. "Why?"

"Hiking websites list Boneyard Beach as Bull Island's top attraction. The sand is littered with dead trees and branches, giving it the appearance of a graveyard of half-buried monster bones."

"Everything fits!" Hi exclaimed. "We must be looking in the right place!"

"But we don't know where to *dig*." Chance's frustration was making him cranky.

"I don't see you helping," Ben said. "All you do is complain."

I ignored the bickering.

There was a stirring deep in my brainpan. The tiniest jolt of recognition. What? Something Shelton said? Hiking? Bonny's poem?

No go. The idea refused to surface.

"Quiet!"

The other Virals stilled. Chance started to protest, thought better of it.

"Let Tory do her thing," Hi whispered. "Trust me, this is our best shot."

I shut out the chatter. Something about that last line nagged at me.

"'Let a clear heart guide you through the field of bones,'" I repeated. "Shelton's right—that must refer to the Boneyard. But the poem directed us to this watchtower first."

I spoke aloud, snapping facts together like Legos, encouraging the subliminal idea to the surface.

"Hold to thy faith, and look to the sea. I'm to stand *here*, but what I want is down on the beach. And I need the cross to find it."

The cross. Why was the cross important?

I rotated Bonny's artifact. "The top tine is bent?" I said. "Why?"

A design flaw? I didn't think so. The delicate curve made the cross utterly unique.

Using two hands, I spun the cross. The crystal in the central ring flashed in the moonlight.

Suddenly, the pieces aligned like the tumblers in Hollis Claybourne's safe.

"Anne," I whispered to the night. "I understand."

The boys watched in silence as I walked to the edge of the hillside.

"'On the moon's high day, seek Island People.'" I recited. "'Stand the high watch, hold to thy faith, and look to the sea.'"

"We did this already." The little patience Chance had started out with was long gone.

The other Virals shushed him.

"The cross *is* the key," I said. "The last line says, 'let a clear heart guide you through the field of bones.'"

"Wonderful. How does that help us?"

"Look at the cross, Chance. *Inside* the ring. What do you see?"

"The crystal? That's the clear heart?"

"Ohmygod," Shelton exhaled. "You've got it!"

Hi shook his head. "I'm lost. How can that guide us?"

"What strikes you as odd about this design?" I slowly tipped the cross this way and that.

"It's bent," Ben said.

"Exactly. *Why* is it bent?"

Holding the cross at eye level, I gazed down at the landscape below.

Felt a charge in my chest, as if someone had lit a match.

Identical mounds of rock rose on each side of Jack's Creek. They seemed wrong, out of place in the lowland swamp.

I aligned the two mounds with the horizontal arms of Bonny's cross.

Perfect fit.

"What are you doing?" Chance asked.

"This cross is going to reveal the treasure's location."

Hi was the first to catch on. "Hold the cross straight up and down. If the arms correspond to topographical features, this hill would be the bottom point."

I did as instructed, but lost the alignment. "I can't make it fit that way."

Ben smacked his forehead. "We're too low! There was a fort on this hilltop."

"The difference in elevation wouldn't be much!" Shelton exclaimed. "Martello towers were basically squatty stone shelters. The floor would've only been a yard or two higher!"

"Lift me," I said to Ben.

"Seriously?"

"Of course I'm serious!"

Chance dropped to a knee. "Hop on. I'm the tallest."

I swung my legs over Chance's shoulders. He rose easily and grabbed my ankles to help me balance.

I raised the cross. From my new vantage point, the mounds clicked into perfect formation.

Heart pounding, I squinted, one eye squeezed shut, searching for the final piece.

The bent upper tine had to align with something.

I pointed to a dark spot on the ridge fronting Boneyard Beach. "Is that water?"

"Moccasin Pond," Hi answered.

"Take two steps left," I instructed Chance. "Now a half step back."

Suddenly, everything slotted true. The curved portion of the cross arced to the center of Moccasin Pond.

I stared hard. The full moon was directly behind me, bright enough to tease details from the shadows below.

"There's an island in the pond!" I yelped. "A third pile of rocks!"

Three mounds of stone.

The crude landmarks triangulated perfectly with the three points of Bonny's cross.

Coincidence? Not a chance.

"Let a clear heart guide me." I peered through the crystal in the cross's center.

And saw nothing.

"Tory!" Hi pointed to the lower portion of the cross. "It's not vertical!"

"Got it." Orienting the cross fully upright, I realigned the three points.

A beam of moonlight shot from the crystal heart and knifed across the sky.

"Ohmygod!" Shelton squeaked.

"Get out!" Hi said.

"The full moon," Ben breathed.

The disk was lighting an object in the distance.

I craned my neck to see, terrified of losing the proper orientation.

The object was a massive tree, bone white, with skeletal branches fanning out like satanic fingers.

"Gotcha," I whispered.

The moon moved in its arc, and the beacon faded. I strained to absorb every detail, knowing I wouldn't get another chance.

"Stop squirming!" Chance placed a steadying hand on my back.

"It worked!" I screeched, twisting in excitement. "I know where to dig!"

Then I was tumbling.

Ben and Hi managed to break my fall. Chance wasn't as fortunate.

"Thanks, guys." Flat on his back, rubbing a shoulder. "Don't worry about me."

"Suck it up," Shelton said. "You dropped our fearless leader."

Chance sniffed. "She wouldn't last five seconds in a chicken fight."

"I know where to dig! I know where to dig!"

"Where?" Spoken as one.

"Get me to Boneyard Beach!"

CHAPTER 53

B en insisted we head back toward *Sewee* and walk along the coastline.

"We can't travel the inland paths at night," he said. "Full moon or not, you can't see anything down in that swamp."

"FYI, those marshes are known as Alligator Alley," Hi added.

"No thanks." Shelton shouldered his pack. "The long way sounds just fine."

We retraced our steps, then followed a deer track along the coastline. The moon now took up half the sky. The ocean was flat and smooth as glass, the air still and muggy. Every mosquito in the county was snacking on our sweat-slicked skin.

After a half hour, we swung back south and reached Boneyard Beach.

"I'll just say it." Hi gestured to the ghostly stretch before us. "This is the creepiest place in the world. So glad we came in the middle of the night."

Hundreds of dead trees lay on the beach, all bleached morgue-white by exposure to sun and salt water. The nickname was perfect. Gnarled trunks. Twisted limbs. The sand was strewn with corroded seashells and the carapaces of long-dead crustaceans. The place looked like a Paleozoic graveyard.

"Spread out," I said. "Look for a gigantic tree with branches spreading like Medusa's hair."

I crept through the Boneyard, stopping every few yards to check the hill across the lake. Finally, I locked onto target.

A petrified cedar, standing all alone.

The weathered old trunk was ten feet in diameter. Two yards above ground it divided into five limbs that snaked low across the sand. Every branch reached inland, as if running away from the sea.

The whole tree formed a lopsided V ten yards across at its widest point.

"The devil's hand!" Ben exclaimed. "Of course!"

"Come again?" Hi said.

"The Sewee legend!" Ben pumped his fist. "Remember what my uncle told me? 'When the night sky burned as daytime, a flaming brand mounted the field of bones, and staked the devil's hand.' This tree has to be it!"

Another piece clicked into place. "Anne Bonny had long red tresses, like flames. The story must describe the night she buried her treasure!"

"The Sewee wove the event into their oral history." Ben squeezed my shoulder. "We dig here."

"Okay, so this chunk of firewood is the devil's hand." Chance was sizing up the cedar. "Where do we stake it?"

Ben made a quick circuit, weaving through and clambering over the twisted, dead limbs.

"The branches all run inland," he said when finished. "Three on the right, two on the left. There's nothing noteworthy on the seaward side of the tree."

I walked inside the V and put my back to the trunk. Nestled between the tree's ancient arms, I felt sheltered and safe, protected from winds and tides.

If it were my treasure, I'd bury it here.

I drew a line in the wet sand. Crossed it with another.

"X marks the spot."

      ⬡   ⬡   ⬡

"We're digging in the wrong place!" Chance tossed his shovel from the hole and hopped out. "It's a dead end."

"Get back in here!" Ben snapped. "We've only gone a few feet."

"And found zilch." Chance stretched his arms wide. "It's been over an hour!"

"I'm barely winded. Don't be such a baby!"

The space between the branches had been converted to a makeshift excavation site. Buckets, shovels, and other implements lay scattered on the sand. Our electric lantern hung from a bough, lighting the inside of the deepening hole.

"This could be the wrong tree," Chance grumbled. "But say

it's not. If we're off by even a yard in any direction we'll dig right past whatever's down there. *If* anything's down there."

Hi and Shelton were leaning against the trunk, ropes in their hands, buckets at their feet. My role was more . . . supervisory.

"This is the right spot," I said. "I'm positive."

"Based on what?" Chance crossed his arms. "Convince me."

"This tree has a substantial root system, but none stretch under this one spot. Also, from here there's a direct line of sight to the watchtower."

"That's it?" Chance was incredulous. "That's your brilliant reasoning? You can see a hundred dead trees from that tower!"

"The cross sighted on *this* tree, and we're excavating the only reasonable location near it."

Chance pointed at Hi and Shelton. "Why can't they dig?"

"They're holding the safety ropes." Ben tossed a shovelful of dirt over his shoulder, forcing Chance to dance aside. "Sand holes are inherently dangerous. If the sides cave in, we need someone to pull us out."

Chance snorted. "Tubby and Tiny here?"

Hi bristled. "We're stronger than we look."

"Keep yapping," said Shelton. "We won't bother with you."

"Enough." I pointed Chance back into the hole. "Dig."

O   O   O

Another hour. Three more feet.

Hi and Shelton were slumped against the tree, taking a break from hauling buckets. Ben and Chance had slowed noticeably.

No one would meet my eye. I could sense a rebellion forming.

And they were right.

I should've called it off earlier, but couldn't handle the disappointment. I'd been so sure.

Thunk.

"Was that your foot?" Ben's voice sounded muffled down in the pit.

"No," Chance said. "My blade hit something."

Thunk thunk thunk.

Clank.

"What was that?"

Hi's question roused Shelton from a light doze. "Wha happa?"

"Holy crap!" Chance sounded funny.

"Find the corners!" Ben ordered.

"Guys?" I stepped to the rim and peered down into the hole. Ben and Chance were on their knees, clawing with their bare hands.

"Get back from the edge!" Ben ordered.

"Spades!" Chance barked. "Now!"

"Okay, okay!"

Heart hammering, I grabbed two trowels and returned to the pit.

"Incoming!" I dropped the implements. "What did you find?"

No reply.

Sand and mud flew from the pit.

"It's wood!" Ben yelled. "I think it's a chest of some kind!"

"Rope!" Chance called. "We'll have to haul it up!"

Shelton grabbed two lengths of nylon rope and chucked them into the hole. Moments later, the coils came flying back out.

"Keep one end up there, you idiot!"

"Sorry dude!" Shelton was bouncing on the balls of his feet. Hi gave him a calm-down gesture with both hands.

I lowered one end of each rope. Ben and Chance worked quickly, exchanging words I couldn't hear, hostilities forgotten.

"Ready," Chance yelled. "Send down the escalator!"

Shelton, Hi, and I hefted a six-foot length of spiky driftwood we'd placed beside the pit.

"Ready?" I asked.

"Ready!" *Jinx.*

Working together, we maneuvered one end of the log into the hole. Ben and Chance seated the crude ladder, then cautiously climbed out.

Once both were safely topside, we withdrew the driftwood. The pit held.

"We found something!" Ben was trying to contain his excitement but failing. "Whatever's down there is *definitely* manmade!"

"We tied lines to handles on both ends." Chance had four ropes looped around his forearm. "We just need to pull it out!"

"Four corners," Hi instructed. "If everyone hauls at once, the pit shouldn't collapse."

We raced into position, everyone bursting with frenzied energy.

"Turn your back to the hole, shoulder your rope, and walk slowly away." Hi had belly-crawled to the pit's edge. "If you move in unison, the load should stay balanced."

"Ready?" Ben glanced from face to face. Everyone nodded.

"Step! Step! Step!" Hi called out the cadence.

I felt resistance at first, then it lessened. There was a soft grating like sandpaper moving on wood.

"Step! Step! Step!"

I inched forward, muscles straining.

Something snagged and my rope went taut.

"Put your backs into it!" Hi urged. "Just a few more feet!"

I leaned my shoulder forward, dug in my heels, and tugged with all my might.

I heard a clonk, then the *shush* of cascading sand.

"It's up!" Hi called.

Ben tied his rope to a branch and raced to Hi's side. A dirt-crusted chest hung suspended an inch above the hole.

"Hurry!" Shelton whined. "I can't hold much longer."

Ben grabbed for the nearest handle and steadied the box with two hands. Hi snagged the other side.

"Shelton and Tory, release on the count of three. Chance, hang tight. Ben and I will pull the chest toward us."

"Uno! Dos! Tres!"

Shelton and I dropped our lines as Ben and Hi hauled backward.

The chest slid onto the sand between them.

Just like that, the treasure was ours.

CHAPTER 54

We gathered around the chest.

Behind it, the pit gaped like an open wound in the earth. The petrified cedar loomed just beyond, cupping our little band like a vast skeletal hand.

The full moon cast long, ghostlike shadows across the beach.

We huddled close, shocked into silence, barely daring to believe that our find was real.

We found Anne Bonny's treasure. It really happened.

As the realization rocketed home, I began clawing away centuries of grime. Other hands joined mine.

The chest was dark brown, constructed of wooden slats nailed to a stout wooden frame. Thick metal banding reinforced its sides and corners. The top was domed, like a small coffin.

Wooden handles were nailed to both ends. A rusty latch and padlock secured the lid. Though clearly ancient, the chest looked rugged and durable, capable of surviving centuries underground.

"Good Lord!" Chance looked stunned. "An honest-to-god treasure chest!"

"Of course!" Hi laughed. "You thought we were digging to China?"

"It just hit me." Chance ran both hands through his hair. "I mean, *look*! We just pulled a freaking pirate chest from the freaking sand!"

"I feel you." Shelton's fists were pressed to his temples. "I never thought we'd actually find something. It's a *whole* different ball game now."

Ben knuckle-rapped the chest. "Sturdy."

"Test the lock." I was too amped to say more.

"They built to last back then." Ben tugged the padlock, but it didn't budge. "We'll need a tool of some kind."

"Try this." Hi tossed him a shovel.

Ben wedged the blade against the hasp and raised a foot to stomp down.

A voice rang out from the dunes behind us.

"Enough!"

Ben spun, shovel in hand.

I sprang to switch off the lantern, then crab-scuttled back to the chest.

Chance froze, uncertain, blinking to regain his night vision.

Hi and Shelton crouched, eyes wide with fright.

"Who's there?" I called.

Before us was a short stretch of beach that led to the dunes. Behind, the snaking limbs of the dead cedar hemmed us in on both sides. Drifting clouds temporarily blocked the moon, keeping the beach dim and obscure.

A shadow moved toward us in the darkness. My heart thudded in my chest.

The clouds parted. Moonlight poured through.

I recognized a familiar figure.

"I won't act like I'm not impressed."

Chris Fletcher stood a dozen yards away wearing faded jeans and a dark CU hoodie. His hands were tucked into the sweatshirt's front pouch.

"I'm serious." His easy smile looked sinister in the pale lunar light. "People have searched for Bonny's treasure for hundreds of years, but you actually found it. Bravo!"

"What are you doing here?" Stupid. It was all I could think to say. Chris's unexpected appearance had frightened me badly.

"Just out for a stroll. You?"

"You already seem to know." Ben's tone was granite.

"True." Chris's blue eyes looked cold in the moonlight. "So maybe we can cut the bullshit."

"Who are you?" Chance was clueless. "Do you work for the Refuge?"

"His name is Chris Fletcher." Ben still gripped a shovel. "He's a grad student at CU, works at the Charleston Museum."

"Don't forget my world-famous ghost tour."

Given the circumstances, Chris's levity was unnerving.

My instincts screamed in warning.

I caught Hi's eye, motioned with a hand behind my back. He

nodded, tugged Shelton's sleeve. Together they inched backward around the pit.

I edged to my left. Chris's eyes followed me, but he made no move.

"Listen up, Grad Student Chris Fletcher." Chance's tone was cool. "This is a private party, and you're not welcome. Run along."

"I don't think so."

"You don't? Ben. Help me convince good ole Chris here that it's past time he left."

The two boys started forward, Ben still holding the shovel.

Chris pulled a Glock 20 semi-automatic pistol from the pocket of his sweatshirt.

The boys stopped dead. Ben dropped the implement and raised both hands.

Shelton gasped. My eyes fixed on the Glock's muzzle, knowing its deadly power.

Chris spoke in a very low voice. "Get the picture now?"

Chance and Ben retreated a few steps.

"Good." Chris craned his neck. "And tell the fat kid and his wimpy friend to stop sneaking around back there."

I took a baby step left. Encountered a branch on its serpentine journey across the sand.

Go. Get help.

I was about to slip under the bough when something clicked in the blackness beside me.

Adrenaline pumping, I turned.

Sallie Fletcher faced me from across the dead limb.

Smiling, she motioned me backward with her own gun.

"They came alone." Sallie slipped around the branch and walked to Chris's side. "Just one boat, anchored near the northern point."

"I expected nothing less," Chris replied. "These kids are incredibly resourceful."

Chance, Ben, and I stood shoulder to shoulder in front of the treasure chest. Hi and Shelton were behind, on the far side of the hole.

The cursed tree had us trapped. The only exit was straight through the Fletchers.

"What do you want?" I asked.

"Let's start with answers. How'd you discover Bonny's escape route? Who told you to look in the Provost Dungeon?"

"No one. We figured it out ourselves."

"It was *you* in the tunnels." Ben's voice sounded menacing, despite our situation. "You tried to kill us."

Chris ignored him. "You just figured it out? Impossible. Sallie and I researched Anne Bonny for two solid years. All you did was swipe a worthless map."

"Map?"

Sallie laughed. "Did you really think you could steal an artifact that easily?"

"I didn't notice at first." Chris sounded amused. "But something about you guys seemed . . . off, so I checked the case the next day. Guess what? No map."

"Why didn't you report it stolen?" I was genuinely puzzled.

"We couldn't believe you swiped it." Sallie shook her head. "The crime was so audacious, so reckless! You had to know *something*. We decided to wait and see."

"Her plan." Chris squeezed his wife's side. "And it worked. Glad I listened."

The situation was surreal. Our conversation was amiable, a friendly chat.

Except for the guns pointed at our chests.

"You guys are tough to follow." Chris scratched his chin. "Boats. Cars. Pawnshops. It got overwhelming. Luckily, you came right to us."

"The ghost tour," Ben said sourly.

"You two suck at espionage." Hi spoke from behind me. "Next time you tail someone, lose the bright red Studebaker."

Chris's brow wrinkled. "We drive a Prius, you dope."

"The ghost tour business is a front, isn't it?" I asked. "You used it as cover to search underneath East Bay Street."

"Looking for Lady Peregrine's roost." Sallie nodded. "We knew Bonny's tunnel had to be near the East Bay docks. But we combed the Provost Dungeon a dozen times, and never once noticed a loose stone. How did you know to look there?"

"What was inside the last chamber?" Greed hardened Chris's voice. "How did you know to come to Bull Island?"

I held out a hand. "Give up the gun and we'll talk about it."

"You'll tell us everything!" Sallie's sudden anger was alarming. "We study and search for two years, find nothing, but you brats solve the mystery in one week? Impossible. You had help. Who? We know others are looking, too."

Silence. No point in responding.

"Not knowing is *killing* me!" Chris said playfully. "When we lost you underground, I was *sure* you'd stolen our treasure. We almost didn't bother plugging the bolt-hole, but Sallie convinced me to keep the faith."

"Always trust your spouse!" Sallie blew him a kiss. "Thankfully, we'd planted a cell phone in your boat. That made tracking you easy. By boat, at least."

Chris chuckled. "We even searched that ridiculous cabin top to bottom. Found nothing. It was very depressing."

"You'll pay for that," Chance promised. "That's Claybourne property."

"Imagine our surprise tonight!" Chris was rolling. "I don't know how you learned the treasure was out here, but thanks for doing the legwork."

"Piss off!" Ben spat.

"Step away from the chest." Suddenly, Sallie was all business. "And hand over the map."

"*We* found the chest," Chance said coldly. "By law it belongs to us. Even if you steal it tonight, we'll get it back. Only *we* know how it was found. Good luck explaining yourselves when the police come knocking."

"Shut up, Chance." Hi was watching the Fletchers carefully. "These two are dangerous."

"Your friend is smarter than you, rich boy." Chris pulled back the slide on his Glock. "Maybe it'd be better if you disappeared. No competing claims that way, right?"

"Just one *incredible* tale!" Sallie's teeth flashed. "Meet the fabulous Fletchers! Hear how they decoded an ancient map, discovered long-forgotten tunnels beneath our city's streets, and found Anne Bonny's lost treasure!"

"Fortune and glory," Chris said. "Modern day Indiana Joneses. We'll be renowned archaeologists before finishing grad school. Not to mention filthy rich."

"People will search for us," Shelton said in a timid voice. "Hundreds."

"But not here," Chris promised. "No one will ever connect Bull Island to Anne Bonny."

"Admit it." Sallie's tone was taunting. "You snuck out tonight. No one knows you're here. When your boat is discovered in Breach Inlet, everyone will assume you drowned after capsizing. One midnight cruise too many."

"Sad," Chris said.

"And look, honey!" Sallie pointed her gun at the gaping hole in the sand. "The kids were thoughtful enough to dig their own grave."

CHAPTER 55

There was no time to plan.

The Fletchers had us trapped between the twisting branches of the cedar. It'd be over in seconds.

I don't remember reaching, but my canine double helix suddenly took charge.

SNAP.

The flare burned like a brush fire out of control.

My senses exploded, battering seams at every level of my brain.

Raw energy sizzled through my body, stronger than ever before. The deluge nearly overwhelmed me.

Full moon.

We had only moments. I scanned our attackers, seeking an opening.

Sallie's chest rose and fell. She licked her lips. Often. Too often. My eyes read "Walther P99" stamped on the barrel of her gun.

Chris's muscles were taut as piano wire. His knuckles bulged white on the handle of his Glock.

They'd do it. More, they'd *enjoy* doing it. I knew this with bone-deep certainty.

The Fletchers would murder us all to safeguard their chance at celebrity.

As before, I closed my lids and plumbed the depths of my subconscious.

In my mind's eye, I stood on an empty black field. Ben appeared beside me. Then Shelton. Then Hi. I felt Coop in the distance, disturbed, tossing in his sleep.

Fiery cables linked the five of us, connecting the group like flashing puppet strings. I reached out and touched the closest one.

Immediately, I heard Ben's thoughts. Racing. Furious. It was the same connection we'd shared in the underwater tunnel, only clearer and sharper.

Excited, I grabbed the lines running to Shelton and Hi. Their minds opened. Their thoughts flowed to me.

Then, for the first time, I noticed myself. Golden light haloed my body, encircling me in a ring of yellow fire.

Why was I gleaming, but not the other Virals?

In a flash, I understood. And didn't waste time. My dream self gathered the fiery cables together. Tugged. The glow spread outward from me to the other Virals.

Focusing all my strength, I willed a message to them.

Chris and Sallie are about to shoot! Prepare to scatter!

The boys tensed as the flares took hold. Ben clenched his fists. Hi dropped to one knee. Shelton moaned softly as tremors wracked his thin frame.

In seconds, six golden eyes blazed like mine.

"What are you doing?" Sallie waived the Walther. "Nobody move."

Chris was staring at Ben. "What's wrong with your pupils?"

Chance turned and met my gaze. His eyes widened, then darted to Shelton and Hi. "Golden eyes!" he whispered. "They *do* glow!"

"Enough." Sallie raised her pistol and took aim at my head.

Time slowed.

Now!

I was coiled to spring when a blood-curdling howl split the night.

Sallie started in surprise.

Chris cast a nervous glance toward the dunes at his back.

A second howl sounded. A third. The noise seemed to come from all around us.

A foreign presence entered my mindscape. Unconnected. *Not* a Viral.

The aura was alien, yet somehow familiar. I tried to make contact. Primal thoughts brushed against my psyche.

We come.

Images flashed in my brain. Ancient memories from another species.

Stalking a deer through a stand of sea oats. Wrestling with

littermates on a chalky white dune. Sleeping surrounded by the warmth of a pack.

A red-brown form appeared in my mind, four-legged, snout up and sniffing the breeze.

White Muzzle.

I sensed the red wolf and his pack racing down the beach.

We come, brothers.

Sallie and Chris were moving with short, jerky motions, unnerved by the baying all around them.

Stooping quickly, I grabbed the shovel at my feet.

The movement caught Sallie's attention.

"Time's up, Little Miss." She aimed the Walther with one trembling hand. "In your next life, remember to mind your own business."

Blood pounded in my ears. No place to run. No chance to dodge.

A brown streak burst from the shadows and clipped Sallie's legs. She screamed as she went down, firing wildly.

Crack! Crack!

Bullets struck a branch above my head.

More howls sounded in the night.

Chris whipped right, then left, unsure which direction to face.

Two blurs shot from the dunes and knocked Chris to the sand. He rolled, futilely searching for targets.

I sent another message to the Virals.

Ben! Take out Chris! Hi and Shelton, distract Sallie!

Moving like quicksilver, Ben dove and tackled Chris before he could stand. The Glock flew, dropped. The two rolled, scratching and clawing to retrieve it.

"Get away from him!" Sallie rose to her knees and leveled the Walther on Ben.

Two more red-brown shapes buzzed close. Sallie cowered, eyes fearful.

Then a fist-sized rock winged past her face.

Sallie spun, cursing.

Shelton chucked again, then ducked behind the treasure chest.

"Bastard!" Sallie screeched.

A conch shell zinged through the air and struck her shoulder. She swung the gun quickly and caught Hi in the crosshairs.

"Blaaah!" Hi dove headfirst into the pit.

"Bad move, you little prick!" Sallie scrambled to the edge and took aim. "Enjoy your final resting place."

I sprang forward and swung the shovel at Sallie's head. The blade connected with a sickening thud. "Nighty night, bitch."

Sallie's eyes rolled backward. She wobbled a moment, then collapsed and lay still.

Hi's voice floated up from below. "Nice cut, A-Rod!"

Ben was still struggling with Chris on the beach.

"Claybourne!" he gasped. "A little help!"

The words snapped Chance from his shock.

Racing forward, he jumped on Chris from behind. Momentarily freed, Ben kicked Chris in the stomach, driving the wind from his chest. Then Chance's fist connected to Chris's temple and he crumpled to the sand.

Shelton scuttled forward and scooped up both guns. "Anyone know where the safeties are?" Then he threw up on the beach.

"Your eyes." Chance was panting, staring at Ben. "Why do they glow like that?"

Ben turned his back.

Chance's gaze shot to me.

"Yours too!" Chance stumbled to his feet. "All of you!"

"Chance." I had no idea what to say next.

"What are you, some kind of cult?" Chance backpedaled, face swiveling from Viral to Viral. "I saw this before. That night, in my basement! It *wasn't* a dream. I'm *not* crazy!"

"If you'd just—"

"Did you summon those animals here!?!" Chance's voice was taut with horror. "How did you all move so fast!?!"

"Relax." I reached out to calm him. "There's nothing to—"

"Stay away!" Chance turned and bolted down the beach.

"Wait! The boat's in the other direction!"

But he was gone.

"We have to go," Ben said. "Right now."

I spread my arms. "And leave Chance out here?"

"No choice." Hi was already gathering tools. "Shots were fired. We don't know who heard, or if these two psychopaths came alone. Time to make tracks."

I groaned, frustrated. But the boys were right.

Working quickly, we broke down the work site, keeping a close watch on the unconscious duo sprawled on the sand. In minutes we were packed and ready to go.

"We just leave them here?" Shelton asked. "They tried to kill us. Twice."

"You have a better idea?" Ben grabbed the chest by one handle, motioned for Hi to take the other. "We can't both escape with the loot and deal with police. I choose the treasure. Otherwise, what was the point?"

"Seconded," Hi said.

"Agreed." I shook my head to clear it. "We can plot our next move once we're safe."

"Okay." With two semi-automatics tucked in his belt, Shelton looked quite the gangster.

"Ready?" Ben hoisted his end of the chest.

"Ready." Hi lifted the other.

Shelton and I shouldered the remaining tools, buckets, and other equipment. With our flares still burning, we had strength to spare.

The boys started off down the beach.

I paused, concentrated hard, and fired one last message into the ether.

Thank you, brothers.

Moments later, canine voices yipped in the night.

CHAPTER 56

B en cut the motor.

    Sewee bobbed in the current. We'd just rounded Isle of Palms and come alongside Sullivan's Island. Ahead lay Charleston Harbor, Morris Island, and home.

Dawn was less than an hour away. The moon was setting, but still reflected off the ocean, lighting the night. With my flare extinguished, I was dog tired.

"Why are we stopped?" I suppressed a yawn.

"You can't be serious." Ben powered the lamp.

Shelton's brows rose. "What are you, some kind of robot?"

"What?" I hadn't a clue.

"Anne Bonny's infamous, long-lost pirate treasure." Hi touched his forehead, then his hand shot toward the chest. "*Right there*. Get it?"

"Time to open this puppy." Shelton rubbed his palms. "After what we've been through, I wanna see some gold bars. Diamond rings!"

I started to protest, then stopped. Why not open it now? There was no real reason to wait, and the boys were clearly out of patience.

"First things first." I pointed to the two handguns. "Over the side."

"What?" Ben frowned. "Why?"

"Because we have to get rid of them."

"The insane curators should be waking up about now," Ben argued. "And we still don't know who tailed us in the Studebaker. We need to protect ourselves."

I crossed my arms. "What do you know about guns?"

"Plenty," Ben said. "My father has a whole rack."

"You willing to hide two semi-automatic pistols at your house?" I turned to Hi and Shelton. "How about you two? They aren't coming home with me."

"The guns could stay in the bunker," Shelton said. "We could hide them in the back room near the old mineshaft."

"We do *not* need guns." I caught and held Shelton's eye. "Are you really ready to shoot someone?"

He looked away.

"I'm with Tory," Hi said. "I get nervous just talking about firearms. We've done fine so far without packing heat."

"It's not who we are," I said. "We don't need guns to protect ourselves."

Ben sighed, then picked up both weapons and tossed them overboard.

"Now can we open it?" Hi wheedled.

I flashed a wicked grin. "Try to stop me!"

"Shoot!" Shelton shook a fist in frustration. "I didn't bring my lock-pick set."

Ben reached for the excavation tools. "Give me room."

We spread out as best we could. Ben wedged a chisel against the padlock and began hammering. For five minutes the lock held. Then . . .

Clunk.

The hasp gave.

"I promise to still hang with you guys when I'm super loaded," Hi said. "The swank life won't change me. Much."

"Open it open it open it!" Shelton squealed.

Ben moved aside. "We found it because of Tory. She has the honor."

"Tory! Tory! Tory!" Hi and Shelton chanted in unison.

After executing a mock bow, I flipped open the latch and pushed back on the lid.

Ancient hinges creaked.

I peered into the trunk's dark interior, the boys crowding close around me.

No one spoke.

No one moved.

We gaped, dumbstruck, eyes transfixed by the sight before us.

The chest was empty.

PART FOUR:
BOOTY

CHAPTER 57

The full moon glowed like a spotlight, illuminating the lonely parking lot below.

Making the job that much easier.

Just one car was present, pulled close to a ramp adjoining an empty dock.

Above, eyes watched.

It was the deepest part of night, that dark period halfway between midnight and dawn.

A rough gravel road descended to the waterfront. On its shoulder, a second car idled, concealed from view.

A match flared inside the vehicle, ignited a tiny red circle. Smoke streamed outward, spread, then escaped in tendrils through a cracked window.

Suddenly, a soft buzzing carried over the water.

Finally.

Another pull. The circle flamed brighter. A diaphanous cloud swirled within the confined space.

Seconds ticked by. The buzzing deepened, grew louder.

A boat appeared in the blackness and slowly puttered to the pier. Aboard, two figures worked to tie up the vessel. They moved slowly, as though underwater or deeply fatigued.

The pair disembarked in silence and trudged up the ramp. Keys jingled. Headlights flashed on the car beside the ramp. A *whop-whop* disengaged the locks.

On the access-road shoulder, a car door opened.

The fiery circle tumbled through the air and landed in a shower of angry sparks.

Go time.

Boots crunched downward toward their target.

CHAPTER 58

I should've just banged my head against a wall.

I'd have gotten the same results, only quicker, and with less pain.

"I'm done with this nonsense." Shelton spread his hands in a wipe-away gesture. "D-O-N-E. Done! Put a fork in me."

His dramatics startled Coop, who padded over to investigate.

Wednesday afternoon. Another bunker meeting, after another all-night adventure. And, once again, nothing to show for our efforts.

The only good luck I had working was Kit's heavy sleeping.

"Calm down!" I said. "We shouldn't rush into any—"

"This thing has gotten *way* out of hand," Shelton blurted. "We almost got killed. Our powers went berserk. And there's no treasure anyway! It's time to throw in the towel."

"You did it again, Tory," Hi said quietly. "Telepathy. Forcing us to flare. And for Shelton and me, it was the second burn that night. Did you learn anything?"

"No." My fist hit the table. "I don't know how I do it. I tried to connect with you and Shelton when we first saw the wolves with Chance, but it wouldn't work. Then later, at the dig site, the contact came easily."

"Any theories?" Hi asked.

I shook my head. "I can't explain how I reached you guys when the Fletchers showed up. I just did."

"Terror?" Ben guessed. "Danger?"

"I was plenty nervous when the wolves circled us, believe me."

"For some reason, Tory seems to flare the strongest." Hi turned to me. "You can tap our minds, but we can't return the favor. Only you can flare twice in a row. Only you can *force* the other Virals to burn. And we have no idea why."

"Did you call those wolves?" Shelton seemed afraid of what I might answer. "Could you talk to them?"

"Yes and no. They might've contacted me; I can't be sure. But I heard White Muzzle's voice in my head, just like I've heard Coop's before." Pause. "At least, I think I heard it."

That was a showstopper. The boys were struck silent.

"I'm getting closer to the answers," I said. "I can feel it."

"You don't even know what you're doing!" Shelton started ticking off fingers. "Let's recap. We're infected with an unknown supervirus. We *cannot* control it. We don't know what crazy side effects might happen next. Our bodies might be spiraling out of control."

My gaze hardened. "We can't hide under our beds."

"You want to keep treasure hunting?" Shelton sounded

exasperated. "Looking for what, exactly? We *found* the damn chest. It's a blank."

"We should call the cops now," Hi argued. "The Fletchers tried to kill us. Since there's no treasure to hide, there's no reason not to bust them."

"With what evidence?" I rubbed circles on my temples. "It's our word against theirs, and we stole the museum's treasure map. The Fletchers can turn us in anytime they want. No one will believe our story."

"We dropped our trump cards over the side," Ben groused. "Those guns would've been useful as evidence."

"Give me a break. I didn't know the chest would be empty."

"Twice we've risked our necks, found zilch." Shelton crossed his arms. "Now insane married treasure-hunter museum curators are stalking us. Tell me the good news."

"I found the phone they used to track *Sewee*," Ben said. "Stashed under the life vests. It's now at the bottom of the Atlantic with their weapons."

"Chris said they don't drive a Studebaker." Hi rubbed a chubby cheek. "Think he was lying?"

I spread my palms. Who knows?

"And don't forget Chance." Shelton was in a state. "He saw our eyes. He could cause *big* trouble now."

Shelton's words reminded me of a topic I'd been avoiding.

"Chance isn't the only one," I muttered. "Two days ago, I made a mistake at cotillion. I flashed my eyes at Madison Dunkle."

"You did what!?" Shelton popped to his feet.

"Tory, no!" Hiram's eyes were dinner plates.

"Quiet!" Ben raised a hand. "Tell us what happened."

I did. Every last detail. When I'd finished, the boys sat mute, considering the implications of my actions.

"Maybe you can play it off," Shelton suggested. "Pretend it was a trick with the lighting. Or funny contact lenses."

I nodded, but wasn't convinced.

"You're *sure* Courtney and Ashley didn't see?" Ben asked.

"Reasonably. I leaned close to Madison for maximum effect."

Hi shook his head. Shelton's gaze found the ceiling.

"Look, it was stupid. I know that."

My statement was greeted by vigorous nods.

"But only Madison saw, and she isn't likely to talk. *Everyone* heard me tell her off, and I was incredibly rude. If she starts saying weird things about me now, no one will believe her. Plus, she'll look weak."

"You can smell people's emotions?" Shelton had retaken his seat on the bench. "Seriously? That's kind of dope."

I shrugged. "Sometimes. Hi and I did some research, and it's not as wacky as it sounds. You just need a crazy-good nose."

To clean the slate, I told Ben and Shelton about my flare at the yacht club, and how I'd used my sniffing power to read Lonnie Bates.

"How many times *have* you flared in public?" Ben scowled. "Ridiculous."

"So dogs *can* smell fear." Shelton scratched Coop's ears. "I knew it."

"We need to keep Chance away from Madison," Hi said. "Both have seen too much, but alone, neither would be believed. Together? Different story."

"Chance saw the most," Ben said grimly. "He's witnessed *two* separate flare incidents. The whole deal. He's a major threat now."

"Maybe an alligator ate him," Shelton joked lamely.

"Plus, Chance is an escaped mental patient," Hi added. "That's not exactly the apex of the credibility pyramid."

"He won't go to the police," Ben guessed. "Chance thinks we found treasure."

"We'll deal with Chance when he turns up," I said. "Right now, we need to focus on our next move."

"Let it go!" Shelton slapped his knees in frustration.

"There's no move to make, Tory." Hi pointed to the empty chest resting against the bunker wall. "We found the treasure, and it's right there. Nothing."

"We can't just quit." I sounded like a broken record. "If we do, I'll be moving to freaking Alabama!"

That got their attention.

"That's right. Kit has accepted an offer. I'll be gone in a month."

"Me too," Hi said quietly. "My dad lined up a gig in Missouri. Some chemical factory. I've been waiting for the right time to tell you guys."

"We're moving, too." Shelton kicked a tennis ball. Coop scampered after it. "Palo Alto. Next month. But hey, West Coast is the best coast, right?"

Worse and worse. My eyes flicked to Ben.

"*I'll* still be here. Only over in Mount Pleasant, with my mom. She's enrolling me at Wando High." Ben gave a tough-guy shrug. "Could be okay."

For a long moment, no one spoke. Each Viral was wrapped in his or her own gloomy thoughts. The meeting now felt like a hospital vigil. Our pack was on life support.

"We have to keep at it." I tried for one last rally. "We can't allow *anything* to split us up! I'm afraid."

Hi crossed the room and placed a hand on mine.

"I wish things could be different, too." His eyes were glassy. "But sometimes you can't win. We're just kids."

With those words, he ducked into the crawl and slipped out of the bunker.

Shelton bailed next, wiping his eyes. Ben followed, unwilling to meet my gaze. That left Coop and me.

I got down and rubbed his snout. Coop rolled to his back, delighted by my attention.

"You won't leave me, will you boy?"

The tension of the last week finally overwhelmed my defenses. Anguish rocked me.

I wanted Mom. Needed the warmth of her embrace. The soothing, familiar comfort of her hands stroking my hair, her arms hugging me, her lips whispering that everything would be okay. That I was safe. Loved.

And I couldn't have it. Not then, or ever again.

I cried and cried and cried, my only comfort the

companionship of my loyal wolfdog. We huddled together on the bunker floor, me weeping, Coop licking the tears from my cheeks.

I'd never felt more beaten.

CHAPTER 59

"Get a grip, Victoria. Stop feeling sorry for yourself."

Coop cocked an ear.

"Not you, big guy." I scratched his snout. "Mommy's upset that everyone threw in the towel."

Maybe the boys were right. What else could we do?

There were no more riddles or poems. No treasure map to follow.

The task was complete. We'd navigated Bonny's trail of clues and successfully dug up her prize. Five feet from me, a pirate chest rested against the wall.

Totally empty.

So why couldn't I let it go? Why was I *convinced* the treasure was still out there?

Intuition? Instinct?

Or was it something less pleasant? Delusion. Denial of reality. Avoidance of a hard truth.

Screw that.

I wasn't quitting until I had no choice. Loggerhead was counting on me.

Save the psychology for someone who cares.

Who knows? Anne Bonny might be my long-lost ancestor. Her treasure might belong to me by birthright.

No backing down yet. Not while I had bullets left to fire.

Palming tears from my cheeks, I scooted over to the chest. It was all I had left to work with.

My fingers traced the trunk's grime-crusted exterior. The frame was still solid, even after three centuries underground.

The lid seemed flawless in design and construction. Bringing my eyes close, I scanned where its lip met the box frame. Unmarred. No divots, cracks, or gouges.

Conclusion: the chest had never been forced open.

Until we popped the padlock, the contents were undisturbed.

What did that mean?

"Two possibilities," I said aloud. "One, the chest was buried empty. Two, the chest was buried containing treasure, dug up later, and then reburied empty."

Neither scenario made sense. Why conceal an empty chest? Why protect it with elaborate riddles and traps? What purpose would that serve?

I couldn't imagine anything less rational than spending time and energy to entomb a vacant trunk six feet underground.

Unless it was a double-cross.

What if someone swiped the booty at the last possible moment?

I frowned. If *that's* what happened, Bonny's treasure was long gone.

My mind shifted to the second theory, which had its own problems.

If someone dug up the treasure, why bother reburying the chest? Why not take the money and run?

Maybe the treasure was relocated for greater security.

Bonny was plainly obsessed with safety measures. She'd already moved her loot once.

My pulse cranked up a notch. If the treasure was moved, and the chest reburied in the original hiding place, there was only one reason.

"So someone else could follow! That means leaving clues!"

Coop looked up at the sound of my voice, went back to chewing his tennis ball.

Excited, I examined the chest with a more critical eye. Rubbed my hands over every inch of its outer surface. Still found nothing.

Opening the lid, I began tapping the wooden slats comprising the frame, hoping an answer would reveal itself. None did.

Then I noticed something.

One corner of the chest held a small mound of debris. Dust. Sand. Dry vegetation. In our dejection, we hadn't bothered to inspect it.

I scooped a handful and probed gently. Three pebbles emerged from the dirt. Small, round, and uniform in size and color, the objects seemed somehow out of place.

Setting the stones aside, I scooped another handful. This

mix contained a number of strange dried leaves. I'd never seen anything like them before.

I thought back to the beach surrounding the dig site. The sand had been littered with seashells and the occasional dead branch, but there'd been no plants growing nearby. And we hadn't opened the chest until safely aboard *Sewee*.

My excitement buzzed to a new level. The leaves and pebbles weren't introduced during our dig. They must've been inside the chest all along.

The remaining dirt held nothing of interest.

I sat staring at the two small piles.

Leaves. Pebbles.

Were these the clues I was seeking?

"Am I nuts, Coop?"

The wolfdog offered no answer to that.

It was a wild hunch that things weren't finished. Only a fanatic would look at a handful of rubbish and see puzzle pieces.

"Then color me crazy," I whispered.

Moving quickly, I tackled Cooper and rubbed noogies on his forehead. He responded by gnawing my arm.

"I may be losing it, dog breath, but we are *not* done yet!"

CHAPTER 60

"Just hear me out!" I shouted.

At my request, we'd reassembled in Shelton's garage. His father's workshop was the best place to examine my finds.

The Allies at Normandy hadn't encountered such determined resistance.

"I don't wanna!" Shelton whined. "You'll start talking, and pretty soon we'll all start nodding, and then the next thing you know, I'm hang gliding off the Eiffel Tower at midnight, being chased by ninja vampires. No deal!"

Ben smacked the back of Shelton's head.

"Inside that crazy rant is a kernel of truth." Hi folded his arms. "We found the trunk, Tory. It's a dead end."

"But think," I urged. "Why bury an empty chest, unless you're sending a message to whoever finds it later?"

"The message was received." Ben displayed his middle finger. "Ha ha. You lose."

"Maybe, but the lid was undamaged, meaning whoever removed the contents had access to the key. I think Bonny relocated the treasure again and left clues for someone to follow."

"Who?" Shelton, voice skeptical.

"Mary Read."

His hands flew up. "She was DEAD!"

"Maybe Bonny DIDN'T KNOW!" I shouted back.

"Enough!" Ben glared at each of us in turn. "Tory's the reason we found the chest. Let's hear what she has to say. We owe her that much."

Shelton rolled his eyes. Hi screwed his mouth sideways, but said nothing.

Ben jabbed a finger at me. "But no promises, Brennan. I'm not wild about chasing pipe dreams, and we almost got killed doing it. Twice."

"This is how it starts," Shelton muttered. "We're doomed."

"Thank you," I said primly. Inside, I was grinning like a well-fed cat.

Shelton was right, of course. Once I got them listening, their curiosity *always* won out. It's what I loved best about them.

"Now." I cracked my knuckles. "There are two things we need to examine . . ."

◯   ⬡   ◯

We regrouped an hour later.

"Let's start with the chest," I said. "Ben and I went over every board, slat, and nail. There's nothing inside, or on the surface. There are no hidden compartments. There is no text of any kind."

Ben nodded in agreement. "The trunk itself is a dead end."

"So that leaves the contents." I gestured to Hi. "Tell us about the vegetation."

"You're not going to believe this." Hi had a bemused expression on his face. "I can identify this plant."

"No joke?" He was right. I couldn't believe it.

"Seriously. It's such a wildly uncommon specimen that, frankly, it was easy. My books were all over it, and I confirmed the ID online."

"Fantastic. Spill."

Hi placed the leaves on the worktable.

"These are the leaves of *Dionaea muscipula*, commonly known as Venus flytraps. I can't believe they lasted that long underground. They must've been predried, and the chest airtight. Talk about craftsmanship."

"How can you be sure?" Ben asked.

"I checked under my microscope." Hi pointed to a red-brown husk on the table. "The leaf blade is divided into two parts: a flat, heart-shaped stalk, then a pair of terminal lobes hinged at midrib, forming the trap. Stiff hairlike protrusions called cilia fringe the edges." He shrugged. "That was all I needed. Not much can be confused with a Venus flytrap. A monkey could've nailed it."

"Gotta love a plant that eats bugs," Shelton quipped.

"Flytraps are awesome." Hi made a V with his hands. "Their leaves are like small mouths that snap shut when a fly enters. Inside the mouth, tiny sensors distinguish between living prey and other things, like raindrops. If a bug taps two sensors in a row, or the same one twice, boom!" His fingertips snapped together. "The jaws close, trapping the insect inside. Then the plant digests at its leisure."

"That's wild," I said. "How did that evolve?"

"Flytraps grow in areas with lousy dirt, like swamps and bogs. The species developed a badass way to make up for the lack of nutrients."

"Very interesting," Ben cut in. "But how does this bountiful plant lore help us?"

"It helps a lot," Hi replied. "Venus flytraps are incredibly rare. These days they only grow wild in a forty-mile area around Wilmington, North Carolina. It's very unlikely that two or three dead ones accidentally got into that chest."

"Excellent work, Hi. Gold star. And you, good sir?"

"I also hit paydirt." Shelton held up a pebble. "These buggers are limestone."

"Explain."

Shelton read from a printout. "Limestone is a sedimentary rock composed of calcite and aragonite, which are the crystal forms of calcium carbonate." He looked up. "Basically, it forms from the skeletons and shells of dead marine organisms, like coral."

"All limestone looks like this?" I picked up one of the pebbles.

"Nope." Shelton's eyes dropped to his notes. "Impurities like clay, sand, or dead sea critters create variations in form and color. Limestone is extremely common, and has been used extensively in architecture. They built the Great Pyramid with it."

"So how did you make the ID?" Ben asked.

"Easy." Big smile. "I emailed a pic to a geologist at CU. It took him about two seconds."

"Nice work," I deadpanned. "When does your Ph.D. arrive?"

"What do I know about rocks? But I get *results*." Shelton dropped his notes onto the tabletop. "Also, he told me to dunk the pebble in vinegar and listen for fizzles and pops. Check and check. It's limestone. No doubt."

"Can you say where the pebbles originated?"

He shook his head. "From what I read, the stuff's too common. But it's doubtful that three identical limestone pebbles were just rolling around on Boneyard Beach."

"So that's *two* oddities," I said. "Plant and rock, neither native to Bull Island."

"Fine," Ben said. "Those things got into the chest somehow. That doesn't make them clues."

"Humor me. Pretend the items were placed deliberately. Where do they lead?"

"Google time." Hi began tapping his iPhone. "I'm using key words 'flytrap,' 'limestone,' and 'South Carolina.'" Pause. "Only one decent hit."

"Edge of my seat here, Hiram." Had I been sitting.

"Keep your pants on. Let me read."

Agonizing seconds ticked by.

"Yep." Hi spoke without looking up. "Dewees Island. According to this nature website, flytraps used to grow there. Gone now, but they might've been around in the 1700s."

"That's great!" I clapped my hands in excitement.

"It gets better," Hi said. "There are no cars on Dewees, so the roads aren't paved. Instead, they're lined with crushed limestone mined from a local quarry."

"That means nothing," Shelton scoffed. "Limestone is almost everywhere. Your search is too random."

"Dewees is the only place that checks both boxes," Hi replied.

"It's at least worth a look," I said. "Bonny might've inserted these items to show the way."

Shelton was *not* on board. "You wanna go all the way to Dewees because it has an ultra-common rock, and a rare plant grew there once upon a time?"

"Yes. I don't believe in coincidence."

"How do we even use that information? Once on Dewees, will the treasure come find *us*?"

Fighting my irritation, I kept a civil tone. "We should explore all possibilities."

"This is pretty weak," Ben said. "Even if you're right, we don't have the first clue where to look."

"How many islands are we up to now?" Shelton squawked. "Wadmalaw. Bull. Sullivan's. Half a dozen more, coming and going! And now you want Dewees. It never stops!"

I refused to respond. I'd made my position clear. The boys

would have to decide for themselves.

Hi came to my rescue.

"Hell, let's do it!" He threw up his hands. "Let's go out to Dewees and goof around. We've got nothing better to do, and a boat trip beats sitting around here, playing patty-cake. I'm in, all the way."

Ben and Shelton remained obstinate.

Hi elbowed Shelton's ribs. "Keep the faith, right?"

"Okay." Ben sighed. "Why not? The Virals set sail for Bonny one last time."

"I *told* you guys." Shelton looked to the heavens. "You can't let her start talking. I'll go pack my hang glider."

CHAPTER 61

I ran home to feed Coop before we left.

Phone check. Kit hadn't called or emailed. I thanked the powers that be for my father's naïveté. In a small way, I actually felt sorry for him.

I was heading back out the door when Coop fired past me and raced down the front steps.

"Coop! Stop! No roaming today!"

A bushy tail rounded the complex, heading for the rear driveway.

"Blargh!"

I found Coop standing beside the mailboxes, his attention focused on something in the woods.

"Let's go, pal." I grabbed his collar.

Coop glanced at me, then turned and barked, legs splayed, fur bristling along his spine.

A feeling of uneasiness swept over me. Was someone out there? Senses on high alert, I scanned the nearby trees.

Chance stepped from the bushes.

My pulse spiked, but I tried to force myself calm.

What to say to him? What had he seen?

As these questions swirled in my brain, my traitorous wolfdog trotted over and licked our visitor's hand. Chance dropped to a knee and stroked Coop's back.

"Tory. Good morning." Still stunned, I said nothing.

"What's that?" Chance cocked an ear, pretending to consider words I hadn't spoken. "Why, I'm fine! Thank you for asking."

"I'm glad you're okay. How'd you get home?"

"Home?" Chance smirked. "I'm between those at the moment. I caught a few hours' sleep at my father's cabin, if that's what you mean."

"How'd you get off Bull Island?"

"The morning ferry. Nine a.m. sharp." Chance thumped Coop's side, then stood. "I gave the captain quite a scare, emerging from the brush and demanding a ride. I'm not looking my best."

It was true. Chance's face was blotchy and pale. A violet half moon underhung each eye. A tic in one cheek suggested barely controlled tension.

Chance had found a change of clothes—an old Citadel sweatshirt and outdated cargo pants—but the grit of a night outdoors still covered his skin.

Most frightening of all, Chance's speech was somehow . . . off. His words sounded high and stretched, and came in short bursts like static from a squad-car radio.

I kept my face blank, my tone neutral. "I'm glad you're okay."

"Are you?"

"Of course. We were all concerned when you ran away."

"Never mind that." He changed the subject. "Where is Bonny's treasure? What was inside the chest?"

I almost didn't have the heart.

"Nothing, Chance. It was empty."

The tic went into overdrive.

"You lie." A whisper.

"I don't." I waved toward Shelton's garage. "The chest is sitting in there. See for yourself, if you like. We struck out."

Chance stared past me to a point out in space. His eyes had an odd look, as if he was battling inner demons.

"That is . . . disappointing."

"It sucks," I said. "We got a raw deal."

Chance's hands rose slowly and rubbed his cheeks. His brow furrowed.

"I've been under a lot of pressure lately," he said. "My breakdown. Father's public humiliation. The trial. While I've been locked away in that asylum, the Claybourne name has been dragged through the mud."

I said nothing. I'd played a pivotal role in those events, a fact of which Chance needed no reminder.

"I'm concerned that perhaps I'm not . . . well. Not fully rested."

"What do you mean?" Like I didn't know.

"I think I might be seeing things that aren't really there. Last night, for example."

"It was late," I said. "Dark. We were exhausted. Then everything happened so fast."

"No!" His fingers curled into fists. "It was *more* than that!"

Chance drilled me with a look.

"I *saw*, Tory. Your eyes *changed*. Became golden. Like the wolves that attacked on the beach."

I searched for a reply, came up blank.

"This wasn't the first time, either. In my basement, the night Hannah—"

Chance flinched as if burned. It was a very long moment before he continued.

"That night, I was on the ground. There was blood everywhere, and the pain was indescribable. But I *watched*. You moved too fast!"

You were hurt," I said. "Confused. And we were fighting for our lives."

"No!" He shook his head. "I know what I saw!"

Chance's breath became ragged. A sheen of sweat appeared on his brow.

"I'd assumed it was my imagination. After all, I'd been shot. Betrayed. Even now those memories are unbearable."

Chance's fist struck his open palm. "But the *same thing* happened last night. Your eyes turned golden. You moved with amazing speed. It was incredible."

What to say? Chance knew. There was nothing I could do to persuade him otherwise.

Then he threw me a lifeline.

"Am I crazy?" His voice had a desperate quality. "Suddenly I don't trust my own senses. My dreams are haunted. I feel like I'm losing my mind."

Chance's hand shot out and grabbed mine.

"Is it real, Tory? Do your eyes change? Or am I in worse shape than I thought?"

Guilt battered me in waves.

I hated to lie. Worse, to chip away at Chance's grip on reality.

But I had to protect myself. Protect my friends.

In the end, there was no choice to be made.

"My eyes don't glow, Chance." I wrapped my hands around his. "They're green, as always."

I held his gaze, hoping the deception wasn't naked on my face. I had to convince Chance I wasn't lying. Wasn't hiding anything. I needed him to believe.

"I think you're unwell." I felt disgust for myself. "Stressed out. Your mind is playing tricks on you."

"Tricks," he repeated numbly.

"It's all in your head," I whispered, driving the dagger home.

"Of course." Chance seemed to wilt.

Coop nuzzled Chance's side, then turned and yipped at me. The wolfdog seemed to know I was warping his new friend's fragile psyche. And did not approve.

I felt lower than pond scum.

"Perhaps I should check back into Marsh Point for a bit," Chance said. "My . . . work there isn't done. They probably miss me by now."

Neither of us smiled at his attempt at levity.

He's better off back at the hospital. Chance still isn't well.

"Let us take you," I said. "Ben can drive."

"I didn't *walk* here, Tory." He waved to a black motorcycle parked down the drive. "There are lots of toys at my father's cabin."

"Will you get into trouble?"

"Trouble?" Chance's smirk suggested some of his old swagger. "I'm a Claybourne. For all I know, my family *owns* that hospital. I expect a discrete reunion."

I walked him to the bike, a Kawasaki Z1000. Sleek and aerodynamic, the thing looked like a spaceship on crack. After strapping on a helmet, Chance reached down and petted Coop one last time.

Then he looked at me. "I'll see you again, I'm sure."

Hammering back guilt, I kept my voice steady.

"Just get better, Chance."

He nodded, straddled the bike, and was gone.

CHAPTER 62

"Poor bastard."

Shelton took the seat beside me in *Sewee*'s stern. "But you did the right thing, Tory. The pack comes first. And Chance needs treatment anyway."

"He's right," Ben said. "You had to lie. Chance can't know the truth about our powers."

"I know." I finished stowing my gear under a bench. "It had to be done."

Then why did I feel so awful?

"Don't beat yourself up." Shelton patted my shoulder. "Messing with Chance's mind is terrible, but we've got to look out for ourselves. Our freedom's at stake. Maybe our lives."

"I know," I repeated. "But Chance was a part of this. We wouldn't have found the chest without his help. And how do I repay him? By convincing him he's bonkers. Awesome karma."

Ben shrugged. "What choice did you have?"

"None." Shelton said firmly.

I tried to focus on the task ahead. "Let's just get going."

I'd make it up to Chance somehow. Some way.

"Where's Thick Burger?" Ben complained. "We said fifteen minutes."

"Here he comes." Shelton rose to his feet. "And something must be wrong, because he's running full tilt."

It was true. Hi was flying down the hill. He hit the dock staircase and nearly tumbled down, then descended as fast as his legs could pump. Five more seconds of sprinting brought him alongside *Sewee*.

"Guys!" Hi puffed and wheezed, his face gone scarlet. "*Guys!*"

"Calm down," I said. "Take deep breaths. You're going to pass out."

"*Radio.*" Hi gasped, hands on his knees. "*Turn. On. Radio. News.*"

"Okay, okay." Ben reached for the dashboard and switched on *Sewee*'s sound system. "Just don't stroke out. Any particular station?"

"News 12," Hi croaked as he crawled into the boat. "Now!"

Ben tuned the dial. A scratchy voice boomed from the speakers.

> *Recapping our top story, a police spokesman has released the names of the two victims of last night's single-car accident on the Arthur Ravenel Jr. Bridge. While department sources won't confirm specific details about the incident, the spokesman*

*identified the deceased as Chris and Sallie Fletcher
of the Radcliffeborough area of downtown
Charleston. According to unconfirmed reports,
a 2010 Toyota Prius belonging to the couple
was found at approximately five forty-five this
morning after apparently driving off the road near
the Highway 17 interchange. The car had crashed
into a bridge abutment and burst into flames. In a
News 12 exclusive, we've learned that the deceased
were graduate students at Charleston University
and curators of the Charleston Museum. We'll
have more on this breaking story as information
becomes available. In finance, Wall Street took
another hit today, as stock prices—*

Ben powered off the radio with shaking fingers. "Oh my God."

"Dead?" Shelton's brows were almost at his hairline. "*Dead?*
As in, the Fletchers died last night?"

"It's all over the news." Hi's breathing was back to normal. "I
was tying my shoes when the story flashed on TV."

"Dead?" Shelton repeated. "For real?"

"They must've woke up on the beach, then left Bull Island by
boat and reached their car." Ben stopped, paled. "Driving home,
they would've been tired, maybe a little woozy . . ."

"It's not our fault," Shelton blurted. "They attacked, and we
defended ourselves. I'm sorry they got killed, but we are *not*
responsible."

I didn't speak. Didn't know what to say. I thought of Sallie's friendly banter at the museum info booth. Chris schmoozing tourists outside the old market. The two of them smiling as they related ghost tales in the soft lamplight of Charleston's streets. They were so young. Their deaths were horrifying.

Then I remembered Boneyard Beach. Chris's coldness. Sallie's gun, aimed at my head. The senselessness of their deaths made me sick, but a part of me couldn't help but feel . . . relieved. And for that, I was ashamed.

That wasn't all. Ben's theory was plausible, and the timeline certainly worked. But my instincts screamed something else.

Foul play.

Hi had the same notion. "Chris said they drove a Prius, and that's the type of car they wrecked in. Meaning someone else was following us in the Studebaker." Pause. "You don't think that—"

"Hold on!" Shelton was nervously shirt-cleaning his glasses. "The news guy said the crash was an accident. There's no reason to think it wasn't."

Hi shrugged. "It just smells funny to me. Did the Fletchers strike you as the type to drive off a bridge? I can't see it."

"Me either." My hand shot up to forestall Shelton's reply. "I'm not saying it wasn't simply an accident. But we need to be careful. Hi's right about the Studebaker. That had to be someone else, and they might still be trailing us."

Hi nodded. "We don't want to have an 'accident' ourselves."

"Are we still going to Dewees?" Ben asked.

"Yes." I didn't hesitate. "Shelton's *also* right. In all likelihood, the wreck is exactly as reported—a tragic driving mishap. We can't abandon our search for paranoid reasons. Too much is riding on it."

Ben nodded. Then Hi. Finally, Shelton too.

"One way or another, we need to finish this," I said. "Let's see if Bonny has any tricks left up her sleeve."

CHAPTER 63

Hi and Shelton untied the lines. Ben eased *Sewee* back from the dock and into open water. "Next stop, Dewees Island."

I tried to shake off the horrid news about the Fletchers. I'd process my feelings later. Right then, we needed to focus more than ever.

"So what do we know?" I asked.

The boys snapped to attention, no doubt sharing the same mixed feelings.

Hi referred to his omnipresent iPhone. "Dewees is north, between Isle of Palms and Bull Island."

"Former Sewee country," Ben added. "My ancestors used to visit Dewees as well as Bull. Its real name is Timicau."

"I remember we passed it last night," I said. "Not many lights."

"Dewees is a very eco-conscious community," Hi said. "Small, and extremely pricey. The island is one unified design, and ninety-five percent of the land will never be developed."

Shelton chimed in. "Twelve hundred acres, so it's less than a third the size of Bull. No bridge, and no cars. The only link is the *Aggie Gray* ferry running from IOP."

"That's twice I've heard no cars." Ben steered into Charleston Harbor, heading north for the Intracoastal Waterway. "How do they get around?"

"Golf carts." Hi answered. "Private gas-powered vehicles are prohibited. It's a sleepy place. No restaurants. No grocery stores. No gas stations. Dewees is like a wildlife preserve, except rich people have vacation homes there."

"Great," Shelton said sarcastically. "Untarnished natural beauty. That means more swamps, bugs, and giant gators. And we've got no idea what we're looking for."

I ignored him. Mainly because he was right.

Conversation died, and I sensed the boys' thoughts returning to the Fletchers. I spoke to keep their attention on the task at hand.

"What else is on the island?"

"Besides private homes? Not much." Hi rattled off a list. "A small lodge, a firehouse, two public-works buildings, a canoe shelter, an old church, scattered fishing docks. Commercial activity is essentially banned."

Shelton couldn't sit still. "You really think somebody killed them?"

Ben gave him a "let it go" look. "So where do I tie up?"

"Wherever," Hi said. "The whole island is private property, so we're trespassing regardless."

Ben forced a smile. "*One* thing we're good at."

We circled the southern edge of Sullivan's Island and entered The Cove, passing the Claybourne cabin for the third time in two days. Dewees lay several miles up the waterway.

"Guys." Shelton's voice sounded tight. "Is that boat following us? It pulled out quickly, right after we passed Chance's place."

Three heads whipped around. A hundred yards behind us, a second vessel trailed in our wake.

"Looks like two people," Hi said. "But I can't be sure."

"It's a summer day in Charleston," Ben replied. "Dozens of boats must be using the waterway."

Nonetheless, he increased our speed.

"Easy," Hi cautioned. "We're in a 'no wake' zone."

"You think I don't know that?" Ben glanced back over his shoulder. "Tell me if they keep pace."

Tense minutes passed. The other vessel failed to fall back.

"Crap." Ben checked *Sewee*'s dials. "I'm pushing the limit, but they're keeping pace. That boat sped up when I did."

"Doesn't sound like Beau and Buffy out for a pleasure cruise," Hi said.

Shelton grabbed for an earlobe.

We passed beneath a bridge and the waterway narrowed. Head-high spartina lined both sides of the channel.

"Hang on." Ben down-throttled and *Sewee* kicked forward. "There's less traffic around here, so I'll risk a fine."

We surged forward. The trailing boat grew smaller, gradually disappeared.

"Can we can lose them for good?" I asked.

Ben nodded. "If someone's following us, they probably think we're headed for Bull Island again, right?"

"Makes sense," I said. "This is the same route we took last night."

"There's an islet south of Dewees called Big Hill Marsh. I'll cut through Bowers Creek and hide *Sewee* behind it. If that boat is headed to Bull, they'll go right by and never see us."

We tore up the waterway, splashing illegal wake, eyes peeled for signs of pursuit. Minutes later we reached the northern tip of Isle of Palms.

"That's the islet." Ben pointed straight ahead to a low green atoll. Steering hard to starboard, he entered a narrow creek, rounded the tiny landmass, and cut the engine. "Keep quiet."

For several minutes, we heard nothing but screeching gulls.

Then, the distant buzz of an engine. The noise increased, and for a tense moment seemed right on top of us. But the boat passed and the engine sound receded.

We exchanged nervous smiles.

"No sweat," Ben said.

"Probably just two dudes going fishing," Shelton joked.

After a cautious interval, Ben cranked the motor and we rounded Big Hill Marsh. Dewees Island appeared ahead, its dock a fuzzy blur in the afternoon sun.

I shot Ben a thumbs-up.

"Take us in, captain."

CHAPTER 64

The main pier was nearly deserted.

"That's called The Landing," Hi said. "It's where the *Aggie Gray* docks. She must be out now."

"Should I pull in?" Ben asked.

Hi nodded. "The Landing has the most slips. Maybe *Sewee* won't be noticed."

Ben selected a space and we quickly secured the boat, acting casual, like we had every right to be there. Wooden planks led up to a quaint covered shelter. A neatly painted sign welcomed us to Dewees Island.

"Nice digs," Hi said.

He was right. Lowcountry marsh stretched in every direction. Pelicans roosted on weathered pilings, wings stretched, basking in the warm afternoon sun. Cranes fished among the reeds and cattails rose from the still water.

"It's pretty here," Ben said. "Even if we strike out, it was worth the trip."

Just off the dock we passed a fleet of golf carts, neatly lined up, waiting to shuttle supplies purchased off-island by homeowners and renters.

Keys dangled from the ignitions of several.

Hi cocked an eyebrow, but I shook my head. Illegally docking *Sewee* was one thing, swiping a golf cart was quite another.

Hi sighed theatrically. I ignored him.

We proceeded onto a wide road that appeared to be made of white gravel. The drive was well maintained, and broad enough for two carts to pass.

"The limestone!" I crouched and picked up a piece of the paving material, then pulled one of Bonny's pebbles from my pocket.

My heart sank.

The crushed limestone composing the road was white, grainy, and very sharp edged. Bonny's pebble was smooth, solid, and drab gray.

"Maybe limestone dulls with age?" Hi suggested hopefully.

"Maybe." But the two samples looked nothing alike.

Just ahead was a circular three-story building occupying a small peninsula. Out front, a flagpole flew the Stars and Stripes above the South Carolina state flag.

"That's the admin building," Hi said. "It also has an educational center, a few science labs, and a post office. That's about it for Dewees."

"So where do we start?" Shelton surveyed our surroundings. "I see two paths."

Hi accessed a map on his iPhone. "Dewees is basically two strips of developed high ground surrounding a large central lagoon. The rest of the island is undisturbed marsh and swamp."

He pointed to three o'clock. "That path leads across the tidal marsh to the oceanfront properties. The clubhouse is also down there."

Hi pointed toward twelve o'clock. "Ahead are the other public buildings, the composting plant, the firehouse, and the old church. They border the lagoon."

"Where would the flytraps have grown?" Ben asked.

Hi shrugged. "I'd put my money on the lagoon. To lure their prey, flytraps need stagnant conditions, with low wind. The swampier, the better."

"Then let's head straight," I said.

"Goose chase," Shelton muttered, but set off with us.

We followed the road about another thousand feet. To our left stretched acres of open marshland. To our right lay the pond.

"It's called Old House Lagoon," Hi said. "It's the largest body of water on the island. Plenty of gators in there."

A small, shallow cove appeared just ahead on the right, an offshoot of the main body of water. Its surface was opaque lime-green, dotted here and there with lily pads. A path skirted the cove, leading to a cluster of live oaks where the inlet joined the lagoon proper. "What's down there?" I asked.

Hi scrolled on his cell before answering. "That's Old Church Walk. There's a tiny chapel tucked in the trees by the lagoon's edge. There's also a fishing dock."

I thought for a moment. "When was the church built?"

Shelton beat Hi to the punch. "Early 1700s. I checked online. It's the oldest structure on Dewees by two centuries."

"It was here when Bonny escaped her dungeon?"

Shelton nodded. "It's a marvel. There was *nothing* else out here. An Irish monk built it, then spent decades trying to convert the local Sewee. He either gave up or died, no one knows. But the building still stands."

"We need to see it." I was getting that feeling. Again.

"A destination!" Hi circled a finger in the air, then pointed downhill. "Onward to ye ancient house of worship!"

With that, he cut off onto the trail.

The church was smaller than I expected. A square bell tower formed the front, fifteen feet tall, broken only by a single wooden door at its center. The rectangular chamber behind had a steep slate roof and two rounded windows on each side.

The entire structure was composed of crumbling stone blocks.

Gray stone blocks.

*Lime*stone blocks.

"Wow." Hi pointed at my pocket. "Check the sample. That has to be a bingo!"

I approached the nearest wall and pulled out the pebble. The pattern and color matched exactly.

"Identical limestone," I said. "Beside a *perfect* lagoon for Venus flytraps."

"Impossible!" Shelton rubbed the back of his head. "No one is this lucky."

"Seriously." Ben sounded uneasy. "Hitting paydirt a third straight time? You're starting to freak me out."

"This building was here in Anne Bonny's time." I ran my hands over the rough-hewn stone. "Built by an Irish monk. Bonny was Irish herself, and obviously very religious. And limestone was very popular with church architects."

"I'm officially excited," Hi announced. "If Saint Limestone here has nothing to do with Bonny's treasure, it has to be the most painful coincidence of all time."

"I don't believe in coincidence," I said automatically.

"We know." *Jinx.*

"I take it we're going inside?" Shelton said.

"Absolutely." I stepped to the door. To my surprise, it swung inward easily.

We entered a small antechamber with ornate stone fountains jutting from the walls. Ahead, an archway opened into the nave.

Two rows of pews flanked a central aisle that led to a simple stone altar. The one-room chapel was obviously still maintained. The floor was cleanly swept, and unlit candles filled brass sconces lining the side walls. In the far right-hand corner, another door exited the rear of the building.

"They must leave this place unlocked for private worship," I guessed. "Good thing the locals are so trusting."

"Sweet Jesus." Ben was staring straight ahead, eyes wide. "Holy crap."

"Don't blaspheme in church!" Shelton whispered. "JC lives in this piece. Bad mojo."

"What is it?" I followed Ben's sightline to the rear of the chapel. Scanned. It practically leaped out at me.

My heart threw an extra beat. Then three more for good measure.

"Mother of God," Hi breathed.

At first glance, the stones of the rear wall seemed uniform in pattern. Careful scrutiny showed that was not the case. White rocks imbedded in the gray limestone formed a pattern.

Five feet tall and three feet across.

A Gaelic cross.

Hi slapped his side. "Tell me *that's* a coincidence."

"Tory, you have psychic powers." Shelton looked thunderstruck. "I will never doubt you about anything. Anywhere. Anytime."

Ben just stared.

"Check the cross!" Shelton was already moving. "There might be something hidden behind it!"

We attacked the wall. Tapping. Prodding. Banging fists. Digging with fingernails. At one point Hi yelled "Open Sesame!"

No good. The stones were impervious to our assault.

I dropped my head in frustration.

That's when I saw it.

Like the walls, the chapel floor was paved with limestone blocks. An irregularity was carved into one of the flagstones at the foot of the cross.

Kneeling, I leaned in close.

The stone was scored with two small lines, one short and

horizontal, the other long and vertical. Together the lines formed a crude cross.

With the top arm curving ever so slightly right.

"Here here here!" I squealed. "Bonny's personal cross! The treasure is under this flagstone!"

"How do we lift it?" Hi was bouncing like a pogo stick. "Who brought the explosives?"

"Wait here!" Ben bolted out the front door.

Minutes passed. Hours? I picked at the stone's corner, knowing it was useless but unable to stop. Shelton paced, hands locked behind his back. Hi drummed his chest, while staring at the floor and humming "I Gotta Feeling."

"Open up!"

Ben was outside the chapel's rear door.

Hi raced over and slid back the bolt. Ben entered gripping a crowbar.

"On the way here we passed a utility shed. I'll return it when we're done." Crooked smile. "Unless I'm carrying too many bags of jewels."

"Get to it!" Shelton squeaked.

Ben wedged the crowbar between the flagstones and pried. Once. Twice. Three times. With a groan, the block inched upward, then fell back into place.

"Get it done, Hercules!" Hi pumped both fists. "You da man!"

Ben planted his feet, jammed the crowbar deeper into the newly created gap, and heaved. The stone rose another few inches, dropped.

KATHY REICHS

Jam. Heave. Drop. Jam. Heave. Drop.

Slowly the block yielded. With one final thrust, Ben lifted the stone's underside above floor level. We grabbed the lower edge and helped flip it. The block tumbled to the floor with a thunk.

"It's a hidey-hole!" I yelped.

We'd exposed a hidden compartment roughly a yard in diameter.

A dusty object rested in its center.

Yowza.

CHAPTER 65

I lifted our find from its hiding place.

A wooden box. Hand carved. And showing lots of years.

A true scientist would've used caution before handling a newly discovered relic, but I was too excited for proper protocol. Aunt Tempe would have to forgive me.

The box was smaller than the chest—the size of a tiny microwave—though equally sturdy. Its lid was sealed with wax and secured by a simple latch.

"This is it guys," Hi gushed. "The end of the road! Payday!" Then a frown creased his face. "If not, I'm going postal. Big time. I can't handle any more rejection."

"Just open it," Shelton said. "Show me the money!"

"Gentlemen," I said formally. "May I present you with Anne Bonny's booty?"

The boys chuckled, eyes riveted on the article in my lap.

I unhooked the latch and tried lifting the lid. The wax held firm.

"Ben." I held out my hand.

Ben slapped his Swiss Army knife into my palm. Moving gingerly, I walked the blade around the edge of the lid. Bits of wax crumbled to the floor as I sliced through the ancient seal.

I handed the knife back and inhaled deeply, positioned my hands, and applied pressure. The wax gave. The lid rose.

Inside were two items. The first was a black velvet pouch secured by a leather cord. I handed it to Shelton, and he began working on the knot.

The second item was larger and wrapped in canvas.

"Why hasn't this stuff rotted to dust?" Ben pointed to the canvas. "That fabric has been underground for three hundred years."

"The hidey-hole was constructed of fitted stone," I answered, "which shielded the box from bugs, soil, and the elements. The wax seal kept it airtight. Whoever hid this took the long view. These things could've lasted another hundred years."

"This is it." Hi's voice quavered with excitement.

Unwinding the canvas halved the bundle's size and revealed a small oilskin parcel tightly bound by metal wire.

"Booyah!" Shelton had conquered the knot and was emptying the pouch.

Gold coins trickled into his open palm.

The crowd went nuts.

"Gold, baby, gold!" Shelton sang.

Hi tried to high-five Ben, who ignored him and snatched a coin.

"One side has Latin words circling a cross," he read excitedly. "The other has a crown and shield, with '1714' and 'Philip V' stamped around it."

"Give me a sec." Shelton was already working his iPhone. A full minute passed, then, "Spanish doubloons! They're called 'eight escudos,' or gold pieces of eight. Probably minted in Mexico."

"How much are they worth?" Ben danced the coin across his knuckles, flipped, then caught it in midair.

Shelton kissed his iPhone. "In good condition, each can fetch thousands!"

"We did it!" Hi started raising the roof. "We're filthy rich! All hail the genius, dog-powered, treasure-hunting, millionaire pimp squad of Morris Island!"

"Not millions." Ben did a rough estimate. "We've got a few dozen here, tops."

All eyes turned to the parcel in my lap.

"Enough with the appetizers." Shelton gathered the coins back into the pouch. "Time for the main course!"

"Open the big boy!" Hi rubbed his hands. "I wanna see some diamond underpants."

"Here." Ben handed over the pocketknife.

Heart pounding, I severed the wire and unwrapped the oilskin.

And stared.

Outside, a gull squawked. Another answered. Somewhere, far off, a dog barked.

Hi reacted first. "What the hell?"

"Really?" Shelton buried his face in his hands. "Really?"

Ben said nothing.

I held a small bundle of pages.

"It looks religious." Even I couldn't feign enthusiasm.

"We're cursed!" Hi moaned. "Pirate treasure is supposed to be *cool*. Valuable. Interesting. And we get a freaking medieval church magazine."

"Let's at least examine it," I said. "We don't even know what it is."

"Have at it." Shelton reached for the pouch. "I'll count the gold coins."

"I wanna hold one." Hi sidled over to Shelton. "Gimme."

"I'm watching you." Ben raised V'ed fingers to his eyes, then pointed them at Hi and Shelton. "No funny stuff."

"Sir," Shelton replied. "You wound me."

As the boys monkeyed with the doubloons, I inspected the pages.

"This is vellum," I said. "The sheets are folded in half and then sewn together at the crease to form a small packet. Looks like ten pages total."

"Uh huh."

"Neat."

Detecting their lack of interest, I proceeded in silence.

The first sheet was covered with Latin script decorated by stylized swirls and symbols. The lettering was elaborate and exquisitely detailed. The author had turned the words into art, singling out snippets of text with artistic embellishments.

The second sheet had a full-page depiction of angels surrounded by interlacing patterns. An ornamental knot filled the bottom corner.

Though slightly faded, the colors were breathtaking. Black. Yellow. Purple. Red. The complexity of detail boggled my mind.

As I leafed through the remainder of the manuscript, a paper dropped from the pages. I scooped it up.

A letter. I recognized the handwriting.

"Well, well."

My change in tone caught the boys' attention.

"What?" Hi asked.

"Nothing that would interest you guys." I waggled the letter. "Just another note from our dear friend Anne Bonny, to her besty Mary Read."

The boys scrambled over, the financial accounting momentarily suspended. We read the message in silence.

Dearest Mary,

> May this missive find you well. I've had no word of your whereabouts since escaping my imprisonment, and worry for your safety and comfort. So many plans have gone wrong. If you are reading this you've found the way, as I knew you would. No other soul could have discerned meaning from the clues I left. I'm rather pleased at my own cleverness.

I write because I must flee Charles Town in haste. Someone has been asking questions, and my freedom is endangered. I will head north to the place we discussed.

In this box is coin enough to see you where you may, even to find me, should you so choose. I have also left your favorite pages as a memento. I take mine with me. When I gaze upon them I shall think of you and remember fondly.

Your Warmest Friend,
Anne

I spoke first. "She didn't know Mary was dead. That's so sad."

"Maybe she wasn't," Shelton said awkwardly. "No one's *really* certain."

"Mary never found this letter," Ben said. "That much is clear."

Hi shook his head. "Anne Bonny's famous treasure is just a handful of coins and some Bible stuff. What a letdown."

I passed around the pages so everyone could see. The boys looked underwhelmed. We'd needed a fortune to save LIRI. Our haul had come up woefully short.

The mission was a failure. Our pack would be fragmented.

"Let's clean up and get out of here," I said. "We shouldn't leave a church messy."

Ben moved to the displaced flagstone. "Shelton. A hand." Together they began pushing the block into place.

"Where does that go?" Hi pointed to the crowbar.

"Utility shed," Ben said. "Fifty yards back the way we came."

Hi hoisted the crowbar and walked out the rear door.

It took a few moments for Ben and Shelton to maneuver the stone into place.

"Jeez," Shelton panted. "That sucker was heavy."

"You're not the one who had to lift it." Ben had both hands on his hips.

"I'll hang on to these bad boys." Shelton shoved the coin pouch into his front pocket. "For safekeeping."

"I already counted them," Ben said. "Lose any, you'll be less a few fingers."

"That's twice you've insulted my honor, Blue. Pistols or swords?"

I was sliding Bonny's pages into my backpack when the main church door creaked open.

"Hi's back." Slinging a strap over one shoulder, I rose. "Everyone ready?"

"Stay put," a male voice called. "We've got some shit to discuss."

My blood froze.

Marlo and Tree Trunk entered the chapel and stood side by side. Neither was smiling.

Each had a gun pointed our way.

CHAPTER 66

"**R**un!"

Ben and Shelton jumped at my barked command. We all bolted out the rear door.

And were stopped short by yet another pistol.

"Good afternoon." Nigel Short smirked, crooked teeth poking in every direction. He wore a brown tweed suit with a solid maroon tie. In his hand was a 9mm Beretta. "Why don't we step back inside?"

"Dr. Short?" Confused. "What are you doing here?"

"I'll be shooting you three in the head, unless you move back into that church." He cocked his weapon. "Understood?"

Slowly, we raised our hands, turned, and reentered the chapel. Marlo and Tree Trunk were standing in the aisle near the front pews. Marlo wore his white tee and jeans. Tree Trunk's current jersey was LeBron James.

Guns in front. Gun in back. Not good.

"You've no idea what it's like tracking you delinquents all over creation." Short pushed his tiny spectacles back up his nose. "Exhausting."

"The rich bitch." Marlo was scanning the room. "He's not here. The fat one's missing too."

"Chance and Hi bailed." I poured everything into the lie. "Too much excitement for one week."

"Hardly," Short said. "They're guarding Bonny's treasure, of course."

"Ya'll are gonna take us to it." Marlo waggled his pistol. "Or this gets . . . messy."

Tree Trunk stood statue still. Mute. Menacing.

"There *wasn't* any treasure." Shelton's voice shook. "The chest was empty."

"Come now." Short's eyes narrowed. "Do you think I'm stupid?"

With a flick of his wrist, Short motioned for Marlo to cover the rear door. Then, unhurried, he walked to the first pew and sat.

I assessed the situation. Marlo at the rear door. Tree Trunk in the aisle, blocking access to the front entrance. We were trapped again.

"It's true," Ben said. "We found nothing. Bonny's legend was a fraud."

"You've *got* to do better than that," Short scolded. "Tell us where the treasure is, and Marlo will make this quick. Otherwise, you'll become acquainted with the services of his brother, Duncan."

Duncan winked, the first readable expression I'd seen on his face.

Stall! my brain ordered.

"Cat got your tongues?" Marlo ratcheted back the slide on his piece. "Looks like I'll have to be more persuasive."

"Wait!" Heart racing, I piled on words. "Why are you doing this?"

I had no real sense of Marlo, but the cold look in his eyes was terrifying.

"For real?" Marlo clucked from one side of his mouth. "Dollars, girl. This is a nice score for my brother and me."

"I met Marlo and Duncan while tracing your steps," Short said. "Imagine my surprise to find so many other people following you."

"The Fletchers," I hissed. "You killed them, didn't you?"

Short gave a dismissive flip of his hand. "Rank amateurs. Obstinate children. Those two believed they were so clever. Such skilled investigators." He snorted derisively. "I've been researching Anne Bonny's treasure for three decades. The Fletchers knew *nothing*, not even what they were looking for! They weren't worthy of the prize."

"You didn't have to murder them."

"They wouldn't listen to reason," Short said matter-of-factly. "But Duncan here got them to chat, and then they had an unfortunate accident. And now we have you."

Short's voice went cold. "We know you have the chest."

"You'd kill us all for pirate treasure?" My mouth was so dry I could barely speak.

"What type of game did you think you were playing?" Short snapped. "Thirty years! Trolling through dusty archives. Painstakingly gleaning clues from archaic documents long forgotten by the living. And then one day you four walk in, wide-eyed and dreamy, with a letter written by Anne Bonny herself." Short tapped the Beretta against his knee. "Asking questions about Half-Moon Battery. Gaelic. Using sample writing from the treasure map. You practically announced your search in skywriting!"

Short's tone was glacial, but madness danced behind his eyes. "I'm a document expert. Did you think I'd missed the bent cross on each of the letter's pages? Or that I wouldn't connect it to Bonny's famous treasure map?"

Think Tory! Time is running out!

"You spied on us." First thought I could verbalize.

"Of course." Short crossed his legs. "After you brought me the letter, I suspected you might know something useful. When you asked to see Bonny's private documents, I listened over the intercom. I even considered stalking you myself, but realized I'd need help." Self-deprecating smile. "I'm not as young as I was once."

Ben glared at Marlo. "So you hired these thugs."

"Thugs?" Marlo stepped close to Ben's face. "Watch your mouth, boy."

"We had similar goals, but the boys lacked direction." Short stood, gently waved Marlo back with his gun. "I lacked manpower. They lacked brainpower. Working together solved both our problems. They're quite adept at surveillance and muscle."

"That's me." Marlo flexed a bicep. "Muscle, baby!"

Duncan just stared.

"The Studebaker," Shelton squeaked. "Ya'll drive that jalopy?"

"*Jalopy?*" Marlo sneered. "That ride is vintage. Dunc and I restored her, piece by piece."

"The pawnshop," I said, finally piecing it together. Why had it taken me so long? "Your father is Lonnie Bates."

"My father's a damn fool." Marlo snorted. "Hates getting jacked, though. Put us on the job the minute ya'll bounced from the shop. I thought he was nuts. Turns out, the old man's still got the skills. Not that he'll see a dime."

"Enough chatting." Behind his glasses, Short's eyes were chips of granite. "Time for some answers. Why are you on Dewees? Why are you in this church? Where is the treasure chest?" He stepped closer to me. "And what's in your bag?"

Out of time.

I closed my eyes. Dug deep.

SNAP.

My powers flooded like water through a breaking dam.

I dove into my subconscious.

Ben and Shelton appeared sharp in my mind. I could feel Hi close, but his image was blurry. Much fainter, at the edge of my perception, I sensed Coop spring to his feet.

As before, flaming ropes connected the five of us.

The golden nimbus surrounded my own image. Reaching for

the others, I tried spreading the glow as I'd done before.

Virals. Listen up!

My message hit the invisible barrier separating our thoughts. Fragmented. I tried again and again. No go.

Why? What am I doing wrong?

Gritting my teeth, I willed my consciousness past the obstruction. Failed. Like our first wolf encounter on Bull Island, I was unable to touch their minds.

Short's eyes narrowed. "What are you doing?"

The image in my brain began to change. Hi solidified, grew more distinct. I sensed him creeping toward the chapel's rear entrance.

A fault line appeared in the mental barrier. I pushed hard, opened a crack. Beside me, Ben and Shelton flinched.

Suddenly, the answer fired home.

Why the telepathy worked sometimes, but not others.

The failures. When practicing flares on Loggerhead, Shelton was missing. When first confronted by the wolves, Ben was scouting ahead.

And when had it worked?

We were *together* in the submerged tunnel. We were *together* fighting the Fletchers on Boneyard Beach.

The power fails when a Viral is missing. When the pack isn't whole.

As Hi closed in, his image grew crisper. The walls separating us weakened.

"Feeling faint?" Short scoffed. "Talk, or you'll have reason to be."

Descending to my id, I projected with all the strength I could muster. Ben and Shelton shivered in response.

"Enough playin," said Marlo. "Time to get serious."

Duncan's eyes bored into me. "I'll make her talk." First words.

Beyond the church walls, Hi crossed a tipping point.

The barrier collapsed. My thoughts exploded outward.

I yanked the fiery lines and spread my flare to the other Virals.

I sensed Hi double over in shock. Shelton and Ben gasped. Inside my head, their figures now burned with yellow light.

"See?" Marlo taunted. "They scared of Dunc."

Dispensing with words, I beamed images directly to their brains.

In seconds, my plan was in place.

I sensed Hi stop, then circle to the front of the church.

"Better yet," Marlo said. "Shoot one of them boys and the chick will sing."

"Yes, of course." Short gestured at Ben, whose eyes were averted. "This one will do."

Marlo's pistol rose.

Now!

Faster than thought, Shelton winged the coin pouch at Marlo's head.

Marlo deflected the bag with a contemptuous smirk. Then his eyes widened at the sight of doubloons scattering over the stones.

Dropping to a knee, he snatched up a coin. "Gold, baby!"

"Look out!" Short shouted.

Too late. Marlo glanced up just as Ben's foot connected with his head. The two rolled backward in a tangle, limbs flailing.

Short aimed his gun at Shelton, who dove behind the stone altar.

Crack! Crack!

Bullets ricocheted. Shards flew.

Crack!

Duncan's shot barely missed Ben's back.

A blur streaked into the chapel and slammed Duncan from behind, knocking him to the ground. Duncan's breath expelled with an audible "Oof!"

With an agility belying his poundage, Hi then whirled and shoved Short with both hands.

Short flew sideways toward me.

I grabbed the Beretta, but couldn't pry it from his fingers.

"Get away!" Short struggled, desperate to free his weapon for a clean shot.

Duncan struggled to his knees. Hi wrapped himself around one enormous leg like an angry badger. Shelton lunged from behind the altar wielding an iron candlestick. Swung with all his strength.

Iron hit bone.

Thunk.

The big man tumbled backward holding his forehead.

In the corner, Ben and Marlo grappled on the floor.

"You have no right!" Short screamed. "You haven't earned it! Bonny's treasure belongs to me!"

I grunted, struggling to wrench the gun from his grip. But

Short's rage was equal to my flare strength. With a growl he began wildly squeezing the trigger.

Crack! Crack! Crack!

Bullets sparked against stone.

Things were spiraling out of control.

CHAPTER 67

Desperate, I launched forward in a wicked head butt.

Stars exploded behind my eyes, but the impact left Short momentarily stunned. Seizing the opportunity, I clawed the pistol free and slammed my knee into his gut. The old man collapsed, gagging and grasping his belly.

I spun, Beretta in hand.

But the fight was over.

Ben was on his feet, aiming a gun at Marlo's head.

"Do we understand each other?" Ben asked quietly.

Marlo nodded.

Ben pointed to the first row of pews. Marlo rose slowly, hands high, eyes never straying from the muzzle pointed at his chest.

When Ben turned, his eyes no longer glowed.

Duncan lay groaning on the floor. Hi and Shelton had backed away to lean against the battered altar.

Hi held a pistol in one shaky hand, panting and wheezing.

"You da man, Shelton. Next trip to Chick-fil-A is on me."

"That was my modified judo chop." Shelton's voice cracked as he set his glasses back in place. "Thank my mom. Those lessons really paid off. The candlestick helped, too."

The boys pounded fists, golden light fading from their eyes.

SNUP.

I shuddered as my own senses powered down. As usual after the canine surge, I felt weak and vulnerable. I did my best to hide it.

Short glared at me with a look of pure hatred.

"Bench." I motioned to the spot beside Marlo. "Now."

"How *dare* you, you little miscreant!"

Wordlessly, I aimed the Beretta directly at Short's nose. He rose and took the seat I'd indicated.

Duncan was on his knees, a blank look on his face.

"Sit beside Short and Marlo," I said. "Now."

Ignoring me, Duncan got to his feet and brushed off his jersey.

"Hey!" I flicked the gun for emphasis. "That wasn't a request."

Duncan extended a palm. "Gun."

"You're crazy."

"Now."

"Butt on the bench. Last warning."

Snorting derisively, Duncan moved toward me.

Crack! Crack!

Bullets struck the stone between Duncan's massive feet.

He froze. A dark blossom spread across the crotch of his jeans.

"Correction. *That* was your last warning. Test me again, and you'll limp for a very long time."

Duncan walked to the pew and dropped beside his brother.

I caught the other Virals in the corner of my eye. "What?"

Ben was staring, jaw open. "Good Lord, Tory."

"Nice shooting, Scarface." Hi handed me Duncan's weapon. "Remind me never to owe you money. Who taught you how to fire a gun?"

"Long story." I wasn't answering "drunk grandfather," true or not.

"Tory's a beast." Shelton had recovered his composure and was collecting the doubloons. "You punks should know that by now."

None of the pew sitters uttered a word.

The boys gathered our things while I kept an eye on Short, Duncan, and Marlo. In moments we were ready to go.

"What's the plan?" Shelton whispered. "We can't just leave them here."

"Cut me a break," Marlo pleaded. "You'll never see me again. That's solid."

"Sorry," I said. "Telling Short to shoot someone was a dealbreaker. Hiram? A moment."

I whispered instructions. Hi nodded, grabbed Shelton and Ben for a conference.

"I'll stay with Tory," Ben said. "Don't want our guests getting cute."

Shelton and Hi shouldered our gear and hurried from the chapel.

Ben and I leaned against a wall, eyes on our prisoners, pistols at the ready. The silence stretched. I grew edgy, worn thin by the pressure of keeping a loaded gun aimed at three human beings.

An eon later, Hi and Shelton returned. Hi flashed a thumbs-up.

"Now run down to the post office," I told him. "There must be some type of security on this island."

Hi hustled off again.

"Police?" Marlo's fingers traced the scar on his cheek. "Come on. We can work something out."

"Dream on. Shop's closed."

"You stole the map from the museum," Short hissed. "You're going to jail, too."

"Maybe. But you killed the Fletchers. You're going to answer for that."

Hi appeared at the door. "You're not going to believe—"

A familiar voice cut him off. "What in the world is going on here!?"

Sergeant Carmine Corcoran whaled into the chapel, sides heaving under a tan uniform stretched to its limits.

Had Bigfoot appeared, I'd have been less surprised.

"Sergeant Corcoran?"

"Tory Brennan." Corcoran's thick black moustache arced down in stern disapproval. "And the rest of the Morris Island hoodlums. Of course. Walking, talking proof that God hates me."

I was still on tilt. "You work on Dewees now?"

"Laid off by the Folly PD." The chubby face reddened

between the mutton-chop sideburns. "Probably because of the embarrassment you brats caused me. It's 'Security Director Corcoran' now."

Corcoran's eyes zeroed in on the guns I was holding. Widened. Moved from me to the trio on the bench. To the weapon in Ben's hand.

"Are those real firearms?"

"These three tried to kill us," Ben said. "Arrest them."

"Who are they?" Corcoran tried to look everywhere at once. "Are you holding them hostage?"

Shelton snickered.

"I'll take it slow," I said. "These people attacked us. We—"

"Freeze! Just freeze!" Corcoran extended one hand, palm out, and yanked a bottle of pepper spray from his belt with the other. "I'm detaining everyone! No one move!"

"You don't understand," I began.

"You'll turn those guns over, right Tory?" Corcoran was clearly uneasy. "No funny stuff?"

I sighed. "Cuff those three, Security Director. Then we'll do whatever you want."

"I'll hold you to that."

Unclipping a walkie-talkie, Corcoran began shouting orders to some unfortunate flunky. When finished, he clamped ZipCuffs onto each of our prisoners.

Satisfied, Corcoran turned. Ben and I passed him all three pistols.

"Wrists," Corcoran ordered.

"What?" I said in surprise.

"You heard me. I'm detaining *everyone*."

Sighing, I extended my arms. Corcoran worked down the line, zipping on four more sets of plastic restraints.

I slumped into the closest pew. Shelton joined me, followed by Hi and Ben.

"What a day."

It was all I could say. The tank was empty.

CHAPTER 68

The rest of that afternoon was a blur.

Interviews. Statements. We told our story over and over, then told it over again. Hours later, I'd had enough.

A director of the Charleston Museum arrived to collect the stolen treasure map. The squirrel went apoplectic when he spotted my writing on the back, was only partially mollified to learn my note was a record of Bonny's cryptic poem.

Threats were voiced, but in the end he decided not to press charges. With two of his curators murdered, our larceny was low on his list of concerns.

A call was made to the Exchange Building, and an inspector was sent to the Provost Dungeon. Once Bonny's bolt-hole was discovered, the atmosphere changed dramatically.

Dubious cops became fascinated listeners. Their stern frowns at our multiple petty crimes morphed into grins at our moxie.

Then Kit arrived.

"Tory!" Wrapping me in a fierce hug. "What's going on? Are you okay?"

"What've you heard?" Testing the waters.

"Nothing! I received a message saying you were at police headquarters downtown. That's it."

"Right. Kit, I uh . . . have some things to tell you." I swallowed. "You're not going to like it."

His face fell. "Are you in trouble?"

"Actually, I don't think so."

"Then why are you here? Did you break the law?"

"Yes. Quite a few." I held up a hand. "But for a good cause!"

Kit's brow wrinkled in confusion. "But you've been grounded all week."

"Yeah. About that. A few days ago the boys and I stole a treasure map from the Charleston Museum. It led to tunnels beneath the Provost Dungeon, so we snuck out Friday night, broke in, and explored them."

He blinked. "What?"

"The tunnels run under East Bay, all the way to the Battery. We found Anne Bonny's original hiding place, but the treasure had been moved. Then someone following us opened fire and we escaped by swimming into the bay."

Kit dropped to the bench beside me. "We had breakfast. You said you were bored."

"The pirates had left a poem as a clue," I continued in a rush. "I called Aunt Tempe because she knows Gaelic, and then we needed Chance Claybourne because his father had purchased

Anne Bonny's cross. We snuck him out of his mental hospital, and he helped us figure out the treasure's new location. Bull Island."

"Tempe? Chance Claybourne? Bull Island?"

"Yes, we went there late last night. Kit, the clues were right! We dug up a treasure chest! But then the shooters showed up again—these whackadoo married curators named the Fletchers—and we got into a scrap. We managed to knock them out and escape, but the chest was empty."

Kit's hands floated to his face. "And?"

"*I* suspected the treasure might've been moved again, and things pointed to Dewees Island, so we went there this morning. Before leaving we heard the Fletchers had been killed in a car wreck, which we thought was suspicious. When we got to Dewees Dr. Short attacked us. He's a document expert. He'd teamed up with the Bates brothers, these thugs who work for a pawnshop guy in North Charleston. It turns out we were right—they'd killed the Fletchers! Anyway, we managed to disarm the three of them and get help. Sergeant Corcoran arrested everyone, only he's not a cop anymore."

Kit winced. "Was anyone hurt?"

"Not on our side. Oh, I borrowed your 4Runner a few times. Sorry."

Kit got to his feet and strode to the duty desk. "Is my daughter being held for any reason?"

"No sir."

"Then I'm taking her home." Kit signed my release forms and

fumbled for his keys, then spoke to me without turning. "Car. Now. No more talking."

I moved as quickly and quietly as possible, pleased that Kit hadn't asked if we'd found anything.

We'd fooled the police. I didn't want to lie to him, too.

○   ○   ○

"I'm taking out the trash," I called.

"Try not to commit any felonies," Kit replied.

"Very funny."

It was the following morning. I'd spent all night telling Kit what happened, down to the minutest detail. He'd taken special interest in how I'd deceived him. Mental notes?

The only thing I'd held back was our powers.

And what we'd found.

In the end, Kit had posed just one question. "Why?"

"Because I don't want to move." Tears streamed my cheeks. "I'll do anything to keep my only friends."

The mood had been more pleasant after that. Kit decided that I'd committed so many fouls—been so irresponsible and reckless—that it was pointless to punish me.

"What you did is incredible, Tory. You're a remarkable girl." Then he'd leaned forward, face tight with concern. "But you risked your life. *Nothing* is worth that. Not a job, not a place, not a treasure. I'm going to trust you to use better judgment in the future."

"I will, Kit. I promise."

I walked to the Dumpster and tossed our rubbish. When I turned, Rodney Brincefield was standing two feet from me.

I jumped backward, mouth open, scream at the ready.

"Hold on!" Brincefield raised both palms. "I come in peace!"

"How did you find me?" I glanced around. No one else in sight.

"I'll admit I did some sneaking, but I mean you no harm. I've lived in this city a long time, and have a few friends on the force. One told me you located my brother's body."

There was longing in Brincefield's eyes. Pain.

"Yes," I said gently. "We found Jonathan in a tunnel beneath East Bay." I hesitated. "He'd been killed by a booby trap. I'm very sorry."

"So he'd gotten close." Though Brincefield smiled, his eyes were glassy. "That's something, I guess."

"He was carrying a stone artifact," I said. "We used it to reach the final chamber. We'd have failed without your brother."

"Was it there? The treasure?"

I shook my head. "It had been moved. Later we found a chest, but it was empty. Bonny's legend was a fraud."

Brincefield's face seemed to crumple in on itself. I could practically read his thoughts. His brother had died for nothing.

Maybe it was unwise, but I couldn't resist. This Bonny-obsessed old man needed closure.

"We did find *something*," I whispered. "In another place. We've kept it secret from everyone."

"Thank goodness! Tell me."

"It's not much, just a bag of gold coins and some old religious drawings." My tone reflected my disappointment. "I think Bonny removed most of her loot when the chest was relocated to Dewees."

Brincefield stilled a moment, then danced a jig, moving nimbly for such a fossil.

I stared at his performance, totally confused.

"Tory, you don't understand! The drawings *are* the treasure!"

"Come again?"

"Jonathan researched Anne Bonny and Calico Jack for years. Collected letters, reports, whatever he could find. He shared his discoveries with the only person who'd listen. His little brother. Me." Brincefield was beaming. "Jonathan knew."

"Knew what?"

"After Jonathan disappeared, I became as obsessed as he'd been. Finding the treasure ate at me." Brincefield's eyes grew distant. "In the end, I had to choose between the quest and my sanity. So, two years ago, I sold Jonathan's collection. For a measly twenty dollars."

The letters! That's *how Bates acquired them.*

"Our chat at the yacht club triggered the old itch," he went on. "I even tried to buy back Jonathan's papers. That's when I learned that a group of teenagers purchased the collection the day before. I knew instantly who led them."

His look became sheepish. "I sorta kept tabs on you after that."

My arms folded. "The ghost tour. Brunch at the country club."

Brincefield nodded. "Sorry."

"Accepted. Now what did Jonathan know about the treasure?"

The gleam returned to his eyes. "In 1718, Calico Jack captured a Spanish galleon sailing from Cadiz. The ship carried a wealthy Spaniard named Miguel de Fernan Ortega. Ortega was traveling to the New World to assume the governorship of Maracaibo."

"Okay." Still lost. "Why does that matter?"

"Because of what he had in his luggage!" Brincefield's enthusiasm was infectious. "Ortega was a known collector of antiquities. Just before disembarking, he'd publicly boasted of a recent acquisition."

I saw where the story was going. "Jack and his crew stole it."

"*Exactly*. When the British captured Calico's Jack's ship—"

"The *Revenge*."

"—they inventoried the hold."

Brincefield held up a single finger. "One item was notably absent."

"The papers we found?"

"Yes! Jonathan burned the king's official report to keep his discovery secret, always believing that Anne Bonny took the document for herself."

"So the pages have value?"

Brincefield's grin stretched wider than the Mississippi. "Of course."

"And you're going to tell me?" I coaxed.

"Yes." The old man's face grew solemn. "You found my

brother. Soon I'll be able to lay him to rest. That's all I've ever wanted. Thank you."

I waited.

"Research the Abbey of Kells." Brincefield winked. "You'll find it worth your while."

CHAPTER 69

"What's this all about?"

Videoconference. Hi sat at his desk, dressed in his favorite Puma tracksuit. "I'm grounded for life, you know. My mother almost confiscated my modem."

Shelton nodded. "If we weren't moving to Cali, I'd be in permanent lockdown. Good thing my parents feel responsible somehow. They think I was acting out misplaced aggression, or some such psychobabble. Works for me."

Ben's face filled a third box on my screen. He was at his usual place on the couch in his father's den, absently spinning a gold coin on the coffee table. "My guess. She wants to talk about the doubloons."

Before turning in Short and the Bates brothers, Hi and Shelton hid the pouch and pages in a locker on *Sewee*. Secrecy seemed prudent. There are few rules regarding buried treasure, and we'd decided to take no chances.

"Actually, that's not it."

I was a bundle of nerves. My news was colossal.

Knowing me as they did, the boys sensed something was up.

"Brincefield ambushed me by the Dumpster this morning."

All three talked at once.

"Relax," I said. "We were wrong about him. Brincefield was just obsessed with finding his brother. He wanted to thank us."

"Not buying it," Shelton was shaking his head. "That man turns up everywhere. I think he's a few beers short of a six pack."

I chose my next words carefully. "Brincefield had some interesting things to say about the pages we found."

"How did *he* know about them?" Ben asked in surprise.

I relayed our conversation.

"That's great!" Hi was pumped. "Between the document and the gold coins, we might still rack up a decent payday. Maybe I could bribe my parents to release me."

I tried to keep my own excitement in check. "This afternoon, I went back to the manuscript library."

"What?" Shelton said. "Why?"

"They have another document guy, Dr. Andrews. I wanted an expert opinion."

Hi nodded. "Smart idea. Could he say what the pages are worth?"

"How'd you get downtown?" Ben frowned. "Did you tell Kit about our find?"

"No way. I took the ferry, then a bus. Kit had a staff meeting at LIRI, so he was out on Loggerhead." I shrugged. "What's one more secret trip at this point?"

"What did the guy say?" Hi asked impatiently.

A smile spread my face. "The pages appear to be a lost section of the Irish Book of Kells."

"That rings a faint bell," Shelton said.

"Dear Lord." Hi's jaw went slack. He knew.

"What?" Ben sounded a bit defensive.

"The Book of Kells is an illustrated version of the Christian Gospels." I tried not to rush my explanation. "It dates to the ninth century."

"Where was it made?" Shelton asked.

"Scholars think the book was created at an abbey on Iona, a small island off the Scottish coast."

"By whom?" Ben asked.

"Followers of Saint Columba." I glanced at my notes. "Later the abbey was attacked and the monks fled to Kells on the Irish mainland, taking the book with them. Then Vikings stole it in 1007. The manuscript was later recovered, but no one knew for sure if any pages were missing."

Ben scratched his chin. "What's so special about it?"

Shelton was totally transfixed. Hi appeared to be hyper-ventilating.

"According to experts, the Book of Kells contains every design found in Celtic art. It's considered the most striking manuscript ever produced in the Anglo-Saxon world. One of the great masterpieces of early Christian art."

"Andrews really believes those pages are from the Book of Kells?" Hi croaked. "No kidding?"

I nodded. "He nearly had a heart attack."

The boys gaped from their squares.

"I'm not kidding," I laughed. "After examining the manuscript for ten minutes, he stood up and grabbed his chest. I thought he was going to pass out."

"So it's valuable?" Shelton was leaning forward, hands on his desk, nose inches from his webcam. "Really valuable?"

"The Book of Kells is the national treasure of Ireland, Shelton. They keep it on display at Trinity College in Dublin. Thousands pay to see it every week."

"What are you saying?" Ben demanded.

"I'm saying we found a lost portion of one of the most famous books in history!" I shouted. "It's like finding the *Mona Lisa*, or the statue of David!"

"We've got ten pages!" Hi ran a hand across his face. "What's that worth, Tory? What did he say?"

"A lost folio from the Book of Kells would be among the rarest documents in the world. Andrews wouldn't even guess, said the value was incalculable. *Priceless.*"

For a moment there was absolute silence.

Then bedlam.

Ben raised his arms above his head. Shelton, Hi, and I started jumping up and down, screaming incoherently.

Then, without warning, Hi disappeared. Seconds later I saw him streak across the lawn outside, shrieking like a madman.

I needed no invitation. In moments Coop and I were running beside him.

Ben appeared next, then Shelton. We formed a ragged circle and spun around like five-year-olds playing a mad version of Ring-Around-the-Rosie.

This embarrassment went on for a full minute.

I was the first to collapse on the grass, breathless and sweaty. The others dropped, one by one. We sprawled in a line, giddy, unable to believe our good fortune.

"I'm going be like that Facebook guy," Hi said. "Or maybe Justin Timberlake. How much does a G6 cost?"

"Hold on!" I had to nip such talk in the bud. "Let's not forget why we did this. We now have the money to save Loggerhead Island."

"But we could be rich!" Hi whined. "Super rich! Buy-Ferraris-just-to-wreck-them rich! We could own a freaking NBA team!"

"We didn't do this to get rich." Ben. The voice of reason.

"That's true," Shelton said. "But you have to admit, millions of dollars is pretty tempting. It's like the dream where you win the lottery. I don't want to wake up."

"If we sold the manuscript and divided the money, our pack would be split." I sat up. "Our parents would move us hundreds of miles from each other. Sure, we'd have tons of cash. But that wouldn't change who we are. *What* we are."

"Virals," Ben said, rising beside me. "Freaks."

"And it's not just us," I reminded them. "What about Whisper and her family? What about the monkey colony, or the sea turtles that nest on the Loggerhead beaches? If we don't come to the rescue, they're all in danger."

"We've found something worth *millions*, and you want to just give it up?" Hi still lay on his back. "I *hate* those endings! We could *buy* Loggerhead Island with that kind of money!"

"You're not thinking straight." I gently poked Hi's shoulder. "It's too dangerous to be a Viral alone. Who knows what could happen in the future? With our bodies. Our powers. Anything. All we can really count on is each other."

"We need to stay low profile," Ben said. "And together."

"They're right." Shelton breathed the world's deepest sigh. "I hate it, but it's true. Our families would scatter. We wouldn't be neighbors, classmates, maybe not even friends. That money is poison."

"We have to be smart." Ben reached across me and tapped Hi's chest. "Guard our secrets."

"But I wanna be a big baller!" Hi threw out his arms. "Make it rain up in the club!"

"You'd choose money over the pack?" I asked. "Fine. We can arrange that. Part of the treasure belongs to you, so it's your choice. No one can force you."

"Gaaaaaaah!" Hi pistoned his arms and legs in the air. "This blows!"

Ten more pumps, then he sat up. "Fine. Crush my dreams. What's the plan?"

"We shock the world," I said, slapping him on the back.

Circling up, we hashed out a plan.

"And Hi, let's be clear," I said when we'd finished. "Our priorities are preserving LIRI and protecting the pack."

Hi started to speak, but I cut him off.

"But that doesn't mean we have to come out empty-handed."

CHAPTER 70

"Tory! I'm back!"

Kit tossed his keys into the tray.

"What'd you do while I was gone?" Grabbing the remote and flopping onto the couch. "Overthrow the government? Find the Loch Ness Monster?"

"Can you please come over here?" I was sitting at the dining room table. "I'd like to show you something."

"Sure." Kit dragged himself to his feet. "What's up? Need to confess a new crime? Your secret life as a Chinese spy?"

Kit's eyes landed on the manuscript.

"Wow. That's beautiful."

"It's a very rare document from the ninth century."

"That explains the metal case." Kit closed his eyes. "Tell me you didn't steal this."

I smiled. "Not this time. The boys and I found it."

"Found it?"

"You should probably sit. I haven't told you everything."

Kit took the chair beside me. "Talk."

"In the end, we actually *did* find treasure." I tapped the document holder. "Anne Bonny left these pages in a box underneath the church on Dewees."

"Why didn't you tell me?"

I ignored Kit's question. "While you were gone, I had the document analyzed by an expert."

"Of course you did." Dramatic sigh. "Where?"

"The Karpeles Manuscript Museum. Dr. Andrews helped me this time."

"Downtown. Where that psychopath Nigel Short worked." Kit shook his head. "I'm putting a tracking bracelet on you. What did the man say?"

"This folio was originally part of the Irish Book of Kells."

Kit's face went pink. I continued before he could interrupt.

"There might be ownership issues, and the Irish government will take a strong position, but Dr. Andrews estimates these pages are worth eight or nine figures. Minimally."

The pink moved toward plum.

"You found a lost folio from the Book of Kells?" Kit's voice was unsteady. "You dug it from the ground?"

"It was under a flagstone. In a box."

"Tory, a father isn't supposed to fear his fourteen-year-old daughter. That being said, you terrify me."

"Don't be silly."

"Is that everything?" Kit demanded. "Is there *anything* else you've held back?"

"No, sir. You've got the full story."

The lie knotted my gut. I ignored the guilt. Some things I just couldn't share.

"I *do* have a plan," I ventured cautiously.

"Of course you do." Kit's eyes rolled to the heavens, then dropped to me. "Let's hear it."

"The boys and I have agreed to give up the folio in order to save Loggerhead Island."

"Give it up?" Kit's Adam's apple rose and fell. "You'd do that for the institute?"

"For the animals." I reached out and cupped his chin with one hand. "But first, you have to make me a promise."

"Go on." The corners of Kit's lips tucked up ever so slightly.

"Promise we won't move. Promise we can stay here on Morris Island. As a family."

"That I can do." Kit sighed in relief. "Somehow, I'll make it work. Whitney's going to flip. And you *will* finish cotillion."

Blargh. "Fine."

"To think that ten little pages can change everything." I ran a fingertip over the manuscript's protective case. "We need to thank my great-great-great pirate grandma."

Kit's eyebrows shot up. "Your what?"

"Nothing. Just kidding."

Maybe.

EPILOGUE

The ceremony was about to begin.

Hi and I hurried to chairs marked with our names on white index cards. Shelton was already seated, and was absently scrolling his new iPad.

"Ya'll are late," he said. "Ben went looking for you."

"I brought Coop out for a visit," I said. "He hasn't seen his mother in weeks."

"I'll shoot Ben a text," Hi said. "He's probably lost."

Shelton glanced at Hi, then started giggling. "Sorry man, but you look *ridiculous*."

"The word you seek is *fly*," Hi replied. "Diamond stud earrings are the bombtrack. This is high-quality bling."

"For the ladies, maybe. For you? Not so much."

"I can't wait until your mom sees that ear," I said. "Please call me when that happens."

A large platform had been erected in the center of the LIRI

courtyard. The entire staff was present, decked out in their finest. The mood was festive, energetic. Smiles were everywhere.

"Too bad school starts tomorrow." Hi fiddled with his newly implanted gem. "I was getting used to being liked for a change."

"Who knows?" Shelton closed out his email and dropped the iPad to his lap. "Maybe the Bolton kids will accept us now. Some must've heard what we did."

"Yeah. Maybe." I didn't want to talk about school.

I hadn't spoken to Jason since blasting him at the country club, when he'd asked to escort me to the debutante ball. Since then I'd completely blown him off, mainly because I didn't know my answer. And I still had no plan for dealing with Madison. I'd be dodging landmines all next semester.

Problems for another day.

Two weeks had passed since I'd shown Kit the manuscript. Events had unfolded quickly, and as well as could be hoped.

Dr. Andrews's team of experts had authenticated our folio as a missing chapter of the Book of Kells. The discovery ran as breaking news on CNN. The art world was still frothing with excitement.

The Irish government had gone ballistic, demanded the immediate return of the pages. Kit had hired an attorney. After days of negotiations, a deal had been struck.

No one would talk numbers, but rumors ran wild.

I spotted Ben hurrying up the aisle.

"How'd you sneak by me?" He slipped into his seat and elbowed Hi. "Nice sparkler, Snooki. When's *your* debut?"

"Philistines." Hi rubbed his rib cage. "You guys wouldn't know class if it died in your bathroom."

"Maybe you got distracted by all of *Sewee*'s new gear," I teased Ben. "She's looking awfully tricked out these days."

"You should talk." Ben adjusted his tie and ear-tucked his hair. "I saw about a dozen packages on your doorstep. How much camping gear did you buy?"

I waved away the comment. "Your eyes deceive, sir."

"Shelton's hoarding car catalogs," Hi said.

"My license is right around the corner," Shelton replied. "Always be prepared. Isn't that the Boy Scouts' motto?"

"Any chance I can score another gold coin?" Hi asked. "I was thinking Gucci for school this year."

"You spent your allowance," I said. "Everything left is for outfitting the bunker. I have big plans."

We never mentioned the gold coins. Not to anyone. The ancient manuscript had been more than enough to preserve Loggerhead Island.

The Virals deserved a reward. We'd solved the riddles and dodged the bullets. We deserved something for our troubles.

"How'd it go with the old geezer?" Ben asked me.

"Splendidly," I said.

After much debate, we'd given Rodney Brincefield a few doubloons. It just felt right. Without his brother's stone disk, we wouldn't have made it through the tunnels. A debt was paid.

"It was nice to see his surprise," I added. "He really is harmless."

"Crazy harmless," Shelton said.

"Why does Chance get a share?" Hi whined. "He's already filthy rich."

"We wouldn't have found the treasure without him. Fair is fair."

I could have also added "massive guilt," but didn't want to be that honest. My debt to Chance was larger than a few gold coins. I intended to make up for playing head games on him. Just don't ask me how.

The dignitaries began taking their chairs. Kit sat behind a long table at center stage, looking extremely uncomfortable.

"Tell me how this works again?" Hi asked.

"It's a rededication ceremony," I said. "There'll be speeches and backslapping, that kind of thing. Later there's a buffet."

"No, I mean the deal your father struck to keep LIRI running."

"First, Kit created a nonprofit trust and donated the manuscript," I explained. "The cotrustees are the new Logger-head Island Foundation, of which Kit is the director, and Trinity College in Dublin, keeper of the Book of Kells. Then the newly created trust secured a loan from the Bank of Ireland. Very nice terms."

All three boys opened their mouths.

"Don't ask," I said. "But the answer is, a lot. A *whole* lot."

"So the trust bought Loggerhead Island?" Ben asked.

"Correct. And not just the real estate. The trust now owns LIRI and all of Morris Island as well. The institute is no longer subject to CU's fickle budget."

Kit had insisted on the purchase of both islands. The State of South Carolina had agreed, with one stipulation. Loggerhead and

Morris would forever remain nature preserves. Neither could be commercially developed. Kit had been happy to agree.

Everyone viewed the deal as a win-win.

"With the Kells folio as collateral," I said, "LIRI will never have funding issues again. In fact, Kit says they may expand. LIRI is poised to become the premier veterinary research facility in the world."

"No wonder they appointed your dad director," Hi said. "He saved Christmas."

"He's perfectly qualified. The position's been vacant since Karsten, and Kit is a member of the senior staff. He's a logical choice."

"Easy there, Lady Defensive." Hi twirled his earring. "Just yanking your crank. I couldn't be happier that Kit is director. He raised everyone's salaries. My father may hang a picture of him in our living room."

"Did you read today's paper?" Shelton asked. "Sounds like the Bates brothers rolled on Short. They copped to the Fletcher murders."

"You still believe Short knew what the treasure was?" Ben asked. "Pages from the Book of Kells?"

I nodded. "He's a rare-document expert. My guess is that Short saw a copy of the same report Jonathan Brincefield did. I think he was willing to kill because he knew the stakes."

Marlo, Duncan, and Short had each been charged with two counts of murder and four counts of attempted murder. My view? Lock the slimeballs up and toss the key.

Kit's generosity had benefited the Virals as well. Though a shockingly long list of museums, landmarks, and wildlife organizations had banned us for life, we'd avoided criminal charges.

Because we were minors, the police had kept our names from the media. Very few knew what had actually occurred, or how and where the folio had been discovered. That was fine with us. Kit could have the celebrity.

The man who gave away a fortune had tongues wagging all across the Lowcountry. Kit had become a local media darling. Whitney was in heaven.

"How's the auction going?" Shelton asked.

"The last doubloons sold this morning," Hi said. "Great price. I shut down the eBay account and moved the money from PayPal. I think we're good."

An AV geek tweaked a microphone. A loud *tap tap* carried over the afternoon air. Kit thumbed a stack of note cards. Nervous.

I caught movement in my peripheral vision. Streaks of silver outside the perimeter fence. I stayed alert, knowing the sighting was not accidental.

Coop appeared, Whisper at his side. Buster and Polo crowded behind, completing the family portrait.

They shouldn't be here. Too risky.

Maybe it was the good vibes, or my giddiness at how things turned out.

It could've been my happiness at seeing Kit receive the recognition he deserved.

Or perhaps it was being with my best friends. My pack.